SINFUL BITE

AN ENCHANTED MATES ROMANCE

SARA OHLIN

Copyright © 2024 by Sara Ohlin

All rights reserved. No part of this publication may be reproduced, distributed, or transmitted in any form or by any means, including photocopying, recording, or other electronic or mechanical methods, without the prior written permission of the author.

This is a work of fiction. The story, all names, characters, places, and incidents are products of the author's imagination. Any resemblance to actual persons, living or dead, locales, or events is entirely coincidental.

Visit the author's website at www.saraohlin.com

Ebook cover by Sara Ohlin

Print Book Cover by Sara Ohlin

Cover Photography by Sara Ohlin

Formatted in Atticus

ISBN 979-8-9903522-4-7 (print for D2D)

ISBN 979-8-9903522-3-0 (ebook)

Contents

About Sinful Bite	VII
Note to Reader	IX
Dedication	X
1. Chapter One	1
2. Chapter Two	11
3. Chapter Three	19
4. Chapter Four	31
5. Chapter Five	41
6. Chapter Six	46
7. Chapter Seven	55
8. Chapter Eight	61
9. Chapter Nine	68
10. Chapter Ten	77
11. Chapter Eleven	84
12. Chapter Twelve	89

13.	Chapter Thirteen	95
14.	Chapter Fourteen	102
15.	Chapter Fifteen	115
16.	Chapter Sixteen	121
17.	Chapter Seventeen	124
18.	Chapter Eighteen	131
19.	Chapter Nineteen	136
20.	Chapter Twenty	144
21.	Chapter Twenty-One	150
22.	Chapter Twenty-Two	157
23.	Chapter Twenty-Three	160
24.	Chapter Twenty-Four	168
25.	Chapter Twenty-Five	174
26.	Chapter Twenty-Six	181
27.	Chapter Twenty-Seven	185
28.	Chapter Twenty-Eight	191
29.	Chapter Twenty-Nine	195
30.	Chapter Thirty	200
31.	Chapter Thirty-One	205
32.	Chapter Thirty-Two	211
33.	Chapter Thirty-Three	218
34.	Chapter Thirty-Four	225

35. Chapter Thirty-Five 230
36. Chapter Thirty-Six 238
37. Chapter Thirty-Seven 245
38. Chapter Thirty-Eight 251
39. Chapter Thirty-Nine 256
40. Chapter Forty 266
41. Chapter Forty-One 269
42. Chapter Forty-Two 276
43. Chapter Forty-Three 289
44. Chapter Forty-Four 294
45. Chapter Forty-Five 299
46. Chapter Forty-Six 310
47. Chapter Forty-Seven 316
48. Chapter Forty-Eight 323
49. Chapter Forty-Nine 330
50. Chapter Fifty 337
51. Chapter Fifty-One 340
52. Chapter Fifty-Two 346
53. Chapter Fifty-Three 351
54. Chapter Fifty-Four 354
55. Chapter Fifty-Five 360
56. Chapter Fifty-Six 366

57.	Chapter Fifty-Seven	372
58.	Chapter Fifty-Eight	375
59.	Chapter Fifty-Nine	381
60.	Chapter Sixty	390
61.	Chapter Sixty-One	392
62.	Chapter Sixty-Two	398
63.	Chapter Sixty-Three	408
64.	Epilogue	413
65.	Acknowledgements	420
	About Sara	421
	Also by Sara Ohlin	422
	Newsletter	424

ABOUT SINFUL BITE

WEREWOLF HUGH WEBB HAS a great life. Dream job with his family's company, surrounded by his siblings in his thriving hometown. What he doesn't have is a family of his own. One scent, one glimpse of Gianna Reily punches him with the knowledge that she's his mate.

Financial analyst by day, assassin by night, and a witch who's hidden her nature, single mom Gianna Reily is no stranger to sacrifice and living a dual identity. She allows herself one night of passion with the incredible stranger Hugh.

Hugh is empowered to find Gia after she sneaks out on him. As fate would have it, Gia is the new contractor for Hugh's company. Although she refuses to date someone she works with, Gia can't help her heart, and with each encounter, she falls deeper in love with her wild and kind hero.

But Gia has many secrets in her search for vengeance for those who murdered her husband. As things spiral out of control, she learns how little she truly knows of her magic. With

Hugh, she can be all she was meant to be. Now, her fragile heart wants to risk it all for love.

Two souls each living half a life. Is love's magic enough to cast them into their enchanted forever, or will the past destroy everything they hold dear?

Note to Reader

Sinful Bite begins around the same time as *Luscious Bite* (Book 1 in my Enchanted Mates Series). You do not have to read *Luscious Bite* to understand *Sinful Bite*. I did, however, write myself into a corner, in a way with some of the scenes in Book 1 where Gia and Hugh appear. I have included those scenes in this book where they are necessary for the story. Forgive me for any mistakes I have made or liberties I have taken with those scenes for Gia and Hugh's sake.

This book contains serious subject matters such as past death of parents and spouse, talk of grief and trauma, anxiety, attempted attack on female character, consensual sex, demons, and suspense.

DEDICATION

*For witches everywhere who carry
the wounds of their ancestors*

Chapter One

Recognition coiled low in Hugh's gut. *Her.* A knowing fed through his bones, stirred his blood as he entered the restaurant at his brother's boutique hotel in downtown Mercy. Friday night and the place was buzzing. Laughter, people murmuring over the delicious food, and the familiar sound of glasses clinking.

The tall windows in the old brick building and the art déco vibe his sister-in-law Harper had designed for the renovations last year gave the place a swanky feel. But the food was an eclectic casual mix of stick-to-your-ribs good ole southern fare. Hugh regularly had a difficult time choosing between his brother's shrimp and grits or the homemade biscuits with smoked honey butter. Although if tonight's menu included lamb shanks, no matter how his brother cooked them, they would win Hugh's vote.

He'd come here for dinner, but now his mind was laser-focused elsewhere.

Low jazz music, small candles on the tables, and the falling snow outside sprinkled the entire setting with magic. *Magic indeed.* There she sat, glowing in the candlelight flickering around her. Nestled in the corner table alone, drinking a glass of red wine, and staring outside as if beyond the glass held all the answers. Immediately, he ached to know every question she sought understanding to.

He took it all in. The melancholy expression on her face, her eyes—he couldn't see their color—were contemplative, dare he say, lonely. She wore a simple black winter dress, made prettier as it curved over her body. A shimmery silver scarf draped across her shoulders. Crossed legs showed off tall, black, high-heeled boots and her wrist was sprinkled with colorful bracelets.

A soft whistle hummed from between her lips and pinged across the restaurant to him. Even over the delicious aromas coming from the kitchen, Hugh could smell her. And she smelled like his. He'd never encountered her before, but in one breath, he recognized who she was.

As he stared, dumbstruck and elated and vulnerable, all at the same time, he let out a huff of laughter. A server delivered a slice of his grandmother's famous black layer cake to her table. Tiny sparks danced over her hands and disappeared. A wide smile blossomed on her face, making her glow. *I feel you, darlin'. That cake's sinfully delicious and addictive.* It was still the cake he requested for his birthday every year.

When she took a bite and closed her eyes, he could hear the moan slip from her mouth all the way across the restaurant, and he was hard immediately. Fuck, his body sure got the message. Loud and clear. He stood in the entrance and watched her eat the cake. And what a delicious torture it was to his body when all his limbs wanted to do was prowl over and taste that cake on her lips. Good thing his brain still had some control. Or was it?

He nearly wept while she ate, giving a quick glance around the restaurant before she took her finger, scraped it across the plate to capture a dollop of frosting that had fallen, and put it right in her mouth. *Jesus Christ, she's going to kill me before I even learn her name.* He put out a hand to steady himself on the doorjamb.

"Hugh." His brother Duncan smacked him on the back, drawing him out of his trance. "You coming or going? Get the hell out of the way. You're scaring the customers." His brother nudged him out of the way, allowing the people behind Hugh to enter and make their way to the hostess stand.

"Sorry." He gave his brother a wry smile, keeping his secret to himself to savor for a bit before his family gave him hell. And they would give him hell. Have a ball doing it too. "I'm overwhelmed by whatever the heck you're cooking back there, brother." Overwhelmed was the truth, but not by the food, not tonight.

"Got your favorite, lamb shanks braised in red wine. Table or bar?"

"Uh, I think I'll just take a Macallan to start." He followed Duncan to the bar, keeping the woman moaning over cake in his sight. He could barely stand to be focusing on anything or anyone else. That's how hard the feeling had hit him. No, hit him wasn't the right phrase. The sensation infused his body, everything inside him waking from a deep slumber or appearing for the first time in what now seemed like an extremely long existence so far. A damn lonely one too.

"Not hungry?" Duncan set the whisky in front of Hugh.

"Starving." The truth. "But I need to speak with someone first."

Duncan nodded, clinked his glass with Hugh's, and downed his shot of whisky. "Tell Casey your order if I'm not out here. Busy night."

"Yeah, man, outstanding crowd. Happy for you." The restaurant was Duncan's dream. Hugh was proud of his brother. Adair's had been busy since it re-opened this summer. Duncan had gone after what he wanted, career-wise and personally. And he'd gotten both. Twins on the way this spring too.

Duncan thumped his fist on the bar and disappeared through the swinging doors into the kitchen with a huge smile on his face. Hugh *was* happy for him, ecstatic. His brother deserved it all. But as he faced the woman by the window, a pang of longing hit him, so fierce it cracked open his chest. Loneliness was a feeling he rarely allowed himself to contemplate. Now it swamped him. He wanted what his brother had, his own family, love, belonging.

He wanted her.

Need had him making his way to her table. Lust nearly had him leaping toward her and carrying her away with him into the forest, especially when she picked up her fork, closed her eyes, and licked every last crumb from it. Then she set it down and her joy vanished; she fingered the stem of her glass and gazed outside.

What haunts you, little one?

"Everything all right?" She started at his words. He might have missed it if he wasn't acutely tuned to her blood and bones.

She masked the startled look on her face, glanced around the restaurant, and then settled the prettiest brownish green eyes on him. Stunning, even though she was doing her best to send annoyance his way. There was not a hint of a smile in her haughty expression.

He offered her a grin in response. Fuck, she was cute. And yes, he could read her annoyance vibrating from her skin in sharp, almost invisible sparks of red.

"You ask every woman sitting alone at a restaurant that question? That the best you got?"

Inwardly, he groaned at how sexy her voice was, or perhaps because it was perfect for his ears. Is this what his brother Duncan meant when he'd met Harper and everything finally clicked into place? *Have I been traipsing through the world asleep for all these years?* Because he was suddenly wide fucking awake.

"Hello?" she prodded, tilting her head.

"Sorry, no." He coughed to cover his laugh. He wanted to laugh and dance and howl. He looked around. "My…uh…my family owns the hotel and restaurant. And I live right around the corner."

"So?" Her brow raised in annoyance. She wasn't going to give him anything, was she? Except, her cheeks warmed into the prettiest rosy flush he'd ever seen.

"I grew up bussing the tables, refilling water, and doing garbage duty, my least favorite." He did give a small laugh then at the memories. How important he'd felt when someone at a table asked him for something. "It's habit, I guess, when I'm here, if someone seems unsatisfied, to see if they need anything."

"Oh." Softness settled over her features, and…and if he wasn't mistaken, longing.

Now why did a woman sitting here enjoying a great glass of wine with the best damn cake in the world gaze at him with longing over such a simple comment from him? She was a hive of emotions dancing in and out of existence. Ones she tried to mask and ones she didn't. She turned her gaze back toward the empty plate and then to the window to contemplate the world outside, or perhaps the state of affairs rolling around inside her.

What troubles you?

"My grandmother's chocolate layer cake rarely makes someone look so miserable." The word was out before he could think, and even though it was the truth, he regretted saying it as soon as the painful expression crossed her face. "It's my favorite. She used to let me help her frost it. I always got more frosting in my mouth than on the actual cake."

"That sounds like a wonderful memory," she said, casting him a quick hint of her soulful eyes and a wistful smile before she tapped her fork on the plate. "I always wanted to be able to make something so good, but I could never...I was never a very good baker."

Her haughty guard down. An admission of sorts. A tiny glimpse of beauty she was offering. And every precious word a lance to his heart. This woman was full of scars. He could hear them in her words, sense them inside her. Rage boiled low in his gut. What had happened to her and why hadn't he been there to help her?

"Hugh," he said, holding out his hand.

"Uh, hi." She carefully put her hand in his as if afraid he was going to capture her and lock her away as soon as their hands touched. "Gia."

He should have been the one worried about their hands touching. Unbelievable. Fire and starlight and passion burned into him in full color. Bright reds, burnished purples, and an orange so multifaceted he wondered if the world's artists knew of its existence.

It took intense control to keep his eyes on hers and his heart from leaping out and proclaiming, "Mine!" She slid her hand away far too soon for his liking. Her guard was back in place, but not fully. Her eyes gave her away, gaze locked on his, hints of green flickering within the brown, interest, desire. Eyes that were now curious and open.

"At the risk of sounding like an idiot again, would you like some company?" He gestured to the seat across from her. And when she nodded, he set his whiskey down, pulled the chair out, and sat, studying her anew from this closer angle. Honey-brown curls danced around her delicate face like they couldn't be controlled, no matter what. Soft, he'd bet, the softest thing he'd ever touch. Or maybe not. That blush of hers exposed the freckles on her high cheekbones. Her skin would be like silk.

A few rainbow bracelets threaded together on her wrist. A long, faint scar ran along the edge of her hairline, ending behind her right ear. Almost invisible. Gears battled in his mind between wanting to know how she'd gotten that scar and how he was going to kiss it when he got the chance.

"So, you're from Mercy?" she asked, sipping her wine. She sent subtle glances around the room as if she couldn't completely settle. Even sitting in this cozy restaurant eating chocolate cake, she was alert, but so calm about it, practiced. Another clue for his safekeeping.

"Yes," he offered, echoing her motion and sipping his drink. She was so fucking cool and he was an inferno inside, but also, certain. And with that certainty came a deep, satisfying breath. "For generations. My ancestors came from Scotland in the early 1800s."

"Oh." Another sip of wine. "The…uh food is amazing here. Your family must be proud."

"The restaurant's been a part of the hotel since it opened in 1890, but last year my brother Duncan and his wife, Harper, took over, refurbished it, revamped the menu, and…" He followed her gaze and took in the joyful din around him, the laughter, the clinking of plates and silverware.

He couldn't smell anything but a unique scent, something elemental to her, a hint of soap, the way her energy flowed through her. No perfume or anything extra. She'd probably consider it frivolous. *What about her life leads her to believe frivolous isn't for her?* "They've done a dynamite job. I'm proud of them. And lucky for me, I get to eat their amazing creations."

"You don't work here anymore?" She quirked her brow at him. One second there, then gone the next. "No more bussing tables?" Was she teasing him?

"No," he laughed. "Not officially. I help out when I can, however they need me. Family business, you know."

"Mm." She studied him. The melancholy returned as well as her guards, as if she'd never allowed him that tiny glimpse inside. "So, you *were* hitting on me, to be fair."

Hitting on you? Oh, darlin' so much more. He smiled. The truth. She was someone who deserved it, and he was the type to give it, although she probably didn't want the whole truth yet. Because, as ancient instincts kicked his pulse into high gear every time her voice met him, *he knew*. Forty-two years old, and he was just now finding his mate.

No, he was certain she wasn't ready to hear that stunner. "I admit, I saw you the minute I walked in." *Recognized you as mine.* It was harder than he thought not to say the words. "And I knew someone as interesting as you, sitting alone, moaning over my grandmother's cake, was someone I wanted to meet. To cake," he said and held his glass toward her. She held his gaze steady, made him wait a minute. The longest damn minute of his life.

"To cake," she said with an almost grin, slightly crooked and out of use. He was surprised when she clinked her glass with his and took the last sip of her wine. Then she yawned the biggest yawn he'd ever seen.

Chapter Two

"Wow." The gorgeous hotshot's eyes opened wide and his smile grew in that sexy way that said he wanted to undress her, or maybe he was already with the power of his gaze alone. Whoa, where had that thought come from? She was about as far from being in a position for that to happen as a dead person. She *felt* half dead inside if she were being completely honest, exhausted, aching...but then he'd appeared.

Towering over six feet, enormous broad shoulders encased in a puffy gray winter jacket, dark brown hair cut close on the sides with an almost mohawk on top, a handsome goatee, and those eyes, piercing and golden. How dare someone be so damn good-looking.

And what in the hell is wrong with me that I can't carry on a conversation with a handsome man? A man not hiding his interest in her. And to him, she was simply a woman sitting alone, not a weary, single mom and lonely widow, so starved for...for touch. And also so completely afraid of it she could weep with the pain.

"I'm keeping you awake." His voice was everything she'd never heard before, beautiful, melodic, deep. It touched her soul. No, it can't be. She must be so freaking out of practice that any cute man's voice directed at her made her loopy in the head.

"Sorry." Her cheeks heated with embarrassment. "It's not that." Not entirely. But he didn't need to know how much sleep she'd lost during the last three years. "Alcohol makes me yawn."

"Ahh, so I probably can't interest you in another glass," he said.

Tired as she was, his voice was so lovely, so gravelly, she could listen to it for hours. Maybe it wasn't such a bad thing to be on the receiving end of his flirting. It was the first weekend she had without the kids since October. She'd dropped them off at her sister, Francesca's, this afternoon so they could have a weekend sleepover with their favorite aunt and Gia could concentrate on her meeting this weekend and her new freelance client on Monday morning.

Her sister was so good to her and the kids and Gia was grateful. Having Francesca close had made the move easier in some ways. What did easy mean anymore? Gia couldn't remember the last time something had been easy, or fun, or exciting. All these forgotten words that didn't fit into her existence.

So many lives she lived, mom, financial analyst, widow, sister, and the two identities worth keeping to herself, witch and...what title was appropriate for what she did under the cover of darkness. Vengeance felt right when she'd started almost three years ago, two months after her husband had been...Christ, why was she digging it up right now? Her goal tonight had been to enjoy herself, or at least try. So much rubble covered her she'd forgotten how to have a good time.

"All right? You went somewhere. I will admit it's been a while since I tried my hand at flirting with a beautiful woman, but I'm thinking boring them to death isn't how I should approach things. I should let you go." He made to stand, but she put her hand on his.

Oh, a shiver moved through her. She'd done that, willingly reached out and touched him as though her hand had been drawn there. And her hand sure did like how it felt. A spark of warmth met her. It was lovely and warm. Something untenable seeped through her.

"Please stay." Where had that come from? Something deep inside her rioted when he'd started to leave. "I'm sorry. I'm...well not very good at this kind of thing. Tell me more about your...uh...family." God, would he realize what an idiot she was if she faceplanted into her hands? She sucked at this. But watching him, feeling his hand underneath hers, his power and desire radiated.

"Mm." He gave her a slow grin and flipped her hand over so he was caressing her palm with his fingers. Fingers so powerful and long compared to her silly little girl hands. No matter what her hands were capable of, they'd always bothered her, how insignificant they seemed. Fascinated by the way he softly stroked her skin, she couldn't look away. He fingered her bracelets and her pulse leapt at his touch. "Pretty," he said. "Gia." He smiled. "Ava, Daniel?"

Mesmerized by their connection, Gia ran her fingers over his as they danced across her beaded bracelets with the names on them. "My kids. My son made them for me. One with each of our names. I don't..." She met his gaze. Sparkling eyes met hers; the golden hue she'd seen initially had been an illusion and now they were deeper than a burnt caramel but nearly...almost...*are they glowing?*

Inquisitive, smoking hot, kind. It was all there in his expression for her to see. The last bit, she didn't know what made her see it, or what made her so relieved it was there, but she was certain down to her bones he was kind. "I don't have...it's just the two of them and me." Her voice quieted to a whisper as she choked back the emotion from admitting that fact to him. It would be three years next month. Why did telling this stranger bring the emotions right to the surface, now of all the inappropriate moments?

He tangled their fingers together, his eyes darkening more, almost as if he was sorry for her. And she certainly didn't want that. But that wasn't the only thing hovering in his expression. Desire and...familiarity or...some elusive emotion she couldn't name.

So much was happening right now, it was difficult to hold on to it all. Sensations floated in and out, twirling around her. Arousal, need. Damn, it had been a long time. She hardly recognized the thread of desire. Him touching her; her touching him. The way he studied her, telling her, if she wasn't completely stupid, that he was absolutely interested.

It was more than arousal coursing through her. What was happening? Everything in the air had her aching to climb over the table into his lap and kiss him, see if he was kind when he kissed too, or confident, or, her blood heated at the thought, a bit dirty.

"Hughy, what are you doing here?" Gia snagged her hand away like it was on fire and clasped it in her lap with her other one, her heart racing out of control. Her usual server, tall, thin, perfect large boobs, black hair up in a high ponytail, bright blue eyes, and stunning cheekbones. All the gorgeousness of someone young and confident. Flirting with...

"Hughy?" Gia inquired, slamming her guard back down, exactly how she'd taught herself.

He had some gall. Flirting with her and the server at the same time. Gia gathered her purse and began tugging on her coat. She wasn't going to wait for his explanation. She'd clearly forgotten herself for a moment. Embarrassment licked up her neck.

He'd touched her in a way that dove under her skin. He'd shared a stupid, probably fake story about his family, his grandmother's cake. Damn it! She'd liked him. It had been there, the beginnings of interest, the stirrings of desire, so much aching desire.

And she'd liked her server. The same one Gia had each time she treated herself to the sinful chocolate layer cake. She loved that cake and this place and…and…she'd never be able to come here again.

She sucked in a deep breath, tried to control her emotions. The door to the restaurant whooshed open and freezing air blew in. The hostess wrestled with the large wooden door to close it. Gia counted to ten, letting her breath out slowly through her lips and the door lost its fight against the storm, closing them all in with the warmth.

"Blustery night," he said, glancing at the door, then standing to give the server a hug. "Sorry, Gia this is…"

Too late, asshole.

"My cousin Catherine. She enjoys teasing me. Hughy is what my sister called me when she was little. It drove me crazy because I was a self-important sophomore in high school, way too cool to be called Hughy. My cousins latched on and never fail to tease me about it. Art school going well, Cath?"

"So amazing," Catherine said. "My professors are incredible." She glanced at Gia. "Another glass of…are you okay?"

Hugh's smile fell. "All right?" he asked Gia quietly, sitting back down and assessing her, contemplative, serious, as if he could read all the thoughts passing through her head. And more.

Gia tried to settle her nerves, or whatever the hell had whipped through her like an angry tornado. His cousin. Family business. Everyone close and lovely and in each other's business.

What would she know about any of that? "I...I should..." What? What should she do? Mortification had her wanting to flee. "I should go."

"Catherine, mind putting her bill on my tab?" Hugh spoke to his cousin but never took his eyes off Gia.

"Sure. Uh, have a good night. See you next time," Catherine said in that pretty voice to Gia, before she walked away.

"You don't have to go. I..." He cleared his throat. "I don't want you to go."

"I..." She probably looked like a child frozen in fear as the clown jumped out and surprised her.

"Pretty outside. We could go for a walk in the snow," Hugh said in a soothing voice that worked its way over her skin and into her body, calming her, rejuvenating her. Gia glanced outside. It was dreamy. Strange memories from when she was a child jostled inside her, the first time she'd seen snow. Fat flakes drifting onto the barren landscape in their backyard. She and her sister had danced in it, tried to capture the flakes on their tongues, tasted the cold magic of snow, and watched it paint the land in a brilliant white blanket.

The memory disappeared as quickly as it arrived. But Gia remembered the feeling it had left her with all those years ago. That snow was more delightful to her than anything in her life at that point, even the fact that she and her sister could talk to each other through their thoughts or her extraordinary ability with numbers and equations.

Gia wanted a tiny taste of that wonder back. Her life was a mess. But maybe for one night, she could take whatever delight she could find. She nodded and stood before rational thoughts got the better of her. To see his face light up in a smile was worth it. Whatever happened next was absolutely worth it. One night of amazingness. It was hers to take, and she was going to grab hold and enjoy every second.

CHAPTER THREE

HUGH TUCKED HIS BEANIE on his head and held his hand out for her as they left the restaurant. She hesitated for a second then placed her delicate hand in his and that sensation of knowing quickened in his blood once more.

"Okay?" he asked her, or perhaps himself.

"Yes," she said, studying their connected hands. Her voice sounded different outside in the snowy quiet. Precious and special. For their ears alone.

Hands clasped together, they walked. How he put one foot in front of the other he didn't know. A frisson of energy zapped between them and all he wanted to do was tug her to him so he could feel all of her against him. He was a fool to think holding hands was a safe, casual idea. But he was never fucking letting go.

He could do this, keep his cool, act normal, not scare her the hell away. They didn't speak, and he felt like an idiot. Words stuck in his throat. It was surreal, the two of them doing something as simple as walking side by side on a winter's night. His past and his future all woven together into his present. A profound reckoning with his soul he'd never felt before. This was how life was supposed to feel.

"It's so beautiful." She spoke so softly into the peaceful silence they were in. He dared glance at her, knowing her face would be more beautiful under snow, and streetlamps, and winter magic.

"Yes," he answered. He wasn't talking about the snowy night, but the woman standing before him. When she shivered, he did the only thing he could. He moved in and wrapped her in his arms. Lifting her with one arm wrapped around her waist, he palmed the back of her head with his other hand. "You're freezing."

He wasn't sure if it was panic or fear that lit her eyes, but he immediately went to slide her down when she rested her hand on his cheek and shook her head. "No, not...not cold...empty. So empty."

The whisper of her words met him like a mournful song, that beautiful humming he'd heard from her before. The flakes swirled around them cocooning them together right before she touched her lips to his lightly, exploring, while her eyes watched his. A stunning caress, as if he'd never been touched before. He hadn't been touched, that is, not like this, never like this. He was stunned.

She pulled her mouth away, studied his face, and traced her fingers over his lips. "Hugh?" she whispered. "Are you...are you going to fill me up?"

Hugh took two steps, backed her up against the brick building, and swallowed her words with his mouth, kissing her as if he needed to do so to take his next breath. She *was* his next breath. She whimpered, wrapped her legs around him, and tugged him closer as they devoured each other. When she arched and opened so fully for him, he wanted to believe he was her next breath as well.

Her lips were warm and needy while she angled kiss after kiss on him. *Take, darlin'. Take whatever you want. I am all yours.* She sucked on his bottom lip, nipped it, then explored his mouth with her greedy little tongue. "You taste like caramel and whisky and..."

Hugh nipped back, stealing her words. This was no time for talking. She was wet and warm. And, fuck, his body vibrated with desire as she kissed him, roaming her hands over his shoulders and chest, her little moans surging into him.

There was so much to explore. How would he ever fucking get enough? He dragged his mouth along her neck, sucking and savoring every single inch while she rubbed her body against him. She threw back her head as he ran his tongue along her collarbone. Blood rushed to the surface of her skin, sending out the tiniest arcs of gold and deep pinks. Her scent was everywhere now, surrounding him, deep and sultry. He shoved her coat and the top of her clingy dress away and licked along the top of her breasts, tasting the snowflakes falling there.

"Hugh," she moaned, and the light caught her eyes.

He pulled away immediately, setting her down gently. Shit, they were outside under a streetlamp for everyone in the world to see. The streets and sidewalks were empty. He was breathless.

"Hugh?"

The shaky question in her voice had him angling into her, meeting her gaze. He grinned to soften the moment. Everything inside of him filled with energy, with recognition, with need.

"Got carried away," he said, tugging her closer as if the inch between them was too much. It absolutely fucking was. "Feel like I've...been struck by lightning, or like I've known you forever." He kissed her again, closing his eyes. "I sure enjoy kissing you." He rested his forehead against hers. "Best kiss of my life. Want to do everything with you."

Fuck, he was shaking too, and it had nothing to do with the cold surrounding them. Where was his calm patience? He was going to scare her away before he'd even had a chance.

"Well," she said, and he opened his eyes to see the green flecks shimmering at him. "What are you waiting for?"

He twirled her around, letting out a booming laugh. "Where have you been all my life?"

"Does it matter?" She tossed out those words as if she didn't have a care in the world about the state of his emotions. "Kiss me," she whispered.

Hugh tossed aside the pang in his chest that this might simply be a casual event to her when it was anything but to him. Carrying her past the building, he turned the corner. "Your kids. Do you need to get home?"

She tugged his head to hers, kissed his earlobe. "They're with my sister for the ...night."

Breathing heavily and mentally thanking her sister, Hugh stepped up the two steps to his door, nearly hidden in an alcove between two buildings. "This is my place." The words came out soft and full of vulnerability.

"Convenient." She grinned.

"Mm," he agreed. "I think I've been headed here since we left the restaurant, but if this is too much too fast..." He'd give her an out. He had to. He'd give her anything, including, most importantly, all the consent.

"Is there an inside?" she whispered against his ear.

His cock, already rock hard, tried to break through his jeans to get to her.

"Take me inside, Hugh."

He had the door unlocked and them through in an instant. She laughed and tugged at his jacket while he stormed upstairs to his loft, where there was another door with another lock.

"Mm," he hummed. He unlocked it while she kissed his neck. Slamming the door behind them, he returned to his one focus, her. He still held her as she shimmied out of her coat and kicked her boots off, laughing as she did. Her laugh was smoky and beautiful. She rubbed against him and brought his mouth back to hers. He devoured her lips, tangled his tongue with hers, and drank in her essence. Sugar and wine and *Gia*, all Gia. Everything in him settled into place. His Gia.

Threading her fingers into his hair, she begged, "Hugh, please, kiss me everywhere."

Nothing was graceful about their movements after that. He tugged at the top of her dress, shoving it out of the way along with her bra. He had to get to her skin. She shrugged out of the long sleeves and with one hard tug, she was bared to him all the way to her waist. Sinewy muscle, graceful body. Hugh palmed her naked back and trailed his fingers over her pretty little breasts, bringing one right to his mouth, nearly cursing as he made contact with her naked beauty. They fell into one of the tall columns in his apartment. "Fuck, sorry, darlin'."

With a dazed smile on her face, she moved her hands under his shirt, trying to get it off him. He moved them toward the bed and fell gently with her. She deserved a soft landing, and he longed to give it to her, but his body, his instinct, his beast wanted to devour her wildly, without control or thought of anything soft.

"Are we getting naked here?" he asked as he kissed down her chest, fingering the dress that sat at her waist now. "I need to know what you want."

She raised up, and this time succeeded in pulling his shirt off. Then, without breaking eye contact, went for his belt. "I sure hope we're getting naked," she said. "If I'm going to have you, I want to see all of you, touch all of you."

Big words for such a little thing. Well, he said he'd give her whatever she desired. Hugh stood and shrugged out of his jeans and boxers, watched her eyes heat as she took him in. Then he leaned down, gently shoved her onto the bed, and whisked away her dress, her sexy black tights and panties. Her bra was in there somewhere too. He tossed them all over his shoulder and she laughed, and he was done. Fuck, pure beauty laid out before him, her laughter singing into his heart.

He crawled over her, dragging one hand along her side, caressing her hip, dipping into her waist, and then her breast. She had freckles sprinkled all across her shoulders and chest, but they ended there. His woman liked the sunshine. He kissed along her freckles to the unmarred pale skin of her. Latching onto one nipple, he nipped and sucked and felt her bow under him, squirming to get closer as she smoothed her hands all over him. Her eyes were closed, and her entire face softened into bliss. All her worries gone. Good, she should never have to worry about anything.

Hugh tugged one of her legs around him as he feasted on her hard nipples, loving how she moved under him, begging for more with her body. He lathered kisses on her belly. Damn it, she'd had kids without him, two babies. And she was all on her own. No longer. *You're mine now.*

"What..." her voice was hushed and shaky, her body arching into him. He threw caution to the wind and gave her the words.

"You're mine now," he whispered below her belly button. Moving down her body was a revelation. Using his thumbs, he explored her inner thighs, and he parted her legs, intent on seeing all of her.

"Yours?" she moaned as he took one long lick against her pussy. "Oh, fuck!" The sexiest laugh-moan came from her as she pushed her body into his.

"Mm," he said and tasted her again. Everything, her scent, her skin, her laughter empowered him, and his beast surged up, demanding more, more tastes, more contact, more bites, more everything. He sucked on her delicate skin, eliciting another moan from her and he flicked her pretty swollen clit with his tongue, feasting. She swelled even more under his ministrations and that powered him on too.

"Hugh, God. I never…how do you…don't stop. Please don't stop." Fuck, she didn't have to beg, but it was the hottest thing he'd ever heard.

"Never," he growled and dipped his tongue inside, using his lips to nip and tease her.

"Fuck," she cried. Her orgasm shot through her, and she rocked her pussy into his mouth. He lapped at her juices and his ego grew a million sizes, watching her gorgeous body shatter.

"That was…what did you do to me?" Glassy, sparkling, greenish-brown eyes gazed at him, and he grinned.

Fuck yeah.

"Come here, I…I need more. I need you."

Hugh knelt, rummaged through his jeans for his wallet, and ripped open a condom. He had himself in hand and sheathed in a matter of seconds, as desperate to get inside her as she was to have him. He hungered to flip her, take her from behind, explore all that skin on her backside, but he wanted to see her eyes sparkle this time when he was inside her.

Hugh stroked his length, watching her watch him. She was so expressive, holding nothing back, eyes wide, smile blooming. She beckoned him, and he gave in, notching himself at her warm entrance, stroking them both now with his fingers and his cock, wetting himself with her juices.

"Your eyes," she whispered, cupping his cheek and running featherlight touches across his eyelids. He tilted his head and kissed her palm. "They're...wow...they're glowing."

"Yeah?" He pressed into her core slowly, savoring every second of how tight she was, how hot, how fucking phenomenal it felt. "They do that..." *Only for you.* Another inch and they both moaned. "When I'm..."

"Aroused," she said on a whispered breath while she arched her back. That movement angled him deeper, allowing her core to take him all the way in.

"Oh, yeah." If this was aroused, he was fucking addicted. He'd never been so aroused in his life. Connected, complete, with his mate. He gripped her head, angling it toward him so their gazes clashed. That's what it felt like, a strike of energy linking them now forever.

"Look at me," he demanded, and then he moved, slowly pulling out, then powering in, soaking up every bit of electric spark in her gorgeous eyes as he sank deeper. It wasn't nearly enough. He tugged her leg closer around him and drove into her.

"Harder," she huffed. "Please, harder."

If she kept saying that, he was going to tie her to his bed right this second and make her stay forever. "Darlin'." Hugh quickened his pace. "Gorgeous woman." He kissed her and moved his fingers to her clit, pressing in and teasing while he fucked her harder, just as she asked.

"Hugh...I haven't. I...so long since I...I don't think I can come again."

"Little liar," he teased, and she huffed out a laugh again, which had her squeezing tighter around him. Fucking bliss. "We'll get you there. Tell me what you need." Hugh pressed his thumb into her clit, teased and toyed with her wetness. "This?"

"Uh-huh," she whimpered. "That's good...and..." She met every thrust moved with him, trying to get closer. "And your mouth...please, I need your mouth on me somewhere, everywhere."

Hugh soared at her request. *That's right, baby. You feel it too.* He moved in and licked a path across her breasts, cupped one, and drew the hard nipple into his mouth, moving and feasting on her, and savoring every moan she gave him. He lavished attention on the other breast, getting lost in her body, the way it tasted, the way it felt gliding against his, the way she smelled, like everything glorious, like spring after a long, cold winter, like his.

Sharp spikes of pleasure drew down his spine. His cock swelled inside her walls. Fuck. this was it. He never wanted this to end. Pressing his body onto hers, Hugh took her mouth, grunting out his thrusts. And as she parted her lips to let him in, she broke apart once more. Breathtaking. She sucked his tongue into her mouth and writhed out her orgasm. He took in the brilliant sight until he couldn't last another second, then he buried his head in her neck, sucked on her graceful shoulder, rocked into her one last time, and let his orgasm annihilate him.

"Gia," he grunted into her neck, buried in her sweet goodness. "That was fucking amazing."

"Mm." Her lazy hum tickled his ear while she danced slow circles on his back with her soft fingertips. "I think you broke me." Her voice was raw and quiet.

He chuckled into her neck then placed his lips there, savoring this too, the aftermath, the rush. "Give me a second and I'll move if I can. Get rid of this condom and come back for more."

"More?" Her laugh rippled through him. "What part of broke me, did you not understand?" Dreamy, soft words. She kissed his ear and down the side of his head. Oh yeah, she wasn't done with him yet either.

"We have the entire night. I'm not wasting a second." He wasn't about to admit he wanted the rest of his life with her. Not yet anyway. Hugh lifted up and kissed and licked his way across her sweaty body. He craved all of her. He slipped his cock out of her. "You're so fucking pretty here." Hugh kissed her pussy. He was feral for her.

"Oh." She shivered. "Sensitive."

"Mm." Hugh smiled into her thigh. "Be right back."

Hugh couldn't wipe the enormous grin off his face if he tried. He wasn't normally one for parading in front of mirrors, but the one in the bathroom showed him exactly how he felt, altered forever. He tossed the condom, washed his hands, and wet a washcloth with warm water for Gia. Then he took a moment to steady his heart that was still trying to leap out of his chest and claim her. He took a few deep breaths. And when he returned to his bed, his beauty was asleep.

Fuck. Hugh put his hands on his waist and chuckled softly. *Tuckered out.* He tossed the washcloth across the room into his hamper. Carefully, so as not to wake her, he climbed in bed next to her, tugged the blankets over them, and wrapped himself around her. "Sleep, beautiful one," he whispered.

Hugh watched the darkness for a while, memorized her sighs and smells. When he closed his eyes and tucked his head behind hers, he heard her, in her sleep, whispering words, an incantation, or spell of sorts to keep her, keep *them* safe.

Hugh tightened his arms around her. *Ahh, my mate is a witch. Spectacular.* He'd wondered when he'd witnessed sparks zapping across her skin. But why in the hell was she weaving protection spells in her sleep? One more thing he aimed to discover about her. Now he would do the protecting. It was his pleasure and his duty. And he was fucking ready to step up.

"I've got you, little one. You're mine. No one can hurt you now."

Chapter Four

Gia startled awake. She was in a bed, no, there was no bed, only a white room or box, with nothing in it but white walls and floors. A dizzy sensation swept through her. She started to spin, and the white changed, color seeping into it. Red bled into the white. Blood was everywhere, and so was Doug. Gia let out a scream and fell.

"Hey, hey there, all right?"

Gia blinked her eyes open. This time she really was in a bed. A massively large, unbelievably comfortable bed, with a warm body wrapped around her from behind. *Hugh. Oh shit.* She'd fallen asleep. Her heartbeat kicked into high gear. The nightmare. She hadn't had it in months. Hugh pressed his hand to her chest and hugged her to him. *That feels so nice.* Heat from his body seeped into her and banished the chill and fear.

"Heart's racing, darlin'. You let out a whimper. Bad dream? I've got you."

"No…uh…nothing…I mean, yeah, bad dream I guess." He nuzzled into her, his lips caressing her ear. Whew, tingles shot through her whole body.

"I'm sorry I fell asleep." How mortifying. She couldn't even do a one-night stand correctly. She distinctly remembered him promising more.

"You were tuckered out."

Who says things like that? But damn, in that low, almost growly voice of his. He could probably say anything to her. The combination of his warmth, the soft bed, and his voice soothed her racing fear from her leftover nightmare. She sank into the comfort. *Just for a few minutes, that's all.* Her stomach decided that was the best time in the world to let out a loud, embarrassing rumble.

Hugh's laughter worked its way through her tired muscles, waking her up. "Hungry too." He gave her body a delightful squeeze, then untangled himself from her. *Boo.* He tagged his gray T-shirt from the floor and had it over her head and arms in a few seconds. Soft fabric that smelled like him surrounded her. Oh goodness, she might swoon right here in his bed. She wasn't a swooner. What had gotten into her?

Hugh slowly tugged on his jeans, grinned at her when she watched the motion, took her hand, and led her to the kitchen. And she simply followed. Albeit with her mouth hanging open at how fucking gorgeous he was and the knowledge that he had not one thing on under those jeans. Jeans that fit him like a glove and were worn in in all the right places.

Damn, girl. "What are you...uh...what's happening?" For crying out loud, she couldn't string a few words together. Maybe he really had broken her.

"Feeding you." He winked and dove into his refrigerator.

Feeding me. She could cry. For three years she'd been cold, although her cold was most likely grief and anguish. And she was always hungry. Her sister fed her delicious things too, but this felt different.

Before she knew it, he had pasta boiling and was making a sauce with lemon, black pepper, and the fluffiest grated parmesan he just—poof!—grated himself. Goddess, why was that so sexy? Mm. His forearms moved with such precision, and she sat there, warm and entranced. Wait. Gia studied his loft space, all grays and dark blues, almost black. Soaring ceilings with all the ductwork exposed, tall, gorgeously paned windows giving a glimpse of the snow falling outside and she was..."I'm not cold," she blurted out, catching Hugh's gaze over his shoulder while he stirred the pasta.

"That's a good thing, right?"

She nodded. *Hugh, whoever you are, what have you done to me?* The scent of sautéing garlic lured her into whatever spell he wove around her with his muscles and his sexy, devilish mouth.

"That smells amazing. I'm not...not used to...um...cooking like that." Huh, she was as loopy as one of the noodles he was cooking, her mouth just spewing anything it felt like.

"Like what?" His face scrunched up in disbelief.

"I'm not a very good cook."

His face softened at that. "Thirsty?" He set a glass of water in front of her and grabbed a bottle of wine from a shelf above the refrigerator. "Wine?"

"I think...probably not." She shook her head and sipped the water. The last thing she needed was to faceplant asleep in whatever he was cooking for her. He grinned as if he knew exactly what she'd been thinking and had uncovered all her secrets.

As if he was the one full of magic, he tossed the pasta with the parmesan, lemon mixture, garlic, oil, and some of the pasta water. The aroma was so intoxicating she wanted to stay forever. *Silly girl.*

"Here we go." Bowl of pasta in hand, he came around the island, sat his sexy butt on the stool next to her, and pulled hers closer. He lifted his feet and set them on the rungs of her stool, claiming her. Goddess, she was in so much trouble, this man had already claimed secret pieces of her, shattered her walls, played her body, kissed her. The way he kissed was what dreams were made of.

When she locked onto his gorgeous brown eyes, a memory hit her from before when he was inside her. The golden ring appearing around his irises. She didn't have time to contemplate that as he held the spoon in front of her and she fucking swooned again at the aroma hitting her. Had she been starving her entire life? Maintaining eye contact, she submitted to the pull, the curiosity, the blatant hunger coursing through her. And she opened her mouth.

"Homly www!" Mouth full of the most amazing garlicy lemony pasta she'd ever tasted. She moaned out her words, closed her eyes, and savored. When she got herself under control and opened her eyes, his were piercing her, all glowing intensity. The gold calling to her, to something unique inside her. *Beautiful. Trouble.* Gia put her hands under her thighs so she wouldn't grab him. And then, she did what anyone in her situation would do, opened her mouth for one more bite. And another. She savored his food along with the look in his eyes that in no way banked his desire for her.

After filling her belly, she asked, "Aren't you having any?"

"Not hungry for pasta," he said. He set the bowl on the counter and dragged her onto his lap. "Woman, the way you eat is one of the sexiest things about you."

"Oh...I... I've never tasted anything so good. I didn't..."

He warmed his hands along her thighs to her butt till he was holding her to him. Then he took her lips in a feral kiss, silencing all her confusion. He feasted on her, marking her. Her body automatically bowed toward him, yearning for his hands and his glorious mouth to touch her everywhere now that she was full and warm and needy all over again. Her libido had been completely dead for three years too, and in one night this man had dug it out of its grave and exploded it into outer space.

Gia shimmied out of the T-shirt and tossed it on the floor, sitting naked on his lap. Straddling a near stranger in his kitchen while he sat there in unbuttoned jeans, lavishing kisses on her body, was erotic and sexy. It banished the rest of the world from her thoughts. He brought her breast to his mouth and growled before feeding her nipple into his mouth. *Ahh, so he is hungry for something.* That thought had her soaring with joy and arching into him.

He dragged his hands up her back to cup her neck, tracing lines on the edges of her collarbone. He followed the motion with his lips, nibbling at her neck and shoulder, leaving soft bites along his path. She raked her hands down his back, tried to tug off his jeans, trying to get all his naked heat against hers.

"Could fuck you right here. Could be inside you so fast."

"Yes." Her entire body flushed and sparkled at his words. His dirty mouth was its own erotic kiss. She moved over him, feeling sensual and sleek. Years of elite training on her body to fight and sneak and perform all her stealth maneuvers and this, right here, right now was power. Open and honest and desirous.

He gripped her butt and lifted her, stalking them to the bed in a few long strides. He was so big and tall, much taller than her, and she was five-nine. He had them down, all his hard muscles powering over her. The way his hands touched her with such ferocious need, and his mouth, sucking at her neck while he palmed her breast, rubbing rough circles around her nipple and growling dirty words to her.

"So fucking needy. My little goddess." His hand moved to her hip, kneading and teasing her butt. His hands were everywhere, leaving a scorching path of excitement behind. He tugged her head to the side and licked the column of her neck, placed impatient kisses along her chest, pinned her hands above her head, took one nipple in his mouth, and sucked hard.

"Hugh, goodness," she panted, unable to form coherent sentences, unable to think.

"Can't fucking get enough."

She laughed, digging her heels into the bed to arch into him. Talk about needy. Why was it so hot that he was as out of control for her as she was for him?

"Hugh." She struggled to get her hands free, and he unlocked his hold to drag his rough palms over her body, mapping her skin. She kissed him, ran her fingers through his lush hair, pushed against him, and tugged him to her at the same time. It was a fight, a glorious, heated, wanton fight. The best fight of her life. She struggled to remove his jeans, her feet sneaking in between the fabric and his skin. His cock was hard and pulsing against his belly. "Off with these, get them off. Condom," she begged.

He kicked them off, fumbled to stand, and swore. "Fuck. Condom. Right." He stalked to the bathroom and let loose a string of curses about needing to go fucking shopping. And she laughed. Tearing the package open and coming for her, he said, "You think this is funny, darlin'? This"—he slid the condom over his beautiful cock, all hard and thick and ready for her—"is the last one."

Oh, she nearly laughed at the pout in his voice. This man had the potential to kill her with his emotions out and open for her to see. And the *darlins* and cooking for her and how he ravished her like he'd never seen a woman in his life, and she was all his glory come to be. Her heart raced a mile a minute. She wanted to revel in the now. He wrapped his massive hand around his cock and tugged.

"One condom…" He came over her then, and she was sad to lose the sight of him standing before her, jacking himself off, but excitement ran through her for what was to come. "Will n*ever* be enough for you and me." He gestured his hand between the two of them right before his body met hers.

The *you and me*, the wickedly important gesture of his hand, the sexy emphasis on *ever*, had fear leaping into her throat. What did he mean? What was happening? The moment paused around her as if frozen. All she could hear was the sound of her heart beating and…and his. How was that possible? She swallowed hard, but before she could think, he was on her, kissing her, touching her, melting her. *So divine,* the way he caressed her pussy. He teased her with his cock at her entrance, back and forth, soft erotic movements, and she barely had time to acknowledge how precious that was before he surged inside her in one deep thrust, grunting out his pleasure.

"Fucking hell, woman. You feel so fucking amazing."

"You…I…" She moved her body in tune with his, while a million sparks glittered in her body, her blood, her skin. Everything pulsed where he touched her now, her sensitive breasts where his beard dragged along her, her neck where he left his marks. Her core shook. He dragged out and powered back in, and all she could do was hold on. Torn between keeping her eyes open to mark every single second of this night, this man, this battle, and closing her lids to lose herself in the feeling.

He took the decision away from her when he surged out and flipped her body over. He raked one big hand down her spine, lifted her backside, and surged back in.

"Fuck," she swore. "That's...I'm..."

"All right?" he growled in that voice of his that was so out of control, yet he was still checking on her as he paused his motions.

She pushed back. "That feels amazing." Her mouth was dry, her words breathy.

He powered in, fucking her faster. He gripped her hips, tugging her to him with each thrust. "Phenomenal. All my life, fuck," he swore. "*Never*...something...someone so beautiful."

She shook her head. "Quit talking," she whispered. "That's...ridiculous."

"Hush." He nipped her shoulder, snaked his hand around her waist, and toyed with her clit, sinking his body lower, pressing her into the bed.

Oh, Jesus. She was impaled between his fingers, doing magical things, and his massive hard body powering into her from behind. She could escape if necessary, but how could she want anything else but to be exactly here? He drove everything from her mind and body except sensations. A current flowed through her, electrical, fiery, explosive. Her entire body shook with tingling sensations. His fingers claiming her, his chest moving against her back, his cock so hard and insistent in her. A riot of colors, deep burgundies, purples, and gold all swirled together in her heart.

"Gia, fuck. Fucking hell," he grunted and stilled, and in a heartbeat exploded into her. She responded, losing control and shattering all around this beautiful man.

***

The sky outside was barely turning pink when Gia slid into her tights and dress. She couldn't find her bra, and her hands were shaking, so she probably wouldn't have been able to fasten it anyway. She took one last glance at the man lying on his stomach on his bed. His long body, huge thighs, and glorious butt. His back was so solid and beautiful. And she hadn't gotten to explore it in the light. His arms were over his head, which was tilted to the side, a loopy smile on his face, even in sleep.

Gia shivered, grabbed her boots and coat, and stole down the stairs before he woke, before he asked her to stay, before she confessed all her sins.

Chapter Five

"Well, good morning, Hugh. You...okay?"

Hugh took a mug from the bar area and set it under the expresso machine. He'd come to the restaurant out of sorts. He ground coffee beans, tamped them into the portafilter, and shoved it in the machine. Leaning his head on the Italian behemoth, he pressed the button to start the espresso. When it finished, he added hot water and reached for the heavy cream. Harper already had it on the counter for him.

"You're here early," he said, ignoring her inquiry. Was he okay? Not one bit. Or, he was amazing but also devastated. He was a mess. It was early. Too damn early. Plus, he was upset at the morning because he'd woken alone. The sun had stolen across his bed, welcoming the day, but as soon as he opened his eyes, the empty loft smacked him in the face. Gia was gone. She'd run away in the night or early morning. He hadn't even had to look around. He could no longer feel her there. The pain that filled him with her absence throbbed like an aching tooth. She'd disappeared.

Harper laughed. "These munchkins sleep very little." She patted her enormous round belly, sighed, and sat at the bar with her laptop and papers spread out. "Besides, I love what the early morning affords me, peace and quiet, and today the bright sound of the snow melting. Spring trying to breathe her way in early."

Harper had a way with emotions and descriptions. She could make you feel something with the exact right words. And she was right. He'd always loved the quiet restaurant after a busy night; old memories simmered into the woodwork, and anticipation for the next service awaited.

And today, the snow, the pristine moment, was melting fast as the temps climbed. It would probably all be gone in a few hours, wiped away from the earth as if it had never laid its sparkling blanket upon them. Normally Hugh loved that about the snow, the pure joy of it. Then it was gone and your heart had to wait until the next time. But this morning, he hated everything. *Damn.* Except his coffee.

"You guys get the best coffee. No wonder I end up here."

"Is that the reason you're here this morning, in particular?" The silly grin she gave him had him pausing.

"Pardon?" Hugh closed his eyes and inhaled the rich scent of the roasted beans. Hiding from her for a few more seconds.

"No sense hiding from me. I see all," Harper said, and let out a husky laugh. She was a powerful werewolf herself. In his life, he'd met few more powerful than Harper Flores Webb. "Walked out with my pretty new regular last night, hand in hand, hmm?" She prodded at him.

"You're messing with your peace and quiet," he said, cranky but amused.

"Duncan's in the kitchen scrubbing the range if you'd rather talk to him."

"Hell no," he admitted.

She laughed at him.

"Not yet anyway. He'll die making fun of me." Instinctively, he'd sought Harper, even while he was almost terrified to admit anything to her, or to himself. "She's a regular?" he asked.

Harper wiggled her eyebrows. "This is going to be so much fun."

He palmed his forehead and attempted to rub the ache away. "Please, Harper."

"Okay, love." She took pity on him. "Anyone who comes to eat or drink here more than once is a regular to me." Harper adored their customers, the locals, and the out-of-towners. She was made for shmoozing, loved it too, and the customers loved her. "But she's special, Gia, I think her name is."

"Mm-hmm," Hugh murmured. Harper knew her name. Of course she did.

"She's been in a few times since September, usually near the end of the month, all by herself. She orders the same thing every time."

"Red wine and Granny's cake."

"Yep," Harper said. "A woman after my own heart." She sighed. "Can't wait to have a glass of wine again soon."

Hugh followed her gaze to the table where Gia had sat last night. He could still see her there, surrounded by the frosty glow in the window.

"And she always looks…"

"What?" Hugh asked, desperate for any little morsel and not trying to hide it. Harper saw everything anyway. It was her superpower.

Harper faced him with that serious, searching expression on her face. "Like she has to face the entire world all by her lonesome. And what she has to face is extremely challenging or full of…" Harper closed her eyes tightly as if to ward off the rest. "Full of anguish, despair. Some powerful, painful emotion is driving her. Yet she allows herself a few visits here to enjoy cake. By herself."

Hugh sipped his coffee, keeping his anger to himself. No sense taking it out on Harper or his perfect cup of brew. Gia didn't have to be alone anymore, and he hated that she'd had to at any point, especially if it meant she'd had to face tragedy with no one by her side. And with babies to tend to.

Harper set her hand on his shoulder and gave him a squeeze. "She's kind when she comes in, although she doesn't talk to anyone except to answer our questions or order. She's a great tipper, and when she's not drooling over your grandmother's cake, she's gazing out the window searching."

"Searching?" Hugh asked.

"Mm-hmm, and I suspect part of what she's searching for is you, even if she can't admit it. I saw your smile when you left together. I hope you had a good night, but now I'm guessing things didn't go exactly as you imagined, or your grumpy butt wouldn't be here sitting with boring old me this morning."

Hugh chuckled and stood. He rinsed his mug and put it in the wash rack. When he came back around, he kissed Harper on her cheek. "You are the least boring person I know, Harp. Love you." He donned his beanie and made his way toward the door.

"Love you too. Be careful," Harper whispered. His exceptional hearing allowed her quiet words to reach him. A warning for him or Gia, he wasn't sure. Both maybe. He'd never been in a situation with such powerful feelings involved. He was both certain of who she was to him, and completely out of his league for what to do now.

The only thing he knew was that he'd found his mate, fallen head over heels for her, then lost her. And he needed to figure out what to do with all that. A day on the farm, helping his parents would allow him the mental space to think clearly. Hard work and sweat and the wide-open land surrounded by acres of lush forests and rolling hills. It would be a muddy mess with all the snow melting. Perfect. He loved a good mess. Making it was fun, and so was cleaning up after.

Chapter Six

Gia still had hours before her assignment, but she was unable to nap when she got home. Her night had been incredible, lighting her up inside. Incredible, invigorating, and, as she swept the floors in her kitchen in her quiet house, she found, lonely. Lonely because it had been only one night. That was all she could allow it to be.

The snow was already melting, and there was rain in the forecast. She could let it melt or be proactive. So, she took her humming blood outside and shoveled the heavy wet snow. If it rained on top of snow, then froze as predicted, she'd have a sheet of ice for a driveway.

At least it wasn't as bad as Boston winters. But Boston also had Doug, or the memories at least. Although she rarely allowed herself moments to remember. Gia paused; his face was there in her mind, clear as day. He'd insisted on getting a snowplow so she'd never have to trudge through the snow to get to their small garage, especially not with two little kids. She'd loved drinking hot chocolate and watching him use that machine. Or shrugging on her winter clothes and boots and teasing him with snowballs when he was trying to plow.

Shivering, she pushed herself back to her chore. She'd left the wonder of snow and the plow in Boston where most of her memories lay too. It was too difficult to resurrect them, especially right this minute after she'd...after she'd had such an amazing night and hadn't thought about Doug once. What kind of widow was she?

The tears came fast while she lifted one pile of snow and dumped it into the yard. The rain started in on her too. *Fabulous.* A shitty widow, that's what kind. And certainly not one with laser-sharp focus. She huffed back her tears and put her joyful experience away in a tightly locked box. She had one mission: vengeance. And she couldn't forget it. She could never forget.

***

"Again!" Orin demanded. Gia leapt to her feet and faced her mentor, jogging in place for a second to shake off the quick flare of pain in her hip. Nodding, she raced toward the padded wall in the enormous home gym he had. It was the size of an actual gymnasium. She ran up the wall, kicked off, and flipped backward, landing on her feet, barely. Sweat soaked her tank top and her face was flaming hot. Damn, she was tired. Suddenly, her indulgence in fantastic sex last night didn't seem like the best decision she'd made. *No, no, no. You are going to tuck that beautiful memory inside for now, where no one else can see it.*

She'd been here now for hours, mercilessly working out, practicing her knife skills, sweating her butt off. Orin pushed her regularly, but today seemed extra difficult, extra, everything. He narrowed his eyes and stalked toward her. He tossed her a water bottle that, thank goodness, instincts had her plucking out of the air before it hit her in the face.

"You are distracted." A quick sneer lit his expression as he trailed his gaze down her body before his face returned to the serene mask of indifference. "I can smell it all over you and it will get you killed. I can't have you distracted, Gianna, especially not for this assignment."

She swallowed the entire bottle of water, keeping her gaze steady on his. When she was finished, she wiped the sweat from her face. "I'm not distracted." *Liar.*

"You're something." He stalked away. That was the third time today she'd seen the unfamiliar expression on his face. *Disappointment? Dislike?* Something ugly crawled along her spine and she had to beat back the shiver that threatened to roll through her body and turn her guts out into the wastebasket nearby. A few silent, almost unnoticeable breaths, and she was okay. He must be extra worried about the upcoming assignment he had for her.

"Come," he commanded. "Time to focus."

Gia followed Orin out of the gym and downstairs to his underground office. The entire building looked out of place in the beautiful blue-green mountains of North Georgia. The Appalachians were old and softened with time. This harsh black building, all angled lines, and very few windows felt sharp against the cushion of the hills. From the outside, it appeared to be a modern home, built into the side of the mountain, with a large almost hidden door at the entryway. The enormous garage sat next to it that housed his car collection along with her torture chamber, or, rather, where he broke her down and built her back up.

For almost three years, she'd been training with him. Being a stealth assassin took more than the ability to kill someone quickly. It took absolute focus, agility, and strength to move in ways most people couldn't fathom. His business office and first-generation torture chamber were located just outside of Boston, where she'd used to meet him. Convenient that his home wasn't too far from her new home in Mercy, Georgia. Although neither she nor Orin believed in convenience or such a thing as coincidence. Most likely with his billions and connections, he'd had it built after he'd found out she was moving away from Massachusetts.

She was his ace. He'd told her repeatedly. And he was her savior. But damn, he was a fierce trainer and unnaturally cranky today. She was going to need a bath to work out these aching muscles. What she wouldn't give for a massage too.

"Meet Laszlov, one name, no surname, the underground Hungarian human trafficker." Orin stood at his wall of computers, using his handheld device to direct the screen. A man's face appeared. Black hair cut short, mustache, ugly mouth, and dead, soulless eyes that gave her another shiver. *It's like he can see right into me. Ugh, impossible.* Maybe she *was* distracted. No good time for that, especially not now, as Orin had said. She mentally shoved everything else from her mind.

"He lives in houses around the world. I'm aware of three. There are more, so well hidden no one can find them. Sit and work your magic."

Was it her extra exhausted state or did the word magic hold a touch of disdain from him? She thought he was proud of her powers. He was one of two people in her life who knew she was a witch. He'd helped her tune into her powers, build her physical strength, and hone her ability to play any role necessary. Normally, he celebrated her skills and put them to damn good use.

"See what else you can find. The file of info is right there, full of his aliases, other known whereabouts, and ancestry." Orin sharpened his tone. "And he previously had ties to Douglas' company."

Gia pulled out a chair and got to work. Lured in by the possible connection between this criminal named Laszlov and her dead husband. She would find Doug's killer one day. The back alleys of computers and code along with mathematics were her gifts. The way some people saw how physical things fit together, she saw and felt how numbers, formulas, and programs aligned.

Soon she tuned out Orin's words, or he left. She wasn't sure. When she got to work and sank into her zone, it could be challenging to bring her out. Her fingers flew across the keyboard. Her muscles ached, her brain hurt, her chest... *Don't go there.* She molded her pain and fatigue into vengeance. She'd been doing it long enough, it hardly took any effort at all.

All right, a bit more effort today than normal, but she admitted that out loud to no one. She never knew how long she stayed tuned into her search in the deep dark web. The computer clock told her it had been hours when she finally found it. The pang in her empty stomach told her she'd missed too many meals. "Gotcha," she whispered, her power tingling through her blood.

She pushed away from the keyboard and stretched. Fuck, her body ached everywhere.

"Well," Orin said. It was uncanny how he appeared right when she discovered something. She'd long since gotten accustomed to his stealth aura, but today it nagged at her along with everything else. She needed sleep, and food, lots of food.

"He's going to be in Prague next month at this location, choosing his own new...victims." Hunger turned to bile in her stomach, thinking about what this monster did. He might not be the man who killed her husband, but he was evil, buying and selling children, and she would end him. While Orin helped to both train her and search for Doug's killer, he also gave her the opportunity to expel evil from the world. Together, they took out terrible people.

"You'll intercept him."

"Right." Her reply was automatic. *What if I don't want to?* She suddenly wanted to cry. *Nonsense, this is what you do. This is who you are.* She'd always done exactly as he'd demanded. Luckily, her in-laws, Francesca, or the nanny she'd had in Boston, had been able to watch her kids when she left on one of her "business" trips. She was lucky, she knew that. But she was…so damn tired and lonely.

"And take care of him, like you always do. This is your duty. Rid the world of scum."

His words were knives he carved into her soul. This was her duty, her path. "Absolutely. Anything current for me on…on…" Fuck. Stuttering in Orin's presence was its own kind of sin. He hated any sign of weakness. "Doug's actual killers?"

He'd already turned and started toward his office, with one slight pause in his step at her words. She almost missed it, except she didn't miss anything. She hated this, hated it all, suddenly. The thought flooded her body. Swallowing the fatigue, she forced her face and body into a state of calm, into a state of vengeance. It was the only thing Orin respected. And if he saw hatred in her, for him, he'd be done with her.

He paused at his desk, poured himself a glass of whiskey. "Nothing. You may go. I'll send you the exact details for your trip to Prague."

Dismissed. Well, she huffed, he'd never demanded she go quite like this. *It's fine.* She told herself. She didn't care. Or perhaps she was simply too exhausted to fight today. It seemed like that was all she did, fight battles. He'd walked out of sight before she could answer and that was fine too. She wasn't sure what words would have come out of her mouth then anyway. Better to keep it shut.

She made her way back to the gym, grabbed her coat and purse, and hurried away. Something uncomfortable had her itching to get away from Orin, more and more these last few months. It was difficult to admit she was tired of the work. Somewhere along the way, it felt like her mission to find Doug's killers had gotten lost. Yes, she was ridding the world of evil. But...she couldn't think straight. Her mind was ashes. She drove home to her empty house.

She held the tears at bay as she unlocked the doors and reset the alarm. She held them at bay when she cobbled together a couple of peanut butter and jelly sandwiches and an apple. Depleted of energy, she sank onto the kitchen floor by herself and filled her belly, wishing she was eating chocolate layer cake and kissing Hugh.

Then she double-checked all the locks, climbed the stairs as if struggling up the steepest part of K2, stripped out of her clothes, and sank to the floor of the shower under the hot spray. When the water hit her, she let the tears flow. She cried for Doug. How she'd failed him, still to this day, unable to find his killer, unable to exact revenge. And she cried for Hugh, a man who, for one night, had given her back herself and made her feel as though she was more than a horrible mother, a woman whose life was a mess, an absolute failure. She wrapped her arms around her knees, let the hot water assault her and she cried angry, miserable tears. So many tears. Would they ever stop? Would she ever not be so alone in the world?

Chapter Seven

She was on time for her ten o'clock appointment with Webb Industrial, barely. Having slept like crap, she wished she could sink right back into bed. Gia loathed getting up early. She'd trained her body to wake at any hour, but her true nature adored sleeping in. What were wonderfully comfortable beds made for, if not for sleeping long, cozy hours?

And well, other things. Her cheeks flushed at the memory of Friday night. She still had memories on parts of her skin from that beard. *Oh my.* Three years was a long time to not have sex. Three years was even longer to be alone. Not that she was ever truly alone, with two kids and her freelance work and, well, her other stuff.

The building before her took her breath away, and she banished all thoughts of sex and loneliness. Webb Industrial, creators of robotics and prosthetics, had been around for over thirty years, started by Drake Webb. But this particular building was brand new and sleek in design, with its asymmetrical metal roof leaping out over the grounds. Beautiful wood beams held the roof up and created shady areas around the four-story building. Enormous metal planters were empty, but a landscaper was currently filling them with soil and small evergreens.

Gia was here, to help their financial systems leap into the current century alongside their amazing products. It wasn't the first business she'd helped improve their financial technology, but it was the first that specialized in robotics and new-age prosthetics. One would think their technology would be top-notch, but they'd grown and burst their britches with their latest core flex module for amputees and hadn't had a chance to bring every department to the next level. Most people weren't good at everything required to run a good business or life, for that matter.

She was no one to talk about balance. After all, her work-life balance was completely skewed. For now, that was how it had to be, seeing as how she'd dedicated her soul to revenge.

At least this job gave her a way to feel good.

It was exciting for her to help a business like this, one that was itching to grow and change and play. Mr. Webb had seemed so kind on the phone last month when he'd called her and commissioned her services. Laughing at how slow they'd been to get their finances in order and how pushy his son had been that they get to it. The love she heard in his voice for his company sold her. Hence, Webb Industrial was her newest contracted client. Beginning today. It wouldn't be a long assignment, but it could be a good one. *Chin up, girl. This is what you're good at. Time to prove it.*

The gorgeous wooden door opened automatically before Gia, so she paused briefly, giving herself a much-needed pep talk, and entered.

"Ahh, you must be Ms. Reily?" A tall Black man with an earpiece and a gorgeous pink paisley tie stood behind the front desk. "So happy to welcome you. I'm Cole."

"Gia, please. It's nice to meet you, Cole. Cool building," she said. The entry had vaulted ceilings with floor-to-ceiling windows maximizing the view of the gorgeous mountains and trees.

"Pretty awesome, isn't it?" Cole shook her hand, then swiped something on his handheld device.

"So is your arm," Gia said. His right arm was black and silver and sleek, with robot-like fingers moving nearly faster than human ones.

He preened and held it out for her to see. "I know, right? My husband thinks it's sexy."

"It totally is." She smiled.

Cole winked at her, put her at ease immediately, and led her through two more stunning wood doors and down a well-lit hallway with offices on either side and a large conference room full of windows at the end. She loved the windows. Her heart gave a happy little sigh.

"Mr. Webb," Cole said, leading Gia into the conference room. "This is Gianna Reily."

"Thanks, Cole. Would you mind checking on my sons? They asked to be here for this meeting."

"On it," Cole said as he left the room.

"Ms. Reily, a pleasure. Call me Drake, whatever you're comfortable with."

His handshake was warm and strong. She liked him immediately. Thick silver hair was cut and smoothed back. And his blue eyes danced as if he'd never seen a drop of sadness in his life. The lines around his eyes told a different story. No one got to his age without experiencing life's emotions, all of them.

"Do have a seat if you wish. Can I offer you coffee, tea, or water?"

She set her bag down and followed him to the sideboard, where an elaborate hot water and expresso maker sat beside an assortment of teas, coffees, and a glass pitcher of water with lemon slices. She took a glass and poured herself some water.

"No coffee for you today? It's organic Peruvian with hints of orange and chocolate." Drake laughed. "Sorry, bit of a coffee snob here."

Gia smiled at him. "I'm worried I'll get the jitters and look like a fool in front of you. Maybe after my nerves settle."

"Ahh, nothing to be nervous about. You've already been hired, my friend. Now it's all about the details."

"Speaking of details, this place is lovely, fantastic, actually. Not sure lovely is the word used to describe a behemoth building made of wood and metal, but you've softened all the edges somehow with the light and the setting, the windows, the plants, even the interior design is comfortable."

"Thank you. I had nothing to do with it. It was all my son. He's the computer design genius around here, among his other talents." Drake Webb turned. "Ahh, here he is now. Hugh, meet Gianna Reily. She's the one who's going to whip our finances into shape."

Oh shit. Gia's mouth hung open. *Other talents indeed.* Holy crap...what was happening? Drake Webb's son was none other than her one-night-stand from Friday, strutting his gorgeous body right into the conference room. He'd cut his hair super short, almost buzzed, and he'd shaved his goatee. She still felt his goatee on her thighs. But his eyes stood out, golden and gorgeous and wide as he studied her. Without thinking, she made to smile, her entire body lit from within with pleasure from his nearness.

Hugh put his hands on his hips and let out a rough laugh. And that shot all her good vibes right out the window.

The. Man. Laughed. At. Her.

"Hugh?" his father inquired.

Hugh made a choking sound. Not very subtle at all, especially since his smile was still there. That same smile that had melted her at first sight the other evening. Oh yeah, it was sweet and sexy and sinful, and...right this minute, it was mocking. If there was one superpower Gia wished she had at this moment, it was to keep her fair skin from blushing. Christ, she shouldn't be the embarrassed one. The jerk laughing at her should. But it never worked that way in real life.

"Sorry, Dad...uh...I..." He pinned Gia with those gorgeous, no, not gorgeous, mocking eyes and said, "I was thinking about something else. Ms. Reily, apologies for my rude behavior." He held out his hand. "Such a pleasure to meet you."

Chapter Eight

He wasn't sure she was going to take his hand. *Fuck.* When he'd realized in that split second who she was, the laughter burst out of him. Joyful laughter, he couldn't believe his luck laughter. But judging by the smoke coming out of her eyes, it hadn't appeared that way to her. She wasn't laughing. She was barely smiling, the polite, controlled look of someone wearing a mask.

"Mr. Webb," she said and shook his hand with a wrestling-tight grip. Her eyes were void of humor or warmth. If a woman could shoot daggers with those beauties, he'd be dead. Nope, not one hint of humor at the situation or at the memory of what they'd shared on Friday.

"I'm here," his brother Grant said, sliding into the conference room. "Sorry about that. I was on a call. You must be Ms. Reily." Grant held out his hand and Gia shook it too.

"Another Mr. Webb?" she asked.

"There are way too many of us," Grant said, winking at her.

Suddenly Hugh wanted to tackle his brother and boot him right out of this meeting.

"Listen, I'm in charge of sales and I have an appointment, but I wanted to say hello. Please call me if you need anything while you're here." Then Grant was gone as quickly as he'd come.

"Right, Hugh," his dad said, patting Hugh on the shoulder. "Can I trust you to show Ms. Reily around and get her set up in her office?"

"It's Gia, please," she said to his father.

"Well, Gia, I look forward to having you here. I'll check in on you later." He winked, gave Hugh a stare, and was gone.

"Gia Reily," Hugh said, grinning. He couldn't help it. This had to be fate.

"It's Ms. Reily to you." She dropped her fake almost smile, lifted her bag, and said, "Please show me where I'll be working." She reached for her glass, but her hand was shaking so she gripped her fingers into a fist and held them at her side.

Short. To the point. All business. Where was the lush, brilliant woman from the other night?

"Are you okay?" He took a step backward to give her space. Something wasn't right. "I'm glad you're here. You left, and I didn't know where—"

"Do you laugh at all your contractors or employees? Let me give you a hint: making fun of the people you're working with isn't professional. I have plenty of clients if I'm going to be an issue for you."

Ahh, shit. He dropped his smile and tried to catch her eyes. "I apologize. I wasn't laughing at you. Never. I was surprised to see you, that's all. In a good way. I thought—"

"Whatever you thought. Don't." She put her hand up. "I can't...I don't...I don't sleep with clients," she whispered, looking around and through the glass walls.

Right. That hint of wary or wounded soul flashed through her. He'd caught glimpses of it when they were talking in the restaurant, and more when she'd woken screaming from a nightmare. A woman with pain inside her. His woman. He was going to have to tread carefully.

"I apologize again. I...uh, would you like a tour? It's a pretty impressive place."

The hint of wary in her expression changed to shock before she slammed a shield over her face. "I'd like to get right to work."

"Right," he said. *Wrong, wrong, wrong.* "We put you in an office this way." Hugh led her to the end of the hall where a nice corner office sat that had yet to have an occupant. Rapid growth was good for sales, but they needed to get the rest of their business aspects up to date. Hugh was delighted his dad was ready to have someone else inspect their finances.

The office was clean and brand new, and it had the chic industrial look they'd been going for, but seeing it now, with her standing inside it, it lacked personality. She deserved more than clean and industrial. He'd have to figure out how to make it warmer while she was here. Was she someone who liked art on the walls? Flowers? Perhaps a soft rug under the desk for when she slipped those high heels off. Or a few more chairs in case her kids came to visit her at work. *Whoa, boy. You're getting ahead of yourself.* She was unloading her things onto the desk, ignoring him, closed in on herself. Damn it. He was such an ass.

"Gia?" He stood in the doorway and spoke softly so as not to hurt her further.

"Hmm?" She looked up, void of expression, except for the blush on her neck giving away her emotions.

"I...can we start over?" He didn't want to start over. He would never forget their night together.

She paused and glanced his way, camouflaging herself with each second. "As business acquaintances, sure. I work for you now and you're in need of my expertise." She brushed him off and turned back to her desk, opening the laptop and sitting down. She was extremely effective in dismissing him. He wanted to laugh at how fucking stunning she was like this too. All business. Looking so damn smart and in charge. He wisely kept that laugh to himself.

So now wasn't the time. But fuck was he glad she was here because he'd intended to spend this week tracking her down and asking her out.

"Desk can raise up if you prefer to stand. Fan, blinds, and thermostat are all wireless and can be controlled from your computer. There's a cabinet behind your desk with a key in case you feel more comfortable locking away your purse."

"Do you have a login for me, or should I contact the IT department?" she asked without looking at him.

"Cole should have texted your login. Once you open the text, it will disappear in five minutes. I would say, if you forget it, IT can help you, but I have a feeling that would be an insult and I'm going to leave now and let you get to work instead of making a bigger fool of myself."

"Thank you," she said.

"Hey." He couldn't resist it. He ached to see her blush one more time before he got to work.

She spared him a glance.

"I'm glad you're here."

Her mouth parted, a tiny crack in her armor. Then she nodded and did her best to ignore him. It was one more brush-off. But as he left and headed toward the on-site gym, he was thrilled with the knowledge that his mate was right here in the vicinity, even if she was seriously pissed at him.

He spared a look at the conference room on his way, did a double take, and circled back. He refilled her water glass, made her an Americano, and used a small tray to carry the water, the coffee, and some cream and sugar to her. It would hopefully bring more comfort to a day that probably hadn't gotten off to the start she'd imagined.

Samantha was wheeling down the hallway, Charlie by her side, when Hugh came out of the conference room. "Ahh, going to check out our new finance guru, are you?" he asked.

"Of course," she said, pausing. "Gianna Reily is notorious for her financial predictions. It's my duty to check out all badass female employees, contractors, whatever." She flicked her hand. "I'm outnumbered here."

"I thought we had a good mix of genders, including those who don't identify as either," Hugh said. "We're inclusive."

Samantha rolled her eyes. Her bouncy blond curls, enormous brown eyes, and lips that seemed permanently tipped up at the corners in a smile gave the impression of a cute, ditzy, happy young lady. Good thing Hugh knew she was a brilliant, shrewd designer with an extremely sardonic sense of humor to go along with her enormous heart.

"Please, don't tell me you think the toxic masculinity of some of the male employees you still have working here can be outweighed by a mere equal amount of genders. Gah! That would take more than you could ever imagine, pretty boy."

"Is it that bad?" he asked, serious now. "My brother isn't like that, is he?"

"You know it's not your brothers, Hugh, any of them, or your father. Good men, all of you. Who's that for?" She changed the subject. "Let me guess, you're checking out the badass too?" Samantha crossed her arms and grinned.

Hugh swallowed his discomfort. "Uh...not exactly. We already met this morning. I thought she might want some coffee." He studied the tray. "But she might have already had enough of my face today."

"Let me take it."

Hugh glanced down the hall and back at Samantha. Probably a safer idea. "He set the tray carefully in her lap. "Okay. Thank you."

"Sure. There's a story here I'm dying to uncover. You know that, right?"

Hugh said nothing. Instead, he saluted her and took off in the other direction. He'd see Gia later. He was confident about that. Better not push his luck this morning. The last glance she'd shot his way said she wanted to push him into the lake.

Chapter Nine

WHY WERE HER HANDS shaking, damn it? He wasn't in the doorway anymore. She'd watched from under her lashes when he left. But she couldn't get herself under control.

First, he'd surprised the hell out of her, and her heart had leapt at seeing him walk into that conference room. Then he'd laughed at her, it had seemed. But he'd apologized and he'd been kind. Then he'd been all subtly intense, nearly flirty again. Good Lord, she felt giddy. And those eyes of his transformed with every emotion he expressed. She certainly hadn't forgotten how soulful and gorgeous his eyes had been. She'd never forget.

And now she worked for him, worse, for his family. One amazing night with the sexiest man she'd ever met, a man so far out of her league in every way possible. She'd wanted to hold that memory precious, would have been grateful for it. He'd offered her a tour and her mind had gone straight to an image of him naked and asleep on his bed, with all his muscles waiting for her to map them, learn them. Yes, absolutely she wanted a tour.

She closed her eyes and took a breath. "Breathe. Hold it. Find that inner strength. Put everything else out of your mind. There you go, let it out. Your heart. Your body. You're the one in control."

"I'm going to like you already." A soft voice startled Gia's eyes open. A woman in a sleek wheelchair sat in her doorway. Her smile was wide and bright, and there was mischief in her eyes. Gia could've sworn. A large brown Labrador Retriever sat beside her with his guide dog vest on.

"I come bearing gifts." The woman pushed a button, wheeled in, and set a tray carefully on the desk. "And yes, you're in control. So glad we have another badass female here. I'm Samantha or Sammy." She offered her hand, but her entire demeanor said she offered friendship and sisterhood and kindness too. Not a hint of shield around her. Either that or she was extremely good at hiding it. Gia knew all about disguises.

"Gia. Nice to meet you. And thank you for the drinks." She gestured to the tray. "I left my water...I mean, wait, did he ask you to bring this because you're a woman?"

Sammy tilted her head, and her smile grew. "Definitely a story," she mumbled. "If the he you're referring to is Hugh Webb, he was actually delivering it himself and I tackled him to let me do it because I had to meet you."

"I bet you could tackle him." Gia grinned. "Sweet ride."

Sammy beamed. "Thanks. You should see my basketball wheels. Sleeker and lighter than these. And they're teal. I was going to go with pink, but I didn't want to hear anyone tell me they were distracted by the color when I beat them."

Gia laughed and held out a hand for a fist-bump. "So tell me what you do here, besides deliver coffee," Gia joked.

"I'm one of the designers." She spun her chair around. "Ta-da."

"Outstanding. You designed that? Wow! You obviously know what you're doing."

Sammy laughed. "I should hope so. With degrees in neuroscience and electrical and computer engineering, I have the student loans to prove I damn well better be good at my job. And you're the numbers lady, huh?"

"I am," Gia said, pouring too much cream into her coffee, the way she liked it. She didn't need more coffee and she should get to work, but talking to Sammy was delightful. And rarely did Gia allow herself to push all the shoulds out of the way. "Who's your friend?"

"Oh!" Sammy beamed. "This is Charlie or Charlie Girl. She's my best pal. Sorry, I forgot to introduce you, girl." Sammy scratched the dog under her chin. "When she's on duty she likes lots of space, occasional paw shakes, and 'Good girls!' Off-leash, she's a fool for belly rubs, snuggles, and treats."

Aren't we all?

"Unfortunately, she doesn't always ask consent before kissing. We're working on it."

Gia laughed.

Sammy leaned over and whispered, "Hopefully, they'll rid themselves of Trent, the accountant, now that you're here."

"Oh, well. I'm not so much an accountant as a financial consultant."

"You're a genius. I read all the accolades." Sammy whirled her hand in the air. "A woman can dream. Listen, I have to get to a meeting, but seriously, watch out for the accountant. He's one of the last MOWM holdouts." She made a grimace.

"MOWM?" Gia asked.

Sammy looked down the hallway and whispered, "Misogynistic old white man."

"I can handle him. Hey, thanks for coming to say hi and bring me drinks. I appreciate it."

Sammy waved and smiled. "See ya."

Gia sat and savored her coffee before she got to work. Ten o'clock already. Time was flying and she hadn't accomplished a thing. She put her earbuds in, turned her music on, and started gathering information.

***

An hour later, Gia was well on her way to categorizing the old investment accounts. Organizing them had been easy, simply because there hadn't been that many. Figuring out how much Webb Industrial had invested over the years and what had been happening with that money would take more time. However, it wasn't so much the past that they'd hired her for; it was the present and the future.

One aspect missing from the past and the present was their basic bookkeeping records. She'd had to dig for those files and once she'd found them, the last five years still had information missing.

If she was going to create a comprehensive investment plan, she had to know how much money they had and how much they were projected to grow. The end numbers of revenue were listed cleanly and succinctly in the report, but she needed more than that. She needed to see the entire picture.

Sammy had mentioned the accountant. Something nudged at the back of Gia's eyes. One quick tick, like having perfect vision, then suddenly experiencing a flash of blurry. A few seconds later, things were clear again. Her instinct honing in on an error, a warning, something that wasn't quite right.

That familiar ghostly ache soured in her gut that she hadn't known to heed it that one time all those years ago. *Will that pain ever disappear?* It shouldn't. She didn't deserve peace.

Pushing out of her chair, she shoved the memories away. *Center yourself. Attack the problem clearly and efficiently.* Orin's words. He'd taught her well; he'd definitely taught her more than words.

No time like the present to meet the man who held the numbers. She hadn't lied to Sammy when she'd said she could handle him. She smoothed her hands over her hips. Even without her secret weapons, she could take a man down in under three seconds physically. Although it was nice to know she had her backup with her today.

Although she wasn't an accountant, she needed to work with him initially, or at least get access to some of his files to do her job correctly. Time to find the man.

She opted for re-orienting herself to the front desk and her new buddy Cole with the bionic arm. Her senses told her he was a good person. Plus, it couldn't hurt to have someone know where she was. Perhaps he could introduce her to the accountant. One more tick flashed through her mind as she wondered why, in fact, the accountant hadn't been to the meeting this morning with all of them.

"Ahh, Ms. Reily, how's it going?" Cole set his tablet down and smiled at her.

"Great, Cole. Could I talk to Mr. Bordin, your accountant? I think he has a few documents I need."

Cole's smile flattened into a grimace. "Unfortunately, he's not in yet, Ms.—"

"Please call me Gia."

"Right, well, Gia. He's not in and I wouldn't be surprised if he isn't in all day today."

"Does he work from home?"

"Oh, God, no. He...uh...he likes to be seen, is the nicest way I can put it," Cole whispered.

Hmm, it wasn't anything she hadn't heard or suspected. What was odd was that he wasn't here today. If he enjoyed being seen, why would he not show on her first day?

"But I'm so glad you came down here," Cole said. "I was about to call you to give you a tour before lunch. The Webbs ordered a delicious spread from Adair's for you today."

Gia ignored the hint of fire in her belly at the mention of Adair's. Where she'd first heard Hugh's voice, witnessed the gold shimmer in his eyes, where... *Get it together, Gia.*

"Wait until you see the gym," Cole said. He showed her a few of the offices like hers, pointed upstairs to a glassed-in area that was the café, and whisked her down an all-windowed hallway behind which was a large room with high ceilings full of open desks, including some large tables and huge monitors where a bunch of employees worked together. "It's the best part."

He led her through a beautiful atrium-type extension full of lovely, lush plants with floor-to-ceiling windows. They were at least two stories above ground, and the view was magnificent. A bright blue sky with drifting white clouds was the perfect backdrop to the mountains. Rolling hills to the northeast glittered with a dusting of snow. While closer to them, the snow had melted, leaving the barren landscape stretching out to forever.

Glass doorways opened at the end to an enormous multi-storied building that felt like the size of an airplane hanger but was one thousand times more impressive. She and Cole stood at a railing, looking down on it all. One level down was a track that ran around the circumference of the place. Beneath that, on the ground level, was a sort of amusement park of exercise and workout brilliance. It simply was stunning.

Several glass-walled areas lined one end, like racquetball courts, but each one was different. There was a field with astroturf where a few kids with different prosthetics were kicking a soccer ball. A climbing wall and basketball court flanked one end. More glass gave a view to two large swimming pools, and in the center of it all were free weights, rowing machines, bikes, treadmills, and random computer stations set on wheels. So many more things she couldn't identify.

"Well?" Cole asked.

"This is incredible!" she said. "I'm so impressed. You don't notice the massiveness of it at all from the front."

"I know right, the hills hide it. Once the weather warms, we'll finish the outdoor parts around the lake. Tennis courts, outdoor pool, outdoor track and field. If Hugh could have conjured a ski slope right here, we'd have that too. But whatever sport or physical activity we can't mimic exactly, we can at least work on the motions of."

Speaking of Hugh, the man took her breath away. He was several stories below her, pointing to something on one of the monitors beside another man who held a curved leg in his hand and was pushing against the end of it. Hugh was dressed in workout gear, a black tight T-shirt, black shorts, and running shoes. He touched the screen, let out a whoop, and high-fived the other man.

Gia sighed like a smitten teen. He was so full of life. He didn't hide one single part of himself. As if he'd heard her sigh, he put his hands on his hips, slowly turned her way, and lifted his head. And the grin that appeared on his face made her heart trip over. *Uh oh.*

Chapter Ten

Hugh raced to make it on time to the lunch they'd catered for Gia. Everyone who worked here was used to the casual environment, especially since many of the employees worked with clients in the gym regularly helping them get a perfect fit on their prosthesis, fix issues, or simply test new versions. But he wished he'd had time to clean up.

So far today he'd run three miles, climbed the rock wall several times, and gotten his ass kicked at HORSE on the basketball court by two high schoolers testing out their prosthetic legs for junior athletes.

He wasn't late, barely. But he was the last to arrive. Gia sat at a round table by the window, smiling and blushing under the attention. Fuck, almost as pretty as seeing her smiling down at him in the compound thirty minutes ago. There was a near constant deep pink aura around her. It changed sometimes, to gold, to magenta when he was buried inside her. *Fuck!* He closed his eyes and breathed steadily, trying to get his raging libido under control.

She was surrounded by Samantha, his dad, his mom, and Cole. Of course she was surrounded. People enjoyed being near her. She couldn't hide all her beauty. She wore a pair of dark glasses he hadn't seen yet, giving her that sexy librarian vibe. He grabbed a plate at the buffet and filled it with Adair's famous crawfish pasta, fresh bread from Sweet Delights Bakery, and some of Harper's peach and burrata salad. He'd have to come back for the chocolate cheesecake.

"May." Hugh leaned in and kissed his mom on the cheek.

"Hi, honey. Have you met Gianna yet?"

"I have," he said. "Gianna," he drew out her beautiful name and gave her a nod. "Having a good day so far?" He pulled out the empty chair across from her. Next to her would have been better *and* worse. At least this way, he could look directly at her.

"Yes, thank you." Short, to the point. He wanted to get her relaxed. He nearly choked on his pasta. This wasn't the place for it, but damn if his heart didn't beat like it was on steroids around her, especially now that he'd had her, his body recognized hers as its mate. He ached to be close to her every second. There was no going back from that. Now he had to find a way to explain it all to her.

"Hugh?" May poked his arm, jolting him out of his thoughts. "I asked you if you gave Gianna a tour of this amazing building you designed."

"I...uh...no." He sucked back his water. Maybe he shouldn't eat and drool over her at the same time.

"I did," Cole said. "Was happy too. I love seeing people's faces when they walk into the gym from the atrium. Never gets old."

"What do you think, Gianna? Good place to work?" May asked her.

"It's all very cool," Gia said. "Hugh did an amazing job."

She sent him a quick glance, and he beamed at her praise. *My heart, she's so damn pretty.*

"I didn't even know it was here. I've only been in Mercy since September. My kids and I." She put a bite of pasta in her mouth and closed her eyes. He could practically hear her sigh from across the table. The pasta was damn good. But he wished she'd keep talking. He was learning so many things about his guarded, brilliant, intriguing witch.

"What brought you to Mercy?" May asked, drawing Gia out. May had a way with people. Hugh was content to sit and listen.

"My...uh sister is a doctor here at Mercy General. She works in the ER."

"Dr. Banetti?" his dad asked.

Gia smiled and nodded. That genuine smile of hers.

Hugh was so far gone, it wasn't funny.

"Yes, how do you know her?"

"Drake had an accident with a goat a few months ago," May said. "Your sister was the doctor who helped us, stitched him up so well his arm doesn't have a scar. She was so lovely. It didn't even feel like being at the hospital."

"Francesca has a…she's very good at taking care of people. Thank you so much for the lunch. It was completely unnecessary but lovely." There she went, shifting the attention off herself again.

"This pasta is to die for," Samantha said. "I might sneak some home for my dinner."

"Yeah, Dad, good choice on the menu," Hugh offered.

"I should do it for everyone more often," his dad said. "Treat the employees here and support Duncan and Harper at the same time. Have you been to Adair's, Gia?" His father asked, and it was her turn to choke on her water. She was much smoother at it than he was.

"I have. I've been several times since we moved here."

"What's your favorite item?" Hugh asked. He leaned his head on his hand and grinned at her.

She got that surly stare on her face that he'd originally thought this morning meant she was upset. Now it read as annoyance and, boy, was she hot when she was annoyed at him. Her eyes got all sparkly. So did her fingers, he noticed, as she gripped her fork. He expected her to zap him.

"I don't know if I've tried enough items to have a favorite." She aimed a quick glare at him, and he sure wished they were alone so he could see what would happen if he teased her a little more. Unfortunately, other employees strolled over to greet her, and Hugh had to settle for watching.

It was a pleasant lunch, delicious, but all Hugh could think about was Gianna. He got up and helped clear some plates. His dad and mom left, along with Cole and Samantha. There were a few other stragglers he spoke to. Then he grabbed a piece of cheesecake and took it back to his table where Gia sat by herself, scrolling through her phone. He sat next to her with the cheesecake and two forks. "Care for some dessert? I noticed you didn't get any."

She placed her phone down and looked around the room. "Hugh. What are you doing?"

"Being polite to the new contractor," he drawled.

She smirked at him. "That's not what you're doing." Her voice was a whisper, and he liked that as much as her confident battle points. She ignored him and dragged the plate closer to her.

He smiled. He couldn't help it. Everything was so fucking awesome. He'd found her. His heart wanted to run and play like a puppy and curl up with her at the same time. "Careful, it's almost as good as my grandma's chocolate cake." His gaze focused on the skin right above her collarbone. He knew how soft, how delicate it was. Her pulse beat right there for him.

She rolled her eyes, and he had to laugh. But the little moan she let out after taking a bite of the cheesecake didn't make him want to laugh at all. "Damn, woman," he whispered and ran his hand over his face.

"Hush," she said. "If you can't behave, you can't sit here next to me."

"Gia, those moans of yours." Behave was the very last thing he wanted to do. But he also didn't want to make her uncomfortable. She'd said strictly professional, and he'd respect that unless she gave him an in. He could be patient. Even if it meant he'd need to run a few more miles after sitting this close to her while her scent stole over him, reminding him of every last inch of her naked body beneath his. Christ, this was going to be harder than he thought.

"It's good cheesecake," she said, all prissy, and took another bite, licking the fork.

And damn if he wasn't rock hard. At least she hadn't kicked him away. He could handle the torture, if that's all she'd allow him for the moment. "Don't remember the eyeglasses from the other night."

Her expression tightened, and she glanced away. "I don't always wear them."

Hmm, now he'd upset her. Because he'd mentioned the glasses or because of something else? "They look pretty, add to your brilliance," he said quietly.

She pushed the plate away and stood. "Thank you, your family, for a delicious lunch. It wasn't necessary at all. I've never…I mean…other companies…well, I'm used to the bare min…I mean, it's unusual, that's all."

Mm-hmm, there she went, giving away another tiny secret about her life. What kind of life had she been leading where the bare minimum was how she measured things? She hadn't actually said it, but he'd heard it, nonetheless. He could read through the lines pretty fucking well. He wanted more for her, from her. More everything, her moans, her delight in wonderful things, her unabashed beauty with no wall separating the two of them.

Crumbs she'd given him today before she'd brushed them all away and slammed the door on anything else personal. He'd take the crumbs for now. Every bit was another piece to her magnificent puzzle.

"I'm going to finish for the day before I go pick up my kids."

He stood. "Danny and Ava, right?"

"You, uh..." Her cheeks flushed and her guard was down for a split second before she recovered. "You remembered their names. I get the feeling you don't forget much."

"Somehow I bet you don't either." He could practically see the streaks of lightning pulling them together. He sure as hell could feel it. Wished she'd let it happen. "Please finish your cheesecake. I'll see you tomorrow." And he turned and left, feeling her gaze on him the entire time. *That's right. You feel it too, beautiful.* And he smiled before he headed back to the track to run off some of this steam.

Chapter Eleven

Gia tried not to slump into her chair, and she refrained from fanning herself, but good lord have mercy, she'd been hot flashing over Hugh as soon as he'd entered the lunch room wearing the same black workout clothes she'd witnessed from that glorious vantage point high above him in the gym. At lunch, he'd been feet, *inches* away from her smelling fan-fucking-tastic.

What had saved her from jumping across the table and begging for his attention in the form of his amazing hands on her was the outstanding pasta from Adair's restaurant. Gah, could she move into the restaurant and eat all her meals there from now on?

And this cheesecake. She swallowed another bite and moaned inwardly this time. She didn't even like cheesecake. But it was out of this world. She finished every crumb while she secretly remembered her night with Hugh, all his glorious skin and muscles, how strong and passionate he'd been for her, Gia

Reily, a tired single mom, a woman who had no business being with someone like Hugh Webb. Lord, for so many reasons.

Never in her life had she had trouble keeping her thoughts PG about a co-worker before. *Maybe that's because you've been half-dead for the past three years. You hush too*, she reprimanded herself. No other coworker had been Hugh Webb. That was the problem and what a problem it was right now. She'd have to avoid him. A spear of pain lanced into her chest at that thought. Tiny pinpricks of gold danced along her skin. She hid her hands in her lap, hoping no one else had noticed. She had priorities and Hugh Webb wasn't one of them.

Taking her dishes to the bin, she grabbed her purse and glanced up. An older, heavyset man with sideburns that said he was stuck in the seventies stood at the back of the café near the doors. Hands crossed over his chest, fake smile on his face. It was the eyes that felt like they were stabbing her. Her instinctual tick sped up. Off the charts. Trent Bordin, she guessed. Good. She'd worn her glasses, hoping to meet him. She had no idea why so many men thought her stupider with glasses. *Not Hugh*. Hmm, something else to tuck away for later. How he always made her feel special.

The man stayed there as she approached the exit. A few other people sat eating their lunches. Good, perhaps this would be an easy encounter. At least there'd be witnesses.

"So you're the financial girl they've hired? And a nice posh lunch to welcome such a pretty young thing."

Lovely. So that's how he's going to play it. Game on. "Gianna Reily. Mr...." She added a touch of softness and lilt to her voice. Hopefully that, coupled with her hair in a bun and the glasses, gave her the air of young innocence. Or whatever the fuck this yahoo needed to see in order to intimidate her.

He took her hand, and Gia had to refrain from gagging. It wasn't simply the vodka oozing from his pores. People said they couldn't smell vodka, but she could. Beyond that was a swirling, awful feeling, a sinking into quicksand.

"Trent Bordin. The accountant." He twisted her hand and leaned in to kiss it when she quickly pulled it away. *Eww.*

She pretended to cover her mouth in a fake sneeze, clasped her hands and gave him the fakest of fake smiles, while his expression slid into one of veiled disgust.

"So nice to meet you, Mr. Bordin. I think I'm supposed to get some files from you, accounting for the last few years. I'm having so much trouble on my laptop trying to find them. You know how it is, being so young and all." She might have been laying it on thick. Hard to assess his reaction since he was swimming in alcohol.

"Mm," he slid his icky gaze over her body. "The files are there. Made sure of it myself. I'll have to get you paper copies. Bring them by your office, shall I?"

"Certainly," she said as he walked away. Knowing full well he was lying. It had become such an easy behavior for her to detect.

As he disappeared, she shed the young and dumb expression she'd projected. That was another thing that had become easy for her, switching between all the aliases she used to perform her jobs. Easy didn't mean it didn't wear on her. She stood, collecting her emotions for a few moments under the rays of sunshine streaming through the windows. When her temper calmed, she headed back to work.

As she turned the corner opening to the bank of hallway windows that gazed out onto the lake, she saw Drake Webb and his wife, May. Hugh's lovely parents. They were strolling toward the forest. Well, Drake was walking. He carried May. She had her arms around his neck and adoration on her face. Gia couldn't hear them but they looked like they were laughing. It didn't take a computer genius to see that. Closeness, joy, belonging.

Jealously spiked from her gut to choke her. She had to place her hand on the glass and catch her breath. The ache was so acute. She watched them long after they disappeared into the thick copse of trees.

When she finally made it to her office, she slowed as she approached the door. Before she reached the knob, she could tell it was unlocked. A door she'd intentionally locked before she'd left earlier.

She filed it away with all the other ticks she'd had. It seems she was compiling a report on more than their financial investments. *Focus. Compartmentalize. Ignore everything else.* More digging around files led her to the same conclusion. She did not have all the files. Every unsettled instinct she'd had today centered around Trent.

Not a good sign for her as she'd unfortunately have to work with him, but more importantly, it didn't bode well for the Webbs that, for all she could tell, their accountant was hiding important company information. Not to mention him being drunk at one in the afternoon at work.

She wondered, since everyone she'd met in the Webb family so far seemed like such good people, and intelligent too, why they had Trent Bordin handling their money. The misogyny and ego were things she could handle. The big red flag was the lying.

She hated lying. It left her unsettled and feeling as though she needed a shower. How ironic that she'd become excellent at it the last three years. She'd told herself it was for the greater good. *Is it?* The pulse started low in her brow, drumming to a full headache. It felt like, with each pretend role she played, each lie she told, each shield she erected around her heart, she lost more and more of her true self.

The throbbing in her head made it difficult to concentrate. Even the ibuprofen she took did nothing to dim the dull ache pressing in on her brain. She had two more hours of work to do before she left to get the kids. There was nothing but to power through what had turned into a strangely emotional day.

Chapter Twelve

Hugh pushed out the front doors of Webb Industrial in time to see Gia make her way to her car. A car that should have been put to rest twenty years ago. *What the hell?* "Gia," he called as he jogged to her.

The annoyed glance she tossed his way made him grin. Damn, did she know how much she rattled his nerves in a good way when she aimed her bossy eyes at him? But he had a mission first before he flirted with her.

"Does this thing still run?" he asked. She had a small bag in her hand and popped a small red candy into her mouth.

She used her key to manually unlock the front door of a baby blue Jeep Wagoneer that had to be at least thirty or forty years old. Ugly was putting it mildly. On death's door wasn't too far a reach.

"What are you doing driving this heap?"

Gia shoved open the door and climbed in, slamming the door in his face.

He grinned.

"Sorry," she said through the glass. "I can't hear you. Have a good night, Hugh." She put another round red candy in her mouth. When she went to start the engine, it chugged like it was dying and it didn't turn over. She tried it once more with another failed result.

He stepped closer and tapped on the window. She gave the biggest sigh, coupled with an eye roll that should win awards, rested her head on the steering wheel, and slowly, because the thing was ancient, used the handle to roll down the window.

"Car trouble?" he asked, leaning his arm on her open window. The sky had been a pristine blue when he came out. Now white clouds raced across it, causing the sunlight to blink above them. A slight wind kicked up. He felt his blood heat too.

"Give me patience," she whispered, turning her head, which still rested on the wheel, to the side to glare at him.

"Are you talking to me or the car?" Hugh's grin widened.

"Both. I'm fine, Hugh. Delly sometimes takes a while when the weather's been iffy."

"First of all, Gia." He looked at the blue sky with enormous white puffy clouds, "If this is what she considers iffy, I'm even more concerned. Second, Delly?"

Gia had taken off her glasses and a piece of hair had slipped from her bun. She brushed it behind her ear and rested her fingers on her lips. Those lips. He had memories of those lips. And not nearly, nearly enough memories. She shifted slightly closer to him.

"Gia?" He leaned in. Slowly, she reached out and ran a featherlight stroke down his cheek. He expected it to burn, with her magic flaring out and over his skin, but it felt fucking right. He felt that touch everywhere in his body, waking him up. His pulse hammered for her.

"You're so beautiful," she whispered, following the path of her fingers with those mesmerizing eyes of hers.

"Hey," he said as he held her hand to his cheek and leaned into her touch. Nectar from the gods. There were dark circles under her eyes and pure exhaustion on her face. Damn it, what caused her so much worry and fatigue? He ached to banish it all for her.

She met his gaze one last time, eyes wide open and searching, before she quickly sat up, turned her head, and pulled her touch away. "But I can't have you, Hugh, please," she begged so quietly, words that held a million meanings. All her wounds exposed for him to see, then closed away.

He ignored her admission that she couldn't have him. "I brought you leftovers." He held up the bag in his hand. "From lunch. Adair's. So you wouldn't have to cook tonight. Thought it could take some of your single-mom burden off."

"Oh." Taking the bag from him ever so carefully, she looked surprised, confused, at a loss for words. "I…that's…thank you."

"I know it must be hard, doing it all by yourself." How inadequate his words sounded to his own ears.

"You have kids you forgot to mention?" she asked. There was her tough side.

He shook his head and took a step back. "No...I..." What did he say? To tell her everything might burden her. But he wanted a life with her and he believed he should start as he meant to go on, being open, being himself. "My mom died when I was little. Cancer. I was 10. My dad was raising five of us by himself until he met May. Got his second chance." Hugh smiled. Drake Webb was one of the lucky ones. Two great loves in one lifetime. May would say she was the lucky one. "So, I don't know what it's like at all, personally." *You look so tired.* He might be dumbstruck in love, but he was smart enough not to say that part out loud.

"Oh." Her gaze softened. "I'm so sorry. That's, that's a tragedy...and a...blessing afterward. Isn't it?" she asked as if she didn't believe, as if she needed him to help her see. He was right here by her side. He'd do whatever she asked.

"Both." He nodded.

"I...well..."

It was a moment of awkwardness she rarely let slip. So he took pity on her. "Go get those kids of yours. I'll see you tomorrow."

She rolled up the window, and he backed away, as difficult as it was, torn as he was between leaving her with all her control and consent, or demanding that she let him drive her home and take care of her. Every cell in his body now cried out to pamper her.

The Jeep started this time. She gave him a slight wave and left. He stood, aching to move, and watched her drive away.

Without a second thought, worried about the heap she was driving, he got in his SUV and carefully followed her.

A few drops of rain splattered his windshield on the drive. Most of the sky was blue, save for a few clouds directly overhead that seemed to follow them. Her car made it to the elementary school near Mercy Park. A little girl skipped from her line to meet Gia, who scooped her up, twirling her around in a hug. Her son, he guessed, walked to her, his gaze mostly down, dragging his feet. Gia's smile dimmed, and she ruffled the boy's hair. Hugh breathed easier when it started right away this time.

Ahh, he thought when they turned onto Emerson Street. This was the Ms. Reily who'd bought the old Turner place. His brother Ian had informed his family when it had finally sold this past September. Said it seemed like a nice young family who'd moved into the place that butted against the Webb's acres of land on the back end. Always good to know who they shared property lines with.

It was an old farmhouse-meets-Victorian style of architecture. The beauty had been vacant for decades and needed some work, inside and out, but the two acres it came with were gorgeous. Hugh smiled. One more box to check off in his favor. They were neighbors, after all.

He watched from a distance as they parked in the driveway near a side door and made their way inside with all their belongings. As the lights came on throughout, he could have sworn the house settled and breathed easier. If a house could do such a thing. He watched for a while, studying the house and thinking.

The front porch sat dark and empty, no quirky wicker furniture or porch swing. Or dog. It was a porch meant for a dog, a big fluffy, happy mutt, and for chairs and lemonade and neighbors on the summer evenings while the sky darkened and the kids chased fireflies.

At some point over the years, some idiot had painted the house a sad tan, the entirety of it, every unique trim and corbel and decoration that gave it it's Victorian charm so that it had become easy to dismiss. The door wasn't true to the house and couldn't have been uglier. From his spot, the entire house sat heavy and almost as if it were trying to hide. But beneath its shroud was...delight and whimsy and happiness waiting to burst out.

The structure pulsed with energy with its little family tucked inside.

It went against Hugh's every nature to leave them. While he drove toward his loft, he wondered why Ms. Gianna Reily who was buttoned up and hiding, except for the night they'd had together when she'd let herself be seen, had purchased a house that seemed with everything he could tell to have matched her. A secluded house, dulled down or told to be dull when what it really wanted to do was shine.

Both ladies were secret hidden gems full of character and charm that were hiding or had been shrouded over with time, due to neglect or outright harm. He didn't know what category Gia fell into, but he aimed to find out.

Chapter Thirteen

Gia changed into her soft gray sweats and hoodie and her industrial-strength wool socks. The old fir floors of their house were gorgeous, or they had been at one time, but they could frostbite her toes in a matter of minutes. She got the kids' lunches unpacked and had gotten firm nos from both kids when she'd asked if they had homework. Ava was perched on the counter when Gia came back downstairs. Poking through the bag of food from Adair's.

"Mama, this smells good. Is this our dinner?"

Gia smacked a kiss on her daughter's cheek, which made Ava squeal. The absolute joy in her daughter warmed her from the inside. It was safe to say Ava's effusive emotions gave Gia a run for her money.

"Yes, it's takeout from Adair's."

"Is there dessert too?"

A child after her own heart. Asking the important questions. "Yes," Gia said. "Chocolate cheesecake."

"We almost never have dessert anymore." Danny's voice from where he lay on the sofa.

Ugh, he was right. She was a horrible baker, cook too, but baking for sure. And after Doug...well she almost never baked anymore. When he was alive, she hadn't been good at it, but she'd done it, trying to make fun sweets. Danny had been her little kitchen helper then, licking the chocolate off the spatulas and playing in the sink with the dishes afterward, that contented smile on his face.

"Can we eat dessert first?" Ava begged. Her eyes were bright green and so big, so open to the world and adventure. Gia had to choke back her sudden tears at the well of grief that rose inside her for all that the three of them had lost. This pain hit her so fiercely sometimes it was a wonder she didn't collapse. But she was a mom, and moms held shit together.

"We can't eat dessert first," Danny said. "That's not how it's done." Now he was her sensible child. Too sensible, Gia worried. Where Ava expressed whatever she was feeling to the tenth degree, Danny kept so much inside. He was in the living room reading his latest science magazine. That was progress, at least. He wasn't shut away in his bedroom.

Which kind of grief did a person choose if there were more than one? That's what she wanted to scream into the void. She'd lost her husband, her kids had lost their father, and they'd all lost security, safety, wholeness. Each of their personalities had been altered. Well, maybe not Ava's. Gia gave her child a hug and squeezed tightly, holding her tears at bay. So, so much had changed. And there were times she wondered if they'd ever get some of it back, if they'd even survive. And that was a kind of grief too, the constant worry that they'd never be whole.

"I think," she said, her voice steadier than it should have been before she smothered her worries and continued. "That Mondays deserve dessert first. Let's start our own new tradition and make this difficult first day of the week better for everyone. What do you say?"

"Yes!" Ava cheered.

"Well, I suppose Aunt Frankie would probably say it's a good idea too." Danny sighed, put his magazine down, and joined them in the kitchen.

"Mm." Gia let out a small smile of relief. "She would. And if she wasn't working tonight, I'd call her and invite her to come join us for our special dessert-first tradition."

"A tradition means more than once," Danny informed her.

"Yes, love, you're right. We haven't done dessert nearly enough since we moved, since, well since—"

"Since Dad died," Danny said quietly, leaning his body into hers.

Gia wrapped her arm around him and held him close. This was as much of a hug as he gave her these days, and she would relish every second. It was getting more difficult to keep those tears choked down. Maybe she shouldn't. Was it okay for her children to see her cry? She didn't know. There was so much she didn't know. A few tears slipped over and rolled down her cheeks, and she let them. She held on tightly to this tiny scene that felt both difficult and almost like a tiny bit of healing, of breakthrough.

"You're crying," Danny whispered.

She had to swallow a few times before she could speak. "I am, love. Happy tears." And they were. They were tears of grief and tears of hope. They sat at the small wooden table in the window and ate chocolate cheesecake for dinner. Three pieces, one for each of them because Hugh had thought of that.

Instead of pondering that gesture and the man behind it, she ignored those feelings and asked her kids about their day, while a few more tears leaked out of her eyes. Steady rain fell outside, and she allowed herself to take comfort in the warmth and safety she'd been able to create for her precious family.

After dinner and a rewatch of their favorite Wild Kratts episode, because her kids were obsessed with animals, she did a bath for Ava while Danny took his shower. Then she read them books and tucked them in. Normal, comforting things.

When her phone rang and she saw her sister's name on the caller ID, part of her was happy because her sister was her best friend, but a hidden part of her, for one fleeting second, had hoped it might be Hugh. Silly, they didn't have each other's numbers.

"Frankie, hi. You on a break?" Gia made sure the alarm was set on the house, even though she'd checked it before putting the kids to bed.

"Hi, honey. Yes. Hiding in one of the closets under a blanket in the dark."

Gia chuckled. "That sounds lovely."

Francesca laughed too. "It's not too bad. I needed the dark and quiet. I love the Emergency Department, but sometimes I get overstimulated."

"Yeah."

Her sister was an amazingly brilliant doctor who loved her job. Gia was lucky to have her, lucky that her happiness spilled out onto Gia and her kids. But Frankie or Dr. Francesca Banetti, as she was known in the Emergency Department, spent a lot of energy healing people through her skill as a doctor and as an intuitive healing witch. A double overnight shift would be especially taxing.

"Thank you so much for taking the kids this weekend. I didn't even think about you having them and then going right into a 48-hour shift."

Francesca's laugh was full and gorgeous. Gia wished to be more like her older sister, to be so free with her joy, to *have* so much joy.

"I would bring those goofballs to work with me if I could. I love having them. They bring so much light into my life. But enough of that, how are you? It's been weeks since we've seen each other more than just you dropping Danny and Ava off. What's going on? You started a new client today? How'd it go?" Her sister fired off questions and Gia held her breath, trying to decide which ones to answer.

I had a one-night stand with a gorgeous man and it turns out he's my client. She did not say any of that. There was so much inside those words she wasn't prepared to talk about with anyone yet, even herself. So she stuck to the surface. "Client is good. It's that cool building on Juniper Hill with the lake and woods behind it. Webb Industrial. They do amazing prosthetics. It's going to be great, I think, if I can get through to the stinky misogynistic accountant I have to work with."

"Oh really," Frankie drawled. "You can handle him. Sucks that you have to, though."

Gia's thoughts exactly.

"Any hotties for you to drool over?"

"Frankie, it's work." Gia huffed out a laugh.

"Mm, indeed, where you and I spend most of our time. Where else are we supposed to find love again?" Both sisters had loved and lost in different ways. Wait…

"You sound a little dreamy. Anything you'd like to share with me, Francesca Banetti?"

"No, no. Nothing solid, just a specific doctor who won't give me the time of day but sends me long lingering looks when he thinks I'm not paying attention." Her sister laughed. "Listen, I have to go. I'm getting paged. But I love you and I love those kids. Talk soon?"

"Yes, thank you so much for having them over," Gia said. "I love you."

After she hung up, the quiet seemed unnaturally painful. The mournful, steady sound of the rainfall added to her dark state of mind. She dragged her worn-out body up, cleaned the kitchen, and checked the alarms on the house one more time.

She should go to the basement and work out, dig around the dark web, and see what she could find, she thought, as she rested her head against the basement door, but exhaustion overcame her and she turned away.

Bed wasn't all it was cracked up to be, though. Bed was lonely, bed was insomnia, bed was all the reminders that she was alone coming together to haunt her. But even her eyes were weary tonight, so she climbed the stairs to her lonely bedroom.

It wasn't until she stepped into the shower that she started crying again. She seemed to be making a habit of it. This time they were tears of both wanting desperately to cling to the past and wanting to let go, to somehow be untethered to it all. When she closed her eyes, Hugh was there in her mind, the gentle lines around his eyes. His beautiful, soulful eyes. It seemed no matter how much she told herself to think of him solely in a professional manner, her emotions weren't getting the message.

Finally, after avoiding it, she climbed into her lonely bed. She snuggled under the covers by herself and tucked pillows all around her body as she'd done ever since Doug died. They made her feel protected, wrapped up in a hug, warm. Only tonight it registered how pathetic she was, seeking companionship and hugs from pillows.

Chapter Fourteen

He was sweaty, exhausted, and frustrated. Fuck, in more ways than one. Hugh chucked the metal knee into the bin.

"Whoa, whoa, that's gazillions of dollars of precious product, there," Hugh's designer Alan said as he gingerly reached in and removed the prosthetic from the trash.

"It's garbage. It's not working. It's not right. We have got to get it right. Not just sort of right, but exact, perfect. We're talking about basic stability here for our clients. This will also affect their gait. In a nutshell, this is garbage."

"We know," Alan said. He set the knee on the table and studied his computer.

"Do you?" Hugh's temper was on the edge. They'd been working on this new knee for months and they couldn't get it right. "Do you know what it's like to have your leg buckle during a run because the fit wasn't perfect? Do you know what it's like—"

"He doesn't," Samantha interrupted, shoving her chair between the two men. "And neither do you, Hugh. You've been a jerk all day, which your team does not deserve and also isn't like you. So take a break and figure out what the heck is going on with your attitude or we will never perfect this version."

Fuck, she was right. He'd been acting like a five-year-old throwing a tantrum because he couldn't go to a party. Only it wasn't a party he was missing, it was Ms. Gianna Reily.

He leaned against the door and let out a long breath. "You're right. Apologies everyone. You're doing a great job. Shit, I didn't realize the time. Everyone go home. Have a great weekend." He stalked out of the office and took off at a jog for the gym. The cavernous place was empty, as it should be on a late Friday afternoon. Half the staff didn't work on Fridays, and the ones who did were there because they loved it or in this case, because he'd been insensitive to his team and hadn't paid attention to the time. He owed them a better apology when his mind was less cranky.

He jogged down the steps from the top level to the track and did what his body needed to do: run. Outside would have been better, unencumbered through the forest, but he didn't relish stepping out into the frigid rain. Plus, after his run, he could hit the bag and hopefully spend some of this pent-up energy.

All week he'd been in Colorado Springs working with a few athletes in the high altitude to test and review their legs. It had been a gorgeous, brilliantly sunny week in Colorado. It had also been hugely successful. He should have had a great time, seeing friends, skiing, watching his team's designs fly. And Christ, it had felt like the longest, hardest week of his life being so far away from Gia, not being able to see her, to make sure she was okay, to hear her voice, to have her act annoyed at him, to catch all the small glimpses of her authentic self she rarely let slip. Today, when he'd gotten back, she hadn't been here.

He ran hard for almost an hour until his chest hurt and he had to stop and bend over to catch his breath. Wiping the sweat from his brow, he stepped down to the bottom level and got busy lifting weights. He'd save the punching bag for last.

Hugh was on his back on the weight bench when her scent swamped him. He lifted his head. Cole, Gia, and her kids stood at the glass railing above him. Cole was pointing things out, and the kids were asking questions.

His hearing wasn't quite as good as his sense of smell, but it was better than most humans. He stayed where he was, breathing in the scent of her, the crisp soap she used with a hint of jasmine. So sexy but so understated. His heartbeat kicked up at her presence.

"Wow," Danny said quietly. The awe was there in his voice, but he spoke with such respect, such reverence.

"This place is awesome. Like the bestest indoor playground ever!" *That must be Ava.* She didn't appear to be shy in her observations at all.

Gia and Cole both laughed. *What a great laugh Gia has, soft and free.*

"Shall we go down and see it from ground level?" Cole asked.

"I...no...it's okay," Gia said. "This is good enough."

"Please, Mama?" Ava begged.

"Could we?" Danny asked.

"Send 'em down," Hugh said as he pushed himself off the bench and came into their view.

"Oh," Cole said. "Sorry, Hugh. I thought everyone was gone for the day."

"No worries. I needed a workout after all that traveling. Gia, I'd love to show your kids around."

"Who's that?" Danny asked.

Gia paused slightly. He could see her warring with what to do.

"That's Hugh Webb," Cole said, and Hugh smiled. "This is his company and he's in charge of making super cool things."

"Did he make your arm?" Danny asked.

"He did."

"It was an entire team that made it," Hugh said. "Come on. I'd love to show you around. If you have time." He sounded like he was begging.

Gia's gaze met his, calm, assessing. "For a few minutes, loves." At that, they raced down the stairs.

"I'll leave you in Hugh's hands," Cole said. "I'm making dinner for my husband. Have a good weekend, all."

Hugh watched the children race down the stairs, and out of the corner of his eye tracked Gia as she descended slower.

She was dressed in black pants that covered those black boots she'd had on the first night. A white blouse under a black blazer completed the outfit and fitted perfectly to her body. The jacket had a little flare out over her…nope, not going there right now.

"Oh my goodness," Ava said. "You have swimming pools!"

"Ava, be careful, honey," Gia said. "She's not a good swimmer."

"It's okay. The pool doors are locked. She can't get in unless I open them."

"Did you really make a bionic arm?" Danny stood a few feet away, arms crossed, studying Hugh.

He grinned. "I did, well, *we* did. There are a lot of cool, brilliant, really nerdy people who work with me. I didn't do it by myself."

"Really nerdy?" Danny asked, stepping closer to his mom. Gia reached out and squeezed his hand, sending Hugh a glare that said a million things.

"Yeah," Hugh said. "Nerds are amazing. You got a thing against nerds?"

Danny let out a small smile and glanced at Gia. "No…I…uh…I think I'm a nerd."

Hugh could practically feel Gia's worry disappear over the path their conversation had taken.

Danny took a step closer to the table beside Hugh. It was in the center of the enormous complex and held parts and prototypes of all sorts of prosthetics they were working on. "You don't look like a nerd. You're huge and strong."

Hugh laughed. "Danny is it?" He held out his hand. "I was your size once, skinnier and smaller with a bad haircut. Couldn't, still can't get enough of astronomy and the moon and especially how things fit together. I don't think a nerd has to look a certain way. Do you?"

Danny gave one more glance to Gia, who had a soft smile on her face. Then he stepped forward and took Hugh's hand. "No, I don't. Nice to meet you. Can I...can you show me some of your stuff?"

"I'd love to," Hugh said. "Here." He pulled a stool over. "Here's a prototype of the hand attached to Cole's arm. We're working on more neural pathways to the brain. And this is a knee we keep failing at. There's something off about each prototype we try, so we're still working that out.

"Wow," Danny did not hide his awe, and Hugh mentally patted himself on the back. The stuff they made was cool. And it was fantastic to see Danny Reily enjoy it.

Ava was by his side, patting his leg. "Can you lift me so I can see too?"

Hugh raised his eyebrows at Gia and breathed easy when she gave him a slight nod of okay.

He lifted the girl and held her, and something settled inside him. Something about this scene felt natural. It felt right. It felt like family, like everything he wanted.

"This is the coolest place you've ever worked, Mom," Danny said. "I'm glad you brought us here."

"I hope it was okay?" Gia asked. "They...uh..." She cleared her throat.

Is she nervous around me? Hugh couldn't tell if that bothered him or made him smile. It depended on what kind of nervous she was. Hell, he certainly was around her, but it was the kind you felt when you'd fallen in love with an amazing woman and didn't know how she felt in return.

"They had a half day today, so I had to leave to get them, but I wanted to check on one last thing here, so I brought them back with me."

"It's absolutely fine, but it's Friday. I'm sure my father or Cole, or someone mentioned you don't have to work on Fridays."

"I know...I..." There was something wrong in her gaze, a flicker of concern or worry.

His senses went on alert. "Everything okay?"

Her hesitation was enough to rattle him. "Ava and Danny," Hugh said. He pulled out another stool for Ava and set her down. "I have a job for you." He gathered a box of the different metal components that went into the knees they made. He put the scale on the table and grabbed a piece of paper and a few markers. "Can you two weigh these parts and record your findings for me? Maybe sketch a small picture of each one next to its weight?"

"Oh, yes!" Ava clapped. "I can do the weighing and Danny can read the numbers and write them because he's much smarter than me."

Danny studied him with skepticism on his face. This kid missed nothing. Hugh gave him a wink. "Seriously. The weight is extremely important in a prosthetic," Hugh said. "It can mean the difference between walking comfortably and falling over a lot. You wouldn't want to be falling all the time, would you?"

Danny grinned at him and shook his head. He took the marker and paper and patiently handed an item to Ava.

"I need to speak with your mom for a quick second."

Hugh gestured across the enormous space to a darker corner that held their juice bar. They could have privacy without losing sight of the children. Without thinking, he held out his hand for Gia's. Her eyes closed briefly as if warring with herself, but then she slid her hand into his. *Best feeling in the world.* When they reached the counter, she pulled away. Maybe he should be sorry, but it sure felt natural to hold her hand, to touch her, to feel her warmth seep through him.

He leaned into the counter and crossed his arms. "Tell me what's going on."

She held the hand that he'd just had clasped in his and rubbed her thumb along it.

"I apologize, Gia," he said quietly. "You asked me to keep things professional."

"No..." She shook her head. "Your hand was so warm. It felt..." She stepped into him, Just slightly shorter than him in that badass, black suit she wore. When she was this close he could see the tiny ruffle on the collar of her blouse.

What? It felt what, Gia? His body reacted, leaning closer. Every single inch of him acutely aware of her scent, the sound of her heartbeat, how erratically it pulsed this close to him, and how their energies pulled them together.

"What, Gia?" he whispered. Hugh cupped her cheek and angled her head so she was looking at him.

"I…I…" She used her hand to steady herself on him, resting those pretty fingers of hers on his chest.

Fuck, his heart was going to crash through his ribs if she kept touching him. She leaned up and closed her eyes. Her scent overwhelmed him, the feel of her hand on him, her breath coming faster, memories of what was underneath all these clothes she had on.

"Hugh…I…"

"Whatever you need. I'm here," he whispered. *I want you too. I'll never stop wanting you.*

She took one last breath, and he thought she was going to lean in closer, but she opened those eyes of hers and what he saw was fear.

"Sorry." She nearly tripped and stepped back. Instinct had him reaching for her arm. But she recovered, and he was both impressed at how quickly she could change and disappointed she hadn't said what she'd really been thinking.

She reached into her pocket and pulled out one of those red candies she liked. Sucking on it for a minute, she finally whispered, "Something's wrong with the accounts."

"Our accounts?" That was the last thing he expected to come out of her mouth right now, but some niggle in his gut had him standing straight. Trent Bordin had never been Hugh's favorite. "Tell me what you know."

"It's more what I don't know, Hugh. In order to do my job, I need to see the basic bookkeeping, preferably for the last few years and before. It helps me see how much money you've traditionally spent on investments and charities, but also how much you might want to start investing."

She glanced at her kids. Hugh looked over his shoulder. They were diligently measuring and tracking all the metal and plastic pieces he'd given them.

"I met Mr. Bordin the first day. I'd already realized some information was missing, and he said he'd get it to me. When I got to my office later, a few files were on my desk, and..."

"Wait, how did they get on your desk? In your locked office?"

She met his gaze. "Good question."

Hugh's hackles rose with his temper. Someone had been in Gia's office without her permission.

"More importantly, they still weren't complete. I'm good at seeing patterns and connections and missing pieces, if you will."

Hugh couldn't help the grin that spread across his face. "Brilliant too, eh?" He had the great satisfaction at seeing her cheeks turn a deep pink. God damn it, he wanted to kiss her.

"I left him a message he has yet to return. I assumed it was because he was traveling with you all week and he was too busy, which is why I came in today. I knew you'd be back and suspected he might as well."

"Wait," Hugh said, confusion running through his mind. "He wasn't with me. He was here all week."

"Oh," Gia said.

Hugh was trying not to be distracted by her eyes, the panther-like glare that bloomed.

"But he said...wait, that ass—"

"Asshole, yeah, I agree," he said quietly, tamping down his anger.

"Mama, Hugh, we finished." Ava ran to them. She threw herself at Hugh, and in a split second, he caught her. "We did good."

"I bet you did," Hugh said, his heart leaping at the rightness of this family he longed to be a part of.

"Can we go eat, Mama? I'm starving."

"Yeah, honey." Gia reached for Ava, and Hugh handed her over.

Danny met them with a crooked grin aimed at Hugh. He handed him the paper with a small drawing of each item next to its weight.

"Well done, Danny. This is super helpful." Hugh took stock of Danny's blush too. These kids were like their mom, desperate for compliments and love. It didn't take a love-sick werewolf to see that.

"Go put all the pieces in the box and we'll go eat," Gia said. When they were gone, she turned to Hugh. "I need to go. They get kind of feral when they're hungry."

"We can talk on Monday about everything else. I'll speak to my father. Things haven't been great with Trent for a while but with the move and the expansion, and…"

"And you trust your accountant to do his job. It's not your fault, Hugh, whatever is going on. Hopefully, it's a simple misunderstanding."

She didn't believe that any more than he did.

She gathered her kids. They yelled goodbyes to him and he stood still, watching them, longing to go with them, to follow them. The kids ran up the stairs talking about what they were going to get for dinner.

"Thank you," Gia said. "For letting them do that. Danny seemed in his element. I appreciate it. It was kind of you."

Hugh couldn't help the smile. Damn this woman. Turns out he wasn't immune to compliments either. And as he watched them leave and listened to the kids chatter, Hugh wished he was going with them.

Once the silence of the place hit him, he walked through the building, making sure everything was locked, especially Gia's office. Hugh needed to speak to his father, but first, he needed food. And he couldn't bear eating alone tonight. After heading home to a hot shower, he dressed and walked to Adair's. Solitude was something he'd prized for a long time, but he couldn't get rid of the ache in his chest tonight. If he couldn't have Gia's company, he wanted the noise and comfort of his family.

Chapter Fifteen

So much for acting like a calm, cool professional in front of Hugh. *You've trained extensively for situations like this. Have you turned into a girl with her first crush?* It definitely wasn't a first crush, the way her heart somersaulted and soared when he was near and burst into stars when he touched her. Or maybe it was. She'd never been that simple schoolgirl. She hadn't had time or anything close to comfort to allow space for things like teenage infatuations.

All Hugh had done was reach for her hand and she'd slipped hers into his as if it belonged there, as if it was normal. While a million wonderful feelings stole through her body and heated her blood and... *Gah! Calm down.*

The kids hadn't stopped talking about him since they'd left. Now they tumbled out of the car and ran with her through the rain to Adair's. She reached into her coat pocket but her sour cherries bag was empty. Darn it. At least she didn't have to make a mediocre dinner tonight.

They'd decided to make lots of new traditions for themselves. Friday night out to dinner was one she was seriously excited about. Tonight was a first, but soooo not the last. They could have gone out for pizza or tried the charming pub in the hills, but her car had led her here. It had become something of a cozy place for her and she wanted to share it with her kids, especially after how much they'd enjoyed the leftovers Hugh had given them.

"Oh, hello." It was the nice pregnant lady who sometimes hosted. "Gia right? I'm so glad you're back. And who are these two lovely people?"

Gia stared. She wasn't used to people being so friendly and open. And this woman was smiling at her like they were long-lost friends. "Uh..."

"I'm Danny and this is my sister, Ava."

"And we're starting a new tradition of Friday nights out to dinner because we haven't had any traditions since our dad died a long, long, time ago," Ava said as she held her belly like she hadn't had a meal in days.

"I'm Harper," the woman said with a huge smile. "And I'm so glad you chose Adair's. I'll tell you a secret." Her voice lowered. "This is my restaurant, mine and my husband's. It's my very favorite and I think this new tradition sounds wonderful. Maybe we can convince your mom to make Adair's your Friday dinner place every week."

"Oh, well...I...um..." Lordy, she'd never been so at a loss for words as she had in the last few weeks.

"Just a thought," Harper said with a smile. She grabbed a few menus. "I have the perfect table. Right here in the corner so you can look out onto the street."

When they reached the table, Ava put her hands on her chest and whispered, "It's perfect."

Gia hid her chuckle. How had she birthed such a dramatic soul? "Thank you, Harper."

"My pleasure. Do you want your regular glass of red?"

"You do remember people, don't you?" Gia said.

Harper sighed. "It's a knack I have. Also, I love my customers." Her smile was infectious. Gia decided to relax and enjoy their evening.

"I'd love a glass. Thank you. And do you have anything special for kids?"

"We sure do."

A server brought them water and a basket of homemade rolls that were salted on top and had flecks of rosemary in them. The aroma alone was intoxicating. There was a small container of soft butter to spread on them and Gia swore they were all drooling while eating. The red wine tasted amazing with the rosemary and the salt. It was like Gia was tasting things for the first time.

She had to put her wine down and suck in her breath to hold in the tears. How long had she been completely numb? Maybe it was this place. The chocolate cake she loved burst on her tongue with its almost burned cocoa and smokey flavor every time she ate it. And now simple rolls made her drool.

"Well hello there, Gia?" She blinked through her thoughts to see May in her wheelchair. A pretty fuchsia-colored comb held her wild black curls to one side.

"Hi...uh..." Gia blushed as if the woman could read all the way through her thoughts to her soul and all her desires. *And there I go with the excellent communication skills.* "May. It's so nice to see you. We...I...brought my kids." *Duh.*

"I see that. Hello. I'm May. Would you all care to join us for dinner? We could pull the tables together."

"I...I um..."

"Excellent idea." That was Mr. Webb, or Drake, as he'd told her. Harper was already gathering servers to help Drake pull tables to connect to Gia's. "Family dinner needs some young ones. Can you tell we're waiting impatiently for the twins?"

"They need a little more time to grow." Harper patted her belly. "But I'm ready too." She winked at Gia.

When had everyone around her developed this ability to wink? And what was happening? The tables were pushed together. Drake lifted May out of her wheelchair and set her down in a restaurant chair beside Ava. Then he sat next to May.

Harper placed more baskets of bread on the table and sat on the other side a few chairs down. "In case I need to get up quickly. Our hostess should be here any minute, and then I can relax."

A man she'd never met came, kissed Harper on the cheek, then pulled out the chair next to Danny. "Duncan Webb, I won't sit long. Have to get back to the kitchen, but introduce me, tell me who everyone is. I've heard about you, Gia, but I have to admit we've never had such fine ladies and gents at our restaurant before. He held his hand out to Danny, who grinned, took it, and introduced himself.

"Are you Hugh's brother? We met him this afternoon at Mom's work," Danny asked.

"Indeed, I am," Duncan said and made a strange face at Harper, who tried to hide her grin, but Gia caught it. "One of them. There are six of us Webb siblings altogether, five boys and one girl."

When he shook Ava's hand, she laughed. "I'm not a lady, I'm Ava."

"Well, Ava, welcome to Adair's. Now tell me, what looks good on the menu?"

"I can't read yet," Ava said. "Not all words." Ava shrank down, and her cheeks turned pink.

"Oh," Duncan tapped his forehead. "Forgive me. Are you sure you're not a teenager ready to take on the world?"

Ava brightened and giggled.

"I'll help you, dear," May said.

"Ah, the family's grown, has it? Good to see you again, Gia. These your minions?" Grant Webb took a seat beside Harper, looking as polished and dashing as he had the first day she'd met him. These Webbs were all so damn handsome.

"And here's our Addy now," May said. "Wasn't sure you were going to make it tonight, but I'm so happy to see you, honey. Gia from work and her kids are joining us now." May said it as if it were a done deal forever. *What is going on?* Gia kept asking the universe, but the universe wasn't answering.

A younger version of May with long hair twisted into a braid, gorgeous jeans tucked into brown leather boots, and a green peasant blouse stood at the end of the table. She had flowers woven through her hair. She blew May kisses and said, "I sent everyone home early cause of the rain. I am so ready for spring. Hello." She sent Gia and her kids a wave.

"You look like a princess," Ava hushed. "I want flowers in my hair too."

"Oh, it's easy. I can show you how," Addy said.

A server brought Shirley Temples for the kids, with two cherries in each glass.

"Can you believe it, Mama? I knew family dinner sounded special."

She tried to hide the panic from taking over her expression, especially when Danny grinned and said, "Yeah, totally cool."

Chapter Sixteen

THE DOOR BLEW OPEN with the wind and the rain slashed at Hugh as he raced under the opening and into Adair's. A blustery night, but a good one. The rain infused his senses and mixed with the garlic and roasted tomatoes he could smell from inside the restaurant, and...Gia. He knew it before he saw her.

When he headed in through the dark entryway, he saw his family, most of them seated at their regular tables along the far windows. Ian and his husband hadn't arrived yet. Who knew about Alexander? And sitting with them, tables connected as if they were part of the Webb clan were Gia, Danny, and Ava.

A fierce pain of longing nearly bowled Hugh down. He didn't know whether to smile at how they'd been roped into family dinner—because, without a doubt, they'd been given no choice from his overbearing but well-meaning family members—or wail his lament at how much of an outsider he felt like in this intimate moment. There they all sat, laughing, talking, eating, welcoming and being welcomed, being seen, being witnessed, being known.

Hugh banished his unruly emotions because all he had to do was walk over and join them, take his place in the family, and belong. He suddenly felt clueless, immature, and confused about how to behave. Almost as if he was the outsider. Something held him back. Fear, white hot and blatant in his chest, fear of not being what she needed, what she *wanted*.

Danny turned and caught Hugh's gaze. The boy started to smile and wave but hesitated, as if sensing Hugh's struggle from all the way across the room.

He couldn't disappoint this child. Hugh battled his insecurities, put a grin on his face, and walked over to meet them all, to his future, or to his doom. He wasn't sure.

He held out his fist to Danny, who was still the only one who'd noticed him for a split second.

The child's shoulders eased and his smile grew into that full crooked one that took over his face. He bumped fists and said, "Everyone, it's Hugh."

"Got room for one more?" Hugh asked, even though he knew the answer. His family always made room for more. Still, his voice held a bit of vulnerability he barely recognized.

Cheers of welcome rang out. Every Friday was different in regards to who showed or who couldn't make it. His dad and May still had everyone out to the farm on random Sundays, but there was something so central and cozy about Adair's. Duncan and Harper had done a magnificent job.

"You made it." His brother Duncan stood and grabbed another chair. "Young Daniel, scoot this way and we'll fit Hugh in between you and your mom. I need to chat you up for another minute before I head back to the kitchen."

"Hello," Hugh said quietly to Gia, who looked gobsmacked. He wanted to grin, but he understood. The feeling was getting stronger and stronger every time he was near her. Gobsmacked was putting it mildly. Her eyes were full of sparks and her pretty pulse leapt under the skin by her collarbone. That special spot he wanted to lick and suck and bite.

"I didn't...we didn't mean...I..."

"Gia." He did grin then and touched her pinky with his. "I'm certain my family saw you and dragged you in, with no way to defend yourself." He took a glass of water and almost held it to his forehead to cool the desire. Instead, he gulped it down and prayed for calm.

"They seem..." She looked around the table and he followed her gaze, catching her eyes when she sent him a soft glance, "Wonderful. But definitely intimidating."

He laughed. "I bet nothing intimidates you, Gianna Reily."

"Mm," she answered and sipped her wine, never breaking eye contact.

Chapter Seventeen

"All right?"

Even without the sound of his deep voice going right to her core, Gia sensed his presence as soon as she stepped out of the ladies' room. Back in this dark, cozy hallway, everything was painted black, the gorgeous trim and crown molding, the old doors. A rich floral wallpaper with bold silver and black flowers swirled over the walls. Gold-framed family and restaurant photos lined the space. And there he stood, leaning against the wall, concern lining his face. He was so immense, so impressive, so imposing.

The heady scent of him, rich and grounding like the strongest fortress, swarmed around her. *Hugh.* This entire night had gotten out of control...his family including them at dinner, the amazing roasted chicken and polenta, the warmth and ease of it all. And every second she'd sat there, her world spinning out of control. What was wrong with her? She felt the tears on her cheeks before she could order them back, order them not to fall in the first place.

"Here," he said and opened a door to an office. Ushering her in. She went as if she had no shields at all anymore. He grabbed a box of tissues and held them out to her.

"My kids...I shouldn't have left, I need..."

He stepped forward and took her hand. "They're good, Gia. My family's got them. They're eating chocolate mousse."

Holding his hand was the most natural and lovely thing in the world. There was a gorgeous tall window framing the rain that had grown stronger when she'd raced to the bathroom, her emotions in a tailspin. "It's all so...you're all so..."

"What?" Hugh tugged, and she went right into his embrace.

"Lovely, peaceful, solid."

"They are that."

He stepped them backward, so he was against a desk. *I want this moment.* It wasn't real. This whole night was a fantasy, like their first time together, all these ripples deep inside that he made her feel. None of it was lasting. *But, Goddess, why does it feel so perfect?*

"Gia?"

"It's..." She looked up at him. "It's too much." She shook her head and damn it, more tears slipped out. Why was she crying?

"Honey." Hugh cupped her cheek, overwhelming her with his scent, his warmth, that rasp in his voice that she ached to cling to as her very own salvation. He swept his thumb across her cheek. "Why too much? How did that upset you?"

Her heart beat a million times a second and her breath was light and quick. He was so solid and powerful right there in her space, energy radiating off him, surrounding her. The ever-so-soft trace of his finger lingered on the skin above her collarbone, burning into her. She wanted him to touch her more. She wanted to put her hands back on his chest, feel how warm, how strong he was, all his unleashed passion bound so tightly now under her.

Huh? She was touching him. Her hands moved of their own accord to slide up his chest until they reached the bare skin of his neck. She could feel her blood racing through her body. Rain slashed against the window.

Hugh sucked in a breath and closed his eyes, lowering his head into her touch. There was power here, but was it his or hers? His intriguing scent was all she could smell, all she wanted to smell.

"Hugh? I…I…" He opened his eyes, and they were molten glowing rivers of richness, sin and shadows, salvation and reckoning. She wanted that gaze on her when he touched her, when he worshiped her, when he drove himself into her, when she came shaking around him, calling out his name.

Gia leaned up. "Please kiss me." He swept his hands around her waist and lifted her, taking her mouth as she rose to meet him. His mouth against hers finally, finally! Fire shot through her body as she opened for him, danced for him. She'd been dead for years. And now the way his hands burned through the fabric of her pants to knead her muscles, the way he leaned into her, tasted her lips like she was divine.

She was dizzy, flying, unmoored, clinging to his shoulders, her legs around him, scrabbling for purchase, burning inside while he kissed her. "God," she swore through the assault.

He growled and traced a path to her neck, licking along her collarbone to that fine thin skin where she was so tuned into him. His lips were a brand on her, punishing, feral, open-mouthed, and hungry, mapping her neck and her face. And she answered him as well as she could, opening for him while he plundered his tongue inside her mouth and tasted. While his hands roamed over her back.

Caught in the riptide, flipped upside down, wild and hot and so, so wet, her whole body came alive for him, tingling and shaking while he used those glorious hands of his on her lower back now to mold her to him as she fit her core to his body. Images burst into her mind as she felt every inch where their bodies touched, a memory and a dream. A desire.

"Please," she begged. "More...I..." *I need you.* "Touch me more, please."

He curved his hands around her waist. The zap of pleasure as he dipped one hand into her waistband, caressing and feeling. *Closer, more,* she begged in her mind, unable to speak, her whole body under his command, flushing and rippling for him. Or maybe...was ...could it be her power engaging? A surge of fire, electric and tingling, flew through her.

He angled her hips closer to him, leaving no space for uncertainty or questioning or confusion. He molded and dug his fingers in and...why were there so many clothes between them? A distant sound of thunder rumbled across the land beyond all the doors and walls. Raindrops flew from the clouds, brilliant, shimmering. As if they began in her.

He tumbled back, tipping them both into nevermore. No space between sin and prayer, no space between pleasure and pain, no space between love and death, as if he was marking her, making her see and feel him, the gorgeous power of him, or both of them together. He slid his hands down her legs, slowly, gently, starting to move and feel, and she wanted it all. Everything. A force greater than both bound them together.

His hands brushed the thin but strong strap around her thigh and her mind shattered.

"No! No...I..." She shoved and stepped off of him, nearly falling in the process. He held his hands up, desire dripping from his eyes. She tried to steady herself. But she'd been tossed off a cliff and was clinging now to one flimsy vine.

His shirt was untucked and half unbuttoned. She'd done that. Her pants were askew; her blouse unbuttoned to her bra. Tendrils of hair slipped from her barrettes. A lone flash of wind blew outside. The silence echoed in her brain.

"Oh...shit." She gulped in deep breaths. Blackness threatened her vision. *Breathe. Get yourself under control.* She tried to remember the words, the tasks that helped her be calm, be fierce, *survive*. Gripping the sides of her blouse together, she channeled Orin's voice, his demands, his sharp tone. But the words wouldn't come. It was so difficult. She was tugging herself out of quicksand...pain pressing down on her...a heat in her belly flared and all she could see was a messy orange darkness.

"Gia? Gianna."

At his voice, she dragged her eyes out of the blinding pain. The beauty of him, the wildness, the...so much she couldn't name in his expression all focused on her.

"Hey." He held out his hands carefully as if she were a wounded animal, ran one hand down her arm, took her fingers, and squeezed. "Hey, breathe, honey. It's all right. Just a kiss. Got away from us. Breathe." With calm fingers, he brushed her hands away, buttoned her blouse, and wrapped her limp body in a hug. "It's okay."

At once, his warmth seeped into her, teasing her with a gift that couldn't be hers. This embrace was worse than the kiss. More devastating than maybe anything in her life.

"Never." She shook her head against his chest. Her breath was coming fast still but more regular. Her vision cleared. She wasn't going to faint or whatever ridiculousness had been threatening.

"I think you're having a panic attack, darlin'. I'm sorry...I..."

She shook her head. "No." She was slumped against him, trying to recover. She had to get out of here, away from him, from all of this. It wasn't hers. It was dangerous, so, so dangerous. She pushed away, and he gave her space, and for one split second, she wanted to weep and beg him never to let her go. Instead, she fled.

CHAPTER EIGHTEEN

Hugh ran his hands through his hair, fixed his clothes, and followed her. She helped her kids into jackets and rushed them out the door, apologizing to his family the entire time. A flurry of Reilys leaving the restaurant, making it all seem like her world hadn't just been on the sharpest edge, like his hadn't. A steady rain fell, a screen shuttering around him.

"Son?" His father's clear voice. One word held an entire volume of meanings.

"I upset her," Hugh said. *Not on purpose, but did that really matter?* He watched Gia and the kids through the damp windows. Steam billowed from the gutters; the streets were shiny with puddles and rain-slicked surfaces everywhere. It was both beautiful and tempestuous. Like Gia. "I have to go." Before his family could say anything else or prod, he was out the door and down the block to his car, chilled in an instant under the deluge.

"Fuck," he swore. And it was a freezing rain too. He preferred the snow, but there was something about this rain tonight, the fervor of it, the wild, angry, hopeless energy of it. He didn't have to follow since he knew where they lived, but something drove him to make sure they got home safely.

That kiss, Jesus Christ. That moment, which felt like the stars exploding in the sky for the two of them, and then the absolute anguish that overtook her afterward. And the panic attack. Did the woman not know she'd been on the verge of a pretty serious one? He sped up. He never should have let her drive in that state, but he'd been…he'd been. He rubbed his chest. His heart was finally beginning to regulate back to normal, or nearly normal, from its chaotic storm of lust and love and devouring.

They were home and inside by the time his truck arrived at her forlorn house, looking all that much smaller and hidden through the walls of water being unleashed from the sky. He parked in front and watched. Perhaps he should be worried that she'd see him. Hell, part of him wanted her to know he was right here, for her, for them, for always. But he also doubted she could see anything through the overgrown evergreen bushes that blocked half the porch along with the magnolia that was so old and gnarly its branches hung onto the roof like it wouldn't be able to stay standing if it weren't for the old shingles themselves.

It was one of the worst symbiotic relationships he'd seen. A damaged old roof entwined with an overgrown tree. Neither one healthy.

"Help! Help! I can't find you!" Danny's voice reached Hugh through the rainstorm. It was muffled and odd. *Dreaming. No, not dreaming, nightmaring.* The sound struck his chest again. "I need help!"

Hugh was out the door of his truck, racing up the front porch steps, and banging on the door before a second thought could cross his mind. "Gia!" he yelled. The door was solid, thank goodness. A flicker caught his eye, and he glanced into the corner of the eaves, a camera. Good, she had a security system.

"Noooo!"

Shit, Danny was tangled in the throes of a nightmare. Where in the hell was Gia? Hugh focused his senses, closed his eyes, and rested his forehead against the door. Danny's tangled cries came to him and the soft sound of Ava sleeping and...the cadence of the shower water falling on Gia while she...wept. It was more than weeping; it was her trying to mask howling cries of agony.

Hugh reared back in shock. What in God's name had happened to her? Danny still cried out and the rain still slashed, and Gia couldn't hear any of it. Hugh did something he rarely did unless he was on his own family's land or in his own space. But the darkness and the rain would have no one out tonight to witness, and he needed to help Danny. He raced to his truck, pulled it down the road at the end of the cul-de-sac, and into a nearly hidden path through the trees. Shedding his clothes, he called on all his emotions and powers, and let the wolf take him.

The pain was an old friend now when his bones and blood changed. In a matter of minutes, he shifted into his other form and raced through the trees on all fours. He paced around Gia's house until his nose led him to beneath Danny's room. He let out a soft howl, drew on every image he had of Danny, and pushed his magic toward the child. And even though he'd been using these powers since he was a teenager, every time it came, it gave him a jolt of energy, of rightness.

He saw Danny. The boy was stuck in a dark, ashy forest, with no greenery left anywhere, and no rain. Only a decimated mess of trees after a long and fiercely burning fire. Desolation was thick. Ashes and smoke coated the air, but Danny spied him through it all. The boy's cheeks were wet with tears. So many tears tonight, as if the rain had conjured them.

A shock jolted Hugh as the boy stepped closer and suddenly Hugh was in the boy's dream too. Hugh gave a soft bark and stepped into Danny. The boy wrapped his arms around him. Eventually, the smoke and ashes disappeared.

"Wow," Danny asked. "Are you real?"

Hugh pranced away and ran back and forth, showing Danny that he was friendly.

"You are real," Danny whispered.

"Who are you?" Hugh and Danny both turned to see Ava trailing into the dream. "A puppy!" she squealed and ran toward him.

Christ, Gia's kids were already powerful witches. He'd never heard of kids their ages dream walking, let alone into stranger's dreams. And if he'd been in human form, he'd have laughed at her calling him a puppy. A four-hundred-pound black werewolf was no puppy.

"Ava, wait," Danny said and grabbed her hand. "It's a dream. You have to be gentle."

"I promise." She looked at Danny and surprised Hugh with her patience and the near plea in her voice.

Hugh approached the two carefully and knelt down so Ava could ruffle the fur on his head and neck. God damn, these kids were going to break his heart. He allowed it for longer than he should have, but seeing their joy and knowing Danny was no longer under the clutches of a nightmare gave him peace. When he nudged them away, they disappeared under a clear sky, safely into the dream world. He'd helped them, but he'd also crossed a boundary. An act that he'd have to explain to Gia, and soon.

Before he left, he silently prowled the edges of Gia's property, making sure nothing untoward lingered or thought to intrude. There was a swirl of darkness hovering over his tiny family. He'd do anything to protect them, but he couldn't do that if he couldn't find the source of evil. It nagged at Hugh the entire way home. He didn't like unsolvable problems.

Chapter Nineteen

"Everything okay?" Gia asked. The kids were whispering to each other in the backseat of the car. Or rather, Ava was trying to whisper and Danny was hushing her.

"It's fine," Danny said. "We're excited about science camp."

"I'm not, humph." Ava sure could pout.

Gia caught the glare Ava sent Danny's way through the rearview mirror. Ava had begged and begged to be allowed to sign up for this day-long science camp when Gia had discovered it for Danny in the fall. Ava had worn her down, so they were both enrolled, but Gia should have known how fleeting Ava's interest would be.

And they were running late. Damn it. They'd all slept in or hardly slept. It wasn't easy to tell, but they'd all looked bedraggled this morning when she'd hurried to get them out the door. She certainly felt bedraggled. After barely being able to step out of the shower last night, she'd fallen into bed, exhausted.

"You'll have fun, love bug."

"I'd rather stay home in bed and dream."

Gia laughed.

"Ava," Danny admonished.

Huh? "Hey, what's that about? She's allowed to say what she'd rather do, even if she is going to camp anyway. You'll both have a great time. I promise. Tonight, we'll cozy under all the blankets and watch a movie." She wanted to turn the car around and bury them all under the covers for the entire day, wrap her arms around her babies, and cuddle out of sheer exhaustion and out of an unsettled feeling creeping around in her gut. She tried to shake both worries off because running errands was so much easier on her own.

Science camp was in the gymnasium of an old Catholic school on the other side of downtown from their house.

"Don't do anything fun without us," Ava said. "Especially not with Hugh or his family. We like them." Ava glared at Danny before he could say anything. Something weird was going on between her kids, but they often had their own language. Sometimes a silent one.

Hugh. His name wouldn't leave her mind, nor would the searing ache of his all-consuming kiss last night. Maybe she could go home and sleep all day, close her eyes to all of it, the man she could never have, the feelings, the love. *No, no, no.* It wasn't that. She dared a glance in the rearview mirror. Her skin was dry. There'd be no getting rid of the dark circles under her eyes, or the hollow look inside them, a thing she tried never to notice. Even though she felt it all the way to her bones.

Shit, this is bad. The kids already liked him too and that could not happen. It was the three of them in life. Gia didn't have time for a stupid affair. She especially couldn't let her kids get attached to him, or his family, lovely though they all seemed in the flickering pretty lights of the restaurant, scooping her and her kids into their group as if they belonged. Ugh, belonging. A foreign word for her. An ache formed in her chest. Ages-old, and it seemed, never-ending.

They arrived a few minutes early.

Across the street from the Catholic school sat a stretch of quaint old buildings. A charming gourmet grocery, a beauty salon, a tiny bookstore, and a few other shops Gia couldn't tell. Right in front of their car was a bakery, Sweet Delights. Its doors were open and the aroma wafting toward them was miraculous. She'd had enough time to grab their lunches for the day and protein bars for breakfast, but the smell of fresh doughnuts and pastries stopped her in her tracks.

"Mommy, can we?" Ava asked.

"We are a few minutes early," Danny informed her after looking at his watch. She was too sleep-deprived to argue. And luckily there wasn't a line. Ava picked a cupcake instead of a doughnut, but what difference did it make? Sugar was sugar, and she was giving it to them for breakfast. She was totally winning as a mom, but she didn't have the energy to berate herself.

"Going to the science camp?" A friendly lady grabbed their treats. She was tall with dark skin and a smile that brightened the entire space.

The kids nodded and thanked her for their goodies.

"It sounds like heaps of fun. Nothing for yourself then," she eyed Gia. "Or come back and have a cappuccino after you drop them off. A fresh batch of doughnuts is almost ready too. They'll be warm from the oven. I'm Willow, the owner."

Gia couldn't think of a lovelier idea, and she couldn't seem to care that it was frivolous.

Getting the kids registered and hugging them goodbye felt like it took eons. Although less than thirty minutes later, she was sitting at a pretty table by the window, sipping the best cappuccino she'd ever had. It had toasty caramel notes and a hint of goddess or friendship, which was an odd thing for a coffee to smell like, but Gia lived her world oddly.

"Darling kids," Willow said, sliding a trio of small doughnuts toward Gia. The sugary aroma was intoxicating.

"Thank you. Um, this drink is amazing." Gia took another sniff and the toasty notes were still there, but now they mixed with the rich whimsy of the doughnuts. Pure joy was what they were.

Willow pulled out a chair and sat. "More of my staff are here now, and I get the rest of the day off. Gosh, that kitchen is hot. I added a touch of my secret toasted chocolate sauce." She pinched her fingers together. "Something about that smokey flavor that goes so well with the coffee. And cream, of course. I hope you don't mind that I used cream instead of milk. I wanted you to get the entire story or emotion."

Gia closed her eyes, sipped, and allowed every nuance in. Her guard was completely down. Perhaps it was the gallons of painful tears she'd shed last night. Ha, last night, talk about the last few weeks. She told herself, in this sunlit space, that it didn't matter, that she could have this. All for her. No one had to know. She ignored Orin's usual dictates that lived in her brain, her always cautious, on-guard brain.

She took a few more sips of her drink before she tried the doughnuts. When she broke into one, a puff of steam spiraled upward. "Oh my," Gia said. "This tastes like magic."

Willow's deep brown eyes sparkled, and her smile grew bigger. "I wondered if you'd get that," she whispered as she leaned in. Taking a quick look around, she continued. "I hope it's okay. I recognized you when you walked in."

Gia swallowed the doughnut, which now expanded like a dry lump in her throat. "Oh." She shook her head. "I'm not...I don't..."

"Hey," Willow interrupted her, setting a hand on hers. "I won't tell anyone. It's all right. But you have to know your power practically sparks off of you?"

The café had a good crowd. The buzz of conversations surrounded them. No one was paying any attention to her and Willow. "I...it does?" She spoke so low she wasn't sure Willow could hear her.

"Sure, honey, can't you feel it? In here?" Willow put a hand to her chest.

Gia didn't tell anyone about being a witch. She didn't talk about it, ever. She and her sister had made that decision years ago. It was safer. Gia didn't even think about it unless she was working, and then she obviously kept it to herself or to Orin for specific reasons. In her financial jobs, if word got out that she was a witch, she'd be called a fraud or cheat immediately. If word got out in her…well her other occupation, she'd be dead. Orin had drilled that into her constantly over the years.

"I'm sorry," Willow whispered. Her words drifted like a sea blue ocean in the Caribbean. "Each one of us has our own path. But at least you know another witch now, me, in case you ever want to talk about it." Willow stood.

"Wait," Gia said. "I'm the one who's sorry." Her heart raced a mile a minute. "I'm not very comfortable talking about it in public." *Or at all.* "But I do…I am…I mean…"

Willow gave a soft laugh. "Listen, we don't have to talk about it. I'm headed down the street to get a pedicure at the new salon. They're having a sale today. Free mani with a pedi. Want to join me? Every woman needs pretty nails once in a while."

Without thinking, Gia nodded and watched Willow's smile brighten the entire room. Gia finished her doughnuts, couldn't believe she'd devoured all three, and wished she'd had ten more. An hour later she sat in a pedicure chair, with her feet soaking in soapy warm water, one hand being buffed, a glass of prosecco in the other, laughing at Willow's tale of the last date she'd been on.

"It's a disaster out there," Willow said and sighed. "Or maybe it's me. You should meet my sister. She's the perfect one. A brilliant teacher. She has an amazing wife who's building her her dream house."

Gia laughed. "Sounds like my sister, Francesca. She's a doctor at Mercy General. Floats around her shifts dusting everyone with fairy sparkles. But I love her, and she cooks for me."

"Cheers to brilliant sisters who make it seem easy."

Gia clinked glasses. "But your bakery is amazing, and those doughnuts were to die for. You're successful too."

Willow laughed. "I suppose you're right. But I'm not inspiring little minds or saving lives."

Gia could smell the vulnerability then, the honesty, the hope for…was it friendship? Gia hadn't had an actual friend aside from her sister in what felt like a million years since childhood. Suddenly, in the delicate center of her heart, she wanted a friend more than anything on the planet. "I hope we're not all expected to save lives, though," she said softly, thinking about how under the cloak of many nights she did the very opposite.

"No." Willow sighed. Her sighs were delightful, full of hope. She reminded Gia of Frankie in that way.

It was probably the delicious bubbly that was putting fantastical thoughts in her head, thoughts of happiness, delight, and friendship.

"You're right, and I adore baking."

There it was again, that scent of kindness and friendship and...it wasn't the doughnuts after all, or not just the doughnuts. It was Willow.

Gia hid behind her glass, begging no more tears to spill, as she wondered for the first time in a long time, what did she love? What was her scent? Because she was afraid she was bleak and hollow, that she smelled like nothing.

Chapter Twenty

Hugh arrived at Gia's house just as her car turned down the block. It was like he'd conjured her. The frown on her face when she noticed him almost made him laugh. It might have if he wasn't worried about talking to her. She looked tired still, but better, with more color in her cheeks. Of course, that could have been her mad.

"What are you doing here?" She slammed the door and faced him, hands on her hips, braced for a fight. He'd love to tussle with her. "How in the hell do you know where I live? Have you been following me?"

Shit. Fear licked through her blood. He could sense her attempt to mask it. He stepped down, so they were on level ground. "Gia..."

"Don't Gia me." Her voice had lost its edge as she stepped closer, and her cheeks flushed. He felt the lure as sure as she did. But she shook herself, took a very deliberate step back, and crossed her arms.

"Do you know Ian Webb?" Hugh asked, deciding not to admit right off the bat that he had followed her.

"My, my realtor? Your brother." The knowledge dawned on her.

"Your yard butts up to my parents' property and when you bought the house, he told us a Ms. Reily and her family had bought this place. I didn't know who you were then..."

"And?"

He really didn't want to confess this part. "And then when your car wouldn't start last week, I followed you to—"

"I knew it." She stormed around to the back of the car and started grabbing bags of groceries. The wind kicked into a fit, angry and slashing, driving her hair in front of her face.

"I wanted to make sure you made it home safely, that's all." He stalked to her to block the wind from her body.

"That's all?" Her disbelief was a live thing, but he could work with that.

"Yes. I was worried about Delly breaking down."

She sighed.

"Here. Let me." Cold wind whipped around them and the rain came too. *Damn infernal rain they'd been having*. He manhandled the bags from her and shut the back of her Wagoneer.

She unlocked the three locks on the house's side door, keyed in her alarm code and swept inside. Hugh followed her angry path and set the bags on the kitchen island. It was large, with an old butcher-block counter that needed resurfacing, but the room itself was warm and inviting.

The inside wasn't as bad as he'd thought based on the state of the outside and how long the house had stood vacant. Old wide-plank floors and higher ceilings. Great windows that needed to be replaced but let in lots of light. The bones were solid. The kitchen opened into a wide living room with an oversized gray sectional full of throw pillows and a few soft blankets folded across the back that said *cozy and family lives here*.

"It's not okay for you to follow me," she insisted. She wouldn't face him. Instead, she began putting away the groceries with shaking hands.

He hadn't meant to make her nervous or scared. "You're right," he said. The bag at his feet held cold stuff, so he opened her refrigerator and helped. Milk, cream cheese, butter, some ice cream. Two kinds, raspberry and chocolate with almonds. Another bag held a bouquet of flowers. He opened a few cupboards and found a jam jar, filled it with water, and began arranging the flowers. So she liked ice cream and flowers. Or maybe the ice cream was for the kids.

Gia huffed and climbed into one of the stools, arms crossed again. Hugh saw the kettle on the stove, filled it, and turned the burner on. He grabbed a mug and a mint teabag and made her some tea while he figured out where the rest of her groceries went. There was a not-too-shabby pantry that needed a fresh coat of paint and a small window to let in more light, but it was a nice place for all her dry goods.

He filled her mug, added honey, and joined her at the island.

"You...what...you put away my groceries and made me tea?" She loosened her arms. "I...that's...thank you."

Hugh hid his grin. Her thank you felt both sincere and reluctant. He tugged her stool closer so their knees were touching. "Pretty nails," he said, running his thumb across her fingers. They were cut short and shimmered with a pale bubblegum pink paint. "They sparkle, just like you."

She set her mug down and twined her fingers with his, watching their connection while he watched her. The pull between them was so strong, more so when they were touching, like an old wound in both of them finally beginning to heal.

"Where are the kids?"

"Science camp," she said, stealing a glance at his face. He got to watch the blush rise up her cheeks. *So damn pretty.* This was the strangest type of flirting he'd ever done, but he loved it. He loved everything with her.

She stood and was right there in his space, fogging his brain. He opened his legs so she could get closer. The wind still fluttered outside. It sounded almost as if it were singing. His arms went around her body automatically and he pulled her in. Her hands landed on his chest and a soft sigh escaped her. She leaned her head into his neck, eyes closed, breath fluttering on his skin.

"We can't keep doing this," she whispered. "I can't..." she rested her lips against the hollow of his throat. "You smell so good and I can feel your pulse and you're so, so warm, Hugh..."

His entire body vibrated with the need to wrap himself around her. He stroked the delicate column of her neck, felt her pulse kick into his caress. She was his. He wanted to consume her, but he couldn't. "Fuck," he swore softly and set her away. He wanted nothing more than to take what she was offering, but he had to talk to her first.

She gasped and stumbled away. "Shit. Right. This isn't what you came for. And I shouldn't be doing this, anyway. God, Gia. You are such an idiot." She ran her hands through her hair. "I...I..."

"No, that's not..." He reached for her, but she stepped away. It wasn't just about telling her he'd seen her kids in their dreams. To explain, he'd have to tell her what he was. And never in his life until now had he been shy about sharing his true nature. Of course, he'd never cared so much about what another person thought. "Gia I..."

There was a buzzing sound that made her freeze. She raced for her purse and tugged out a phone. All color and emotion disappeared from her face. She straightened and blinked away any shimmer from her eyes. In a matter of seconds, she became a different person.

"What's wrong? The kids?" He stood. A current of danger zapped through the kitchen.

"The kids are fine." All traces of his Gia disappeared. "I have to be somewhere. You need to go." An icy tone slid into her words.

"Gia?" Hugh made his way around the island to her. *What the hell is going on?*

"No." She held up her hand. "I need you to leave." She walked to the back door, held it open, and waited. The chill from the day seeped in, lacing the quiet between them with something heavy. "I'll...I'll..." One minuscule stutter to her words, and then she recovered. "I'll see you at work, and that has to be all."

Hugh watched her face for any sign. She wouldn't meet his eyes. Her expression was completely frozen.

"Fine," he said. "I'll leave you alone." *For now.*

He pulled down the street and waited in his truck for her to leave. He'd never seen anything like it, the ability to turn every single emotion off. Twenty minutes later, she hefted a duffle bag into her Jeep and drove away. Hugh sat in contemplation. The wind and rain had stopped, leaving a solid wall of gray clouds across the sky, low and heavy with loneliness. It was an odd thought to have, but it narrowed in and pierced him. A full moon tonight. Hugh didn't need a clear sky to see that. It was in his blood and bones. But something else was coming too. His skin prickled with warning.

Chapter Twenty-One

"You're late," Orin said as soon as he beeped her into his home.

Feels more like a fortress.

"I came right away," she said, walking the corridor that led to his inner office. From the outside, the sleek modern asymmetrical look of his place screamed, cool, modern living. Inside, everything was stark. Not one piece of art or photograph. Orin didn't believe in anything frivolous. There was no mention of the sun. Everything was a waste of time as far as he was concerned when villains were out there needing to be caught and killed.

Only, we never simply catch them. That thought flittered through her mind. A mind that was still clouded with the scent and feel of Hugh, of how much she longed to be in his arms. The warmth, the passion, the safety.

Safety is an illusion. That's why she was here to fight the world's wrongs.

Orin didn't bother to look up when she entered his office. He was typing away at his computer. "You smell awful. What have you been doing?" he criticized.

He didn't expect an answer. He never did. He was her drill sergeant, and she respected and accepted that. There was no way in hell she was going to mention Hugh. Something inside locked tightly around the moments she'd had with Hugh. As if her most important assignment was to keep him hidden, to keep him safe from Orin. Anger licked at her belly, like a tigress protecting her pack.

"Wasting your morning, is that it? Getting your nails done?" His words were caustic as he finally took in her appearance.

Gia fought the need to hide her hands behind her back. Hands that had been warm and entwined with... *No, shut it down. You are strong. You are in control.* "They've been painted before for assignments."

"They have been painted according to my instructions for each disguise you wear."

Right, even her nails belonged to him. She'd never been annoyed at him before. She needed to control her shit.

"And you look weak. Perhaps taking on freelance work is too hard for you. Perhaps you should think about what's really important."

"My freelance work is important. I have to have a job, Orin, to pay my bills, or at least the appearance of a job and a paycheck, to be seen as a normal member of society." Those words were especially difficult for her to say. When had she ever been allowed to be normal?

"You came to me, remember? To help you find Doug's killers. And we are getting close. I can feel it. I'm here to help you. Together, we've done the world many favors. But you can't get distracted now. You must stay focused."

Finding Doug's killers was all she wanted. She had come to Orin, hadn't she? Or had he found her? That time in her life was a blurry mess. Gia took a deep breath and shunned the memories from three years ago. Maybe she was getting distracted. "I can maintain my freelance work and stay focused." She'd have to stay away from Hugh. She'd already been awful to him. Most likely, he wouldn't want anything to do with her again. The pain that caused her, like bones breaking, was more difficult to hide than she could have imagined.

Orin studied her. It was a battle of wills, a staring contest. She had to let him see exactly what she allowed. A skill she'd perfected over the years. She shoved away the disgust that caused her and stared back at him. He blinked, not losing one bit of his fierce scowl, tossed her a folder, and gestured to his closet where a garment bag hung. "This one shouldn't be too difficult for you, as long as you are at the top of your game tonight."

"Tonight?"

"Is that a problem?" His scowl had turned into a sneer, an expression that suddenly chilled her bones. He could be lethal if she weren't on his side. She masked the shudder that ran through her.

"We agreed I need enough notice to find childcare. This has been part of our deal since I started..." *Since I started killing for you.*

"Can you manage to figure it out?" Had his voice always been so condescending?

"Give me a moment." It took more than a few deep breaths for her to calm the instant rage that rose in her. Gia walked away and called her babysitter Ashley. She was a senior in high school and the kids loved her. Then she called the camp and arranged for Ashley to pick the kids up. There, done.

Exhaustion wrapped its gnarled fingers around her. Was this truly her life? Reluctantly she began learning her last-minute assignment, all while maintaining the ice around her heart. Reading the folder gave her a jolt. "This guy worked for the same company Doug did, Future Growth."

"I thought you'd appreciate that," Orin said, his voice now dripping with ego.

"But what does it mean? Is this him? Is this who killed Doug?"

"Gia, Gia, Gia, how many times have I told you to remain calm? It's how we accomplish our goals. He did, in fact, work with your husband. He's no longer with Future Growth, but he is still embezzling money."

"Still? You mean, he did it at Future Growth too?"

Orin nodded. Maybe a piece of the unfinished horror puzzle of her life was finally slipping into place.

"So, he could be responsible for Doug's death. Is he?" Sickness churned in her stomach.

"He's a connection, however close or far. Do you want to finish him or not?"

Of course she did, didn't she? This was as close as she'd been in years. She wanted the truth. But after all this time, after all the money involved and the treachery she'd witnessed, she realized she might never have all the answers. Orin had taught her they'd still take their revenge wherever and however they could.

"This is a light assignment. No killing involved." Orin sighed as though he was disappointed. "We get access to his money, which will eventually be the death of him, anyway."

No killing involved. The words chilled her. She wanted to weep with gratitude for that small mercy. Revenge and vengeance had lived so long in her belly that they'd become companions. But those weren't the friends she longed for anymore. A surge of energy simmered in her blood. A long-forgotten ally stirring. Her magic, but not the kind she used with Orin. Instinctively, she masked it. Shuttering her emotions and energy, she faced Orin.

"You need to get close enough to him and his computer so we can access his money. He resurfaced last month. Idiot doesn't even have his hidden accounts offshore. Lucky for us, he's taken a liking to top-shelf bourbon. The ego always gets them in the end."

Orin's smile reminded her of a snake catching his prey in an undetectable snare.

"If you can attach this to his computer without him noticing. We will end him. His money will be gone, and his employees will be alerted to his...shall we call them sins?"

Gia memorized the information Orin gave her, then shredded the documents.

"And there will be no talking to him, no interrogating."

The argument was on the tip of her tongue. He was one step ahead of her.

"He's not your husband's murderer. He's too flawed for that, too immature. He's not like you and me, Gia. You must get in and get out. You don't want anything to happen to you. Who would those kids have then?" Another snide smile, there for a second, then gone. "I'll leave you to get ready. I'd say good luck, but I'm sure you won't need it. Remember the end goal." This time, his directive hit her like a threat.

Orin swept out of the room and shut the door behind him. It wasn't for modesty's sake. He had cameras everywhere and could watch her change if he wanted. It was simply because he was finished and didn't need to bother himself with this task anymore.

She tried to control her inner seething while she changed herself into a tall blond with light blue eyes and some extra padding in the important places, all the ones men liked to grab. Her dress was navy to match her heels. *How magnanimous of him to show concern for my kids when it has to do with obeying his orders for the evening. He doesn't care about my kids.* She'd long since known that. Why, then, was it bothering her so much?

Gia took the small electronic device the size of a flat black pea and her bag of clothes and left. It wasn't until she was a few miles away that she pulled over and strapped her knives to her inner thigh and across her shoulder, fitting it under the dress Orin had chosen for her. Tonight's job might not be an assassination, but she'd be prepared for anything, just in case.

CHAPTER TWENTY-TWO

HUGH SHED HIS CLOTHES, bowed his head under the moonlight, and felt the stirrings of change. He'd been feeling it all day, the need to let his body morph, to howl, to run. There hadn't been a drop of rain since this morning. But the crisp, clear night and few clouds hovering near the moon didn't settle well in Hugh's gut. The frigid air whipped over him as he sprinted through the forest on his family's land.

A powerful force was afoot, more powerful than his entire family of wolves. He ran to get his frustration out; he ran for knowledge.

Perhaps it was because of his last encounter with Gia or all of them put together, but the sizzle in the air felt related to her and her kids. Perhaps he simply wanted to be near them. Cresting the top of a steep hill, he circled toward her house and cursed himself for not telling Gia about the kids finding him in their dreams. He could console himself with the knowledge that he'd tried and that he would again the next time he talked to her.

Now in his agile wolf form, Hugh raced through the night to the back edge of Gia's property. He slowed and quieted the pads of his paws into silence while he approached. Ages of instinct and lineage allowed him to travel nearly undetected.

From his stance between two ancient cedar trees, he watched the house. Lights were on and the drapes were closed. A warm glow shone through, which eased Hugh's nerves until he noticed her Jeep was missing.

Hugh took one silent step closer, then stopped, nearly leaping away at the menace startling him. A void not born of night, but of evil. An essence born of malice. It wasn't human, witch, or werewolf, but he couldn't tell exactly what it was. It swirled around the house in an almost lazy circle, watching and...mocking? The thing had no clear shape. Hugh waited it out and eventually, it disappeared. The malice and mocking were gone. But Hugh felt them as surely as if they'd seeped into his soul.

It wasn't long before she pulled that shitty car into her driveway. A few moments later, a young woman exited and drove her small Honda away. The downstairs lights soon disappeared and new ones flickered in the back upper corner. Her room. Hugh stepped over the fence line, keeping to the trees as he made his way closer. There was no trace of the darkness that had haunted this house an hour earlier.

There was, however, the sound of weeping. Hugh's ears pricked. *Gia.* His heart rushed at his chest to find her, soothe her, but another sound met his ears.

"Oh, it's you again." Danny appeared in his own dream, discovering Hugh. *How in the world?*

"Oh, goody!" Ava was there too. All Hugh had to do was step forward and he'd be in their dream.

Both children held a unique power he'd never encountered in any witches, not even full-grown, trained witches. Remarkable. He needed to leave before he overstepped further.

"It's so much nicer when you're here," Danny admitted. The child who was close-lipped and serious. "It feels safe."

"Very safe," Ava echoed.

"Will you stay with us?" Danny asked. "Until we fall back asleep?"

How could he say no to that? Hugh stepped forward into their dream.

After they were both sleeping and their dreams were quiet, Hugh slowly walked away. All the while keeping the sound of Gia's tears in his heart.

Chapter Twenty-Three

WEBB INDUSTRIAL WAS QUIET on Monday morning. Cole was on the phone when Gia arrived, but he gave her a smile and a wave as she made her way through the stunning lobby and down the hall to her office. She stopped when she saw Hugh waiting at her door. *Why does he always look so hot and cute and warm?* So, so warm.

"Made you a coffee," he said as she approached her door. Every time she got close to him, she wanted to fall into his arms and let all her stress disappear.

"Were you just going to stay here until I arrived? What if it had gone cold?" She yawned. Of course she did because sleep was little to be had this weekend and coffee was exactly what she craved.

He hit her with his smile. It did something fierce and beautiful to his eyes, and the lines around them, the way he enjoyed the hell out of life. Another foreign concept to her. Gia ached to lean in, reach up and touch those lines, kiss them, pull them into her dreams, and learn every single story he had to tell.

"I know what time the elementary school starts and how far it is from there to here. I gambled." He moved aside so she could unlock her door and when she'd set her stuff down, he handed her a still-warm Americano with the perfect amount of creamer.

"Thank you." She sighed when the aroma of rich coffee met her tired brain. It wasn't fair, damn it. How did he sense what she needed *and* do it for her even while she tried to push him away?

He studied her with his arms crossed as if inspecting every inch of her expression. Eventually, he spoke. "Would a meeting with my dad right now be okay? I explained what you told me, but I think he'd like to speak with you about it. We can talk in the gym office. Trent never makes his way down there."

Gia nodded. "Let me grab Bess. May as well take my stuff with me." She slung her big purse over her shoulder. "In case someone makes his way into my office again."

"Here." Hugh took her laptop bag from her. She swore he was going to take her hand, but instead, he brushed her fingers with his, gave her a soft expression, and motioned for her to lead the way. "Bess?"

"My…uh…my purse." She patted her bag and moved her gaze from his. *Oops.* Hadn't meant to admit she'd named her purse.

"Hmm." His hum worked its way into her tired bones.

"Did you...uh...have a nice rest of your weekend?" she asked as if she hadn't tossed him out of her house Saturday morning.

"Mm," he glanced at her as they walked side by side. How could a look unnerve her so? "It was interesting. You?"

"Oh, mine was...everything was fine. Pretty boring. Single mom, two kids." She gave a fake laugh. "You know."

"Gia," Hugh said, stopping them as they got to the main floor of the Compound. "I don't suspect one single thing about your life is boring. Exhausting maybe." He leaned in and lightly brushed his thumb over her forehead and down her neck to that place she loved when he touched her, as if he was stroking her, claiming her, worshiping her. "But never boring." Then he turned and opened a door to a small office. His father was already there.

Drake stood. "Ms. Gia, thank you so much. This isn't the ideal way to begin Monday morning. But I'd like to know everything you told Hugh."

It didn't take long for Gia to relate what she'd discovered. Drake followed every word.

"I also didn't get a chance to ask Hugh on Friday, something else I wondered about," she said.

"Go ahead," Drake said.

"In our first phone consultation, you mentioned you wanted me to evaluate the charities you were donating to and if there was more you could do on that front."

"That's correct," he said.

"The Veterans Aid is there, as you know since you hold the auction every year and work with the veterans specifically," Gia said and faced both men. "But I couldn't find any evidence that you'd been contributing to the other two charities at all." She placed a few documents in front of them and used her pen to point. "The accounts are here," she said. "But the money isn't going to the charities. Something felt off to me, so I checked with the organizations."

"Where is the money going?" Hugh asked.

"I suspect you'd have to ask Mr. Bordin that question."

Both Hugh and his father sat back in their chairs. No one said a thing. No one had to.

***

Hours later, Gia sat at her desk and watched out the corner windows as security escorted Mr. Bordin out of Webb Industrial for the very last time. Drake stood outside watching him, his wife, May by his side, their hands linked, pain in both their expressions.

Gia uncovered truths and untruths through numbers and accounting and people's financial statements all the time. People thought numbers could lie, but they never did, not in the end. Mr. Bordin had been stealing from his friends indefinitely. A thorough investigation would reveal how deep his betrayal went. She'd rooted out another bad guy. Unfortunately, today didn't feel like a victory. Anger and sadness sat heavy in her gut.

She'd begun to care about the Webb family, and although Trent was now gone, his betrayal would cut deep.

Without letting herself second-guess her decision, she went in search of Hugh. She found him in the gym. He was at the ground level in the pool, racing down the length in a powerful freestyle, all his back muscles showing off. He executed a perfect flip turn and continued, slicing through each stroke as if he were punishing the water.

Gia wrapped her arms around herself, stepped back, and quietly returned to her office. A mess had been made and now she had to help right the wrongs. Hugh was off limits, no matter how she ached to comfort him.

***

"Could this day get any w…" *No, don't say it.* Things could always be worse. But after what she'd had to disclose this morning to the Webbs, watching the betrayal and not being able to do a thing about it, to now, listening to the awful noise her car was making, she could scream. "Come on, Delly," she begged the old car.

The sky was a miserable shade of gray, and the air smelled like snow. A thick layer of frost already glittered across the ground and the wind sliced through her hair, when she stepped out and slammed the door. She huddled into her jacket and carefully made her way toward the door of Webb Industrial when Hugh stormed out.

"That thing finally dead?" Anger licked across his skin. She'd seen him bank it during their morning meeting and try to expel it while he swam, but it wasn't gone, not fully. His eyes were dark pools of emotion, pain, and longing. He started to reach for her, then stepped back, and tossed his hands on his hips.

"I can't get it to start," she said, her own anger replaced by compassion for him. "I need to call a tow truck and see about getting a loaner. My insurance will cover it."

"Come in here out of the cold. Call your tow. I'll give you a ride home."

"Hugh? No—"

"Your insurance going to have a car here for you this afternoon?" He crossed his arms, vibrating with unspent energy, his gaze never leaving hers. The heat of it singed her.

She swallowed. "Probably not."

"Give me your keys, please." He softened his tone, taking a step toward her. "Call the tow. I'm going to have a look under the hood."

In the end, she was too cold to argue. And too lost in his fraught gaze, the way he saw so deeply into her. She was also annoyed. She could be both. What a man thing to do, order her around and look under the hood. Fine, let him be miserable in the freezing temperatures.

When he returned to the lobby, the cold rushed in with him. "Sounds like the starter. Could be expensive to replace."

The tow company had just taken her off hold and was speaking in her ear. "Three hours?" she said. "No, I—"

"Here." Hugh took the phone from her. "Never mind. We'll get it figured out another way." Then he hung up and whipped out his own phone.

"Hey," she demanded. "What is wrong with you? I need that tow?"

"Three hours, if that. In this weather? Could be longer. I'll get my brother to tow it to the farm. He'll fix it for you too, most likely."

"No, I can't...that's..." She hated not being in control. What was happening?

He raised his eyebrow at her. How dare he. She glared at him. A hint of a grin cracked his angry expression.

"Yeah, you at the farm? Got time to tow a Jeep Wagoneer out there? Yeah. Thanks. I owe ya one. I'll be out there tomorrow to help you fix it. If it can be fixed. Yeah, the starter. Yep. Thanks."

"I don't need your help." Gia tried to speak calmly, but she could feel the steam rising from her head.

"Yes, you do. You just don't like it. That's fine. I understand. Come on, let's get your kids and get you home. I'll give you a ride in the morning if you don't have your fancy rental by then."

He held the door for her, and the wind swirled in, blowing small flakes of snow and sleet. Georgia was supposed to be sunny. Peaches and sunshine. Southern hospitality.

"Storm's coming. Could be icy, dangerous. Gia?"

She shoved away her annoyance for now and tried to ignore how her body warmed to his voice. "Fine," she bit out and walked into the cold, feeling like she'd lost more than control over her car situation.

Chapter Twenty-Four

"Warm enough?" Hugh asked her as she sighed into the passenger seat.

"Seat warmers?" she asked and glared at him.

He could see the words she'd wanted to toss at him, *"No fair!"* And he didn't give a damn. He wasn't playing fair. Stubborn, beautiful woman needed help.

"Yes, welcome to a car made in this century."

"It's a little big don't you think? Overcompensating much?"

He barked out a laugh. The tension and anger from the day left his body. "I'm a big guy, Gianna." He sent a wink her way. He loved the sound of her name. "I have big siblings. I'm also often hauling equipment around."

"Hmm, equipment, huh?" She faced the window before he could catch her expression, but he'd caught the flirt in her tone and he'd take it. All he had to do apparently was take her for a ride in his car and warm her up.

"I like your laugh," she whispered.

This woman was going to be the death of him.

Hugh reached over and took her hand, let their connection settle him further. He'd needed to expel his anger earlier at the betrayal, at the disgust and defeat he'd seen on his father's face. And now he needed this. Christ, how he needed this. That she allowed it comforted and confused him. After this weekend, he wasn't certain she'd even speak to him again. How cold and stone-like she'd been ordering him to leave her house. Not like his Gia at all, and yet...

They drove in silence for the few minutes it took to reach the elementary school. Huge snowflakes had begun to fall, making visibility worse. And the heaviness settled into his heart when they pulled into the parking lot because he still hadn't told her about the kids' dreams.

He parked and let her run in to get them, keeping the car warm for them all. But when he saw them approaching, he got out to help her.

"Hugh!" Ava yelled and ran to him, talking a mile a minute. He quickly buckled Ava into the car seat they'd grabbed from Gia's Jeep.

"Hi," Danny said, a small grin breaking out over his face. "You have a huge car." He climbed in and buckled himself.

"It's a little scary," Ava said with a huge smile. "Fierce. I like it."

"Oh, Lord, help me," Gia whispered and rolled her eyes.

Hugh chuckled.

"I love the snow," Danny said. "Makes everything quiet and sleepy."

"Yeah." Gia looked at her son. "We don't get as much here as we did in Boston."

Danny gazed out the window. "I miss it."

Gia glanced at Hugh.

"My parents have a farm with lots of land not too far from your house," Hugh said as he drove this precious family home across the slippery streets. "You should see it when it snows, like rolling white blankets for acres."

"Does it have animals?" Ava asked.

"All kinds," Hugh said. "A few horses, pigs, cows, chickens, some barn cats and dogs, lots of dogs."

"Horses?" Ava breathed. "Could we...do you think we could meet your horses? Someday?"

"Ava," Gia said.

"Yes," Hugh answered. Checking his rearview. "If your mom says it's okay. I'd like that. And I bet Betsy, Chocolate, and Marshmallow would love to meet you."

"You have a horse named Marshmallow?"

"Yep," he said as he pulled into their driveway.

Gia sent him a glare that turned into a small smile before she got out of his car. Hugh helped her get the kids and all their stuff inside.

"Can Hugh stay for dinner?" Danny asked. "Maybe he can help me with my science project, since you're not very good at science, Mom."

"Wow," Gia slipped her heeled boots off and rubbed her feet. "Way to sell me out, kiddo."

Hugh watched her move around her house, putting her purse down, rechecking the alarm at all three doors, those tired eyes of hers not one bit hidden from him.

"How about if I make dinner?" He had to talk to her anyway, and he wanted to stay, be surrounded by their warmth, their chatter, their openness.

"Are you a better cook than Mama?" Ava asked as she climbed onto a stool. Gia grabbed juice and poured both kids a drink.

"Hey," Gia said, poking Ava in the side and making her giggle.

"I can cook." Hugh grinned. He checked the tea kettle to see if it had water and turned it on, finding her tea and a mug.

"Right, but you don't know what ingredients I have. Don't you need a recipe?" Gia asked.

Hugh opened her fridge and freezer and checked in her pantry. "Sometimes a recipe helps, but I grew up working in the family restaurant. After bus boy I graduated to prep chef, then line cook. Cooking is in my blood." The kettle screamed, and he turned it off and poured it over the lemon tea bag.

"Oh," Gia said.

When he glanced back at her, she seemed so small and lost. Her hair had partly come out of its ponytail and was still wet from the snowy rain. She stood there, shivering.

"Go take a shower and I'll figure dinner out. The kids can help me if that's okay?"

"Oh…"

"Yes. I want to help. I'm very good at stirring," Ava said.

"I can help. I help Mom and Aunt Frankie all the time," Danny chimed in.

Hugh came around the island and put the warm mug in her hands. "Go get warm. We'll be fine." He found everything he needed for simple chicken cutlets, defrosted some buns in case anyone wanted to make theirs into a sandwich, and started slicing potatoes to bake some fries. Simple, good food he hoped they'd all enjoy.

He set Ava up at a station to pound the chicken breasts and Danny helped him bread them and fry them while Ava got distracted and tugged out a basket with a million stuffed animals to play with on their enormous sofa. He checked the fries and set the table while Danny flipped the chicken. And he could hear Gia upstairs moving around and showering. He listened for the sound of her tears, but they didn't come tonight.

When she came back down, he couldn't help the smile that spread across his face. She was in the softest gray sweats, her hair down around her face, no makeup, cheeks rosy from the shower, looking relaxed and warm.

They ate cutlet sandwiches with toasted buns and an aioli, and fries with ketchup around her old wooden table. Then Hugh helped Danny work on a project about sound waves and motion while Gia read to Ava on the couch, tucked under a soft looking pink throw blanket. In Gia's lap, she had a tiny bowl full of those red candies she was always eating.

"I should go," he said when she was corralling the kids upstairs for baths. He didn't want to go. "I need to speak with you."

"Let me put the kids to bed. You can...wait if you...I mean, if you don't have somewhere else to be."

"I'll wait." His relief was enormous. After that ice queen had come over her on Saturday, he'd been confused and rattled. Tonight she was warm and soft, even when she was cranky.

Hugh put the books on the shelf and tossed the stuffed animals into the basket. He and Danny had done the dishes already, but he put everything else away and rinsed out the sink. Her small bowl was on the counter with one candy left. He popped it in his mouth. *What sweet did his witch like?*

Hugh bit back a curse and spit the sour cherry candy out in the garbage. He filled a glass with water and sucked it back. *Not sweet at all.* Sour as hell. Fuck, he chuckled. She was full of surprises.

He sat on the sofa, leaned back, and rested his eyes, listening to them above him. Letting their sounds wash away everything bad that had happened today. Letting their warmth surround him.

Chapter Twenty-Five

"Hey," she whispered.

Hugh's eyes opened clear and bright. Those gorgeous brown orbs studied her in silence before he took in the scene around him. He was stretched out on her sofa under the blankets she'd tucked over him last night. She handed him a cup of coffee.

"I fell asleep. Damn," he said. "Sorry about that." He twisted his legs to the side and sat up, taking the mug from her. "That smells amazing. I haven't slept that good since that night with you." He finished the last part quietly, staring at her across the rim of his mug.

Gia stepped into the kitchen, where she got cereal and milk set out for everyone. She'd make some toast too when the kids woke up. Two simple things she could make. She could admit she'd been disappointed after putting the kids to bed to see Hugh asleep too. Part of her longed to join him on the couch, even just to cuddle. But cuddling and casual weren't for her. So she'd covered him with blankets, turned off all the lights, and taken herself to bed alone with only her pillows for comfort. Secretly, she'd enjoyed knowing he was in her house. She'd lain awake for a long time trying not to think about him. Eventually, exhaustion had taken her under.

How nice it had been to have him here, making them something delicious to eat, fixing her tea. It wasn't the first time he'd noticed her chill and made her a warm drink. He'd done the dishes, helped Danny with science, cleaned up their messes. It was so easy to get lost in a dream of him.

"Kids still asleep?"

"Yeah. I'll wake them in a while if they don't get up on their own."

"What can I do to help?" Here he was suddenly, taking up space, still smelling amazing, his voice resonating through the house. Standing so close to her by the sink.

"Nothing, you can sit or go," she said. "Thank you for...d d doing everything last night. I owe you." Why was she stuttering her words? It had to be his scent. She was acutely attuned to scents, and his was irresistible. Power and gold and strength and desire and something else deeply unique she was having trouble identifying, a sort of soul-stirring.

"You don't owe me anything. I enjoyed doing it."

"Cleaning up after a strange woman and her kids?" Gia scoffed as she sliced bread, her hand shaking. What was wrong with her?

"You're not a stranger."

"I..." she hadn't said *stranger*. But he'd corrected her. Making a point.

"Mind if I take a quick shower? I've got a duffle with clothes in my car. Comes in handy when I'm at work too long. I can give you all a ride this morning unless that rental is coming."

"No, uh...no rental today, at least until tomorrow. They said."

He was out the door to his car and back, brushing snowflakes off his shoulders.

"You can...uh...use mine...my shower, um...here." Gia led him upstairs to her bedroom and bath. "I don't think you'd fit under the other showerhead. It's pretty...small. Neither one is great."

They were both in her bathroom, which itself felt a million times smaller as he took up every extra inch of space. Exactly what she wanted...no she didn't...she couldn't. But she was having trouble remembering why she couldn't. "I..." Gia stepped toward him, silent, standing so close, unable to voice her desires. "Hugh?" Her plea came out in a whisper. It was impossible to fight the lure of him.

"Gia." He stepped into her. His smile turned to heat.

Her hand made its way to his jaw of its own accord. "Your beard grows fast," she whispered.

"Mm." He nuzzled his face into her hand and closed his eyes. "Like it when you touch me, Gianna."

She stretched and reached her other hand into his hair, arching her whole self into him. "I shouldn't." She shook her head but ran her hand through his hair, thicker and longer now than it was when she'd started work. He responded by wrapping his arms around her and lifting. Her legs went around him automatically too. Even while her brain was trying to maintain some distance, some rationale, her body so obviously had other ideas. He walked her to the counter and sat her down, closing his eyes and leaning in.

"May I?" he asked, and she nodded, too scared to let her voice be her guide. Warm lips met hers, heating her whole body instantly.

Lust sparked up her spine. She held him close, never wanting to let go. Maybe she'd never speak again. He towered over her. She had to lean back at the force of his kiss. It wasn't soft. It wasn't calm. It was demanding and devouring and everything, giving and taking. He dove his tongue into her mouth to taste her while her legs tightened around him, dragging him in closer. She couldn't get enough. It would never be enough.

When he opened his eyes, they were no longer that soft golden brown, but...were they...

"Your eyes?" She whispered, stretching into him. "Are doing that thing again."

He ignored her, taking over her mouth like she was the very essence he needed to live. Pulling his mouth away, he swore, tugged off her sweatshirt, and brought her naked body to his mouth, teasing one nipple as she sighed into him, begging and pleading. "Yes, please, Hugh."

He snaked his wonderfully large hands down the back of her sweatpants, palming her bottom, caressing and kneading, holding her tightly to him. Her nipples beaded for him, hard aching points, and he nipped at them, eliciting a moan from her. Somewhere in the back of her mind, she knew she should push him away, but she couldn't.

Perhaps he was using magic on her. She nearly laughed at that thought.

"Let me look at you. Let me kiss you. Let me make you feel good, Gianna." He wasn't asking, he was commanding, and she obeyed. With his mouth at her breast and one arm wrapped around her, he brought the other hand around to her thigh and inward, exactly where her body cried out for him, cupping her with his warm hand, branding her. He stroked a finger through her wetness. "So wet for me," he whispered against her ear, scenting and tasting her, and she bowed for him.

He worked her up, one finger gently teasing, sliding in and out. He added another finger, dragging her higher, so tight, so good. Everything inside her hummed, arching against him, towards what his fingers promised.

"I...Hugh...I..." She couldn't find her breath and seconds later, she was bursting and trying not to shout as she shoved her face into his neck. She spiraled into nothing and everything.

"Fucking beautiful," he said, holding her to him. "So fucking beautiful in my arms."

They were as close as two people could get with half of their clothes on, or at least he still had clothes on. His did nothing to hide the state of him. Every single inch of him was hard and vibrating under the layers of fabric as if one more second would be his undoing.

"Mama." Ava's voice came from down the hall.

"Shit?" She scrambled out of his arms and dressed in a flash, having to tug her sweatshirt off and around the right way when she glanced in the mirror. Her cheeks were glowing. Her hair was a mess. She shoved Hugh and his delicious smirk toward the shower, tried to hide her ridiculous grin, and exited the bathroom.

"Is Hugh still here?" Ava was tiptoeing down the hallway with her horse stuffy hanging onto her neck.

Boy, is he. "He's taking a shower, love. Let's go make toast and tea, shall we?" Gia scooped her daughter up and carried her downstairs, so grateful that this darling child still loved hugs and cuddles. Danny was so stoic these days, so old, or trying to be. He was already downstairs with the kettle on when she and Ava arrived. Her sweet son, taking care of them. She ruffled his hair and kissed his cheek as he tried to squirm away.

"You have to make four teas, one for Hugh," Ava said and leaned her head into Gia's.

Danny glanced at Gia.

"He fell asleep on the couch when I was tucking you two in. He's in the shower, but yes, let's make him some tea too."

"Awesome," Danny said. "He can give us a ride in his sweet, warm car. We won't have to wait for Delly to take twenty minutes to warm up."

Gia closed her eyes. Maybe it was time to buy a new car. She could afford it, but she hated to spend any of the money she made in connection with Orin. She didn't do what she did for him for money. In fact, she hated that money and only touched it if she had to. That was another reason she clung to her financial clients, so she wouldn't have to depend on blood money to care for her kids.

Suddenly the euphoria she'd been riding, since Hugh had grabbed her and kissed the life out of her, drained away and she was left with her lonely, harsh reality. *Suck it up. Lonely's better than dead.*

CHAPTER TWENTY-SIX

HUGH WAITED IN THE car as Gia walked the kids into school. The snow had stopped, and the sky was a hint of blue under a flimsy layer of clouds, but it was still fucking cold. A dusting of frozen snow covered the land and blew across the road. Coldest winter they'd had in a while.

He wanted to take them to the farm, show them his family's land, the barren, stark beauty of it in winter. How it changed in spring and came alive, and was flush with growth during the summer. How it often took on a different barrenness at the end of hot, rainless summers. And then the graceful way the trees and land drifted into death during fall. So many layers to it all.

So many layers to her, he thought as he watched her rush back to his car, tugging her black wool coat around her. Too big for her by far. One more way for her to hide. He got out to open her door. A melancholy hit him. Why *was* she always trying to hide from him, from life? He was certain she would push him away farther after he told her about her kids. He'd planned to tell her last night but he'd fallen asleep.

Then this morning, well, just thinking about this morning had his blood heating. When she let herself be free for him, it was everything.

Now would be a good time to tell her, in the car without the kids.

"You didn't have to do that," Gia said, shoving aside his gesture and climbing into his SUV, which made him smile. She was so efficient and unneedy and he wanted to give and do everything for her. To care for her, treat her like precious gold, dig his way into all her secrets, and hold them carefully in his heart. He wanted her to fly, knowing he would be her soft place to land.

Hugh climbed into the driver's seat, buckled his seat belt, and took her hand. She let him, which surprised him again because with every step forward he made with her, she shoved him ten steps backward, putting on her mask, protecting herself. So many wounds carved into her bones and he still hadn't touched the surface of them. Would she ever let him? Tension ran through her blood. Something wasn't right. "Okay?"

She glanced at him. A good night's sleep hadn't dimmed the dark circles under her eyes. Maybe she hadn't slept well after all.

"Danny hates school. The teacher pulled me aside this morning."

Hugh squeezed her hand. "What's going on? You can tell me."

She sighed. "He's not very outgoing, especially since...uh...since our move. And some of the other boys make fun of him. There have been some tense moments at recess," she said. "He usually loves school and learning...please don't tell him I told you any of this. He seems to like you, and I don't want him to know I told you."

"I'll hold your secrets. You can tell me anything."

She brushed a tear away and shook her head, taking her hand from his. "He doesn't have any friends," she whispered. "Do you know how hard that is for a mom to witness? And I know it's not about me at all, it's about him, but it hurts." She rubbed her chest.

They'd arrived at work, and he parked the car but left it running. "I can't imagine what that feels like. He's a great kid."

"Oh, we're here. I'm sorry to spill all that on you. I never...I don't..." She shook her head as if she'd found herself in some alternate reality.

Hugh took her hand again. "Hey. You can tell me anything. I meant that. I want you to share."

"I'm totally failing at this mom thing," she whispered, and he could visibly see her trying to hold her tears in.

"Gia, both those kids are incredible. You are a single mom doing it all on your own, doing a great job."

"I...thank you. I...need to get in to work. So do you. Thank you for everything."

Hugh sighed and followed her out of the car. There she went, shoving him back. "You don't have to thank me.

Oh,"—he caught up to her—"my brother texted. He has your car parts and can have it fixed by this afternoon. I could help you get the kids and run you out to the farm."

"I don't know. I..." She glanced at the door to Webb Industrial, shivering under her jacket. She gestured between them. "This is...I'm not sure I'm in a position to have this. With anyone right now."

Hugh gave her an out for now. The woman was freezing, and they were at work. "No stress, Gia, just helping you get your car. The kids'll like the farm. I guarantee it." *I'm hoping you will too.* Each tiny step forward with her, he'd take. Whatever he could get.

"Okay," she ducked under his arm that held the door for her, gave him a soft smile and then she was gone, disappearing to her office.

He was smiling like a fool until he remembered he still hadn't had a chance to tell her about what he was, and that her kids were apparently capable of drawing him into their dreams.

CHAPTER TWENTY-SEVEN

GIA'S HEART NEARLY STOPPED at the breathtaking beauty before her. She knew Georgia was a pretty state, the northern part especially with its gentle mountains. But she hadn't paid much attention to it all during the last few months. Apparently, she hadn't been paying good attention to anything. Her kid was getting in trouble at school and she hadn't had a clue he'd been so unhappy.

Now they'd pulled down a long tree-lined drive that circled and meandered into the most stunning view. An old white farmhouse sat on a slight rise and to the left, flowing out beyond, were softly rolling hills and flat lands that eventually led to a treeline, every inch covered in snow. It was less than five inches, but the freezing day today had set it all into a gorgeous scene that might have whispered despair to some, with the empty tree branches and the snow rolling across the land under the guidance of the low wind. But to Gia, the serenity and peace eased every single thing inside her. *Magic.* Whispers of joy fluttered inside her. *You've forgotten your connection, Daughter.*

What? Gia glanced around. But the words had come from within her.

Smoke puffed from one of the three chimneys in the farmhouse. Two enormous gray barns sat in the distance and next to them a large shop, big enough for cars and heavy farm equipment.

May came onto the porch, followed by three enormous dogs who tumbled down the steps and barked and played around Hugh as he exited the car. He scrubbed behind their ears and leaned in to give them kisses, and Gia couldn't help her smile.

"Wow, cool dogs," Danny said. "Are they friendly?"

"Hugh wouldn't let us around unfriendly dogs, Danny."

Ava was most likely correct, but what an odd thing for her to assume.

Gia got out and the dogs raced toward her, tails wagging. *Gosh, they're soft.* Two Golden Retrievers, and an enormous chocolate Labrador that wiggled slowly to Ava. Ava gently wrapped her arms around the Lab, who threw furious licks on her cheeks.

"Why does she look so funny?" Ava asked.

"She's pregnant," May said. "Due in a few weeks now.

Danny was surrounded by the Golden Retrievers who were acting like he was their playmate, as they danced and butted their heads into his body.

"My goodness, what a pleasant surprise," May said. "Come on in where it's warm. I'm making homemade marshmallows to have with cocoa. Connor's here somewhere. He'll be happy to see you kids."

The kids raced up the steps, and the dogs followed.

"I wasn't sure you'd ever want to see me again," Gia said.

"Oh, honey," May said. "That rat bastard stealing from our company was not your fault. I'm grateful to you for discovering it, Gia."

The laugh bubbled out of Gia, easing her tension and worry. May was as cantankerous as she was regal. "It's lovely here," she said.

"Yeah," Hugh said, breathing in the cool air. "One of my favorite places."

"Mine too," May said with a huge smile.

"Come on." Hugh reached for Gia's hand and she let him tug her into the gorgeous old farmhouse after May. The charm and warmth wrapped itself around her. While her brain told her she *couldn't* have this, her body blossomed with everything Hugh brought to her life.

After the best homemade cocoa and marshmallows, Hugh helped May dig out old work boots in her kids' sizes, and Hugh took them out to see the animals, most of them keeping warm in the barn. Three horses were in the smaller barn with several enormous barn cats. In the second barn were a handful of goats, who didn't seem to care that it was below thirty degrees outside, cows, and even a pig who was, Hugh mentioned, ready to give birth any day. *Fertile place, this farm.*

Her kids hadn't shown this much excitement about things in as long as she could remember. Hugh introduced her to a few of their staff members who helped with the animals. They left the kids with a woman named Hannah who gave them treats to feed the horses. Then Hugh led her to the shop where her Jeep was waiting along with a man who must have been another brother.

"Ahh, there's Webster now," Hugh said.

"You have a brother named Webster Webb?" Gia raised her eyebrow and shook the man's hand.

Hugh grinned. "How'd you know he was my brother?"

"Come on, you all look alike." She waved her hand up and down. "Enormous muscles, that unruly dark hair, except when you cut yours short, and eyes that…"

"Eyes that what?" His brother choked back a laugh. "This I've got to hear."

"No teasing her, man," Hugh said with a grin.

"They seem to…" She got lost in Hugh's eyes. *See all the way inside me, even to the parts I haven't shared.* Was that it? Was that what was so special about his gaze on her? That shimmer that went all the way around his irises, lit with enjoyment. She looked at his brother, embarrassed now. Webster's eyes weren't the same at all, they were dark and assessing.

"You must be Gia." The man wiped his hands on a shop rag and held one out to her. "You're right. I'm the oldest, Alexander.

Webster's an old nickname. You can call me Alex. This guy likes to tease, don't you, Hughy?"

Laughing, Hugh dodged a punch to his shoulder.

"Your car's starter died. You also needed new brake pads, so I replaced those. You'll need tires soon. Between my brothers and me, we know everyone in town. Could help you get a deal on a new car."

"Thanks," Gia said. "But I'm good." Delly was from her life before…before…

"I get nostalgia, but there's also freezing your butt off in the middle of winter." Alexander crossed his arms and looked at her like she was two steps away from the loony bin.

"Thank you for your input, Alexander. How much do I owe you?" Gia ignored his well-meaning but overbearing words. She had enough of that from one Webb.

He grinned and shot Hugh a glance. "Consider it a favor. May's baking ribs. Better hurry and get to the house if you want us to save you some," he said before leaving them alone.

It was the two of them in the warm shop, while the air whipped around outside.

"Gia, I need to talk to you," Hugh said.

"Mama," Ava and Danny ran into the shop along with another child, a boy, tall, skinny, jet black hair and serious eyes.

"Ms. May said we could stay for dinner. Can we? Can we? She has the bestest breadsticks ever that she made with butter and salt on top. I could die they smelled so good." Ava's words rushed out. "And we made a friend too!"

"My nephew, Connor. Alex's son." Hugh introduced. "Got a hug for your uncle."

Connor rolled his eyes and gave Hugh a side hug. "Cool Jeep," he said. "You guys should stay for dinner. Grandma May is a culinary genius. And I could show Danny the bike I'm fixing up later."

Danny's smile hadn't been this big in years.

"Can't beat May's cooking," Hugh said. "Bet she has scalloped potatoes too."

Ava took Hugh's hand and led him out of the shop. "What's scalloped potatoes?" Ava asked as Danny and Connor followed. And then it was Gia standing like a fool by herself. She stuffed her hands in her pockets and followed them to the warm house. It glowed from the inside now with lights and laughter and connection. Something she wished for. Something elusive. Something she'd never believed in.

Chapter Twenty-Eight

"Wish I was driving you home again," Hugh said while he switched Ava's car seat from his Yukon back to Gia's Jeep. *Wish you knew we're meant for each other.*

"I appreciate everything, Hugh, your help, your family's help. And I will pay Alexander back. But I have to get home to…my reality."

She was pushing him away again. He could feel it in the clip of her words. He could practically read her mind as she stood there shivering. She needed a hat and gloves and to not be standing outside in the cold with her legs bare under her skirt, even with those sexy leather boots she wore. She teased him without knowing it. Showing glimpses, then pulling away.

"Going to let me kiss you goodnight?"

"Hmm." There was a small smile on her face to match the tone of her voice.

She might have barriers, but he sure loved it when she let them down for him. He swung the door shut and wrapped his arms around her waist, leaning against the car with her in his arms.

"I'll keep you warm." He'd love nothing more than to keep her warm forever. Damn him for falling asleep on the couch last night.

"What were you trying to tell me earlier?" she asked as she ran her hands over his head.

God, that felt good. The way she dragged her nails across his scalp sent tingles through his whole body.

The door to the house opened, and the dogs spilled out with Danny, Connor, and Alex. Ava was asleep in Alex's arms.

"Got a tired one here," Alex whispered. Gia untangled herself from Hugh's arms and opened the door while Alex buckled her in.

"Please send me a bill for the car," Gia said to his brother. "I don't like to have debts."

"Mm-hmm." Alex crossed his arms. Hugh knew he'd never send her a bill. Didn't mean she wouldn't try and force money on him, his proud and independent witch.

"See you guys soon, I hope." Connor waved and went back inside.

Hugh stepped back from her car as they drove away, feeling like he'd let something important slip through his fingers. It felt wrong, them leaving without him. And once more, he'd failed to tell her the truth of things. They both had secrets they were keeping. And his had the potential to make her furious at him, at the least.

"Good little family there," Alex said. "Fell for a witch, did ya?" His brother smacked him on the back. "Gonna be a challenge. Good for you."

"Hmm," Hugh answered, watching the car until it was out of sight. Then he glanced at his brother. "I don't think she's aware I know she's a witch. It's not something she ever mentions. She keeps everything locked inside. It's like she's hidden it so deep she.... We uh...we haven't talked about it yet."

"She know what you are?"

Hugh shook his head. "I don't think so."

"Better tell her. Something special like that isn't something you want to fuck up." Alex's eyes grew stormy. Alex's wife had left him years ago. "Better say my goodbyes. Time to get Connor home."

"Yeah," Hugh said to no one, or perhaps to all the ghosts that had drifted across this land and his family's heart.

He stood in the darkness breathing in the cold for a long time after trying to figure out how he was going to explain everything to Gia and not lose her in the process. The crisp air burned his throat and made him restless. He knew exactly where his run would take him this evening.

And if it was an excuse to make sure she got home safely, so be it. He still had a nagging feeling of danger from that weird essence at her house. Evil was the word that kept appearing in his mind and it was too damn close to her and her kids for his liking.

The ground was tiny frozen shards beneath his paws and he welcomed the awareness it sent through his body. How he had to work harder to get his muscles loosened in the cold, the puff of his breath through the forest. The way a punishing run in nature purged the stress from his body.

When he got to her yard, he forced himself to sit and wait in the tree line. Lights were on and he could hear the murmur of their voices. He steadied his breath while their chatter washed over him. Lights went out upstairs and he waited for the sounds of crying, for nightmares to appear, but all was quiet. Even the sky and air outside were peaceful, as the three most important people in his life fell asleep inside their cozy house.

He wanted to walk closer, see if the kids would draw him into their dreams again, but he didn't. They didn't need him tonight.

Tomorrow he'd tell Gia his secrets, one by one, until they were all exposed. So that what lay before them were all his truths, his heart, his soul, and his nature. All that and his love. Hugh walked back toward the farm, taking a longer path and thinking about the life ahead of him, about everything he wanted, and whether he was worthy of it all.

CHAPTER TWENTY-NINE

S ITTING IN HER OFFICE, Gia was putting the finishing touches on her report for Webb Industrial when she felt the presence of an angry energy, familiar too. Fingering her ear pods, she shut the volume off. She might work well with music, but she never had the volume that loud. Nope. She was always absolutely fully aware of her surroundings. It had been lanced into her. It was a part of her now, an old scar that would never fully disappear.

Worry, instinct. A knowing. Carved deeper into her three years ago when she'd turned into her bedroom doorway and found her husband murdered in their bed. Although it had actually crept upon her the entire drive home that fateful night from the airport. There'd been a clanging in her gut, ringing slowly over and over. She'd known something was wrong before she'd pulled into their garage. Their neighbor, Mrs. Giovanni, had been out on her porch and Gia had asked her to watch the kids.

Then she'd gone inside and that awful scent had hit her. Upstairs to her bedroom, Doug lay there. One heartbeat in her chest and she'd realized the scent of death. Not the smell of blood or decomposing human body, just death, a thing she'd recognized in her soul.

It was the same scent ground into her when the intruder had killed her mother all those years ago. It felt like it was an essential part of her being. A life no longer. Snuffed out forever. A painful absence. That was the moment her instincts had forced her never to be completely at rest again. Fourteen years old and on guard for the rest of her life.

She'd grown comfortable, lazy with Doug. Then his murder had reinforced it, clamped onto her gut, and singed deep. Memories coalesced in an instant. A burning signaled behind her eyes. *Come back to the present, Gia.*

She glanced up. Trent Bordin was in her office. He shut the door. The loud click of the lock reverberated through the room.

It wasn't the smell of death she smelled right now. It was disgust. Murky, indignant disgust.

He fingered one of the black and white photos on the wall. "Trent, you're not supposed to be here." Her senses homed in on her environment. *Locked door, no one else around, mostly soundproof walls.* The sick aroma of stale alcohol matched his unkempt appearance, and his eyes seethed. If eyes were the only part of a person Gia could see, she could tell so much. Gone was the expensive suit and trimmed hair. Today he wore a black shirt and pants with no belt, loafers with no socks. He'd half-dressed himself this morning. His emotions spilled out all over the place.

"Look at you in your posh office, a bit much for someone so new to the company, wouldn't you say?"

"Trent—"

"Although you got me fired, anyway. Hugh probably had his hand up that skirt by now, that it? You think you can play with numbers. You're gonna get burned, girlie."

"You need to leave. I'm calling Cole right now."

"Cole, pft. Little man with an even smaller dick. What's he gonna do?" Trent laughed. "Bionic arm me to death."

Gia lifted the receiver with one hand and hit the button for the front desk. Cole would know what to do. Trent wasn't supposed to be here. Where was her cell phone? She caught sight of it from the corner of her eye on the far edge of her enormous desk.

Trent weighed more than her, but with one quick study, she could tell he wasn't skilled at fighting. Sometimes, however, that didn't matter. A man with more weight and motivation on his side was scary for most women.

"Now, Hugh might be able to take me. Too bad he's busy playing with his plastic knees, pimping to the big guns, showing off, ignoring everything important. Yeah, tight already, I'd say, the two of you. Is it tight when he stuffs into you? I bet it is. Little girl like you."

She stood, needing the height, needing to move. Every word out of his mouth made her sicker. She was used to the vilest men on the planet, but never had it been directed personally at her. "You need to leave, now."

"I don't even have an office this nice, with two windows facing that view." He casually strolled behind her desk and tapped his fingers against the window.

You don't have any office anymore. Gia's heart rate kicked up. She faced him, with her office chair between them.

She set the phone down quietly and inched her way around the desk, never taking her eyes off him. Gia could handle him. He had no idea what her hidden skill set was. But the beginnings of fear crept in. Fear kept her on guard. Fear was every woman's first piece of self-defense.

He thought she was the numbers girl. She was so much fucking more.

Her training had given her the ability to be fully prepared in any situation, whether or not she could see a threat coming. And she could always see the threat coming. Waves of disgust rolled off Trent. He wasn't here to whine or insult her. He had nothing left to lose, the sign of a desperate man.

He slid the chair out of the way and followed her. He was fast for someone so out of shape, knocking her cell across the room with one swipe of his hand before she could reach it. Kicking stupid people's asses was for her other job. But she wasn't about to be this guy's punching bag. Suddenly, she was pissed. Let him try. Her heart was still beating fast. Fear and anger mixed together now, a heady combination that surged through her. *Bring it asshole!*

He caught her wrist as she made it around the desk. Dragging her to him, he moved and had her pinned to the desk. *So he thinks.* She'd use the desk as leverage if she had to. A quick look showed no one in the hallway still. Of course. She was down a long hallway in a building with several empty offices. They'd put her somewhere quiet on purpose. There wasn't going to be anyone waltzing by.

He leaned into her, his hand still clasped around her right wrist. Good thing she was ambidextrous. His breath reeked of alcohol. This situation kept getting worse.

"Get off me," she said clearly. "And get the hell out."

He scoffed. "I'm a senior accountant here. I can do whatever the hell I want, bitch. You don't tell me what to do." His sleazy eyes made their way over her body as he dragged his free hand to her breast.

Fuck. He left her no choice. Gia carefully placed her left hand on her hip and lifted her skirt. Even while her heart pulsed out its warning, she tried to breathe calmness into her body and mind. *Goddess, give me strength.* She placed her hand on the hilt of her knife.

Chapter Thirty

Hugh ran on the track alongside Alphonso, a former NFL linebacker and now two-time gold medal-winning Paralympic in track and field, and a sixteen-year-old named Bethany who'd lost her leg in a car accident. This morning, after Hugh had handed off the perfect Americano to Gia and wished he could kiss the surprise off her face, he'd come to the gym. They'd fitted Alphonso and Bethany with their curved carbon-fiber legs and brand-new knees.

All three of them had stretched, lifted weights, and done sprints to test the knee that Hugh had helped design. These two clients had been working with Webb Industrial for months. The knee had been the problem, acting like a spoiled child. Countless designs littered the trash, but this one was it. Now Alphonso and Bethany were testing out their other legs, the ones meant for running long distances. Each piece was also waterproof. Amazing.

Alphonso could afford the equipment. Bethany could not. Luckily, Webb Industrial offered scholarships and financial assistance whenever they could. Everyone deserved prosthetics. Gia had also run some fabulous ideas by them for more charitable work. And with her ideas, they were ready to get the ball rolling.

"So you got a 5 on the AP Bio test?" Alphonso asked Bethany. "As a sophomore?"

"Yes," she said, and Hugh could hear the grin in her voice.

"Sophomores taking AP Bio. Damn girl. Impressive."

"Thanks. That's my third 5 on AP exams. I have two more AP classes this year. And I'm taking college classes to get my Associate's Degree before I graduate High School."

"That's badass. Wait, don't you have time for fun?" Alphonso asked.

"Oh yeah," she said and laughed. "Beating your assess is super fun." She took off ahead of them.

Hugh started to laugh when something sharp stabbed him in the chest and he doubled over. *Gia's in trouble.*

"Hugh, you okay, man?" Alphonso knelt by him.

Hugh shoved the pain aside and focused. "My ma...my...Gia, she's in trouble." He looked at Alphonso. Then he ran. Pain and exhaustion were nothing. *Get to her now.* He raced down the track and took the stairs two at a time, his lungs burning. He burst into the main building and sprinted when he saw through her office window.

"Get off me." Her faint voice hit him in the chest.

Trent Bordin had Gia pinned against her desk. And he was fucking touching her. Everything slowed, time, sound. Everything except scent, fear, anger, and…power. He glimpsed her lifting her skirt and the—*Is that a knife tucked into her garter?*—right before he crashed down the door with one lunge.

His hand was around Trent's neck as he threw him across the room. Blood thundered through Hugh. He lunged for the man, not satisfied with the noise his body made hitting the wall and crumpling to the ground. But Gia grabbed his shoulder.

"Hugh, no, stop. It's okay now. I'm okay."

Deep breaths, Trent moaning on the floor, Gia's touch, soothing and strong. The state of things slowly whirled into focus. Alphonso and Bethany stood in the doorway. Gia had wrapped herself around Hugh's arm.

"Dude, that was some speed and power," Alphonso said.

Hugh ignored him and turned to Gia. He carefully took her wrist in his hand and studied it. "Are you hurt?" His words were harsh and dry as if he'd sprinted across the country to get to her. Felt like he had.

As gently as he could, he raised his hand up, fingers suddenly trembling beside her cheek. But he didn't touch her there yet. He needed to wait until she said it was okay.

"I'm okay," she whispered and moved his hand to her cheek, holding it there, holding his gaze as well.

"Can you"—he faced Alphonso—"find my father and call the police?"

"I'll do it." Bethany took off running.

"I'll make sure the asshole doesn't go anywhere." Alphonso put his prosthetic leg on Trent's body to hold him down. "I dare him to try anything with me."

The shaking in Hugh's hand filtered through his entire body. She'd almost been hurt. She'd been cornered, and who knows what the hell Trent had done to her before Hugh had arrived.

"It's all right," she said, soothing him with her soft voice. She placed her hand on his chest and he took a deep breath. "Can you maybe give me a hug?" she asked, her voice unsteady and small through her breaths.

He gently wrapped her in his arms. The feel of her warmth seeped into him. Her heartbeat pulsed in rhythm with his. *She's alive. She's...* "Gia, fuck," he whispered. "He hurt you."

"No." She shook her head against his chest. "I think he wanted to, but I...you came. I...I think you broke the doorjamb. What was that? I've never seen anything like that."

Without letting go of her, he glanced over his shoulder.

"Son, Gia," Hugh's dad was there with police officers. "What's going on?"

"Get him out of here," Hugh managed to sound professional, though his wolf threatened to snarl and lunge. Sweat dripped from his forehead and his muscles ached with the need to shift and pummel his enemy into the ground. He hadn't felt this type of rage since he was in his teens and changing for the first time, confused about what to do with all his power and hormones. Only difference now was that he knew exactly what he wanted to do.

"He attacked me," Trent whined to the police.

"Wrong answer," Hugh said. He crossed his arms and spoke to the police. "This man assaulted this woman. He locked her in here, cornered her, touched her when she specifically asked him to get off her."

"We saw it too," Alphonso said. "Hugh had to break the door down to get to her."

"All right," a police officer said. "Let us do our job and figure out what happened." They hauled Trent into the hallway. Then, one by one, in separate rooms, they questioned everyone starting with Gia. Watching her walk away without him was the second hardest thing he'd done today. The first being refraining from killing Trent Bordin.

Chapter Thirty-One

Nausea churned in Gia's stomach as she walked into the lunchroom. Across the room, she saw a familiar face and sighed. "This seat taken?"

"Gia!" Sammy cried. "I heard something happened. But no one will say for sure. Are you okay? Here, sit." Her Lab, Charlie, rested at her feet.

Gia slumped into the chair. Her adrenaline was fading quickly now that she was finished describing everything to the police. She pulled out her thermos of hot tea and poured herself a cup. "Trent came back. Not sure how he made it into the building. He confronte...he attacked...he tried to attack me."

"Oh, no." The color drained from Sammy's face. She put her hand gently on Gia's. "What happened? I'm so sorry. Here, have a protein cookie and some orange juice. You're shaking. It'll help."

"He cornered me, locked the door..." Gia suddenly realized how bad the situation had been. She'd certainly been in worse, but somehow none of that mattered when her blood sugar plummeted. She'd almost had to use her knife on him.

At Sammy's intake of breath, Gia continued. "Hugh broke the door down and uh…threw him across the room." Gia took the juice and had to switch it to her left hand. "Damn it, I guess he did hurt me." Her wrist was throbbing, not broken, thank goodness, but bruised and sore from where Trent had grabbed it.

"Wow," Sammy exclaimed. "That's a pretty massive door."

"Yeah." Gia huffed out a laugh. Everything was coming back to her now, a slow-motion replay. Hugh had broken down a solid wood door with one kick. It had torn the doorframe off with it. *Who has that kind of power?*

"Wow, skilled designer, nice guy, powerful, *and* good-looking."

"Too good-looking," Gia said, then covered her mouth. This crash of adrenaline made her lips loose.

Sammy laughed. "No joke. You should see his brother."

"Which one?" Gia fanned her face. "I've met a few of them, at family dinner and…the farm…Webster…I mean Alexander and Ian." She was having trouble remembering the rest at the moment.

"Oh, really?" Sammy said and leaned in, offering her cookies, which Gia gladly took. The sugar was helping. "We need a coffee date or a wine date soon."

"I…I…would love that. They're kind of overwhelming, the Webbs." Overwhelming and perfect and kind and loving.

"Can you believe five boys and one girl? Poor Addy. She's her own badass, though. Guess you have to be in that family."

Charlie started to wiggle, and Sammy's cheeks turned pink. Gia glanced toward the door and watched Grant Webb approach their table.

"Ladies," he said and knelt down.

Sammy unhooked Charlie's harness and gave a gentle command, and the dog leapt at Grant.

"How's my good girl, huh? How's my Charlie girl? Being good to your mama?" Grant sent a hurried glance in Sammy's direction. "Gia, you okay?" He stayed on his knees, showering his love on Charlie, who basked in the sun that was Grant Webb.

He was the suave brother if Gia had to label them. Dressed to the nines in a gray suit that cost more than most cars, sleek loafers, and his hair, brown and normally unruly, she imagined, like his brothers, was slicked back with some product. He still wore his sunglasses. Maybe the sun did follow him.

One look at her friend and Gia realized Sammy was in big love with this Webb brother. He hadn't been around the office as much, traveling to sell and demonstrate their products. And Sammy was so quiet suddenly, holding herself in, not taking up space with her joy and her self-confidence the way she usually did.

That's no good. Even though Gia was an expert at that same technique, it didn't feel right to see her vibrant friend dim herself. *Is that how others see me?*

"Gia?"

"I'm okay, Grant, thank you."

"He's gone now. The police took him into custody."

Gia allowed herself to relax a fraction. "Thanks for that."

"Well, here comes big brother. You ladies take care now." He stood. "Yes, you're still my favorite girl." Grant showered more scrubs on Charlie before he walked away.

"I'd say someone else wishes she was his favorite," Gia whispered to Sammy, who'd turned a perfect shade of pink.

"I…uh…should go." Sammy whipped Charlie's harness back on and escaped the lunchroom as if the room was on fire.

"Okay, bye," Gia whispered to thin air right before Hugh pulled out a seat and sat beside her, leaning in close.

He carefully took her bruised wrist and held it in his hand, running his fingers over it in a whisper of a caress. "Needs more ice," he said gruffly. His voice caught, and he swallowed a few times before he continued. Gia could still feel his heart leaping and snarling even without touching him.

"It's over," she said softly.

"It never should have happened," he insisted.

"It's not your fault." Gia cupped his cheek, unable, it seemed, to stay a safe distance away from him. Although safety was something she felt in his presence. It was such a foreign concept to her. One she'd had to carve out for herself almost her entire life. With Hugh, everything was so different. Her heart could be incinerated into ashes by being with him, but every motion of his said he wanted to keep her protected.

Would *he* be safe with her? That was the important question.

"It damn sure is," he said. He opened his legs and tugged her chair in, leaning his head into her chest. Automatically, her hands went around him. Why did it feel so amazing to be connected to him? His hands went to her waist, and she felt them, heavy, warm, and strong through her clothes. Gently, he slid his hands to her hips, using his thumbs to rub gentle circles across her skin.

She wanted to stay like this forever, but reality crashed into her. Gia pushed his hands away and stood. "I need to pick up the kids."

His gaze fell to her hips, then back to his hands, before he stood too, a confused look on his face. "Let me drive you. You're hurt. Please let me take care of you."

This sweet, overbearing giant of a man. Sometimes standing beside him, witnessing his beauty, it stole her breath. So many things unspoken shimmered between them. So many she could never mention, while at the same time, she wanted to know every secret he kept hidden, every fact he'd never told another soul. She longed to be that person for him. To be strong enough. To simply be enough.

"My wrist is okay to drive, Hugh—" *It's already healing, but my emotions are a hot mess.*

"It's not. You need to ice it, then wrap it and rest. None of which you can do while driving." Anger, like she'd never witnessed before, sparked from each word he spoke, even while his tone was gentle. He still blamed himself.

"Hugh, I..."

"Please." He leaned his forehead against hers. Every inch of him vibrated with emotion. Even like this he was he was so, so careful with her. *What a powerful feeling*. She was simply unable to walk away.

"Okay," she whispered.

"Give me your keys and I'll have my brothers get your car home. You can still take pity on me and let me drive you, but I suspect you'll feel better knowing Delly is there." Hugh stood and offered his hand. She hesitated for a second, ignored all the reasons this was an awful idea, put her uninjured hand in his, and let him lead them home.

Chapter Thirty-Two

"I don't know what groceries I have at home," Gia said. I was...we were going to have cereal for dinner. I think."

Hugh might have grinned at her cute voice, but she sounded nervous and weary. She was a master at ignoring her exhaustion. He could see right through her pride and strength to the worn layers of her emotions.

As the weather was clear and dry today, the kids were waiting outside in the carpool line. Hugh put his hand on Gia's to stop her from getting out. "I've got 'em," he said, putting the car in park and jumping out to help the kids.

"All right, everyone," he said, climbing into the driver's seat. He felt a sense of calm wash through him at having them all safe and sound within his reach. "Your mom hurt her wrist at work today, so we have to be very careful and help her, okay?"

"I love helping," Ava said, and Gia smothered a laugh.

Hugh grinned. "I bet you do."

"How did she hurt it?" Danny asked, very stiff and forthright.

"I'm okay, honey. I sprained it when a door shut on it accidentally." She gave Hugh a stern look.

"So," Hugh said. "We need to make sure she can rest and we need to get her some ice to put on it. Think we can do that?"

"Yes," both kids chimed in.

"And how does it sound to go to the farm for dinner tonight so she doesn't have to cook, and you two can check in on the dogs?" Hugh took her hand while he carefully drove out of the school parking lot.

"Hugh, no. Your family has had enough of me to last them a lifetime. I caused—"

"You obviously don't know my family very well." *And nothing about today was your fault.* He too kept his words to himself so as not to worry Danny and Ava. His blood pressure rose at the image of Trent pushing into her, the mix of fear and power radiating off her face. The bruise on her wrist and the way she shook in his arms afterward were going to kill him. Jesus Christ, if anything more had happened to her.

"Hugh. Hugh." She squeezed his hand, and he realized he'd stopped the car.

He let go. "Sorry. I—"

"Can we really go to the farm again?" Danny asked. He held himself so stiffly, aware, most likely of the tension in the air.

"Yes," Hugh said.

Gia was holding her sore wrist to her chest, leaning her head against the headrest with that crooked smile on her pretty face that made him fall in love with her every time he saw it. He refrained from rubbing his chest because he welcomed the pain that loving her caused. He would do anything for her. And he needed to tell her the truth, all his truths.

"Will you...will you make sure it's okay, so we're not barging in?" She asked so quietly he almost didn't hear her. Her smile had turned to anxiety in an instant. He reached over and smoothed the worry lines on her forehead. Then he dialed his dad's number from the car.

"Hugh? Everything all right?"

"Yeah, Dad. I've got Gia and the kids with me. Heading to the farm, if that's okay?"

"You don't have to ask. You bring that family here so May and I can spoil them. And they can taste-test my chicken and dumplings. Make sure the recipe's good enough."

Hugh smiled. His dad had been making Hugh's grandmother's chicken and dumplings since he was a child. The recipe was as good as it was ever going to get and it was amazing. "Sounds good. Thanks."

"Anytime, Son. See you soon. Be careful with them."

"Always," he said.

***

When they arrived, Hugh helped Ava out of her car seat so she and Danny could run and greet the dogs. Gray clouds whipped across the sky above and if it had been different circumstances Hugh might have laughed. Her power was magnificent, and he was almost certain she didn't know she had it, at least not the storm connection. He'd never met a storm witch before. And he certainly hadn't met a witch whose powers were so strong, yet...almost out of control, or so unknown.

When he turned back, Gia was still sitting in his SUV, holding her wrist, her shield fallen, and all the worry and anxiety appeared for him to see as she took in the farm. *What the fuck?* She was freaked. He stalked to her. He'd give a million dollars for her to open to him, to trust him. *Goes both ways, idiot.* Tonight. He'd tell her tonight.

"Hey." He couldn't help it. He wrapped his arms around her gently. She was bone cold. *Damn it.* "Let's get inside. Whatever it is. I promise you, I'm here to take care of you." For one brief, beautiful moment, she allowed herself to sink into his embrace.

When she pulled away, her tears had disappeared, and she nodded. Shoring up. His woman was constantly shoring up her defenses against the world. She was fucking amazing, but she didn't have to do it on her own. Time to show her she could trust him. "Come on." He took her uninjured hand in his and led her inside. Ava and Danny were in the corner of the living room, peeking over the short wall to where his mom's Labrador was napping.

"No puppies yet," May said. "I promise to call you when they arrive."

Hugh walked Gia to the wide sofa. She sat down, still stiff and wary. "Please relax. What can I bring you, tea, wine, whiskey?"

"Now," May said. "You kids, hang your coats and we can see what smells so good in the kitchen. I have hot cocoa ready for you two." Ava ran toward the kitchen. Danny came to check on Gia first.

"Are you sure you're okay, Mom?"

Gia settled into the sofa. "I'm gonna be fine, honey. And I'm so glad we're here. Go get some hot cocoa. It's your favorite, and it looks like Mr. Webb..."

"Drake," Hugh said. "You can all call him Drake."

"Drake might want help in the kitchen. You'll enjoy that."

Danny hugged Gia, gave Hugh an assessing stare, and then slowly made his way to the kitchen.

Gia looked at Hugh like she had so much to say. He wished he could whisk her away and have her all to himself. They needed time alone. She kicked off her shoes and tucked her feet underneath her. Hugh grabbed the soft throw blanket and covered her.

"Could I...uh, have tea and then wine?"

Hugh's heart was continually flipping over around her. All these vulnerabilities she rarely showed. And he was taking stock and taking care with each one. He leaned in, kissed her forehead, tried to calm the nagging instinct that something awful was about to happen, and went to get his woman some drinks.

***

The sky was calm as he drove them home through the dark streets of Mercy. All three of them were asleep and something in him itched to keep driving, to take them all away from…from what he couldn't name. There was an instinct beating relentlessly inside him to keep them safe.

He got the kids inside quickly, the chill of the air stealing into him. Or perhaps it was something else, something dark and dangerous. He wanted to believe whatever negative feelings he had were simply leftover emotions from an awful day. But it didn't feel like that. As soon as he got both kids into bed, he hurried back for Gia.

"What's happening?" She snuggled into his chest, eyes still closed, while he carried her upstairs.

"You fell asleep in the car?"

"What?" He felt her stiffen. "The kids?"

He gave her a small shake. "Gia." Her eyes met his. The terror that flashed in her gaze startled him. He knew there were layers of emotions and grief and trauma to her, but what the hell? "They're fine. They're both in bed asleep. I got them there before I brought you in."

"Oh…I…I should check on them."

"Here." Hugh turned around and carried her to each bedroom so she could see both kids asleep in their beds.

"Okay," she whispered. "Thank you." She relaxed in his arms.

Hugh set her on the bed and carefully tugged her shoes off.

Gia wrapped her hands around his neck, opened her eyes, and whispered, "Don't go."

"Gia."

Chapter Thirty-Three

"Please stay with me tonight." Gia knew this thing between them was dangerous. But her body and her soul didn't want to be apart from him. So many things felt wrong when he was far away. She just wanted to be safe in his arms, to feel his heat and his naked body moving with hers in their own sensual dance. To forget about everything difficult in her life and appreciate this night.

He smiled a soft, almost sad smile and nodded. "We need to talk anyway, without anyone interrupting us."

He was so serious, so resigned, and she couldn't bear it tonight, whatever it was. Not one more serious thing to fit into her brain, which already felt on the edge of collapsing. She was bone-deep tired, and she ached for the physical pleasure that could, even for a few seconds, wipe everything else away.

"No talking," she whispered. "Please, not now. In the morning." She didn't know what the morning would bring. They didn't make any sense together, but... *Please want to keep me.* The thought fluttered from her heart to her lips, but she held it in. "I want to feel you. I need you." The words were a plea. "Please, Hugh." She tried unbuttoning his shirt with one hand, frustrated that her fingers encountered a T-shirt underneath.

He seemed to flinch at her touch, closing his eyes, but when he flicked them open, they were that shining gold again, a sign she recognized as his desire for her.

He didn't answer with words. Instead, he took her sore hand and caressed it with his magical fingers. Then, with his eyes closed and swearing her name, he placed soft kisses on her wrist, breaking her heart into a million pieces. He cupped her head and kissed her with the lightest fluttering touch, then deeper until he was licking and sucking, peppering attention along her neck to her collarbone, chanting her name with each breath he took, lifting her emotions. He spun her world into fireworks of the most brilliant kind. All her desires, all her aches, her fears, even her grief, they all tumbled and wove together to make her feel...whole.

"Oh." She pulled her lips away, still swaying from the momentum. *No,* there was no whole for her. Why did her rational thought always have to be right there under the surface?

"Gia?" He sat next to her. His skin vibrated with warmth and desire. She felt it under her lips, under the fingertips of her uninjured hand, the way he held himself so tightly bound, waiting for her to be okay, but still so needy. That itself was a heady feeling. He would do anything for her.

She caressed his cheek. "Make me feel, Hugh. Make me forget," she begged.

One flick of his gaze and his glowing golden eyes fired up. He could excite her with a look. She wasn't tired anymore. Climbing over, she settled on his lap so she was straddling him. He whipped off his shirt and had his hands under hers, peeling it off so carefully so as not to hurt her. He tugged her close so their bodies were pressed against each other.

"Yes," she whispered. Gia arched into him, sending her core tight against his hard cock while he licked and sucked at her mouth, his warm hands roaming her back, holding her close.

"Gia, Gia, my...what am I going to do with you?" He set her away, stood, and tugged off his pants so he was naked before her. She stood on unsteady feet and carefully pulled her skirt down, thankful that her knife harness was sown into this skirt so it was still hidden in the fabric, hidden to him. Even more thankful that she had enough sense to remember she still had her knives on at all. That would have killed the mood.

She should not be doing this. She paused, rethinking everything, but then his arms were around her, lifting her and facing her away, pressing her back to his front. Bringing his hand around to her front, he ripped off her panties and cupped her pussy with his talented fingers. Wrapped in him, while he sucked at her neck, she melted, her entire body alive and tingling every time he touched her. Hugh set her on fire and right now she wanted the inferno.

She tilted her neck so he had better access. He clamped his mouth down right there where her neck dipped and met her collarbone. And it was like her body blossomed for him in that space.

Hugh growled, flipped her around, and laid her gently on the bed, climbing over her to leave no space between them.

"Yes, please." She offered herself, pleading with her body for him to touch her, kiss her, taste her.

"What in the world have you done to me, woman?" He kneed apart her legs and settled on her with one leg in between hers. Gripping one breast, he teased the other with his mouth, kissing her sensitive skin, then taking her nipple into his mouth, sucking and nipping at her, bringing her higher, drawing soft begging moans from her.

"What do you need, Gia? Tell me."

"Everything. All of that, what you're doing, touching me, tasting me...I can't think, don't want to."

"Taste you here?" He teased his tongue around her breast, lingering on the underside.

Oh, how sensitive she was.

"Or here?" He licked at her nipples, first one, then the other, all the while trailing his hand up and down her side, over her hips, and around to her butt, tugging her to him, dragging her leg along his hard cock. His other hand gripped her neck, one lazy thumb stroking that lovely spot on her neck that was already sparking from his earlier kisses. It felt as though he touched and stroked her everywhere. He consumed her.

"This beautiful skin here." He moved down her body, leaving kisses along her belly. "And here, this favorite of mine." He skipped her burning, aching core and settled his lips against her inner thigh, twirling lazy circles with his tongue.

"Hugh, please," she begged. Every cell in her body pulsed and waited for his touch.

He sat up and gripped her hips. His eyes were ripples of gold. They were so powerful and beautiful, glowing for her, and, for an instant, her heart exploded for him.

He brought her core close to those beautiful lips of his. "Gianna, mine," he whispered before he set his mouth on her pussy.

"Fuck," she swore. It was a good thing he held her because her body wanted to leap off the bed. His mouth, his tongue, his power surrounded her, brought her body to a humming. Everything inside her surged toward him, called to him, begged him to give her everything. Her orgasm slammed into her, her whole body shaking with the force and the sensations.

Hugh held her and licked at her, taking everything she had, demanding more until she was whimpering. Then he slid up her body, claiming her, kissing her, demanding more.

"Can you take more?" he whispered. "That was magnificent. You are magnificent. Was it too much or can you take me now?"

"Yes." She nodded and kissed him. "Please yes, Hugh."

He rolled away and rummaged through his wallet. Sheathed in a condom before she had time to blink, he was back on her in a flash, and with no more words, he surged inside her.

"Oh, my," she hushed. He was so hard.

"So fucking perfect," he hissed as he settled into her. Tugging her head to the side, he licked along her neck and growled out his words. "You are so fucking beautiful. Stunning. Do you know that?" He surged in and out. "Can you feel how good this is? You and me together? I can feel you taking me in, wrapping around me. How tight, how perfect."

His teeth at her neck, his words whipping across her skin, his body claiming hers. She wanted to, *had* to touch him. Finding space between them, she ran her thumb along his shaft as he pulled out and surged in.

"Fuck, yes." He dropped his head into her neck, pumping faster. "Touch yourself. Give me one more orgasm."

Hugh had her doing things she'd never dreamed of. But she wanted desperately to please him, to please herself, so she obeyed. She wrapped one leg around his hips, opening herself further to him, and used her fingers to rub against her core. "Oh, that feels good."

"Yes," he hissed. "Give it to me, Gia. I'm close, so close."

So was she. One more swipe of her fingers and she was tunneling toward everything. She tightened her hold around him and, locking them together, cried out her release. He followed, shuddering, all his powerful muscles shaking, his glorious scent surrounding her, sensual, familiar, hers. *Mine,* she mimicked him, only wishing it could be true.

Chapter Thirty-Four

Gia stirred in his arms while faded light filtered through the curtains. *Morning.* Why did the weight of the world feel like it was pressing down on him? He'd gotten up last night to dispose of the condom and when he'd returned, fully ready to have an important conversation, she was smiling and relaxed, eyes closed, asleep. Beautiful, vulnerable, exhausted woman. So he did what he needed. He climbed in next to her, pulled the covers over them and wrapped his arms around her. When she let out a sigh and settled into him, his worries flew away.

Unfortunately, every single one now returned. Ever since his body had changed into a wolf, he'd learned to lean into and listen to his instincts and they were telling him something bad was about to happen. His energy glitched with it.

"Hey," he whispered into her neck, breathing in the scent of her. "Good morning."

For an instant, she snuggled into him. Then he felt the change as her body stiffened.

She jumped out of bed. "Shoot, what time is it?" Grabbing her phone, her eyes widened. "I have to get the kids to school. They can't be late. Shit, shit, shit. And I have to pack for my sister's…"

"Gia, it's okay." He sat up. "It's only seven. I can help. Let me take them to school. You're nearly finished with your contract at Webb. Take the day off and rest. A lot happened yesterday. And I want to talk to you." He rested his hand on her hip. There was such heat between them when they touched. A spark of it flittered through her eyes.

"I can't rest…I…I…" She leaned into him, her body contradicting her words again when her phone buzzed.

She studied the screen, and all that heat and spark inside her vanished. She morphed into a different Gia again, right before his eyes. The same one from the other morning. A chill settled over him. Stepping away, she walked to the closet door, grabbed a robe, and tugged it around her body, tying the sash in a hurry. And he felt her closing herself off to him as surely as she'd just closed her body.

"I can't rest. I have another job."

"What other job?"

"Another client." She was like ice, standing there before him.

"Someone like Webb Industrial?" God damn it, it was like pulling teeth now to get her to answer.

"I can't talk about it."

"Why won't you tell me?" He raised his voice a bit, frustrated with her shutting herself off to him.

"Why is it any of your business?"

"Because I care about you." He stood and tugged on his boxers and jeans. "You're mine." He knew it was the wrong thing to say as soon as the words left his mouth, but it was the truth.

"I'm nobody's." The disgust with which she sent his words back was a slap in the face.

"You are. You're mine and I'm yours, damn it." He grabbed his T-shirt and slipped it over his head.

"No." Gone was the ice queen, but what was in its place scared him more. A glimpse of her truth, tiny and broken and so fucking scared. Before she tried to hide it. He'd seen that snapshot one too many times now.

"I love you, Gia. Why won't you let me in? Let me in all the way." He made to walk closer, but she threw her hands in between them, shaking her head furiously.

"No," she commanded. "You don't love me. You *can't* love me."

"You can't tell me who to love or not. That's not how it works. If you don't reciprocate, that's another thing." His heart thudded against his chest, trying to get out, to get to her. "But I do love you. I fell in love with you the moment we met." *Recognized you from a soul-deep longing.*

"You're crazy," she said, her face blanched white like a ghost had walked across her heart. She stepped back, trying to get away from him. "You can't love me. You can't. I need you to leave, now."

"Gia," he pleaded, everything inside him breaking. The pain was unbearable. "Talk to me. Why do you look like someone died? Why do you keep pushing me away like this?"

"Please, go," she begged. "And never come back. This was a mistake. All of it," she whispered before she ran into the bathroom and locked the door.

What the fuck just happened? His wolf screamed inside him to get out, to get to her. It took every ounce of strength he had to hold himself still. He wanted to yell and scream at her, but reason won out, barely. He needed to calm the fuck down before he acted like a raging, pissed-off animal striking out. He grabbed the rest of his stuff, leaned his head against the bathroom door, and said, "This isn't over, Gia." He waited, the longest minute of his life. Then he left before her silence drew another slice across his heart.

"Oh, hi, Hugh?" Danny startled the hell out of him. He was in the kitchen making tea when Hugh walked downstairs. The boy smiled, all the sunshine of his mother. "Want some tea? I didn't know you were here, but I can make another cup." He hurried to grab another mug.

Fuck me.

"I can't stay, Danny. There's...uh..." Fuck, he hated to lie.

"Oh. Okay." Danny's face fell and Hugh longed to take his words back and let the boy make him tea. He wanted this life with them here in this crooked, cozy house with an ache he'd never felt before. He didn't know, in this quiet moment, who was more disappointed.

"Another time, Danny. I'll be back. I promise."

"Okay, well. Goodbye then."

It went against every instinct Hugh had to turn and walk away, but he did it. He needed space and time, and Gia did too. But no way in hell this was finished between them. And no way in hell them finding each other was a mistake.

Chapter Thirty-Five

"Brrr." Gia shivered and buckled Ava into her car seat. The rain had stopped, but the freezing air bled through to her bones. A calm, chilly day. She shoved the old omen, *calm before a storm,* far away. "How was school?"

"We didn't get to have recess in the rain." Ava sighed and rested her head on her car seat.

"Monkey?" Gia nudged her son.

Danny was silent, gazing out the window. He'd hardly spoken a word to her since this morning when he'd asked about Hugh, and she'd told both kids they probably wouldn't see him anymore. Well, that had hurt, uttering those words as if speaking them would make him disappear from their lives completely. *Stupid, stupid.* But what choice did she have?

Love? Goosebumps rose on her skin while she drove. How could he love her? No, absolutely not. He was delusional. But he sure didn't seem delusional. She was the one who felt crazy and out of sorts and achy. While keeping her eyes on the road she fumbled through Bess for her candies. *Don't tell me I'm out of my sour cherries.*

"Don't call me Monkey anymore. It's for babies," Danny said.

"Uh, okay, hon...uh, Danny." Ugh. Another slice to her heart.

When she'd seen Orin's text this morning and checked her encrypted account about her assignment, she'd known she'd done the right thing in sending Hugh away. There could never be anything lasting between them. No matter how much she ached for him, she couldn't allow it. The risk was too dangerous. What if something happened to him because of her? What if he...

Then why did she want to curl into a ball and cry? The pain in her chest was so great she almost hadn't been able to breathe. She'd dropped the kids at school and spent the rest of the day preparing her mind and emotions. She practiced with her knives, but even the fact that her wrist was fully healed and posed no threat to her mission didn't ease the agony in her soul.

Now, although crystal clear on her upcoming mission, a nudge inside her, perhaps from her heart, begged her not to go. When was the last time she listened to her heart? *Every day, Daughter. Your heart beats fiercely for those you love.* Her body tingled with awareness. Her magic, a guide, a comfort? Speaking to her now after all these years?

Furious clouds raced across the winter sky as she drove to her sister's house. An omen? Something was barreling down on her, but she couldn't understand the message. *Deep, steady breaths.*

She had to get through this job and get home safely. That was the mantra she fed through her mind on repeat. Gia wasn't expected in Europe until Saturday, but she liked to get the kids settled before she had to leave. It helped settle her too. Selfishly, Gia also wanted a few hours around her big sister, who knew exactly what to say and how to comfort.

***

"My Boo and Monkey. I've missed you so," Francesca said, as they shrugged off their coats and boots in her small hallway.

"Danny says you can't call him Monkey anymore," Ava announced. "He's too old and important."

"Too old, huh?" Her sister's thoughts were clear in her mind. They'd been able to talk to each other this way since they were teenagers. It had come in handy more than a few times over the years.

"New school. New kids. I think it's all getting to him." Gia wasn't about to open the Pandora's box that was Hugh to her sister right now. Gia needed to keep her emotions hidden for her mission. It was all about control. Gia didn't keep many secrets from her sister, but this one was tangled and confusing.

Francesca gave her a sympathetic look and an enormous hug, then announced they were having breakfast for dinner. One of her kids' favorites. One of Gia's too. Her sister made the best damn pancakes on the planet. Francesca set Ava on one of the kitchen stools and ran her hands through her hair.

"Owwww," Ava moaned.

"Sorry, Boo," Francesca said. "Still struggling with tangled hair?"

"I swear," Gia said. "It's never-ending. Exactly like when you were a girl. Nothing works. Not conditioner, not special pillowcases. I swear she rolls around on the top of her head and mashes it into the worst tangled mess she can manage."

"Oh, Mommy. I do not," Ava said. "I fly in my sleep to the clouds."

"Do you now?" Francesca asked. *"I'll mix some of my special shampoo later for her, see if that helps."*

"May the angels bless you if it works." Gia sighed. Her sister was so talented and so good to her and her kids, and here she was keeping secrets. It weighed on her.

Francesca got busy making pancakes and enlisting the kids' help.

"I do fly, Auntie Frankie," Ava said. "And sometimes I take my dog with me."

"Your dog?" Gia asked. What was her daughter talking about?

"Yes," Ava said. "He's black and furry, very soft fur, not tangled at all like my fur." Ava burst into giggles. "And he's very quiet for how enormi he is."

"Enormi?" Gia tickled her daughter.

"Danny made it up. He makes up the bestest words ever."

"I've seen him too." Danny's words were much quieter than Ava's. He gave Gia a quick glance before returning his concentration to the pancakes.

"Oh, really?" Francesca asked. "In your dreams?"

"Mm-hmm," her son said.

Holy shit. *"Are they too young to be dream walking?"* Gia asked her sister with her silent communication. Could her kids really dream walk this young?

"I don't know, but for how smart they are and how much energy they have, I wouldn't be surprised," Francesca said.

Something strange was happening here. Stranger than her babies being able to dream walk at their age. Gia couldn't put her finger on it. Instead, she dove into her pancakes.

***

Gia finished saying goodbye to her kids before she went downstairs to join her sister. On her way to the living room, she double-checked that her sister's alarm and security system were engaged and that all the doors were locked.

"Are they asleep?" Francesca asked. She handed Gia a shot of bourbon and they cuddled on her sister's couch. Francesca tucked the blanket around them.

"Ava is snoring away. Danny's still reading."

"So serious, that one," Francesca said.

Gia set her glass on the coffee table and rested her head on her sister's shoulder. "Mm, more and more so, especially since the move. It's been months, but it hasn't gotten better." Wrong. It had felt better with Hugh around. Danny seemed to relax and laugh and not keep track of everything and everyone, like an adult. "Did I do the right thing?" she whispered. In her heart, she was asking about sending Hugh away, but Francesca wouldn't know that.

"Oh, honey. I think so, but what do I know? I love having you closer, but that could be purely selfish. You were drowning and lonely in Boston. The kids weren't happy either," Francesca said.

"True, but at least it was an unhappy they recognized. Now it's new schools, new people, new house. Maybe it's all too much." *Hugh wasn't too much. He was the perfect amount.* She yawned. God, she was...so, so tired.

"I think it's going to take time," Francesca said. "You know how Danny processes things. But they have you. And you all have me. And I think they enjoy coming to visit me as much as I enjoy having them."

"They love it." Gia sighed, which turned into another deep yawn. "So do I. I wish I could stay."

"I'm glad you can bring them to me easily now."

Gia snuggled into her sister's side.

"Where are you going this time?" Francesca whispered. "Don't get me wrong. I love having them. And you know my neighbor Katie adores watching them on the days I have to work. I just worry."

"I'm not sure." Small white lie. She would never divulge exact locations to her sister as a matter of safety. She explained what she could. "I'll be gone before the sun comes up."

"You don't have to do this." Francesca's plea sank into her bones.

"I do," Gia whispered. "For Douglas's sake. I can't let his murder go unpunished. I won't." That right there was the most important thing to focus on. She had to. There was no other path even if her heart and soul had been wishing, with the tiniest smidgen of hope, that there could be. *Someday.*

"I do it for Mom too." After their mother was killed, their lives flew into a chaos-filled spiral of awful foster homes until Francesca had gotten them out. With a full ride to college and an apartment, the two of them finally had a safe place. Those early days in foster care didn't bear remembering. If Gia had been quicker that night...maybe her mom would still be alive. If only she'd been smarter...she...

"We never talk about her," Francesca whispered back. They spoke so softly to each other, as if not wanting all these truths of their lives to be revealed.

"I know." Why was it so difficult to speak about their mother? Fear slithered over Gia's heart. "I miss her so much."

"Me too," Francesca said.

Gia closed her eyes and let the warmth soothe her. "You're not disappointed in me, are you?" Sometimes it was easier to hear the truth in the dark with her eyes closed, while guilt flooded her.

"Never, Gi."

"Hug them for me every day, will you, Frankie?" It was the last thing Gia remembered before she dozed off, safe and warm in her sister's arms.

Chapter Thirty-Six

Hugh gave Gia a week. He even refrained from visiting her yard to check on the kids. It was the longest fucking week of his life. He couldn't remember a time when he'd hated work, when he'd been so short-tempered, when people had actually gone out of their way to avoid him.

Every night after work, rain or shine, he'd run for hours, punishing himself, trying to work out his emotions or not feel them at all. One or the other. Didn't matter. Nothing helped. Right now, he was in the gym cleaning weights and organizing shit. He'd sent everyone home so he could have privacy and work on mindless tasks. It wasn't helping.

"All right, asshole." His brother Grant smacked him on the back.

"Not a great way to address me right now," Hugh said, vibrating with anger.

"Tough shit." Grant shoved a pair of boxing gloves into his chest. "Asshole is exactly what you're acting like. Come on, let's fight."

Fuck. Hugh hated boxing, especially with his brother, who was ten times more powerful than Hugh and quicker on his feet too. "I am not in the mood—"

"That's why we're going to do it. You and me. It'll take a shit ton of focus and energy for you to beat me if you even can," Grant taunted him, stepping onto the mat and dancing around. "I don't know what's going on since you won't talk about it, but maybe you can get your anger out this way and figure the rest of your shit out."

Hugh tossed the towel into the bin. *What the hell?* He had nothing to lose except his dignity. Fighting Grant had the potential to wear him down to nothing. Maybe that's what he needed.

"Headgear too," Grant commanded.

"You gonna punch me in the head?" Hugh asked.

"Not on purpose. But your lazy ass brain may fall into my fist."

"Right," Hugh chuckled.

Grant was merciless. He was probably born boxing, or dancing, or both. And he came at Hugh with all his power. Over and over again. It wore Hugh down until he couldn't take any more.

"Fuck!" Flattened on his back on the mat, sweat pouring down his face, Hugh tore off his helmet and gloves. "I give. You win."

"No surprise there." Grant reached out a hand to help Hugh. "You ready to talk about it?"

Hugh nodded.

"Good. Let's get showered and head to Adair's for happy hour. Ian's meeting us there and Callum's back in town. Has been for months. He'll be there as well."

***

"Damn, it's been a long time since you've been in Mercy. What, ten years?" Hugh hugged his old childhood friend Callum at the corner table in Adair's. Grant was at the bar ordering drinks and food from the bartender. Hugh suspected Duncan would be out any minute from the kitchen once he knew they were here.

"Yeah, man, too long. Glad to be home," Callum said.

"What brought you back?"

"I never felt right being away from here." Callum shrugged. A dark expression crossed his face. He looked worse than Hugh. "It was time. I finally opened my own pub, up near Franny's Woods."

"Can't wait to check it out," Hugh said. "We missed the hell out of you."

"Are we finally going to talk about our feelings?" Hugh's brother Ian arrived and pulled out a chair. "Is that Callum? Christ, you got huge." Ian pulled Callum into a hug. Callum had left town more than a decade ago. Hugh had seen him a few times over the years during his travels, but some of his family hadn't seen Callum in almost ten years.

"We better fucking talk about our feelings. Hugh's about to take everyone's heads off at work and we need to help him get his shit sorted." Grant delivered a round of beers and took a chair next to Ian, just as Alexander walked through the entrance.

"Oh shit, Webster?" Callum rose and gave Hugh's oldest brother a hug.

Grant had pulled out the big guns. Alexander hated going out to eat. Or going out anywhere in public. It was even rare for him to show at Adair's. Hugh felt a pang of guilt. Normally, he was open with his siblings, but he'd mostly kept his feelings about Gianna and all the complications swirling around her to himself.

"All right, Hugh, what's got you so pissed off?" Ian asked. "That's rare for you."

"Pissed off. Frustrated. Worried," Grant said.

"It's gotta be relationship woes," Duncan arrived with a platter of fritto misto and some homemade dips for them to snack on. "Let me guess, Gianna Reily and her adorable kids?"

"Wait, the woman I sold the house to that borders the farm?" Ian helped himself to some fried goodness.

"Yeah," Grant said. "She also spent the last few weeks contracting at Webb Industrial to get our finances in order."

"Oh, shit," Ian said. "She's the one who uncovered Trent's embezzlement."

"Yes, and he fucking attacked her too," Hugh said, barely keeping the rage out of his voice. He took his hands off his beer and ran them through his hair. Fuck, he missed her hands on him. When she caressed his scalp, it had a way of soothing him.

"Thought things were cozy with you and her," Alexander asked after he took a sip of the tea Grant had ordered for him. "Happiest I've ever seen you, Hugh was with her the other week. And that's saying something since your normal setting is pure fucking joy." Alexander gave him shit all the time for his positive attitude, but Hugh knew he was teasing. As the oldest brothers, they'd been thick as thieves before and after their mom had died. At least until Alex's wife had left.

A server set down a tray with platters of food. Spicy pasta with sausage, lamb chops, polenta, goat cheese ravioli, bread, and salad. Hugh was suddenly famished. He filled his plate and switched to water. Beer was messing with his brain and he needed that like he needed a hole in the head.

"Didn't you bring her and the kids to the farm after she got hurt?" Duncan asked. "Shoot, kitchen beckons. I'll be back."

Hugh swallowed his food and told them all how she ended things with him. "I think she's afraid of something, but she won't tell me. I...she..." He wanted to confide everything to them, but some of it was Gianna's to tell, not his. "Her past is pretty awful, and I'm guessing it's hard for her to trust."

"Difficult when you give yours freely," Ian said.

Hugh nodded.

"And when she's your mate," Alexander said softly.

"You could tell?" Hugh asked.

"Even with her being careful, it was like a shimmer around the two of you."

"She doesn't know." Hugh rested his fork on his plate.

"That she's your mate?" Grant asked.

"That and...well...everything."

"You haven't told her what you are?" Callum asked. "And she can't sense it?"

"I don't know what she can sense or not. She's a powerful witch, but I get the impression that she isn't fond of her powers or keeps them hidden."

"So you haven't seen her in what, a week?" Grant asked.

"I thought I should give her space and time."

"Well," Grant said. "Maybe you've given her enough. You could check on her without being creepy about it."

"Hey." Hugh shoved Grant, which did absolutely nothing to his beast of a brother.

"First though, cake." Duncan set another platter down. "Grandma's chocolate cake heals all woes. Then you can go get your woman."

Hugh wanted to race to her instantly, but he loved being surrounded by his brothers, his friends. He'd needed this. This support, a bit of confidence boost, because he had no idea what would be waiting for him when he finally tracked her down.

***

The house was dark, which wasn't odd, considering it was late, but her Wagoneer wasn't there. Sitting inside his truck with the windows up, he couldn't get rid of the feeling that something was wrong. Hugh stayed for hours, his instincts never settling. Eventually, he drove away.

It wasn't until he was in bed, right before he dozed off thinking of her, that a stab of pain so sharp and all-consuming crumpled his body. It dragged at his insides. Evil. Emptiness. Like she was gone from this world. Almost. He couldn't get a clear sense of her. Danger and grief pressed on his soul, on everything around him, the land, the air, his connection with her. Something was dangerously wrong, and all he knew was that he had to find Gianna now.

Chapter Thirty-Seven

"My dear, sitting here all by yourself on such a momentous night."

Momentous night. He's certainly creepier than normal. That's almost funny. Normal in the world of human trafficking criminals.

"You must not be from here." Laszlov practically breathed his words, standing too close to her at the bar as if he had permission to press into her space. It was what she came for, but all the goddesses above she was so sick of this horrid game.

Gia blinked, pretending she'd never seen the man before, pretending he was her heart's desire, luring him in before she bit, or in this case stabbed. The simple pasta she'd had soured in her gut. *I do not want to be here.* That thought would get her killed. Willing away her fragile emotions, she did everything she could to stay in character.

"Pardon?" Batting her eyelashes at him, she gazed around the room before she settled her innocent look back on him.

"Yes." He smiled. "You and me meeting like this. The most beautiful woman in the room, in my bar. I have never seen you before and yet here you are."

Yes, asshole. Here I am.

"You are too pretty to eat alone. Would you do me the pleasure? Besides, I have a feeling. Tonight is going to be my night."

Too bad for him, he had the wrong feeling. She'd already rerouted the delivery of his shipping container contents to be discovered by the CIA. All the victims he'd planned to sell were safe now. But he didn't know that yet. This time, her smile was genuine.

"I'd…I'd like that," she said in her fragile too high-pitched voice. Playing right along. She stepped down from her stool and had to choke back her vomit at him putting his hand on her butt.

"Something more private."

"Oh…well…" Gia pretended confusion.

"My apartment upstairs. You won't be disappointed." Christ, she was surprised his ego hadn't gotten him killed yet. "I promise."

She nodded, too afraid that if she spoke, she'd punch him in the face and ruin the entire mission.

Fuck. He didn't waste time. Once the elevator doors closed, he put his key into a slot and hit the top button, then grabbed her and sealed his lips to hers. She wanted to bite his lip off. She felt the vibration of his phone in his coat pocket. He ignored it, slamming his tongue into her mouth. It rang again, and he paused.

Gia was grateful for the interruption because fake kissing this disgusting man was the worst thing she'd done so far in her quest for vengeance. She hated it, suddenly, this path, hated herself. But she needed to get him to his apartment. She rubbed against him, but Laszlov took his phone out and answered it.

"Igen." Yes, in Hungarian, then nothing else. His face was stone. He ended the call, returned his phone to his pocket, and smiled at her. "Where were we? Come."

The doors opened, and he pulled her along. His grip on her wrist was nothing abnormal, yet Trent's attempted attack slammed back into her mind. Unease snaked its way down her spine at Laszlov's hold on her. Casually she tried to pull her wrist away, but he twisted it harder, slammed the apartment door shut, and had a gun under her chin before she could blink.

Fucking hell!

"Convenient, me finding you in my bar on this night. I almost thought you were my perfect present, but then the call. My shipment is missing. Nothing is ever perfect. Who are you? Where are my goods?" His voice slithered over her, menacing, dangerous.

She shook her head, trying to use her free hand to slip into one of the hidden slits in her pants to reach her knife. *Careful, slowly. Don't panic. You've almost got it.*

He shoved her into a table. *Fuck, that hurts.*

"Don't play dumb with me. You are dead. It's only a matter of how nice I am to you before I kill you. Now tell me where my goods are."

"Goods?" She tilted her tiny dagger, and, using every shred of strength she had, slid it into his chest. "Not goods, human beings. You'll never get them. You're finished."

"Fucking...whore!" His words came out garbled.

She did what she had to do, coiled her muscles, bit back the bile in her throat, and twisted the knife deeper.

"Segítség," he cried, as he fell on her, blood spilling between them.

The door burst open, and a team of his men entered.

Oh fuck, she barely had time to blink before a man stabbed a syringe into her neck. One breath later, she was out.

***

So thirsty. Mouth dry and cracked, throat burning. "What?" Gia couldn't lift her head as she surfaced to consciousness. Her tongue was stuck to the roof of her mouth, desperate for water she tried to call out, to find her glass. Where was her water? Where was she?

A memory, her wrist being twisted. Trent, and someone...someone, saved her. Hugh. Shit, where was Hugh? She wanted to be wrapped in his warm arms, even though his arms didn't belong to her. Ha, ha, ha. So funny. Obviously, his arms didn't belong to her. She meant...she meant...*Why can't I walk?*

I'm sitting. Legs and arms tied. Why? Her heart raced, and she was so confused about why she couldn't get off this chair.

"Gia?" She heard her name in her head.

Her sister was here. *"Frankie?"*

"Gia."

She breathed through the pain that throbbed in her head and her wrist, both wrists because they were...they were tied roughly behind her back to a chair. Was she awake or asleep? She and her sister could talk in their dreams.

"Gia, what's wrong? Where are you?"

"I'm a little stuck at the moment." Why was her sister in her dreams sounding upset? *"I should be asking you what's wrong, Fran...Frankie. I can feel...your...heart...beating...I mean..."* What the hell was happening? She couldn't form complete thoughts or sentences. Her whole body felt floating and dizzy. *"Damn it...I'm struggling to..."*

"Gia, why can't I see you? You're there, but you're not."

That was how she felt. She finally lifted her head. It was so heavy. Everything was so wobbly. She was going to be sick. She leaned over, parted her knees, and vomited on the floor. *Fuck, fuck, fuck.* Tears leaked out of her eyes. She felt too hot, but shivering at the same time. This was not good. Something was wrong. Orin. Prague. Laszlov. Shit! She opened her eyes. But all around her was darkness.

"Gia?"

"I'mmm okay, or I'm gonna be." She had to be. "This partic...particular job is proving to be more...difficult than I... Are kids okay?"

"Listen to me Gianna, I know your work is important, but something happened. I need you to come home. Everyone's fine, but we were in a car accident. I think someone was after the children."

"What..." No. *My kids. My babies.* But they were safe? Francesca. Where are you? Her heart raced. Her throat burned. Everything in her hurt and she couldn't...she couldn't...she tried to move her bound wrists and ankles. She couldn't move. "Danny, Av—"

"Gianna!" Her name thundered through the space. Suddenly, a shocking blast exploded around her and tossed her over. The chair she was in slid along the floor. Her head slammed onto the ground. Heat licked along the walls. Fire. Walls crumbled around her. *Danny...Ava...Francesca...Hugh. Help me!*

Chapter Thirty-Eight

Hugh blew a large enough hole through the building to get in, but something else was happening simultaneously. Another much bigger explosion, along the far side of the warehouse. Christ! He was on her before the initial explosion finished. In his wolf form, he sliced his teeth through the binds on her arms and legs, carefully tucked her into the harness he'd strapped around his body, and then he ran.

Dark flames spread over what was left of the building. Someone had doused it with gasoline, then sent bombs in. With her still inside. Fire licked at his fur as he raced up metal shelves to where he'd entered, out through the crumbling ceiling, into the night, through the thick ugly fog. He ran faster than he'd ever had to, away from that foul black hole of despair.

He used his power, fear, and anger, allowing everything to center in his chest and propel him on. There were beautiful thick woods he hardly noticed. He crossed wide, surging rivers and snowy mountains, down into the outskirts of a city, covering ground quickly before morning arrived. Traveling under the cloak of midnight was the safest for both of them. His home might be friendly to werewolves, but the entire world was a different story.

He ran until he reached the van his friend had loaned him that Hugh had left across the border in Germany. They were safe, or nearly so. He wouldn't feel one hundred percent until they were back in Mercy. Quickly, using his teeth, he cut Gia from the ties that held her to him. As carefully as he could, he set her in the van. Fuck. There was blood everywhere and in the van's light, he could see bruises forming all over her still unconscious form. Her pulse was there, but rapid. He needed a doctor immediately.

"Hugh?" Her eyes were closed, and she reached out an arm to him, running it down his forearm.

She was alive. Thank the fucking goddesses. Her touch both centered him and scared the living daylights out of him. He'd nearly lost her to...what? Some macabre nightmare? This was the first time she'd touched him as his wolf, and it was not how he'd expected it to happen. What the hell was she doing here?

He quickly shifted and dressed, got her safely buckled in, made a call, and drove, putting the exploded factory and whatever the hell Gia was tangled up in, far, far behind them.

***

Hours later, they were both clean. Well, she was as clean as he could get her without taking her unconscious body into the shower. She slept now. His friends, a husband and wife team of doctors, had come and gone, leaving her attached to an IV. He'd shuddered with relief to discover most of the blood covering her wasn't hers. She'd been beaten but hadn't lost much blood at all.

As far as his friends could tell without taking her to a hospital, the drugs that had been injected into her were worse than the beating. And how long she'd been left alone, tied up in an abandoned warehouse. As if they, whoever had done this to her, had abandoned her too. Then the explosion, the gasoline everywhere, the fire. Had they left her there to die like that? Fury shuddered through him.

After his friends had left, he'd napped fitfully, his hand on her back to feel her breathing, but he was awake now, having gotten enough sleep to restore his strength and his anger. The drugs would take a few hours longer to leave her system. They were safe in a clean apartment in Munich. She wasn't dead, and her outward injuries and bruises from being beaten would all heal. This information had soothed his temper, barely.

It was his current discoveries that had his anger and confusion surging back up. He sat next to her on the bed, keeping track of her breathing because she was his life and he'd nearly lost her. In his hands, he held two black leather garter-like contraptions he'd found strapped to her thighs. Attached to them were small but extremely sharp knives. There were four spaces where knives could be, and only three knives left, which meant she'd lost one, used one?

Small images fluttered through his mind. Blurry memories. That day at Webb Industrial floated to the front of his mind, when Trent had her cornered, right before Hugh smashed down the door. A flicker when her skirt rode up, and her hand. He blinked that image away as another memory sought to make an appearance, but it wouldn't come. Was it another time he'd sensed or felt her weapons?

Fucking weapons. The woman wore knives around her thighs. Deadly, hidden knives. Why the fuck? Those few times she'd gotten weird texts in his presence and switched personas instantaneously, kicking him out of her life. That ghostly void in her eyes. It was the same expression staring back at him now from a passport with her photo, but someone else's name on it.

Hugh wanted answers. He wanted to wake her and demand she tell him everything. He was losing his fucking mind.

"Goddess help me," Gia whispered. "Find my loves. Enclose them in your magic embrace. Something's coming. Worry...worry. Take my gratitude. Keep them safe."

"Gia?" He rested his hand on her arm. She wasn't awake. *Talking in her sleep again.* Dreams or... it sounded more like spells. Protection spells.

Fuck. Were her wounds buried so deep that she only whispered spells in her sleep? Or was it a conscious choice? One more thing to hide from him?

Chapter Thirty-Nine

A DULL THROBBING ACHE radiated through her entire body. Gia blinked. Sunlight stole in through some wispy curtains, leaving a pretty crisscross pattern on the floor from the multi-paned window. She lay on her stomach, one arm down her side, the other one off the side of the bed. Wait what? Whose bed? She made to move and let out a low moan instead. Carefully, taking stock of her injuries and battered body, she turned to her side. The hand lying over the side of the bed was attached to something. An IV?

"Good. You're awake."

"Hugh?" Gia swallowed carefully through the throbbing in her side where she'd been...punched. The fist had slammed into her while she'd been tied to a chair. *Fuck, that hurts.* Her voice was scratchy. When she blinked back the pain, his face came into focus. The bed depressed as he sat next to her and took her hand in his, looking at his watch. Taking her pulse.

"What? What happened?"

"That's exactly what I'd like to ask you?"

Gia's mind was a fuzzy, swirling mess of memories. She closed her eyes to see more clearly and covered her eyes with her hands.

"Don't," Hugh said, his voice low and demanding.

"What?" She couldn't make out what was happening. In her dark mind, the hotel bar, Laszlov? Her knife, the pinprick of a needle, and then...nothing.

"Don't hide from me. I pulled you out of a burning exploded building where you'd been beaten, drugged, and tied up. And I think..." He swallowed and ran his hands through his longer hair.

It was longer on top again with the sides shaved close. She loved his hair. "You think...what?" She reached out to touch him, and he stood and backed away from her. *Why is he here? Why am I with him? Where am I?*

"I think you were left to die in that explosion. I think they meant to burn you alive."

Burn her alive? Christ, her stomach roiled with nausea. She couldn't put all the pieces of the past few days together. She closed her eyes again. Every bone in her body ached like she'd been...she couldn't...she didn't know.

"Gia," he swore her name.

Carefully, she opened her eyes. Holy shit, she'd never seen Hugh angry, not like this. "I'm not hiding...I...I'm trying to remember. When...when I close my eyes, I can see better...I can see my memories...I. Oh no, Francesca..." She tried to sit up but everything hurt, and she was so, so weak. "My kids. Danny, Ava. Hugh," she pleaded. "I have to get to them."

"Hey." Hugh was there again by her side. "Hey. You're okay. You've been out for two days. Take a deep breath and we'll figure everything out."

Oh. He's being nice to me. Gia slumped back on the pillow and sucked down the glass of water he handed her. Best thing she'd ever tasted, soothing her mouth and her dry throat. She was starving too, and she had to go to the bathroom. "I have to use the bathroom."

"Here." Hugh carefully unclipped her IV and lifted her.

"I can walk." *I think.*

"I'm not so sure you can, but fine." He set her down by the toilet and closed the door behind him. "Call me when you need my help."

Huh. He was being bossy. But when she finished peeing, she realized he might be right. Her limbs were wobbly and worn out and much fucking weaker than she realized. She managed to wash her hands and almost died at her frightening image in the mirror, but when it came time to open the door, she barely had enough strength to twist the knob. "Hugh," she said. Invisible razors cut at her throat. *More water.*

He was there in an instant, swooping in and lifting her again. He was so beautiful, but different somehow. Everything felt too difficult and painful. And she wanted to be near him. She raised her hand to his chest, and he flinched. He returned her to the bed, clipped her IV back in, and stepped away, arms crossed, staring at her.

"Hugh? I don't feel too good...and I'm freezing...what happened?" Gia closed her eyes for a minute as she tried to calm her racing heart over the lingering glimpses of a mission that had gone horribly wrong. A heavy blanket draped over her, Hugh's big hands tucking her in, swearing her name and she couldn't stay awake.

***

"Gia, you're okay?"

Her sister was here in her dream.

"What the hell happened? I was so scared. You were, you were tied up and drugged it felt like, then there was an explosion and it blew me out of your dream. I've been so worried."

"Frankie. I'm so, so sorry. I don't know everything that happened. I got...someone found out who I was." She still hadn't had time to sit with this knowledge. She'd gotten burned. But how? *"I got out."* Someone saved her. So many things didn't make sense.

One image kept returning to her. Black fur, coarse and soft together under her fingertips, warmth seeping into her body, flying through the air, or...no, running. Flashes of the elevator with Laszlov, her knife, being beaten. Then a wolf snarling and snapping and carrying her. She was still weak, even in her dreams. She wanted to tell her sister everything. Francesca could often see the complete picture better than Gianna, especially when emotions were involved.

"Are you there, honey? Gia?"

"Sorry, I'm still weak, but recovering..." Something warm and strong moved beside her, stirring her from sleep, from dreams.

"We're all okay," Francesca said. *"Gia?"*

Her babies were okay. Her sister. *"I'll see you soon."*

Gia blinked and opened her eyes. It only took a second to remember. The ache throughout her entire body had lessened, and nighttime met her through the windows now. Cars honking and people talking, a door shutting. Her right side still ached, and she assumed the bruises on her jaw and abdomen were a brilliant shade of puke green or purple at this state, but the nausea and shivers were gone. She took a breath and...ugh; she smelled ripe. There was also a hint of...something warm, lovely...

Gia pushed herself up, slowly this time, and froze. Patting her side and her bare legs, she... "What the hell am I wearing?" A soft oversized T-shirt she'd never seen covered her, although it...it was the source of the pleasant scent. Her underwear was her own, she hoped.

Laszlov, fuck. She'd killed him, but he'd stabbed her with something, or someone had. The last glimpse she remembered was him falling on her, her knife protruding from his chest before she'd lost consciousness. *Oh shit.* She scrambled.

"Looking for these, Divinia Chase."

Gia whipped her head to the side. Fuck, the movement hammered her head into a million pieces. She breathed through her nose, through the pain. Hugh sat next to her on the bed. Her fake passport in one hand—which she'd had taped in plastic to her side during her mission—and her black leather garters that held her remaining knives.

"Those are mine." She tried to lunge for them but he was healthy, huge, and swift, tossing them off his side of the bed, then twisting so he was over her, straddling her, and pinning her to the bed with so much finesse, he barely touched her. Yet, she wasn't certain she could escape if she tried. And she could always escape. God damn it, she hated being weak.

He leaned in, carefully laced her fingers with his, and raised them above her head. He sniffed at her neck, his body rubbing ever so lightly against hers

"Don't," she pleaded. "I smell..."

"Alive," he whispered against her neck, trailing his nose along her skin one more time.

She arched into him. How could she feel turned on right now? "Hugh?"

In the blink of an eye, he pressed away and off the bed, his eyes burning golden with dark pulsing rings of black. "You smell fucking *alive*, which you almost weren't. Want to explain anything to me, *Gianna*?"

"No." *Yes. I want to tell you everything. But I can't.*

"Or is it Divinia?" he spat. "Who are you?" he demanded, his lush but angry voice reverberating off the walls. "Fake passports, glasses with no prescription. Knives dangerous enough to kill with."

"I'm no one," she answered, her heart beating in a frenzy. She had to get away, but she was fucking stuck.

He came back slowly, his gait sure and steady and quick, too quick for her. He was on her in an instant, almost as if he pounced...flashes of jumping through the landscape, over rushing rivers and across mountains. No it couldn't be.

"I told you before, you're mine. And I'm yours."

The warmth of his body, how hard every inch of him was, the pure masculine smell of him, but how he also held himself above her, barely touching her so he wasn't hurting her. The power and discipline it must have taken. She wanted to be his, desperately. But fear choked her. She couldn't breathe. "I'm no one's." Her voice was small when the words came out. *Damn it!* "Get off me."

"You would tell that to your children? To Danny, to Ava, to your sister who you dream walk with? That you are no one's?" The incredulous disbelief in his voice was difficult to hear. "What about your ancestors, Gianna, whose hearts still beat inside of you?"

No, no, no. Her usual refusal threatened to crawl up her throat, but her heart disagreed. Her heart spun with his words. She was so confused and angry at the world, at herself for almost getting killed.

"What were you doing in that warehouse? Alone, beaten, tied up, left for dead? What are the knives for?" His voice had slowed to a whisper, cooing at her, seducing her. He leaned in, scenting her, and she wanted to give in.

She ran her hand through his tawny hair with flecks of silver, his golden ember eyes burning into her. Another image. Asleep or something, strapped to his...Wait, what? She shoved him. "Get off."

He moved away immediately, and she stood and paced around the room, putting space between them.

"You're a...you're a werewolf?" Turning to face him, she didn't know what to expect, but a grin was the last thing.

"Aye. All of us Webbs and many others in Mercy. All around the world."

He stood, and she shivered, but not from fear. No, she knew fear all too well to recognize this wasn't it. Exactly.

"As you are a witch, Gianna Reily. A very powerful one." So he knew. Good, great. At least she wouldn't have to explain that to him when she barely understood it all herself. But she didn't want to talk about herself. Down that path lay a hollowed-out shell of a woman. She focused on that pompous grin of his.

"When were you going to tell me?" She lashed out.

His grin disappeared, but his eyes? No, his eyes stayed that beautiful gold, sparking in heat. "Not when I was rescuing you from a crumbling, burning building, but a million times before then and now." He shot back.

"How convenient that you simply didn't."

He stepped toward her, and she stepped back. "I would hardly call our relationship"—he enunciated the word in a way she couldn't tell was good or bad. Did she want to know?—"Convenient, now. Would you?"

"Right," she snapped. Had she been that much of an inconvenience to him? Her heart hurt more in that instant than after she'd shoved him away before her mission. She thought she'd been, that they'd been... Goddess be damned. Tears formed in her eyes and she did not want to cry in front of him.

"Gianna..."

For Christ's sake, why did she love it when he said her full name? It sounded like the finest whiskey might taste, full of honey and beloved secrets.

"There are many things I want to tell you, need to tell, but..."

"But what?"

He hesitated, studying her like she was a cornered, wounded animal. Damn it again. Where were her shields and power? "Would you have believed me, love? If I'd told you what I am?" A hint of unease or vulnerability coated his words.

Would I have? Love. He confused her so. She shook her aching head and backed away.

"Christ, Gia, there's so much we need to talk about."

"No. I have to get to my children." The rush of tightness threatened to burn her from the inside out. "I have to shower, please. I can't... We can talk later."

"Mm," he said.

What does that mean? She wanted to scream at him, throw a tantrum and beat on his chest, beg him to tell her everything. But fear pressed in on her from all sides.

She rushed into the bathroom, locking the door because the force of his gaze, how he could see everything inside her, made her want to vomit. No one knew the real Gianna Reily. It wasn't safe for anyone, least of all a maddening, gorgeous beast of a man who made her heart want to soar and hide in equal measure. She didn't want to hide anymore. But she didn't know how to be her true self, how to be brave.

Chapter Forty

She was quiet as she ate the soup he'd made her and the tea full of too much honey for any normal day. But nothing, not one thing about Gianna Reily or this day or the past few weeks was normal. She needed easy, quick fuel for her depleted body.

He was also quiet, studying her, giving her space, at least the emotional space she cried out for. She wore the fresh set of clothes his friends had dropped off. He almost laughed at the outfit, but he refrained out of self-preservation. A bulky, soft white sweater that could almost be called sweet, paired with dark blue jeans that hugged all her curves, and a pair of tall brown boots. Not one inch the guarded badass. Instead, all precious, gorgeous woman. Too fucking exhausted to maintain her barriers, but...alive.

God damn it. He was furious with the memories of how he'd found her. How he almost hadn't in time.

When she finished, he wanted to carry her to bed, strip her naked, make her divulge all her secrets, then curl up around her, and sleep for days. Her body could use the sleep. It was evident in her expression and how she tried but failed to hide the fatigue from him. But she was also desperate to get to her kids. He would feel better too once they were all safe with him.

She cleaned her dishes in the sink, dried them with the towel, then turned to him, hands on those fucking amazing hips of hers. Here she was, ready for battle. Too bad she didn't know he could also be stubborn as fuck. And anger still licked at his bones. Anger at her for putting herself in danger, and anger at still not knowing what the fuck she'd been up to. And he was fucking pissed at himself for taking so long to find her. He'd never had to track someone across oceans and continents before.

"I need to go."

"*We* need to go."

"I can get home by myself," she insisted. She was pissy and cranky this morning. He'd take it over the Ice Queen any day.

"With no phone, no wallet, no money. Good thing you still have this." He held her fake passport and when she reached for it, he pulled it away. "Is this going to be a problem, Gianna? Or is it Davinia? Have I been falling in love with the wrong person all this time?"

She stared at him, that flash of shock on her face. Then her snotty expression returned.

Good, at least she's healing.

"Maybe you have," she said, stabbing him in the heart with her words.

A beat, then two passed between them. He tossed the passport her way along with a winter coat, grabbed his own jacket and a large black bag, and said, "Let's go then, ma'am."

"I'd like…" She cleared her throat. "I'd like my knives back, please."

"Not sure how you've been traveling, but you can't walk on a plane with those. They'll be fine in here till we're home." He slung the bag over his shoulder and held the door. "After you."

She hesitated, and led the way out of the apartment, standing proud, brushing by him in all her glory. He was locking the door when she backed into him abruptly.

"Whoa." He squeezed her shoulder. "It's okay. I forgot to tell you, we're in Munich. Far from where you were being held," he said softly. Skittish kitten she was, claws ready to strike, but soft when she allowed herself. "This is us." He found her hand, linked it with his, and helped her into a rental car.

The drive to the airport was silent unless you counted the clanging cloying tension between them. She wrapped her arms around herself and rested her head against the window. As they drove out of the city, she whispered, "I really am Gianna."

Hugh sighed. He was glad to know, and he believed her. The strange thing was, he couldn't tell if she was telling him or trying to convince herself.

Chapter Forty-One

"I could have had my knives all along." Gia sulked beside him in the passenger seat of his SUV. "Hmph. Private jet."

He was breathing a whole lot easier now that they were back in Mercy. She'd fallen asleep on the way to the airport in Munich and stayed that way until they landed outside of Mercy. It was amazing how she could stir him up, make him want to laugh and yell in equal measure. She was like someone who had had to grow up extremely fast and was doing an amazing job taking care of everything but had never been able to enjoy childhood. He wanted to give her that delight back. He wanted to give her everything.

"You need them all the time?" The road curved into the mountains, leaving neighborhoods and shops behind.

"You have knives too? Or rather, swords?" she accused. She'd seen them in his bag when the plane had landed.

"I do. Years of Martial Arts practice. The techniques are excellent for discipline and potentially saving loved ones." He raised his eyebrow at her. The ground before them leveled out when they neared some farmlands and estates as he followed the address she'd put into the GPS.

"Did you…did you need them when you rescued me?" Gia gave him a brief look.

Hugh swallowed. He hated any memory attached to that night, but he couldn't shove it down. "No. Right before the explosion, I shifted. I used my wolf strength to get you out."

"How…how did you find me?"

"Your scent. It's a part of me now, in here." He patted his heart. "Because we're…" *Mates.* "Linked. And you…you said something about Prague, in your sleep."

"I what? No way." She shook her head and looked out the window.

Hugh let her be in denial. He opened the console between the seats, took out a bag of sour cherries, and tossed it in her lap. "Here."

"You…I…" Gia fingered the bag and held it to her chest.

He started to reach for her other hand when the hairs on the back of his neck rose in warning. He braced as they parked in front of a beautiful old stone house with separate wings stretching out to both sides. Surrounded by land and forest, it looked like had been here for hundreds of years. He took a deep breath and scented Danny and Ava, reassured to hear their hearts beating. But he sensed something else too.

Gia was racing out of the car and to the door before he could stop her or warn her that something was wrong. He strapped his swords on and rushed to catch up with her.

"Gia, wait."

"They're here, Hugh. They're here." Before she could knock, Danny was opening the door for her. She picked him up, swung him around in a hug, and carried him inside. Hugh followed, his instinct tripping over the scents of witches and canines... A woman ran down the stairs.

"Auntie Frankie, look!" Danny yelled.

"Gia." The tall woman with flowing red hair swooped Gia into her arms.

Her sister.

"She's home." Ava ran toward them and fitted herself right between the two women to cling to her mother. "Mama always comes home. Look, Danny. She brought our dog."

Uh oh.

"What?" Gia asked her daughter.

"Hello, who are you?" Her sister asked as a man came down the stairs behind her. The warnings from Hugh's instincts all swirled together in one massive cloud. The absence of scent. No heartbeat. *Vampire.*

"You!" The vampire surged forward and grabbed Gia's sister, wrapping his arms around her.

"You're..." Hugh snarled, grabbed Danny, Ava, and Gia, tucked them behind him, and drew his swords.

"What the hell is happening?" Gia shoved her way to the front.

"Niko's a vampire," Danny said. "We already know. He saved us. He's friendly." Danny set his hand on Hugh's back, patting him gently as if he'd announced they were having vanilla ice cream for dessert.

Hugh hadn't realized the kids knew his wolf form was him. *What the hell is going on?* Werewolves, witches, and even some demons had coexisted for centuries. But vampires had been a thing of dark lore to Hugh and his siblings. Where vampires were, people died.

"He hasn't shown us his teeth yet, though," Ava said, grasping Hugh's arm and attempting to climb it.

"What...I..." Gia was dumbfounded.

"You knew?" Niko said to Gia's sister.

"I tried to tell you," Francesca whispered to whoever this Niko character was.

"What the hell are you doing in the home of this vile creature?" Hugh demanded. "All of you?"

"You dare," Niko swore and lunged. "Get out of my home."

"It's all right," Danny said, holding his hands out between them. "Niko protects us the way you do, Hugh. He saved Aunt Frankie's life, and he brought us to his home to make sure the dark shadow couldn't get us. He has two hounds who aren't as big as you, but they watch over us, and they like to play fetch outside. Wait until you see Niko's land. We like it here." The voice of a child, a child who was smarter and more intuitive than most adults.

Hugh's brain was having a difficult time tracking everything. He sheathed his swords, knelt beside Danny, and carefully ran his hands over the boy. *He's all right.*

"This is Hugh," Danny continued to the others. "He, or rather his other form, watches out for us too." *They knew the wolf was him. Powerful little witches.* And, shit, he'd meant to tell Gia so many times, but here it was, the truth. He braced for another explosion, this kind from the woman he loved.

"What the hell is going on?" Gia demanded. Her eyes were lit with fire, beautiful when angry. But also, maybe a bit dangerous.

"He's the pretty black dog in my dreams," Ava answered.

"You've been spying on my children?" Gia accused. "How...why...?"

"He wants to keep us safe, Mama," Ava said before he could get his words out. He rested his palm on her small head.

"I've been watching over you," Hugh said. "The three of you." *Ever since I knew you were my mate.*

"Without telling me?" Gia's anger was mixed with hurt.

Fuck, he hadn't meant to hurt her.

"Just because we... I...we work together doesn't give you the right to invade my home, my children's dreams."

"I didn't invade. And you're not safe," he shot back. "They're not always safe. I can feel it. And I thought we were way more than co-workers."

"You should have told me." She pulled Ava in for a hug.

"Would you have allowed it?" It took all his strength not to yell. "Would you have listened to a thing I said, stubborn woman?" He ran his hands through his hair again. It was longer and way more out of control than he liked. "I've been trying to tell you for weeks—"

"You're not my keeper. You don't tell me anything." Gia turned away, dismissing him. He was in the wrong, not explaining sooner. But damn, he was tired of her turning away from him whenever she was too frightened to have tough conversations.

"Whoa," Francesca said. "Let's take stock. We're all okay. We're happy you're here and we have a lot to tell you."

"We were in an accident."

Gia sat down on the ground, tugging both kids into her. "I know, loves. I'm so sorry. Let me look at you."

What the hell? She knew, and she hadn't told him.

Danny pulled away and stood next to Hugh. "There was a dark shadow at the accident. It was awful. I could sense the evil. It tried to hurt us. I yelled and got Aunt Frankie's phone and called an ambulance." He fell into Hugh's leg and Hugh didn't hesitate to wrap the boy in his arms.

"So brave," Hugh said. "You should be proud of yourself."

"I was terrified," Danny cried into his arms.

He glanced up and caught Gia's look of pure anguish. That alone caused more pain to his heart than any one moment of her shoving him away. He would fight a million demons to banish that expression from her face.

Chapter Forty-Two

The day flew by and now her kids were asleep upstairs in a charming room in a charming house and Gia should be relieved. She should climb into a bed piled with blankets and sleep for the next year. But there was so much information flying around her. Niko's housekeeper, Marie, was apparently her long-lost cousin, also a witch. Francesca was sleeping with a vampire, and Gia, well, she had a sexy, meddling, overbearing werewolf shoving his way into her and her kids' lives.

She was furious, and she had so many questions. And a werewolf...wow. A gorgeous, powerful werewolf. How incredible! *Damn it! No.* She needed to remember the fury. He apparently *also* had an appreciation for swords. Another secret he hadn't told her. She headed downstairs because Francesca and Niko were going to explain the accident and everything that came with it, which they'd waited all day for so they could talk without worrying the kids. She reached her hands into her pockets...empty. Of course, because she'd left her sour cherry candies in his car. He'd even bought her her favorite candy.

Following the sounds of voices toward the hallway, Gia nearly ran right into Hugh before she sucked in a breath, sidestepped him, and stalked into the library.

"Could you stop for a minute, woman?"

"I don't need a follower," Gia snapped. His heady gaze burned her, as it had all day. She wanted to beat at his chest and demand he tell her everything. She wanted him to wrap those massive arms around her and hold her close, keep her safe, for evermore. She wanted to not be afraid to want him.

Her emotions were a riot, a tangled bird's nest of confusion. *He would never hurt me or the kids.* That thought steadied her.

Francesca was making cocktails and Gia didn't see Niko at first, but she could feel his presence. Interesting that a vampire, essentially a creature who was dead, could have such a noticeable scent. It was a mixture of old wood, rain-washed land, and...and her sister. *Huh?*

"I'm trying to have a conversation." Hugh and his voice trailed in after her.

A conversation? How in the world was he always so calm? "You can start by apologizing."

"For what, making your son feel safe, protecting you?" Eyes glowing molten were the only indication he was fired up as he carefully leaned into her space.

"For interfering in my life and not telling me!" She grabbed the bourbon from Francesca's hands, took a drink, and sagged onto the sofa. "You went into their dreams?" Damn it, her voice shook.

"Not exactly." An enormous sigh ran through Hugh's body.

He was so handsome standing there, but...also so tired. She'd never seen him look tired before. *The past few days, what...what must that have been like for him?* She'd hardly been at her best physically or emotionally to see anything outside of herself, her fear, her worry. But he'd tracked her across the world, jumped through fire to rescue her, made certain she was safe.

"The first time was after I met them, that one night." He rubbed his heart. "I could hear Danny...having a nightmare. I knocked, but you didn't answer. You were uh...I could hear you in the shower. I couldn't sit by and do nothing. I promise you I would never hurt those kids." He stepped closer.

Shit, she'd been in the shower crying so hard she'd barely been able to function.

"I waited outside his window, tried to urge my calm onto him. *He* found *me*, from his dreams, somehow."

Gia gasped.

"I'm not sure how it happened," he continued. "Surprised the hell out of me, honestly." He stepped away, ran his hands over his head. His beautiful hair. How quickly it grew wild and long. The sides were growing in as well. He was so beautiful and caring. Helping her, helping her children.

Her hands shook. Carefully, she wobbled the glass to the table and set it down. She gripped her head; her left temple pulsed with a headache. Her son, her beloved little boy. What was happening? "His nightmares are awful." She'd been too busy falling apart that evening. What she hadn't been doing was comforting her son. She hadn't even heard Danny crying.

Niko stalked toward Hugh. "So, you entered the dream of a young child. Some strange man taking advantage of a boy in pain."

Hugh faced off. "Never. I went as a—"

"Your beast." Talk about fury. It radiated off Niko, this man...vampire she'd just met. Another person who'd been taking better care of her children than she had.

"Look who's talking, bloodsucker," Hugh hissed, anger rolling off him in waves. "I was simply a big, friendly dog to Danny, one who listened and walked by his side. Ava appeared later...and acted as if she'd known me her entire life. They found me. I'm aware it wasn't the best way to handle it, but I was worried, and I would *never* do anything to harm or scare those kids."

"All right, you two." Her sister pushed the two beasts apart. "It's obvious you both care a great deal about those children. Niko quit being a jerk. I know you have friends who are werewolves. And Hugh, Niko has kept us all safe. There's nothing to worry about. Please put aside your dislike of each other so we can all talk." Frankie was so good at this, staying calm, and being joyful in the face of everything that life threw her way. Gia loved her for it, even while she was jealous. Francesca curled up on the sofa next to Gia.

Gia gripped her hand. "The accident, Start there. Why didn't you call me immediately?"

"Because she was undergoing surgery for a collapsed lung and multiple other injuries, including a broken arm," Niko said, his voice low and angry.

"Oh, Frankie. I'm so sorry," Gia said. Her sister had been hurt far worse than she'd realized.

"I'm okay now. You know I heal quickly. But I think whoever, or...whatever did it was after the children."

What in the hell? God no, she couldn't lose them too!

"A demon bent on destruction or something I can't quite put my finger on," Niko said.

Gia stood. "What? How do you..." Everything she'd been working on for the past few years, all the danger she'd put herself in, had it...no...it couldn't have...it was impossible...it was... "What makes you think that?" She could hardly get the words out as fear squeezed her chest. "It's all my fault."

"No, stop. None of us knows for certain," Francesca interrupted. "But there was this evil presence at the accident. Niko sensed it. And it seemed...it seemed like Danny recognized it. Niko also discovered it at my apartment after the accident, and..." She stood and turned to Hugh. "Your scent was there as well, wasn't it? Preventing the evil...protecting me?"

"I had a bad feeling. Couldn't get ahold of Gia. I know who you are, Francesca. I went to your place... Something else had me on edge too. My instincts were correct." He sent Gia a hard, fierce glare. "So I did everything I could to find Gia."

"You were in our dream that night too at that warehouse, weren't you?" her sister asked.

"I blew a hole through the side to get Gia out before they..." Their eyes met and held.

"Before they killed you," Francesca whispered, wrapping Gia in her arms again. "You were almost killed, and he saved you."

A wolf saved her. She held his stare. His wolf. An integral part of himself he'd never told her about, until, until he had to. That hurt. She didn't know why, since she'd banished him from her life when he'd told her he loved her. *The fool.* No one should love her. She wasn't worth it. "I don't know who saved me. I was unconscious."

Hugh broke their stare and raised his eyes to the ceiling as if begging the Heavens for patience. Francesca got up and hugged him.

"Thank you for saving my sister, Hugh. I was so scared when I couldn't get to her. Nothing good was happening, and she was in pain."

"I don't have a clue who'd want to hurt the children," Gia said. "I...I mostly target humans, not ...uh...other creatures. And you know how careful I am to let nothing I do bleed back into our lives. You *know*." Who was she trying to convince? Herself? Guilt and fear ate at her.

"I do, honey." Francesca took Gia's hand. Immediately the warmth and soothing touch her sister had wove into Gia. "The whole thing is strange. Whatever it was—"

"A hybrid demon." Hugh stepped forward, a sharp look on his face. "If I had to guess. Shapeless or able to change shapes. It left behind a distinct tar-like substance at your house, Francesca. My sense of smell never fails me." He raised his eyebrow at Gia. "And this one was weird."

"It started tailing us after I took the kids to the bird sanctuary," her sister said. "I noticed nothing out of the ordinary before that. I certainly didn't detect its scent at my home."

"It can change shape?" Gia asked.

"Yes," Hugh answered. "But it's more complex than that."

"Oh, great, a complicated demon." Gia huffed.

"Indeed," Niko began. "It was off. Something about its makeup. There was such rage present at the accident site. Not to scare you further, but it's important you know what we're dealing with."

"It reminded me of something," Hugh said, puzzled concentration centered in those mesmerizing eyes of his. They were eyes she recognized not just from their first meeting, but a long time ago, it seemed, like ancient lives colliding. They were eyes she wanted to learn more about. He paced the room. "But it was difficult for me to tell. It was cloaked in layers to distract. To hide its truth."

"Yes," Niko said. "Shit." He faced Hugh, rage illuminating his dark face. "A relative of Asmodeus."

"Fuck," Hugh swore, swinging his gaze back to Gia.

"What is it?" Frankie asked.

"Francesca." Niko pulled her up and wrapped his arms around her. "I don't think the demon was after the children."

"I...that's a good thing. Right?" Francesca asked.

A dangerous look passed between Niko and Hugh.

"Asmodeus and his descendants are demons of lust. Your car, your apartment. It was a simple coincidence the children were with you when...when it attacked. I think the demon was after you."

An uncomfortable hush fell over the room.

"Oh, shit." Her sister tried to pull away from Niko, but he kept his hold on her. "So I'm the reason the children were nearly killed? I...I..."

"No. Never your fault." Niko shook her gently. He rested his head against her neck. Fear and worry laced Francesca's expression.

Aside from this serious conversation and all the danger swirling around them, her sister looked good with Niko.

"None of this is your burden to carry. I've got you," he whispered to her sister.

"But it's still out there," Francesca whispered, the two lost in their own intimate world. Boy, Gia had missed a lot while she'd been gone.

"I'll find it," Niko swore.

"How?"

"I can track it," Hugh insisted. Gia swung her gaze his way.

"No," Francesca insisted. "I'll not put another person in danger because of me. If It's me, it's after. I'll draw it out."

"You mean use you as a lure?" Gia said.

"No fucking way," Hugh said.

"Over my dead body," Niko swore at the same time.

Gia stood in between them now. "You two Neanderthals do not get to order us around. Christ, typical." She had to move. So much had happened. So much was unsettled inside her, around her. The room practically beat with all the emotions and passion. "When women try to take charge, the men get pissed. What are we supposed to do, stay barefoot in the kitchen baking cookies?"

Her sister covered a laugh. Her eyes were huge. *"I mean, barefoot in the kitchen baking cookies did end well for me right before you arrived."*

Gia gaped at her sister.

"I'm teasing, kind of." Frankie turned toward the men. "Of course I don't want to be told what to do while the men do all the grunt work. Whatever we do, we do together. Don't cut us out and don't for one second think you can order us around."

"This is extremely dangerous. It almost killed you once," Niko said. "And I...we"—he gestured to Hugh—"have special powers, strength."

"Yes, yes..." Gia was annoyed now. And for the first time in a long time, ready to claim her powers in front of others. "Big, strong vampire and werewolf. Go beat your chest somewhere else. Francesca and I also have special strengths, if you will." An enormous yawn overtook her.

Hugh stepped forward as if to catch her. "You're wiped out and still healing. You need to sleep."

"Don't you dare try to run my life now," she snapped. He was right, of course. Why was she still snapping at him? Her body felt overflowing with energy. Prickles of sparks zapped inside her and along her skin.

"Hugh's right, honey," Francesca said. "You're exhausted. We all are. It's late and I feel in my bones that we are safe here for now. Let's call it a night and see what the morning brings." Francesca wrapped Gia in a hug. It wasn't Hugh's arms, but it sure was steady and comforting.

"I should…I should go," Hugh said. His gaze still bore into her, but his vulnerability was right there for her to see. It pulsed from him.

Don't go, Gia almost pleaded.

"Nonsense." Frankie patted Hugh's shoulder. "It's late and there's plenty of room here. I'm sure Marie already got a few extra bedrooms ready for you both."

"Francesca," Niko said.

"We're all safer here together with you and Hugh both protecting us."

"Oh, lord, Frankie, way to lay it on thick," Gia said.

"Too thick?" Her sister giggled, and Gia couldn't help but smile at her.

"Goodnight." Gia snuggled into her sister's hug and then turned to walk out. "I'll check with Marie about bedrooms." She sent a glance Hugh's way to find his eyes following her, flecks of gold shooting out of them. *Follow me, please.* The words were on the tip of her tongue.

"I'll make sure she makes it to bed safely," Hugh said, stalking swiftly after her.

Oh boy. What had she gotten herself into?

***

"If you don't want me here, I'll go," Hugh said. The room was dark, save for two small lamps on either side of the bed. The entire house had a lovely, old, but with modern conveniences cozy feel. But right now, all Gia felt was cold.

"I don't want you to go," she whispered, afraid to look at him. The thought of being alone after the last few day's events was more than her soul could handle.

"If I stay. I stay with you in that bed. I need to hold you, feel you. What about you, Gia?"

"I don't know what I want." Her voice was thready. She hardly recognized it. *Yes, you do*, a voice in her head urged. *Don't be afraid to ask for it.* "I want you to stay."

"Get ready for bed." He gestured toward the ensuite bathroom.

She took a quick hot shower and ached to linger under the gorgeous rain shower head but she could hardly keep her eyes open. While Hugh took his turn in the bathroom, she towel-dried her hair as best she could while her arms felt like jelly. She put on underwear and one of his T-shirts from his bag and climbed under the covers into a seriously comfy bed. Her shivers started and then he slid in next to her, his boxer briefs still on.

"Hugh." She reached for him. His hard, hot body was so close to hers. All she wanted to do was feel him and nothing else, not the throbbing pain from her bruises, or the lingering shakes from whatever she'd been drugged with, not the fear that her kids and sister had been in a horrible accident, not the deep worry about a demon stalking them. Simply his warmth surrounding her.

"You're beat," he said, efficiently turning her around so her back was to his chest. He gently rested his hand on her hip. "And still healing."

"I'm not." She could hear the pout in her voice. Why were all her ugly childhood behaviors rearing their head suddenly? "Can you just hold me?" She sounded pathetic, even to her own ears. And she knew it was wrong to beg him, then keep pushing him away. It felt as though the Gia she used to be was slowly being unraveled one thread at a time and she didn't know what to do, how to stop the mess she was becoming.

He sighed but wrapped his body around hers. His beautiful warmth seeped into all her bruised and broken parts.

"Hush now. Sleep." Even when he was being overbearing, his voice was so nice, so soothing. His legs tangled with hers.

One arm snuck under her and rested on her stomach, banding her to him. The other stayed on her hip. His fingers drew slow circles on her.

"I don't know if I can sleep…there's so much…going on. I can't…" God, now her admissions were just spilling out. She had to get a handle on her shit. She wrapped her arms around herself, closed her eyes, and tried counting her breaths. The darkness helped. His heat radiated into her. And she wanted it with a desire that scared her so fucking much.

Chapter Forty-Three

Within seconds, she began to close in on herself. "Gia, please don't disappear on me, not when I'm right here with you. I know you're scared." He wished he could pinpoint exactly what she was afraid of. He could guess, but that did no good.

Carefully, he untangled her arms, wrapped so tightly around her body, and laced their arms together. Christ, she'd nearly been murdered, and her kids and sister had survived an accident and an attack by a nasty demon. His wolf was a snarling, angry beast at all that had happened. It was a side of his wolf he rarely saw, but he was in full-on protection mode now that he'd found his mate. All his emotions were heightened.

"What is happening?" she whispered. "I mean, how can I keep up with everything…I…"

She didn't have to do it alone, stubborn woman, but now was not the time to insist on that. He wanted to ease her mind about things, not force her into a corner and make her lash out.

"Will you talk to me, Hugh, until I fall asleep? Your voice soothes me."

He'd never heard her sound so lost before, and it nearly broke him. His strong, brilliant witch was struggling, yet still offering him tiny glimpses into her soul. It was time to clear the air about a few things. Perhaps that would allow her to sleep. One step at a time.

Leaning closer, he spoke against her head. "I'm sorry for not telling you about the kids and the dreams. I should have done it immediately."

Gia braced and for a second, he wondered if he'd made a mistake, but then she squeezed his hand. "I should have been there for Danny that night. All the nights. I usually am, Hugh."

"I know, honey. You're a wonderful mom." He gave her a gentle squeeze. He'd tell her as often as it took for her to believe it. He hadn't known what to do, who to help that night. Danny and Ava pretty much made that decision for him. It had lanced his heart to walk away from her even though he'd been able to help the kids instead. "Does he have them a lot?"

Her head shook back and forth gently. "No. After my…husband died, he had them. We had a therapist in Boston. I didn't know he was still experiencing them. I used to sleep in his room…to make sure…I…"

"We're going to figure everything out together. I promise," he vowed. "Trust me, lean on me. I was made to be yours." It was risky to utter those last words when her guards down, but he'd tell her again. The next time they sparred about mates and true love, he wanted her at her best. He wanted her to fight all right, to fight for them, for herself, for love, for the idea that they deserved each other.

"I think I need to move off of my side," she whispered.

He'd been hard since he climbed into bed beside her. His blood stirred with a vengeance. Desire and fated prophecies. But...fuck she was still hurting.

"Here." As gently as he could, he rolled her to her stomach. Her allowing him was going to be his complete undoing. "Need any more painkillers?" His voice shook. It was a privilege to care for her, and it gave him time to rein in his emotions. It was probably lingering effects from the drugs she'd been injected with, the shivering and then the sweats, her body working it all out. The fury that swarmed in his vision at what had been done to her. He had to bank that too, for now.

"No." She shook her head, rested her cheek on one hand. "That feels much better. Thank you." He lay down beside her, his head propped in his hand, and stroked his fingers through her damp hair. He shifted her shirt so he could gently rub her back.

"So you're a dream walker too?" she asked.

God, he liked this, this intimacy. "I've only ever experienced something like that once before Danny and Ava found me in their dreams."

"Hmm."

"I was a teenager and learning how to shift into a werewolf, learn my powers, my strength, my lack of it. I was egotistical, proud, stubborn, ridiculous."

Her body softened beneath his touch.

"I was running, got lost, was exhausted, couldn't find my way home to the farm. I fell into a fitful sleep. My father found me in my dreams and guided me home."

"Wow," she said.

"Mm-hmm. I thought it was a one-time thing. Once I was home and safe. It never happened again, not until Danny and Ava. Your kids are powerful, Gia. They surprised the hell out of me."

"They... got to see you... You let them see your wolf? But not me." So soft, he almost missed her words.

Fuck. Hugh closed his eyes and placed a gentle kiss on her spine. He traced the purple bruise on her side and back. She had another on her chin. He'd hurt her too in a way. Never his intention, ever. "Gia."

"It's okay," she rushed out. "I...I push you away...I...why would you want to show me that side? I understand keeping things close, special things." She was drifting off.

"Mm." There was so much to unpack with her words. And Christ, did she not understand? He *did* want to show her. He longed for her to know everything inside him.

A loud moan came from somewhere in the house. Hugh angled his head and tuned his ears. Another moan, and then more sounds of pleasure.

A sleepy giggle escaped Gia. "Well, someone else is having much more fun than we are." Her yawn melded with her words this time, and she closed her eyes.

"We'll get to that. Soon. I promise," he whispered against her back. He laced his hand with hers and rested his head on the pillow.

"You shouldn't...shouldn't make promises you can't keep."

His grin was automatic. "Never, Gianna."

Chapter Forty-Four

Oddly, Gia had woken refreshed and feeling like she'd had the best night's sleep of her life. Hugh had stayed with her, his warmth and solidness a comfort, a soft cocoon she'd slipped into and never wanted to leave. Now her worries were flinging out everywhere.

The cold window helped to soothe her anxiety. Hugh was driving her and the kids home this morning. It was necessary, but she'd hated leaving her sister alone. She'd had a good talk and snuggle with Francesca this morning. Her sister was in love.

"You all right?" Hugh asked from the driver's seat. "You said you wanted to get to your computer, start researching everything you can about... the..." He glanced in the rearview mirror.

She wasn't close to all right. In the past week, she'd blown her mission, almost gotten killed, discovered Hugh was a werewolf, learned her sister was in love with a vampire, that they had a cousin who was a lovely, powerful witch, *and* that some evil demon was still out there. Oh, and apparently her kids could walk into other creature's dreams, and they knew Hugh was a werewolf. She hadn't spoken to Orin yet. Kind of difficult to do with her mission phone gone and an overbearing werewolf hovering in her space.

And, she...she twisted toward the window. Well, she might be in love with her werewolf. And it scared the living crap out of her. She thought she was breaking out in a sweat again, but not from lingering side effects, from the need to escape. Goddess, just thinking about her next conversation with Orin and trying to explain everything to Hugh about what she was. A killer. How could she love someone when she wasn't brave like her sister, when she, Gia Reily, was a complete chicken and a...a fraud?

"Gia?" Hugh took her hand and, my goddess, she let him.

"I'm worried about my sister," she blurted. Much easier to talk about Francesca than her own life. "She's...well Niko..."

"Want me to turn this car around and go get her? We'll bring her with us, hide her...anything."

Her heart melted. She patted his arm. "No, no...well she's in love. And I guess Niko might be too. Who wouldn't love my sister?" *But Niko is...afraid.* She couldn't even voice the last part, probably because it so aptly described herself.

"Niko's a good guy," Danny said from the backseat. "You don't have to worry about him, Hugh. I can tell, and he's been taking care of us, protecting us."

"*And* he took us to meet his good friend, Mr. Callum, and get the bestest French fries in the entire world," Ava said.

"Callum?" Hugh asked.

"Yes," Danny answered. "At a pub in the woods. It's really cool and it has games."

"What's Callum's last name?" Hugh asked.

"Don't know," Ava said. "But he has big black tattoos on his arms and three small silver hoops in his right ear."

"Ah."

"What's going on?" Gia asked, trying to follow the conversation.

"Callum's a good friend of mine, of my family. It appears he's friends with Niko too. I guess I have to give the vampire the benefit of the doubt." Hugh sounded grumpy, admitting those words. She kind of adored grumpy Hugh. How in the world was she supposed to fight these gooey feelings she had for him?

"Niko took us to his house to protect us," Ava said. "Are you going to take us to yours to protect us, Hugh?"

"Hey," Gia said. "I protect you."

Ava giggled. "You are the bestest protector in the world, Mama. But you always say, 'More help is better help.' right?" Ava's voice got quiet. "You used to say that when we'd help you clean. When you were happier."

Gia couldn't handle one more dagger to her heart today. "I..." She had to swallow back her tears. "You're right, honey. I forgot about that. We used to sing a song about it. I'm so glad you reminded me."

"I'm not taking you to my house. I'm coming home with you to yours. Maybe it's better for you all to be home. I'd like to stay." He sent a quick glance Gia's way.

Why did she have the feeling, from the steel in his gaze, that this wasn't up for negotiation?

"Yes!" Danny and Ava cheered together. Well, she'd lost this battle. For now. Did she ever really want to fight it?

"I do like your farm, though," Danny said. "Especially all the dogs."

"Mm," Hugh said. "The farm isn't my home, though not anymore. It's my parents, who I guarantee will be excited to have you visit anytime, especially when those puppies arrive. I live downtown. I'll show you sometime if it's okay with your mom."

"I—"

"I really want a puppy," Ava said.

Gia glanced back to see pleading in both her kids' eyes.

"Mr. Webb, I mean Drake, said they have to find homes for them somehow. Good homes with good people who will love them," Danny offered with hope in his voice.

"He did, Mama," Ava joined in.

"Those'll be good pups. Good for kids. Good family dog."

Oh lord. "Puppies take a lot of caring for and cleaning up after," she said.

"Well, if Hugh moves in with us, he can help us clean up too, Mama. Then you won't be so stressed all the time."

"I can definitely help clean up. I am an expert cleaner," Hugh said, sending her a huge grin and a sexy wink.

She was so, so screwed. "We'll see about the moving in part. That's hardly necessary," she said.

"We'll see about it indeed," Hugh echoed, but she was certain his plans were not at all the same as hers.

How had things gotten so out of her control? She had no idea how to shove everything back to how it used to be before…before Hugh. Gia stole a glance at him and decided she'd worry about that later. Or maybe never.

Chapter Forty-Five

G IA WAS HUGGING A pillow to herself and staring at her bed when Hugh entered her bedroom. It was after eight. She'd put the kids to bed and had never returned downstairs. He wasn't surprised. She was a scared animal knowing she was about to be caught, equal parts hiding, and spitting and clawing out in fear. How could he explain to her he wasn't out to hurt her but to love her? If she'd simply let him.

"Oh, sorry. um...thank you for bringing us home and spending the day with us. I...um...goodnight. I mean..." She held out her hand.

Hugh raised his eyebrow, took two steps toward her, and batted her hand away. He lifted her. She wrapped her legs around him and he hid his grin. Sitting on the bed with her on his lap, he said, "I'm not leaving. Stop doing that. Stop brushing me away."

"You don't have to stay. I don't need you to stay." *Liar.* But Christ, she wounded him with little effort.

He cleared his throat. "*I* need to stay. I need to make sure you and those kids are okay. Please give me that."

"It's *my* job to make sure they're safe." One more strike to his heart. She didn't even wield her knives, and yet she struck. Her knives, that was another issue they needed to talk about.

"It's my job now too. There's a demon out there, Gia, a dangerously unhinged one."

She met his gaze. He could practically see her contemplating everything.

"And there's something else."

Her expression grew serious. "What, Hugh? What else?"

He spoke quietly but succinctly. "I've sensed something evil around your house when I came as my wolf. I don't know if it's the same demon." He suspected not. "Or something else." Which worried him to no end. "But until we figure it out, I want to be here with you three." *I want to stay forever.* But that would be winning the entire game and, for now, he had to think inning by inning.

"Why didn't you tell me? No more keeping secrets."

Does she even realize what she just said?

She squirmed on his lap, and he grabbed her hips to still her. He raised his eyebrow. He itched to kiss and nip that snarky expression off her face. Something to look forward to when their lives had calmed down. One hand went around to her back of its own accord, tugging her in tighter. She settled there right over his cock and gave another wiggle, her eyes drifting closed and open. A flush blossomed up her neck to cover her cheeks.

Christ, it was difficult to have a serious conversation with her sitting on his lap. Rookie mistake. One he wasn't too upset about as her warmth seeped into him, lighting him on fire. Maybe he'd fuck her into a state of euphoria and she'd give him all her secrets. "I'm telling you now. It's the first chance I've had alone with you, not counting last night when you'd had a lot thrown at you and you needed your sleep." He spanned her back with his hand and caressed the base of her spine with his thumb. The delicate, but powerful bones of her.

Gia closed her eyes and arched into him, letting out a whimper.

"Gia." He cupped her cheek and whispered. "Tell me how you're feeling. Still in pain? I don't want to hurt you. I should tuck you into bed and let you sleep."

"Shh." She kissed him, soft sweet lips.

The taste of her shot right to his cock, and woke every cell that wasn't already standing at attention for her. He kissed her back, angled her head so he could drag his lips down the pale column of her neck, to the center of her throat where her pulse leapt. Then up to the bruise on her jaw, he peppered featherlight kisses there and whispered, "I'm not the only one keeping secrets, now am I? What were you doing in that warehouse? A fake passport? Your knives? Do you wear them all the time? Anything you'd like to share with me? Why you're living every day in fear?"

She braced and stumbled off his lap, a frightened kitten once again. "Those aren't secrets. Those are a part of my life *not* available for discussion."

Hugh hung his head and sighed. His aching cock was the least of his worries. One, two, three strikes she'd shot at him tonight. Good thing this *wasn't* fucking baseball. Boy, but did his heart hurt. He took one more look at her and willed her to talk to him. "Right." Hugh stood and started to walk out.

"Where are you…where are you going?"

"I'm going to sleep on the couch. You don't trust me, Gia, and that…that cuts deep. I know it's not your fault. You have a lot going on, but I want to help you and you won't let me in." His instincts screamed at him to tuck her into his body and sleep soundly beside her, but he needed some space.

"I…I can't…I don't… Please stay here." She was using that vulnerable voice, and it cut him to the quick. He paused and walked back toward her. Apparently, he was into self-punishment.

"I'll sleep on the floor." He reached around her and grabbed a pillow from the two million she had piled on her bed.

"You can't…that's not comfortable. It's hard."

"Wolf, remember? I'm used to sleeping on the ground." Alone, he almost added, but he was trying his hardest not to lash out at her. He wanted to offer to stay if she told him all her secrets, but that was a petty way to act. He'd have to *show* her she could trust him with anything. She was so bent on keeping him at arm's length that, not for the first time, he wondered if she was even honest with herself.

She climbed into bed and he shut the lights out, making himself as comfortable as he could on the floor, his eyes wide open, his body primed for her. It was going to be a long fucking night.

"You can sleep up here," she whispered through the dark.

"Hush. Close your eyes and your mind. Tomorrow's another day to fight, love."

***

A sharp scream woke him. Hugh was on the bed instantly, gently shaking her.

Gia struggled against his hold, flailing and beating. "No!"

"Gia."

She scrambled away from him, nearly falling off the bed.

"Whoa." He grabbed her. "Gia. It's okay. You're dreaming."

Her eyes opened and she settled her gaze on him. She blinked a few times and rolled to her back on the bed. "Fuck," she swore. "I'm...I'm sorry."

"Don't apologize. Are you all right?"

"I'm all tangled." She tugged at the collar of her T-shirt, which he realized was one of his shirts. This woman and her confused, tender heart.

"A shower might help. Soothe your tired body." She must have still been exhausted because she stared at him with all that vulnerability on her face and let him lead her to the bathroom. He stripped the rest of their clothes away, turned the water on, and tugged her into the steam in what was a poor representation of a shower, but the water was hot. She closed her eyes and brought her face toward the water, letting it spill over her. Then she hung her head and turned, face-planting into his chest. He grabbed the sponge and some soap and cleaned her body.

"You don't even want me now." Her pout was adorable.

Hugh barked out a laugh.

"Don't make fun of me. I don't think I can take it," she whispered. "Especially not while you're taking care of me and I'm so...not myself...I..." Her words trailed away.

"Not making fun, Gianna, my love. I'm laughing because I want you, always, with a fever, woman. Open your eyes and look at what you do to my body."

"Oh." She braced her hands on his chest, her gaze down. Every inch of him was hard and ready for her.

"Now look at my eyes. They only do this for you."

She reached up tentatively and traced a path around his eyes, studying him. He rinsed the soap from their bodies, turned off the water, and grabbed towels. After he dried them off, he swept her into his arms and carried her back to bed. He ached for her. But he hadn't lied. She was still healing, and now having her own nightmares. And a canyon of secrets sat between them. It wasn't until they lay together in bed once more that she spoke.

"Thank you. I don't know what's going on. I slept so well last night...with you. I always sleep well with you. The nightmare, I was back there...being tied to the chair, drugged so I couldn't...I couldn't fight."

"Nightmares aren't logical." He didn't feel too fucking logical himself right now, knowing what she'd been through, that someone had beaten her, tried to kill her. He wouldn't have survived himself if she'd been... "Fuck." He buried his head in her neck.

"Hugh?" She wrapped her arms around him.

God, her warmth, her heartbeat, the blood pulsing through her.

"I'm okay. It's okay."

"I almost lost you."

The soft caress of her hands stroking up and down his back soothed him.

"I'm right here," she whispered, sliding her leg over his. She sure fucking was. Right there naked and open for him and...

"Gia." He took her mouth. She was so wet and warm, begging for him with her body, the way her scent stirred his wolf, who was pacing and growling. All he needed to do was inch up and he could slide right inside her heat. The kiss turned hungry, hot, and wet as he nipped at her lips and tasted her. She held his head and kissed him back, meeting his hunger.

"Yes, Hugh. Yes. I'm here. For you."

He hiked her leg up higher and she moaned. "Am I hurting you?" He rested his lips against her neck, trying to control himself. His wolf demanded he mate with her right this instant.

"No. I'm okay. I heal fast, like my sister. It's one...one of my better qualities."

He huffed out a laugh, which brought his aching cock right there. Everything in him pulsed for her, reached for her.

She slid a hand down and gripped him, and it was his turn to moan. "Woman. My self-control is shredding here. I don't want to hurt you and there are issues..."

"I know so much is swirling, but I want to feel alive with you."

"I'm grabbing a condom or going to sleep on the floor." Holding her like this, side by side, naked body to naked body, all their heat swirling together, stepping away would be madness, but he'd do it for her.

"I have an IUD and I...I..." She paused and met his gaze with her hazel eyes clear and shimmering with desire. "I haven't been with anyone but you and my late husband, Hugh. There's never been anyone else."

A secret. She'd given him so much with that simple admission.

"Gianna Reily, you are so beautiful, this heart." He kissed the fragile skin over her heart and nipped at her breast on the way down. "This body." He lavished kisses on her belly. "This soul." He bowed his head against her pelvis. Her bruises were completely gone. "You shatter me."

"Hugh. I don't want to hurt you. I'm so...my life is not...I—"

"Shh," He moved lower and kissed her core, licked at her wetness, breathed her in as she arched her body to him, and cried out.

"Hugh, I need you inside me. Feels so good. Please..." she shook her head, gripped the sheets by her side.

He sucked and caressed, teasing, drawing her higher and higher. And she nearly shot off the bed when her orgasm slammed into her. He could make her come again like this, at his mercy, while she let herself go, but he wanted inside her. He crawled up her body.

"How do your eyes do that?" she whispered, face flushed, voice hoarse.

"It's because of you," he said. "You and I are connected. My body recognizes yours."

She closed her eyes and kissed him.

"I've always used a condom, Gianna. I also haven't been with anyone in a while, and I got tested after that first night you let me in."

"I know..." Her voice shook. "I know you think I don't trust you, Hugh, but I do, with so much."

Something flickered inside him, lit up, and settled. He lined up his cock, rubbed through her wetness, watching her moan and try to move closer, and then he angled her hips and slid inside, so, so slowly.

She took his mouth and kissed him and moved with him as he stole out and drove back in, picking up the pace with her whimpers and pleas to go faster. Her hands roamed his back, sending heat through him.

Reaching his fingers down, he found her clit, rubbed his thumb over it, coated it with her juices. He could smell her everywhere. He should please her more, take care of her first, but his body wanted to stay right here, as connected to her as he could be in body and heart, while she wasn't hiding anything from him, while her eyes were locked with his, while she was showing him everything she could.

"Gianna, your eyes light up for me too. Did you know that?"

She shook her head, so many expressions crossing her face. Surprise, wonder, confusion. It was too much for her to process. He could feel it, but this moment here was a step forward. He broke their stare, giving her the mental space she needed, and placed gentle kisses along her jaw, where her bruise was almost gone.

"Hugh, I need..."

"What, love? Tell me."

"That, keep doing that, slower, with your hand and your body. Your body is so powerful. You make me feel...I..." She arched into him.

"What, Gianna? Give it to me. I make you feel?"

"Hugh," she cried and buried her head in his neck as another orgasm slammed into her.

He held her tightly, used his hands to move her hips as he drove into her one last time, and let the tremors of her release pulse around him and tug him into ruin with her.

Christ. He held her and caught his breath, felt her delicate but talented fingers flit along his arm.

They drifted connected for an immeasurable amount of time. Perhaps time meant nothing in the dark of night with confessions and love-making. He slipped out of her and made his way to the bathroom to clean up. When he returned with a warm cloth, she was out, sleeping softly, a gentle smile on her face. Memories of their first night. Love. Belief. Warmth.

He cleaned her, murmuring sweet nothings. When he finished, he checked to make sure the kids were asleep, double-checked the locks on all the doors and windows one more time, then climbed back in bed with Gianna. Wrapping his arms around her, he whispered, "Mine."

It may have been an hour or two later and still dark out when Gia spoke in her sleep, snuggled beside him. "Free, Hugh. You make me feel free."

Precious Love. How much he ached to hear those words from her when she was conscious.

Chapter Forty-Six

Gia's eyes flew open, and she flailed her hand out. Hugh was still here. His voice came from downstairs, where he and Danny were making breakfast. *Deep breaths.* She'd dreamt he'd been buried alive, and she was shoveling through the dirt to get to him in time.

For the last few days, he'd stayed with them. He'd held her as she'd slept, but he hadn't made love to her again, and every morning he'd been up before her, making breakfast, and helping her kids get ready for school.

Like all the nights he'd slept beside her, she'd slept soundly. She should have been making up for all her years of sleep debt, but her body still ached with exhaustion. She thought she'd known fatigue before, but this was different. This was loaded down with too many worries, confusing emotions, and fear.

There were moments during the night when she thought she'd heard Hugh whispering soothing words to her in her sleep.

Was he holding sex away from her to get her to talk? No. Gia didn't believe that. He was nothing if not open and honest. He wasn't the one hiding things, not anymore. But her secrets were...her secrets got people killed.

She climbed out of bed and dragged herself to the shower. The scalding water woke her as the gnawing in her stomach churned. Her nightmares weren't getting better, only worse. She had to keep reminding herself that Laszlov was dead. It was over. And yet...why hadn't Orin answered her calls, any of them?

She'd been burned, her identity found out. How much did they know about her? Had Orin been burned too? What had happened? Was he dead or hurt? Shit, and she hadn't done enough to try to find him. She toweled off and threw on some sweats. Then she slipped into her closet, shut the door, and dug out her secret compartment hidden behind her shoe boxes that kept her burner phones and the special one Orin had instructed her to use only in an emergency, furious with herself that she hadn't thought of this earlier.

"You dare call me?" Orin hissed through the phone.

Gia was so shocked she dropped it.

"What?" She fumbled to grasp it back to her ear. "Orin? Are you there? Are you okay? I've been so worried. I'm...I'm okay...I..." *Thought you'd want to know.*

"You destroyed a mission, failed at your one singular job, the most important job you have in this life, and you think I want to hear from you? You could have destroyed our entire operation, our entire end goal. You are a failure." he seethed.

What? "I...I..." So many thoughts and images rang through her mind.

"I don't have time for your petty distractions and amateur mistakes."

Silence met her. A whoosh rushed right through her body. Then a ringing started in her ear. Something invisible pressed in on her chest, a hollow squeezing pain. Fumbling, Gia set the phone in the box and shoved it aside. She barely managed to get the closet door open, then slumped to the floor and put her head between her knees.

"Gia?" Hugh called up the stairs. His voice was coming closer.

Help. The squeezing was harder, fiercer. She couldn't breathe.

"Gia!" He was by her side. "What happened? Fuck," he swore. "Another one."

What? She tried to speak, but there was no sound, no breath.

"Hey." Hugh sat and lifted her onto his lap, where he rested his hands on her back and pressed her chest to his.

It was faint, but she could feel their hearts beating against each other. Slowly, he moved his fingers in that gentle circular motion that soothed every scar inside her.

"Stay with me, Gianna. Breathe in. Feel my heart align with yours."

Gia closed her eyes and let the life force of him slip into her and ease her anxiety. She got a breath in. It fucking hurt. And out. And another one. She felt her body relax against his big strong one and she reached her weary arms around him and held on.

"Okay?" Gently, he held her head so he could gaze into her eyes.

Everything was spiraling out of control. Except this. Every time this man touched her, held her, looked at her, something furled open inside her and radiated peace. Something that had been dead a very long time. Longer than she cared to realize.

"What happened?"

She shook her head. "I...I was in the closet and...and then I couldn't breathe."

"Usually something sets it off?"

"It?"

"Your panic attacks."

"No." She tried to stand, but her legs wouldn't work. "Shit."

"Yes, Gia. You are having panic attacks. Since I met you. How long before that have they been happening?"

"I don't...I don't know. Honestly."

"Hmm."

"Are the kids...school?" Christ, she was coming undone.

"Kids are fine. Danny said no school today, teachers' in-service."

"Oh, right." Leaning into him, feeling the rumble of his words through his chest, her breathing finally slowed to normal.

"They're washing the dishes?"

"What?" She raised her head and met his gaze. His eyes were dark brown now, so serious.

"Yeah. I filled the sink with soapy water. Ava's on a stool washing and singing a song she said you used to sing them."

"But we have a dishwasher?"

"They said they like to play with water. It seemed fun. Not okay?"

"It's fine," she said. "They used to do it in Boston. We didn't have a dishwasher. They loved it. They'd put their tiny plastic animals in and make it an underwater zoo. It's a mess, but it was always worth it."

"Ahh."

Can I just stay here forever, warm in his arms, talking about silly things?

"Tell me what's going on, please, Gia," he begged.

He was so stalwart, so strong, so good. Something hard in her deflated. She wanted to tell him, to unburden herself. But what could she say? She was so fucking afraid that he would leave her, in one way or the other. Pushing him away had seemed like the only course of action because the alternative...didn't bear thinking about. But pushing him away wasn't right either. Her instincts were screaming at her. Maybe it was time to heed them.

"I messed up," she whispered. "At my...at the job in Prague. The most important mission I had, the most important job, and I messed up."

"Gia, listen to me." Hugh brought her face up to meet his gaze, his warm, solid hands cradling her face. "I don't know what you're talking about if you won't confide in me, but the most important things in your life are those kids and you. I want to be important to you too, the way you three are to each other, but even I wouldn't put myself before your kids. Think about all of that, Gia. What the hell is going on?"

His words hummed through her bones and into her soul. He believed in her, supported her. What the hell was she doing? Fuck, she really had messed up, but not in Prague, with her life.

"You can tell me anything. I promise."

A shiver worked its way through Gia, and she untangled her arms. "I want to, Hugh. I...I'm afraid," she admitted.

"Of me?" Hugh's expression hardened.

And a pain ripped through her at how he must have been feeling. "No, Hugh, never. Of...of..." *Things I've done. Who I've become.* "Myself," she whispered and squeezed his hand gently before she left him sitting there on the floor of her bedroom and wondered how she was going to tell him the truth that would either send him running or potentially put him in grave danger. How was she supposed to make that decision?

Chapter Forty-Seven

"Ahh," Niko said, eyeing Hugh, who stood behind Gia as they walked into Niko's house. "Welcome back, I suppose."

"Aren't you glad to see us?" Ava asked, leaning into Niko for a hug. "I missed you." The vampire's entire countenance softened. Hugh understood. These ladies got a lock around your heart and never let go.

"Absolutely," Niko said. "But you know who's really going to be delighted? Lollie and J. They're out back. Go on now and see them." Danny and Ava ran through the house. Hugh could hear them saying hello to their aunt and then making their way outside to play with Niko's hounds.

Hugh's anger, annoyance, frustration, all of the above, had been at a low simmer all day. Francesca had called when they were cleaning the kitchen that morning when Gia had gone silent again. She invited them all over for the day. Hugh included. He had a million things to do, including trace the phone he'd found along with several burners in Gia's closet after she'd left. He'd never been a snooper before. And he found he didn't much like it now. But she and possibly her kids were in danger and he would be merciless in protecting them. Plus, where they were, he wanted to be.

"So glad you all made it," Francesca said, wrapping Gia and then Hugh up in hugs before she linked her hand with Niko's. Niko gazed at her with stars in his eyes.

Hugh understood. He was just as gone for Gia. It hurt that she'd spent the last several hours putting space between them.

"Come into the kitchen. I'm almost finished making brownies. You can help me, Gia." Francesca kissed Niko, then took Gia's arm and whisked her away.

"You don't want my help, Frankie," Gia said.

"All you have to do is stir, love, that's it."

Hugh held up the bottles of wine Gia had insisted they stop for on the way.

"Well, you'd better come in too." Niko sighed, taking the wine. "Gia looks..."

"Exhausted, yeah."

"Everything...all right?" Niko asked.

"She's been having nightmares since we got home from Europe." He hadn't meant to blurt it out, especially not to a vampire, but damn, he was exhausted too. Every night almost. Either a nightmare or her speaking in her sleep. Some nights were both.

"Ah, yes, Francesca hasn't been able to speak to her sister in dreams much this week. I suspect that's what the invite today was about, to check on her."

"Something ugly's going on."

"You mean the rogue demon," Niko seethed.

"I think it's something else, something additional."

"Shit," Niko swore. "Anything to do with how you found her?"

"I think so. I..." Hugh studied Niko. They'd gotten off on the wrong foot, but Gia's kids trusted him, Hugh's best friend Callum trusted him, and Francesca and Niko obviously made each other happy. If things went in Hugh's favor, they might be family someday. He'd heard about vampires having special powers. He didn't enjoy going behind Gia's back, but maybe Niko could help him keep his woman alive. "I could use your help."

Niko studied him, set the wine on the entry table, and said, "Follow me."

***

Thirty minutes later, Hugh stormed out of Niko's office.

"Ahh, Hugh, this might not be the best way to..." Niko's words trailed off as they entered the kitchen.

"Care to explain this to me?" Hugh demanded. He slammed the papers and phone on the kitchen table.

Francesca was taking brownies out of the oven and Gia jumped at his tone. Good, maybe he startled some fucking sense into the woman.

"Gianna?"

"What?" Gia glared at him. "What is going on?" She brought the papers closer to read for a few seconds before she dropped them like a hot potato. "What the hell did you do?" Ghost-like fear blanched her expression. She palmed the phone and stuffed it in her pocket.

"What the hell did *I* do? Were you ever going to tell me? That you've been working for a mercenary?" He was in her space, pushing her boundaries.

"How dare you. It's none of your business." Fiery red sparks shot from her eyes.

"I was worried!" He yelled, then stalked away, raking his hands through his hair. He faced her then. She was wearing her tight black pants and that soft fucking sweater from Germany. That sexy dichotomy of curves and sharp edges. Was she wearing her knives even now? That pissed him off too. Would she ever tell him what they were for? She practically vibrated with anger. Well, good. He was fucking angry too. When the hell was she ever going to fully trust him?

She stalked toward him, spitting mad and lashing out. "You don't have to worry, Hugh," she snarled, sparks leaping out through the air. "I'm good at my job."

"No offense." He leaned in. "But numbers and finances and whatever"—he flicked his hand through the air—"you do on your computers didn't help you not get caught and almost burned alive in Prague." He stabbed the papers. "And they're not going to help you here with a madman." He was right in her face, towering above her, this close to kissing that anger off her face, but he wanted more, he wanted...

In an instant, she tossed herself into an almost invisible quick twirl in the air. So fast it was hard to tell, but in a furious blur of color, she had Hugh on the floor, arms pinned under his back and one of her knives at his throat.

Fucking finally. He tried as hard as he could to hide his smirk. *Gotcha.*

"Offense taken," Gia whispered. "But don't worry. I'm not only excellent at numbers. I excel at killing, in my other job. As an assassin. So don't *ever* condescend to me." She pushed off him and leapt away, sheathing her knife in some nearly hidden pocket on her hip as if it hadn't just been pressed against his carotid artery.

Hugh flipped himself to standing and crossed his arms to prevent himself from hauling her over his shoulder and escaping with her until he could fuck all the truths out of her. No. He shook his head. That wasn't the way. That was his wolf pushing for dominance, and he'd never do that unless it was what she wanted too.

An assassin. He'd suspected after how he'd found her in Prague. And now discovering Orin Zeleb's identity, thanks to Niko's worldwide connections. Hugh thought he knew a lot of people, but there were advantages to being a centuries-old vampire.

His tactic had worked. He'd provoked, and she'd shown her secrets. Now he had to get her to talk to him, explain everything.

"Gia," he said.

Her fury was slowly diminishing. Poor thing looked like a starved animal. Not to mention the fireworks leaping and charging from her skin in a myriad of colors, mostly reds and pinks, those pretty deep oranges.

"I...shit...I..."

"I think you and I should take a break from the guys and go visit Marie," Francesca said. "She's down the path in her cottage. She hoped you and I might come talk to her when I mentioned you were all coming for dinner. Let's go, honey." Francesca sent Hugh and Niko a wide look and disappeared out the patio doors with Gia.

"Feeling bad about your choices?" Niko came to his side while they watched the women disappear.

"Not in the slightest," Hugh said. "Stubborn woman."

"Both of them," Niko admitted. "I gather their childhood and adolescence, perhaps their whole lives they've been battling for survival. Difficult to trust when that's the case."

"True," Hugh agreed. Guilt worked its way into his chest.

"Tell you what," Niko said. "We know where Mr. Zeleb lives. I can trace myself to his house, poke around outside without anyone realizing. If you stay here and guard our families, I'll return in a flash."

Hugh stared at Niko. "I'd appreciate that." It appears he wasn't done being sneaky yet. Not until he was certain Gia and her kids were safe.

Chapter Forty-Eight

"Wow," Francesca whispered.

Gia wasn't sure whether to be embarrassed or angry, or...no...she could not be aroused by Hugh. The way his chest had heaved when she'd had him pinned down. The almost smirk on his beautiful mouth. Yes, she could swear he'd been smirking at her. The beauty and grace with which he'd flipped his enormous body back up, the lack of fear or...surprise in his expression.

A weird, almost orange wind whipped around Gia and her sister, twirling leaves into a mini tornado before them. The evergreens sent off a swishing sound swaying with the frantic air. Off in the distance, the sky flashed as if lightning were hiding behind the clouds and toying with them.

"Hugh totally played me," Gia said.

"Mm, he did something to you all right." Francesca's voice held a bit of humor and confusion. She looked from Gia to the woods.

"Oh, ladies, how lovely to see you." Marie opened the door when they stepped onto her porch steps. "Oh, my goodness, Gia. You're..."

"I know right, she's been sending off these sparks for the last few minutes. Ever since, well. Hugh sort of got under her skin."

"What are you talking about? I got under *his* skin," Gia insisted.

"Mm-hmm," Francesca said in that indulgent tone.

"Your powers are quite brilliant," Marie said. "But...why...they're..." She rested her hand on Gia's cheek, then drew back the curtains and glanced outside. "You've been hiding them, but it's not working anymore, am I right?"

"My what?" Gia whispered as a shiver ran through her, a warm, familiar shiver, or shimmer pulsing from her. She couldn't tell. "My powers aren't like that. I don't have any except my ability to see numbers and patterns, and I can dream walk."

Marie's eyes grew huge. "You don't know..."

"I don't know what?"

"Gia." Marie led her to a full-length mirror where Gia could see gold, purple, and deep pink sparks shooting from her fingers and her eyes, zapping along her arms. "What exactly do you know about your powers?"

"What the hell is happening?" Gia asked and stepped closer to the mirror. "I don't have powers, nothing like this." She raised her hands for a closer look. "What is this?" Memories twirled in her mind, long ago and more recent ones. Moments she'd ignored or brushed off. Colors twirling from her body. "I thought...I thought this was just part of my makeup as a...witch, like what color eyes people have or something...I..."

"Mm." Marie smiled. "You're a powerful witch, Gianna Reily. Very powerful indeed."

"How can you tell?" Her body hummed.

"Well, I can see it and feel it when I touch you. I sensed it last week when we met. Your ancestors live in you. Their powers are coursing through your blood. Remarkable." Marie scanned Gia's body, gently took one of her hands, and studied it. The wild, colorful sparks zapped and leapt, but Marie seemed unharmed by them. "Weather or storm witch is the one I can see and feel trying to shove her way forward. There's more too. I'm not sure what exactly, but how fantastic to discover."

"Storm witch?"

Marie nodded.

"Look outside, Gia," Francesca said. "The wind and the heat lightning off in the distance."

"I can't be doing that...I'm not responsible for..." Gia's blood stirred, poking at her. It was a feeling returning to her. A familiar old presence set free.

"I think you can and are," Francesca said. "The sky was clear and calm when you arrived this evening, actually until Hugh stalked into the kitchen a few moments ago. I felt the change. "

"What happened a few moments ago?" Marie asked.

"That werewolf snarled at me," Gia said, and gold sparks shot out of her fingertips to the table. Disappearing in a poof. *Holy shit.*

"Ahh, provoked you, did he?" Marie grinned.

"You could say." Gia sent a quick shake of her head to Francesca. The fewer people that knew Gia was an assassin, the safer for everyone.

"Gia," Marie said. "It's not a good idea to keep your powers locked away, repressed. They won't stay that way. You must exercise them and practice with them in order to control them." Marie sat in front of her. "Take a few deep breaths. Let's see if we can calm the energy inside you."

She obeyed. "I didn't even know I had these powers...*have* them," Gia whispered, taking a sip of the tea laced with bourbon and honey her sister set before her. "I mean, I thought my skill with mathematics and computers was my power."

"Oh, dear," Marie said. "Your mother wasn't able to explain before she died? Or you weren't manifesting them yet, perhaps. Hmm. And then you two had such a difficult time trying to survive. I imagine you buried them without realizing it. Trauma can alter us. Not to mention you bear the trauma of witches going back generations. We all do. It's in our blood whether or not we accept it. It appears circumstances in your life are stirring things up. I suspect Hugh and love are some of those things."

Gia wanted to deny it, but she was shaken, to say the least, so she listened, hoping for some answers.

"Hmm." Marie smiled, gathering both Gia's hands in her lap and closing her eyes. She whispered words of a spell Gia had heard before, in what felt like many lifetimes ago. Memories squeezed her chest and tears filled her eyes. She and Frankie hadn't heard a spell in decades. "Oh, heavens, I sense moon witch energy in you too. Very robust and quite fitting, don't you think?"

"Moon witch?"

"Oh my goodness, you and your werewolf are meant to be," Francesca gushed.

"Hush with your soulmate wishes, Francesca." Gia's heart raced. *Hugh. Love? Soulmates?* Nothing scared her more.

"Don't be afraid," Goddess whispered.

"I also see danger inside you, Gia. You deal with terrible men. They surround you...you..." A shadow crossed Marie's face. "You eliminate them."

Gia gasped. So much for keeping her identity a secret. "How can you know that?"

"Like I said." Marie held Gia's hands, palms up now, rubbing them gently with her fingers. "I can feel things. I view the world in pictures: the past, the present, and the future. And I feel many wounds here." Marie's fingers stilled at Gia's pulse. "Every time you're around one of these men, you open a new cut. There's a powerful one still open and ...it's like..." Marie dropped her hand and stood. She hurried around her kitchen, collecting herbs and little bottles, a bowl, and some kitchen utensils.

Gia looked at Francesca. "Like what?"

"It's poisoning you or...I'm uncertain. It's confusing me." Marie sat back down, took both Gia's hands in hers again, and closed her eyes, whispering ancient words. Gia leaned into the comfort, the old familiar.

"I was...I was drugged on my last mission." Gia hadn't had much chance to talk to Marie last week when they'd returned. She hadn't even hugged her, still in shock over having a relative she and her sister had never known about.

Marie opened her eyes and studied her. "That could be what I'm sensing. You're doing better, clear eyes, but its lingering effects are still inside you. I'm going to make you a special tea to drink for the next few days to purge it from your system."

"Her teas are magical," Francesca said and gave a small laugh. "Pun intended. But seriously, she helped me heal after my accident. Oh, this is so cool. I can't wait to learn from you, Marie. Can I help?"

Gia let the two converge on Marie's stove. She wanted to learn too, but her head was spinning. She, quiet, invisible Gianna Reily, had special powers she'd never known about. Francesca obviously knew Gia was a witch. Marie could sense the powers inside her. Even...even Hugh knew she was a witch without her telling him. How could that be?

Worse, she had no idea how to use her powers or control them. Another familiar had stirred in her when Marie had mentioned moon witch. But it came with an ominous cloak. It was something she couldn't put her finger on. Confusion swirled and pulsed through her. And fear. Something was coming. And Gia had never been so scared in her life.

Could she really unearth her powers? Become familiar with them? Embrace them? A part of her whispered, "Yes." But the broken pieces of her heart were cowering in fear. She didn't know if her magic would be her salvation or her doom.

Chapter Forty-Nine

Hugh fingered his phone, then tucked it into his back pocket and went to find Gia.

A text had come in while they finished dinner with Niko and Francesca last night, but he'd forgotten about it. She'd looked shell-shocked when she'd returned from Marie's cottage. It was all he could do not to carry her away somewhere and let her sleep, protected for the next few decades, especially since Niko couldn't tell anything from Orin's residence.

Gia infuriated him and worried him to no end. He'd broken through one of her shields last night and, although he was glad to have the information about her knives and why the hell she wore them, it also made him realize how little he still understood.

"I have an idea," he said.

It was late morning. Gia stood by the window sipping tea, watching small snowflakes drift from the sky. He came up behind her and wrapped his arms around her. She stiffened for a second, then relaxed into his arms.

"Let's go to the farm for the weekend. May and Dad invited us. Puppies came yesterday afternoon. Kids can't hold them yet, but it's amazing to see them at this age with their mama and then as they grow. Plus, it's beautiful in the snow and this might be the last we get this year. There's plenty of room. Family dinner on Sunday at their house this weekend because it's Harper's birthday."

"I feel like I'm coming undone," she whispered. "Like I'm losing myself. Last night...I..."

He tightened his hold. "I don't think you're losing yourself, Gia. I don't think that's it at all. I think maybe you're finding yourself."

"You do?"

"Mm." He rested his lips on her head. "I do."

Soft like this, fierce, joyful, sexy, angry, sad, he loved every part of her being. He wanted to give her some peace. And he still had work to do, apparently to prove himself to her.

***

"Oh, how beautiful," Ava whispered in awe as she gazed into the caged area with the seven newborn puppies.

"One day old," Danny said in awe. "They're so tiny."

Gia had her arms around her kids while they all watched the puppies sleep curled around each other and tucked into their mama. "I've never seen a puppy this young before."

"I think today sounds like a good day to make popcorn and watch a movie," May said. "Later, if it keeps up, we can go play in the snow."

Hugh's dad came in from the back. "Coming down nicely out there now," Drake said. "Not too wild, peaceful."

"I love watching the snow fall," Danny said.

"Me too," Ava echoed. The kids climbed onto the padded window seat.

Hugh put his hand on Gia's back and nudged her toward the back door. "Come with me? For a bit?"

That shell-shocked look from last night was still there, not as strong, but she was struggling with something, with many things he suspected.

He found an old beanie of his and put it on her head. Her curls stuck out at the end and damn, she was cute. Now he needed to rosy those pale cheeks and coax some life into her. He passed her an extra pair of boots and Gia obliged him by kicking off her sneakers and stepping into the basic black rubber boots lined with gray fur. A pair of yellow mittens followed.

"After how I lost my temper last night, you still want to be around me?"

His heart couldn't take her vulnerable offerings. "I always want to be around you, Gia. I want to know all of you."

"Okay," she whispered. A concession, finally.

He tugged her outside and wrapped her in his arms so they could watch the snow together. He whispered, honoring the quiet of the land. "You make a cute snow bunny."

She gripped his arms. "I remember my first snow." Her voice was hushed, reverent. "I was seven, I think. Gosh, I haven't thought about that in a long, long time. It was my mom, Francesca, and I. We woke up and the world was covered in white and I couldn't believe how beautiful it was. It was one of those wet snows. My boots were too big, and they kept getting stuck in the snow, so I'd lift my foot to walk and my boot would stay behind."

"Good memory." he said.

"The best," she whispered. "I don't have very many of...well...I think I shoved a lot of memories away along with...I think I used to have a connection to the snow, a special one, and I don't even remember that anymore."

"Mm." He nuzzled into her neck. Another clue about how difficult her life had been.

"I don't know how or why, but I want..."

"You want what?"

She turned to face him, holding his hand. "To make new memories. Ones I can hold onto."

He smiled. Hugh wanted to make memories with his pretty snow bunny too. "I want to show you something." He twined his fingers through hers and silently led her across the field toward the forest.

"Hugh?" Gia asked. "Do you think..." She paused to study the landscape turning white around them. "Am I doing this?" She lifted her eyes to the sky and her hand to catch the white flakes drifting to the ground.

"The snow?"

She nodded.

"I don't know." He squeezed her hand. "It doesn't feel like it. Your pulse beats differently when your magic appears. And your eyes often shimmer. And when...when your magic is out of control, or heightened, maybe, I'm not sure, sparks light along your skin, or leap from your eyes."

"I didn't..." She shook her head. "I learned...saw...last night. Lots of things. Marie said it's not good to keep my powers shunted, but I didn't realize I had them. I don't *know* myself. I don't really know you, but I want to. Please don't...please be patient with me."

Please don't leave.

He could practically feel her heart beating with those words. Didn't she know? He'd never leave her.

"There's a lot we haven't talked about, but learning about your powers seems pretty monumental. How does it feel? How do you feel?"

"Electrified. Shocked, Curious. Scared. Marie said she'd help me learn and practice. Both Francesca and I lack so much knowledge."

"Does it feel insurmountable?" he asked, taking both her hands.

"No. Maybe." She huffed out a laugh.

"So, we have some things to work on, some things to learn about each other, some things to help each other with, so many things to talk about."

Tentatively, she nodded.

"You said you don't really know me, and that's why I brought you out here." They stood at the edge of the forest. "I want to show you. I'd like to keep showing you until you have all of me." He nudged her farther in.

Eyes and smile wide, she said, "You're sure?"

"I've been wanting to, Gia." Suddenly he was feeling nervous. People might say they were fine with it, but saying and seeing were two different things. "I'm comfortable with my wolf, but not everyone in the world is. But you...you are my mate." There, he'd said it.

She didn't balk or run scared. She simply softened and smiled at him, like he'd given her a gift.

"Please show me," she whispered and stood on her toes to rest her warm lips on his.

Hugh kissed her, taking her warmth and devouring her mouth. This, this was what he craved, this frenzy moving through his blood for her. Desire so deep it was elemental. Cupping her head, he kissed and nipped at her lip, moved his lips down her jaw to trace the fine skin of her neck, every beautiful part of her beating there for him.

Then, before he lost all control, he stepped away and let go of her hands. Stripping, he watched her eyes rake over him and heat. Watched pricks of her light swirl around her. He could feel his body changing. His wolf always started in his eyes first. When he was naked, he said, "Ready?"

At her nod, he stepped back several paces, ran, and leapt, twirling through the air while the changes spiraled through his body.

Chapter Fifty

B EAUTIFUL SOARING BRILLIANCE. A fierce energy rang through the forest as her mate changed before her eyes, from a man to a wolf, a werewolf. Gia stood still. She held her hands, palms open, at her sides and watched the enormous werewolf land on all four paws. Powerful muscular body. His fur was jet black with flecks of silver and goldish brown. He pawed his way toward her. His eyes were purely golden now, aimed right at her, seeing, she felt, with her whole being, to the heart of her, knowing her, loving her.

The power was overwhelming. Desire, dreams, the beating of fated souls struck across the forest floor with each step he took. His power into hers, hers into his, pulses of lightning illuminating the sky, each strike an intense, eye-opening, heart-shattering love. Her heart sang their song. Quietly, he made his way to her, stopping with his head close enough for her to touch. It was up to her. She took the final step, reached out her hand, and caressed his cheek and up to his head.

His fur was coarse and soft, a beautiful blend. When she scratched his head, he let out a huff of relief, desire, love. Then he bent and leaned in until he was touching her collarbone with his nose, sniffing at her, nuzzling her.

A joyous laugh burst out of her, and she wrapped her arms around his neck. He pawed at her and nearly knocked her down, but captured her before she hit the ground, tumbling with her gently, holding her, keeping her safe in his limbs. He set her on her feet and nudged her toward his back.

Without hesitation, Gia grabbed hold of his fur, climbed on, and wrapped her arms around him. He stood and walked a few paces, then she gave him a squeeze to let him know she was okay. He trotted, raising and lowering his head playfully. Finally, with her holding on, he ran.

Gia had never felt anything so wondrous and fantastic. Air rushed over her, through her, his power beat under her hands, the strength of him. He ran through the woods as if he had the ground beneath him memorized, as if it was in his blood. She supposed it was. Never once did she feel fear or worry. Her body melded to his, moved with his across his ancestors' land, alongside a rushing creek and snow-packed banks.

At first, she held on tightly and watched the scenery pass before her, learning not only her love in this shifted form but the world he shared with her. And even in winter, the land beat with a life force, with a crisp, electric energy, with a whole new meaning. The scent of pine needles underfoot, dampened by snow, the clean, shocking splash on her hands when he leapt through a stream, the peaceful quiet of nature at rest.

After a while, she tucked her cold face in the fur at his neck and breathed him in. Snow had crusted on parts of his fur, but buried in deep he was still so warm, radiating that heat that she loved fiercely. He was beautiful. He was love. He was hers. And she held on and breathed, and dreamed of a love like this, his love, that could really belong to her.

Chapter Fifty-One

"Come into work with me, please," Hugh said. "I have to be at Webb Industrial today for an appointment. Dad and Grant want to talk to you about doing more work for us to accelerate our investing and charities." They'd left the farm this morning, full of May's cinnamon rolls, after a peaceful weekend of family, kids, celebration, and loving. He hadn't wanted to leave.

A pang of warning tunneled through his body when he woke this morning. It got worse as they dropped the kids at school. Every cell in his body screamed at him to keep Gia safe, more so than what felt normal. He couldn't settle his anxiety; it was live and on edge, pulsing in his eyes, thundering in his brain.

"It sounds like you're inventing things for me to do," Gia said. Her face had more color, and she had a sleepy, joyous expression. "I do not need a babysitter, especially not three of you." She laughed.

He wanted to bathe in her laughter, but he…he… Fuck, was he the one having a panic attack this time? "I'd feel better with you close." The clanging warning in his head nearly made him scream the words at her. Could she not hear him?

"I can take care of myself, Hugh." She reached out and took his hand. "And I have to find Orin and talk to him."

"The hell?" He removed his hand and put it on the steering wheel, trying to control the shaking fury at her statement. "I tell you I'm worried about you and your first response is to say you're going to find the mercenary you've been working for?"

"I have to," she insisted. Her own anger was no match for his at this moment. "I have a few choice words for him. And I want closure."

"Gia! He's a madman!"

"You don't even know him." She huffed and faced the window.

Do you? He took a deep breath. "You've been running around the world, what? Killing people at his request?" Christ, he couldn't understand any of it.

"You have no idea what I've been working toward!" The air between them zapped with electricity. Sparks shot from her fingers.

Beautiful, frustrating woman!

"Because you don't trust me enough to tell me! Meanwhile, you're putting yourself and your kids in danger."

"I'm doing this to keep them safe." She exploded out of the SUV as soon as he'd parked in her driveway.

"Going after who, criminals?" He followed, nearly breaking his car door with the force of his anger. He was incredulous. She unlocked her door and stormed inside. Fuck, how many heart attacks was one man supposed to endure over his love?

"Yes!" she raged, finger in his face, cheeks flushed, magic humming around her.

God damn. It wasn't fair that every time they fought, he wanted to fuck her.

"You think they've been safe with some crazy man walking around this earth?" she yelled.

Crazy man? "What are you talking about? Leave the criminals to the police, the international whatever, CIA, FBI."

"Oh please!" she scoffed. "They do nothing. They don't *know.* Nobody does." Her body shook with the force of her anger. "Is it because I'm a woman, that you don't think I'm capable, that you—"

"No!" It was his turn to explode. "Because you're precious! And I don't want anything to happen to you!" He felt like he was missing something, but no fucking way was she going to see Orin. "Gia, please listen to me. I need you to be safe. I need you. Listen to reason, please. Don't take you away from me. Don't risk that."

Her phone rang.

That god damned phone!

"Leave it. Talk to me, Gia. Right here, right now."

"My..." her phone buzzed again at the same time his did.

"Fuck," he swore and let her go. He could barely hold his hand steady to read the text that had come in from Niko.

"It's Francesca," Gia said. "She's at the hospital. I have to go."

"I'm going with you."

"You need to go to work, Hugh."

"Gia, I swear, one of these times we will not be interrupted. But right now, they need both of us. No way in hell I'm letting you face a crazed lust demon without my help. Don't you want your sister to have all the help she can?"

"Fine." She ran upstairs. He suspected to put her knives on, and he stalked to the car to wait for her. He texted his father and asked him to cancel his appointments or see if Grant could work with them. He couldn't wait for the day when his biggest frustration was a wonky gear on a prosthetic limb, for Christ's sake.

She raced to the car with her laptop bag and a scowl on her face. "Is it okay for me to say I don't want anything to happen to you either? Or is that reserved for overbearing males?" She huffed. Deep red flicks of light snaking out with her breath.

Hugh couldn't help it, even as pissed as he was, he grinned. "I would be delighted to hear you say you don't want anything to happen to me."

***

Police had set up a checkpoint at each hospital entry. Something serious was definitely happening.

"Detective Mason, good to see you," Hugh said with Gia by his side. "This is Gia Reily. Her sister works here, Francesca Banetti."

"Yep, you two can go on in. Be careful. Bad shit happening. Another serial killer victim."

Hugh nodded at his friend and led Gia inside to find her sister.

A violent smell of evil met Hugh when they entered, which meant it was worse than he'd thought because the hospital was already a hotbed of potent scents for a werewolf. He had to take steady breaths and soothe his wolf to calm the fuck down. It didn't work. Neither he nor his wolf were anywhere close to calm.

"Where are the kids, honey?" Francesca's voice stole through the madness.

"At school," Hugh answered. "They're protected."

"I already cast a basic protection spell around the school," Gia huffed. "I don't need your help."

"You do," he shot back. "You're not safe." *Not here and not at your home.*

"I'm as safe as I've ever been," she insisted.

He scowled at her. From the state of things, she hadn't been *safe* in a very long time.

"I promise, I would never knowingly put my babies in danger," Gia whispered, leaning into him. "You know that."

Hugh closed his eyes and breathed in her warmth, her scent. "I do." He was practically growling. This place, the situation they were in, all the unsaid things left between them were getting to him. He needed this to be finished, then he needed to fuck her into next week and spend hours taking care of her and her kids, giving her the safe, joyful life she deserved. "I...I care. And something extremely dangerous and old is at play here and..."

Foul demon! His wolf was trying to claw his way out in a frenzy. His eyes burned out of control. "Don't leave the hospital. Don't go anywhere without me," he ordered, then strode down the corridor, following the ancient scent of Asmodeus. He was running by the time he found the morgue. Niko and the pathologist, Augustus Clarke, stood over a grotesquely destroyed body.

"What the fuck?" Hugh swore.

"Holy shit, Hugh Webb?" Augustus asked.

"You know this asshole?" Niko said. And Hugh might have smirked if the situation wasn't so dire. He and Niko were practically friends now.

Augustus was speaking, but all Hugh could hear was the ringing in his head. "I recognize that scent," Hugh said. "That body is covered with our lust demon's scent."

Chapter Fifty-Two

Gia took steady breaths on the eerily peaceful sunny afternoon. She'd trained extensively to go unnoticed. She excelled at it. And now that she was learning more about how her energy moved through the world, she was intent on maintaining control of her emotions during this mission.

They'd determined who the lust demon was, a doctor who worked with both Francesca and Niko. A demented creature out for Francesca's blood, but hell-bent on creating chaos before Francesca succumbed. None of them were going to let this demon kill Francesca. Right now, Gia, her sister, Niko, and Augustus all followed Hugh who was tracking it.

Hugh. He'd said he was hers and she was his. A mantra she ached to believe with all her heart, with every sin in her soul that damned her to be alone for the rest of her life. A fate she'd been resigned to until he'd sauntered into her life and pushed at every excuse she gave him. Every moment since they'd met, her heart had been weaving its way into his. How had she ever thought she could stop it? And this weekend, seeing his wolf. No more brilliant magic had she ever witnessed. Magic to behold and love, not to hide and shun from the world. He was teaching her things she'd thought herself too afraid to hope for.

Without speaking, the five of them crept along a worn path into the woods by Crystal Lake, where most of the victims of this evil creature had been found. Thankfully, they'd all agreed that Hugh would not go alone. They were in this together and they would go as a powerful team. No way in hell she was letting Hugh go off on his own to battle something so malicious.

As difficult as it had been for her to admit because fear had sliced a cold shard into her heart at the thought of loving Hugh only to lose him, she wanted to keep him safe too. She wanted to tell him everything, to share all the broken parts of herself with him. He'd shown her his wolf. He'd loved her from the beginning, cared for her, brought her back to life. And she wanted to grab onto that life and soar with him.

Maybe it's time to give up my quest for vengeance. Maybe she could rest now and simply enjoy the life she had and all the gifts she'd been given. Maybe it wasn't her responsibility to fight every last evil. She needed no closure from Orin; it was her responsibility to be finished with that part of her life. An enormous pulse of negative breath seeped out of her with the knowledge

She was lighter, freer. Pretty magenta sparks spiraled from her fingertips. A small smile lit her face. After today, she would tell Hugh everything. She couldn't wait to see the smile on his face when she finally gave herself to him, heart, mind, and soul, no matter her wounds and trauma. He's said he'd care for them and she believed him. Love. True, heart-spinning love. It was hers for the taking. She'd never been so lucky in her life.

Joy and worry tumbled together inside her, but now was the time for focus. Everything else, all her pent-up emotions, her need to expose her truths to Hugh, could wait. Their group turned toward the crowded trees, losing the sunshine when they made their way farther into the forest.

The scent of hate assaulted Gia, and she nearly cowered at it. Bold, vicious, hovering.

"Wait," Hugh ordered, and for once she obeyed him.

That smell...a tangled root full of disease dug into the soil, so deep Gia couldn't see its origin. *It can mask its scent.* Was it doing that now? The world blurred before her. She focused on her inner visions and tried to see, but as she followed the scent, it connected like a coiled rope of poison right into her sister's heart.

As she opened her mouth to scream, a fierce wind blasted through the air, taking all her breath. Everything spiraled and flung out around her and she tried to reach into her own powers, but a limb snapped off a tree and pummeled her.

Pain. Evil. We're surrounded by evil.

"Nooo. Gia." She heard the words in her mind, in that voice she loved. Warmth and safety surrounded her, tunneled with her into a jarring, cushioned fall.

***

Warm breath on her shoulder, panting, a paw on her face. Hugh?

Agony tore through her head. Memories surged and invaded. A baby, alone, doing nothing to help as her father was killed. She'd shed no tears, hiding from...something. Blank pages inside her for so many years. Afraid to make memories. Finally, a few safe ones with Mama and Frankie. Then fear, running, being chased. More hiding. Her mother's screams. A man sneaking out the window. Alone with her sister. Trusting no one until a warmth snuck past her defenses. Doug and babies. But then red blood was everywhere, someone stabbing her with a knife to the heart over and over. Silent screams sucked down deep. Always afraid. And the pain came, pushing on her heart, reminding her, warning her.

"Gia? There you are. It's Hugh."

It hurt to open her eyes; it hurt to keep them closed. Hugh was there, furiously putting on his clothes, and then kneeling by her side, holding her head still.

"Christ, you're okay?" So gently he rested his forehead on hers.

The warmth was immediate, the pain too, stabbing into her head, crippling her heart. "No." She shook her head. *I can't do this. I can't have this. A singed orange warning. This beautiful man can never be mine.* She tried to take a breath, but a weight squeezed her chest. Her whole body hurt.

"Over here," he turned and yelled. "She hit her head."

Paramedics were there, jostling her. *Oh, fuck!* She turned her head in time and threw up in the forest.

Someone put a water bottle in front of her, and she rinsed out her mouth. It felt like she'd spent hours running for her life.

"Hey." Hugh was right there brushing the tears off her cheeks. "It's okay. It's finished. We're going to get you checked out."

"No."

"Yes," Hugh insisted.

She turned away from the blanch of fear in his eyes. Her stomach rolled again, but she took short breaths to stem the nausea while she answered the paramedic's questions. She was oozing out annoyance and fear at everyone around her, but by the goddesses, the pain was excruciating.

Everything that had just happened had been a warning to her. She didn't deserve any more good in her life. Especially not Hugh. She couldn't stomach losing him, and she couldn't put him through losing her. Gia closed her eyes to him, to love, to everything.

CHAPTER FIFTY-THREE

HE. WAS. FURIOUS. THEY'D been home from the hospital for two days. Two days of him caring for her and her bearing it in silence. She spoke to be polite, barely. And she wouldn't meet his eyes. Fuck polite. Fuck avoidance. And fuck this silence.

She seemed to be getting good sleep, which helped her body, but maybe she was simply using sleep to put distance between them. Putting all those guards up again, or trying to. She was doing a piss-poor job of it, though, because he didn't need to see fear in her eyes to know she was afraid. The scent of it leaked from every pore on her body.

The kids, he suspected, also sensed something was wrong. They were abnormally quiet, and Danny was back to being a stoic old man. Both kids glued themselves to Gia's side every second they were home from school.

He needed to run before he lost his very last shred of control around her. So he'd called in reinforcements. Niko and Francesca stood in the doorway.

"Didn't invite you," Hugh said. He was only half serious. Honestly, he was grateful to leave the kids with as many powerful beings who loved them as he could.

Niko raised his eyebrow and held up the rectangular box in his arms. "I have a game to win against Danny. He's beaten me twice now."

Hugh wasn't surprised that Danny had beaten Niko. The boy had wiped the chess board with Hugh every time they'd played like a grandmaster who had been practicing for fifty years. He *was* surprised the vampire admitted losing. But Hugh suspected being in love with Francesca had softened him.

"How is she?" Francesca asked, wrapping him in a hug. She radiated healing even when she wasn't in her doctor's scrubs.

"Stubborn," Hugh said, then tried to soften his tone and offer her more. "Physically, she's doing better, I think. What the hell do I know?" He studied Francesca. The two sisters were close. "Maybe she'll talk to you. Thanks for...uh...thanks for coming. I have to go." He grabbed his jacket and keys to his SUV. On the way out, he made eye contact with Niko.

"Nothing will happen to them while I'm here," Niko swore.

Hugh nodded. "Thank you."

Quickly he drove to the road connecting the Webb family farm and Gia's property. When dusk hit, he left his clothes, and he ran. He ran for hours, through the massive red cedars clustered so tightly together hardly anything grew underneath them, through the new growth white pines rising from the ashes of a fire that had decimated a hundred acres during a summer years ago, onto where the boulders spilled into the river, up over the cliffs and across the fields. He was alone. And he fucking hated it.

The night was cloudy, but calm, peaceful, almost, except for all the turmoil in his mind and body, in his heart. His instincts resonated that he still had a battle to fight, and with no knowledge of how to fight it. He pushed his body beyond what he was used to, and then he ran farther, punishing himself for not being enough for Gianna Reily.

When he'd exhausted every bone in his body, he walked the trail back, sweaty and contemplative. And with his anger spent, he tried to formulate a plan to become worthy of her, to shatter all her barriers, and finally get her to share all of herself with him. This was like no battle he'd ever fought. It felt like it would take more than magic for him to be good enough for her to love him.

Chapter Fifty-Four

"Honey, you're crying." Francesca stepped out onto the back porch where Gia sat on an old wicker sofa she'd found at a secondhand shop in the hills. She and the kids had recovered the cushions with fabric printed in bold, red strawberries. Ava's pick. It wasn't perfect but it was comfortable. Or it usually was. Not so much when she hadn't slept in days, because, because…her fear had been eating her alive.

"He left," Gia said through her tears, wiping them away as they came. His anger and hurt had been a thriving energy in the house since they'd fought Francesca's demon, since Gia had been knocked unconscious, since she'd thought to close herself off from him. It hadn't worked, but she was so weak, she'd let her fear overtake her. And now…

"I mean…" She tried to fight the onslaught, but it wouldn't stop. And she wasn't alone in the shower this time, where no one could see her tears. It was impossible to shove them away.

Even as she tried to focus and understand what the hell had happened to her emotions over the last few days.

"I pushed him away. I did this...keep doing this. I know why he left, but it hurts so damn much. I didn't expect this ripping in my heart. I...I..."

Francesca sat by her side and wrapped Gia in a hug, pulling her head into her chest. How the hell was everyone else so warm, and she was so cold? Francesca's magic wove into Gia's frozen body, reaching out with its healing threads.

"You thought if you didn't tell him, didn't let yourself believe it, that it would mean you didn't really love him."

"How are you so smart? I'm so...so weak and dumb and I'm a coward!" Her words were muffled in her sister's body, but distinguishable.

"You, my beloved sister, are brave and amazing. You are not a coward. You are not weak, honey. Your heart is excruciatingly sensitive, and you have endured enough heartbreak to last ten million lifetimes. Of course you're scared to let him in. You don't believe your heart can bear to lose another person. The truth is that your heart can't bear *not* to love that man. He illuminates your world, my love. Literally. Sparks fly between the two of you." Francesca let out a small chuckle.

"True," Gia whispered. "How weird is that?"

"Not weird. Freaking wondrous. Magical."

"Yeah." Gia sighed into Francesca's warmth. "Magical."

"To see your special powers emanating from you..." Francesca wiped her own tears. "It makes me so happy, Gi. It's been so long. Too long."

"It's time to study our gifts, isn't it?" Gia whispered.

"Yes. Now...why are you not letting me pull away?"

Gia held tight and spoke into her sister's chest. "Because I got snot and tears all over you, and I can't bear to see how I ruined your pretty blouse."

Francesca laughed, gave Gia one more squeeze, then untangled herself. Reluctantly, Gia let her. The damage wasn't too bad, but she sure missed the warmth.

"Listen, we are not alone anymore. You are not alone. We have each other, we have Niko and Marie, we have those adorable kids of yours, we have more friends and family than we've ever allowed ourselves to dream of. And if you want it, you have Hugh. There's no way that man is letting you go this easy. He didn't abandon you. I think he needed some space to figure out how to battle your stubborn misbelief that you're not good enough for him. Now is our time to come into our powers, our true selves, and to be happy. We deserve it, Gia. We have lived hidden in silence and alone for too long."

"You believe that?" Gia looked to her big sister for knowledge, for strength.

"I feel it in my heart and soul and in my own magic that is pulsing to life."

"And that all has to do with your vampire?"

Francesca grinned. "It has to do with love and acceptance. And some of the lessons I've had with Marie. I finally get to be my true self. But mostly love. Love is a powerful force all on its own. I think it's what kept you and me going all those years. The love we have for each other. Don't you?"

Gia nodded and took a big gulp of air before she started crying again. The air changed around her. It wasn't coming from within her. No, it...he...

"Look," Francesca said, turning Gia to face the backyard.

He came back. Hugh stood at the edge of her yard, still half in the trees, nearly covered by darkness, formidable, and...he looked fucking exhausted. Otherwise, Gia couldn't tell a thing from his expression. It was one she'd never seen before, almost blank. He'd closed himself off from her. And it was her fault. She'd done that.

"I'll leave you two alone. Yell if you need anything." Francesca slid off the sofa.

Right before she went inside Hugh said, "You and Niko feel free to take off now."

Frankie glanced at Gia, then at Hugh. She winked and then she was gone.

Was Hugh sending them away so he could break her heart while she was alone? Was he going to do it quickly, then leave too? She stood, the blanket falling around her. She sat back down. She didn't know what to do. Frankie had talked about love being powerful, but to Gia love and magic felt similar, parts of herself she'd shoved so deep inside she felt incapable of retrieving them. Worse, they were twisted up with guilt, with shame.

"You left," she blurted out.

"I thought that's what you wanted." He wasn't giving her an inch, and he was still so far away. Not touching her was too far away.

What did she want? That was what she had to ask herself. No, she didn't. She knew. It started as a spark the night they met, and no matter how she tried to smother it… "You came back. I thought…I thought you left for good."

"Never," he vowed, walking toward her.

Hope warred with the fear inside her. He reached for her and ran his fingers along her cheek, catching her tears. She melted her body into his. "Hugh."

He tilted her head so they were gazing at each other. "I had to run, had to get some of my frustration and anger out."

"Anger at me?"

"Yes, woman. You keep pushing me away, locking me out. What in the goddess's name do I have to do to get you to trust me, open to me? You are mine," he growled, cupping her face gently with his warm hands. He was so careful with her, even when he was mad. His eyes were on fire, like his wolf was trying to come out. "And I. Am. Yours. I want to be yours so much, Gianna Reily."

Fear tried to leap to the surface, but so was something else. Her magic, pulsing, thriving, not beaten into a dark hole. It was shooting those beautiful sparks off of her in brilliant magentas, in passionate reds. Even the orange was vibrant and alive, a phoenix climbing out of the fire.

"Talk to me, please," he begged.

There was so much stillness around them. She could hear their hearts beating. "I want so badly for you to be mine," her words were the quietest hushed whisper. Another tear slid down her cheek. "But...but...Hugh, everybody I love gets murdered."

Chapter Fifty-Five

With one hushed sentence, she broke his heart into a million aching shards. Silence ripped between them. Like after a fighter jet rips through the air and is gone in a flash, taking all the air with it. Whoosh. Knocking over everything in its path. For those split seconds, everything is suspended.

In an instant, his entire world changed.

"What?" he whispered, holding her head closer, sending all his warmth into her, looking deep into her eyes. Eyes that were partially shadowed, with hints of green trying to break through, and the fiery flecks shooting out. The fire was on her skin too. And he didn't have to see behind him to feel the wind whipping around the house.

"First, my dad was killed when I was a baby. I was too young to remember, but somehow I do. I have this image of a sweeping arm cutting a line across my dad's throat. It was a thunderstorm outside. I think that's why I remember it. That's the sole memory I have of him. I didn't even...I didn't even cry, Hugh, to alert anyone."

What was she talking about? A baby alerting someone?

"Years later...someone killed my mother. I was fourteen. She made Francesca and me hide, but I snuck out and ran downstairs in time to hear her scream. Her killer stole out the window, almost as if they were flying like in a dream or rather a nightmare, out into the pouring rain. I knew something bad was going to happen that night. I knew. And then..."

Hugh locked her in his arms. Her tears spilled out with her words. God fucking damn it. He knew she'd been scared to love him, but this was, this was... "And then?" he asked, afraid to hear the answer, but knowing he had to let her speak it. And he would hold it, whatever it was, for her.

"Someone murdered my husband, Doug, three years ago. I...I...we were gone, the kids and I. I didn't feel right when we were gone. And when we got home, I could smell something...wrong. It was the dry cracked earth of a thousand-year desert, or old broken bones if they have a smell. A heart snuffed out under the burn of liquid fire. That's what I smelled. It was awful. I was the one who...I found him in our bed.

"And...I think all of them are connected to magic, to my magic, to me, somehow. I'm the link. So I hid...I hide who I really am. When I found Orin, I thought I could uncover Doug's killer, the crazy man I mentioned. I got caught up in taking down evil men for revenge. I learned to kill with knives.

They became my security. I'm so ashamed. I've been awful to you because I'm so afraid, Hugh."

All he could do was clasp her tighter and wrap himself around her. He tucked her head into his chest and held on. He wasn't sure when his tears mixed with hers.

"My Gia, my love. I am so, so sorry." How in the world was she still surviving, moving, and functioning each day?

"*I'm* sorry." Her tears choked her.

"No, darlin'. You don't have a thing to be sorry for. And you haven't hidden all of you from me. You've given and given, trusted me even when your furious mind told you not to. You trust me with your kids, to care for you, with your emotions. Even when you're fighting me, you lean into me."

"I do?"

God damn it, she seemed so broken, so vulnerable, so small. Yet at the same time, she was fierce and brilliant. "Yes." He chuckled. "You even offer parts of yourself in your sleep. You talk in your sleep."

She gasped. "No."

He nodded. "Sometimes you cast spells. Often it's a phrase or two. You told me...you told me..." Now it was his turn to be vulnerable. "I make you feel free," he whispered.

"Oh, Hugh." Her crooked smile broke out of her face. "You do. It's...you're so good at everything and so good to me, and I ache to have you. And I tried not to. I tried hard to push you away. I did, Hugh. I swear. I'm such a failure. I'm not good at anything. I failed and I...can't feel bad about it, because I want you so much."

Even now, she made him laugh. He lifted her and sat on the sofa, curving her body onto his. He ran his thumb over her bottom lip. "I'm glad you want me. I'm glad you told me. And you are not a failure. You are the strongest, fiercest, bravest person I've ever met. I'm in awe." He pulled up the weird-shaped blanket that was usually inside on their sofa and placed it around her shoulders. "What is this anyway?"

"Sylvia, a blanket I tried to crochet," she said. "You're probably good at crochet too." There was that adorable pout of hers again. "I tried to be good at it, to be a good mom, do the things moms do." She fell into his chest and pulled the blanket over her head.

He chuckled. "Gia. You're one of the best moms I've ever met. You shower them with love. You take great care of them, protect them, hug them, and read to them. You make sure they have a happy, safe life. Those are mom things. You're doing it all by yourself."

She let him rub her back and, as the minutes fell away, her heart calmed with his. The sparks were threading into her skin. "I don't have many memories. I think...somehow I taught myself not to make any."

"Gia, love. You're killing me here. Is that why you name inanimate objects?"

"What?"

"Delly, Bess, Sylvia? Friends who will never hurt you or be hurt by you?"

"God." She hid her face in his neck. "I'm ridiculous."

"No, honey. Precious. And lonely."

After a moment she whispered, "I worry every day that the kids will be next, or Francesca...that... What if I can't keep my family safe? What if I can't keep you safe? What if I let myself love you only to lose you? That's what I can't bear. That's why I'm so afraid to love you. But I do, Hugh. I love you so much I can't help it anymore. I don't want to fight it. I've been fighting so hard for...for all the wrong things. I can't do that anymore. I want you and me and my kids, together."

"You're not alone anymore, Gianna. I'm here to help and support you and love you. Listen to me, not one of those awful tragedies was your fault, okay?"

She took a few deep, shaggy breaths. "Okay," she finally whispered.

They sat in the silence of the dark night, wrapped in each other, letting the warmth calm them.

"I'm ready to be done with my quest for vengeance too," she whispered, pulling away slightly so they were eye to eye. The emotions felt lighter around them with her admission. "I want to...can we try to have a normal life?"

He huffed out a laugh, and she joined him.

"I mean, I don't know how normal a witch, a werewolf, and two witch kids can honestly be," she said softly.

Hugh rested his forehead against hers. "More kissing and laughter, less chasing evil?"

"Yes, please," Gia said and then she kissed him, lighting up the night around them with her brilliant sparks. "I love you, Hugh Webb, more than the moon and the stars and all the snowflakes in the sky. I'm yours and you're mine."

His heart beat for her now, more fully than it ever had. And he could feel her love spilling into him. Mates forever.

Chapter Fifty-Six

"You okay?" Hugh asked, putting one hand on her hip to draw her inside and shut the side door. He traced his fingers along her cheek and down her neck as if that was his way of checking in on her, taking the pulse of her. She couldn't help but lean fully into him, gravitating toward his body warmth.

Her hair was wet, half her clothes were soaked from the rainstorm she'd started and then directed across the backyard of Niko and Francesca's house. But it didn't matter now. Nothing mattered except where she got to come home to, *who* she got to come home to. "Perfect," she whispered and stretched up to her tiptoes to kiss him.

He returned the kiss like she'd been gone for months, not hours, taking the kiss deep and heating her up quickly, sending her into a million warm shivers.

"Good day?" His voice rumbled through her lips and straight to her core.

"Amazing." She'd spent all day with Francesca, Willow, and Marie learning about her magic, practicing spells, figuring out how to unbury her witch instincts. They'd been gathering once a week for a month now. Gia was already feeling more confident, and Marie had said that's because it was natural for them to know their powers, not hide them.

It helped her to see Francesca embracing and loving her own powers. And while Marie was an expert and very patient, Willow brought whimsy and fantastical delight to their practice sessions. She also brought her spring strawberry doughnuts Gia was certain were sprinkled in magic.

"Kids are asleep. They had a blast. Got to ride horses." Hugh led her to each bedroom door so she could see for herself. He knew her well, her need to see with her own eyes that her kids were okay. He didn't seem to mind this quirk of hers as he liked to check on them too. But truthfully, he didn't seem to mind any of her quirks. Her absolutely awful knitting and crocheting that she was determined to get right someday, her need to be touching him throughout the night. She was touching him now. No, he never seemed to mind her touching him.

"What did you learn today, love? Hmm?" He twirled her into his arms after they shut Danny's bedroom door, walking her backward down the hall. His fingers ran through her wet hair, and he kissed raindrops from her cheeks.

She loved sharing with him all the things she was learning about herself, her sister, witches in general. But as Hugh nuzzled her, kissed her, and snuck his fingers under her shirt to the bare skin above her leggings, teasing her so well, she didn't want to talk now. Then he snaked his hand between the fabric and her body, bypassing her panties altogether, palming her butt, making her whimper with need. "Hugh?"

"Love." He called her that often now, with that sexy shimmer in his eyes. He reached his other hand in too until the bare skin of his hands was branding her, sending strips of fire across her. He chuckled, and she felt that too, zapping through her.

"Love the way you light up for me, beautiful woman."

Gia gave a small jump and wrapped her legs around him. She threw back her head as he kissed her neck. She did light up for him, and she was no longer afraid to show it. Ahh, it was amazing to be herself, to be free with him, safe and full of desire, letting all her emotions show, showering him with love the way he did her.

He had her leggings and underwear off in a whoosh before he set her on their bed, in their dark bedroom. Gah, she giggled. Their bed. Together. Because since that night she'd told him all her secrets, he'd never left.

"Love the way you light the dark, how your colors twirl and spin in delight." It was true. The way her magic flamed with him, for him, was pure joy and passion and love. Everything had changed. Her ability to control and wield her magic and the way her true self, her witch responded to him, performed for him, even in everyday normal life. Although, she would hardly call their life normal. But she could call it extraordinarily beautiful.

When he came over her, he wasted no time diving his hands under her sweatshirt and swooping it off.

"Hugh." God, he could play and charm her body with his smooth agility. He was so skillful. Man or wolf, she loved watching him move. He pressed his body into hers, peppering kisses along her skin, snagging her bra down, and teasing her nipple with his tongue, while his eyes caught hers and heated.

She arched toward his talented mouth, while everywhere his fingers touched her, sparks leapt and twirled off her to him, her magic reaching for him. With deft hands, he flipped her body over and she let out a huff of a laugh again. She didn't mind feeling weightless in his arms because he would make her soar, and then bring her back, always grounding her to him.

"Need you naked, right now. Missed you." He whipped off her bra and sighed as he smoothed his hands over her back.

"I was only gone a few hours," she said, but her words lacked any sense of ridiculousness because she'd missed him too.

"I miss you anytime you're separated from me. That's the power of our mated bond. That's the power of our love. I want you to go and do and fly, but I also ache when I can't touch you."

She turned her face to the side, smiling at him. He smoothed his thumbs over each notch in her spine. The feeling was incredible. The way his touch sent heat zapping all the way to her soul.

He caressed and massaged each muscle, whispering words into the night. "Beautiful, soft skin." Lighting her up with each breath.

He repeated the movements until his thumbs trailed in between her thighs, teasing, marking her. He came over her this time as his hands made their way back up her body, linking his fingers with hers and raising her hands above her head, pressing the full length of his body into hers. He placed small kisses along the back of her neck and shoulders.

A tickle fluttered through her and she laughed until he licked and nipped at her neck, causing her to moan as shivers of desire danced along her skin. His hard cock rested against her. Clasping both her hands with one of his, he brought his other underneath to wrap around her waist and nudge her body up enough so he could slide his fingers into her wetness. Hot and aching and so wet for him. He toyed with her there, driving her up and, without making her wait, he guided his cock into her from behind.

How big and hard he was, slowly pushing inside her. One achingly beautiful thrust after another as he kissed and sucked at her neck and shoulders, praising her with his touch and his words. She could feel every inch of him inside her and the weight of him sliding along her body.

Her magic responded in a flurry, linking to him, to their bond, the one he spoke of often and so fondly, like a man who'd been waiting for his true love for ages and been absolutely delighted to have found it in her. That's what he brought to their lives, among so many things, pure delight and love. She shivered under his touch, under all this glorious love. Hugh tightened his hold and sped up his thrusts.

"Mine," he whispered, trailing his hand down her side, his body bowed over hers. He snaked his fingers back around to her front, finding their connection. He pulled her hip to the side, opening her further to him, and then used his fingers to tease her clit, while he moved in and out of her from behind, holding her preciously between him. She was high and languid and floating, fluttering against his hand.

"More, please. I need you."

"You always have me."

With each movement, he grew harder inside her, speeding up, forcing her to feel the rasp of his body along hers, every glorious inch until she exploded and her magic flew apart around them.

"Fuck, Gia," he swore as his entire body stiffened and he came with her, swearing his love to her.

Chapter Fifty-Seven

Gia couldn't find her way out of this dream she was in. It was different from her usual vivid dreams or the times she slept without them. Exhaustion dragged at her every step as if an oppressive force squeezed her. Her muscles moved through thick sludge, yet she was walking all the same. No, she was floating, or...hanging? *What is going on?*

She wasn't hanging, but something fierce pushed at her. There was a deep void in her horizon, a colorless, empty space, frozen but with no reason for it. Each step felt like battling a storm she was blind to. A buzzing started in her head. It was her pulse racing faster and faster. A warning, an alarm.

Gia woke sucking in air. She took gulping breaths before she realized something was wrong. The world around her was her world, but everything smelled different. Everything smelled wrong.

"Hugh?" She scrambled to his side of the bed. He lay on his back, sleeping. But he made no movement when she touched him. She shoved herself away in surprise. He was freezing. Unnaturally so. *What's happening?* She took another breath and then, as the aura finally filtered through her nose and into her brain, she screamed.

She jumped off the bed and ran toward the kids' bedrooms, first Danny's. Empty. Then Ava's. "No!" *Where are they?* Even as she raced downstairs, praying they were both watching TV, she knew they were gone. She'd sensed it the minute she'd woken. Her house held a hollow aroma, just like her dream. The flickering yellow joy and wonder of Ava was gone. And Danny? The rock-solid momentum and deep teal of his brain, absent. Both of their scents vanished. *Fuck, fuck, fuck!* Rage and anger bloomed inside her and she raced back upstairs.

"Hugh!" She scrambled onto the bed and tried with all her might to shake him into consciousness. His scent was wrong, altered somehow, even though he was still here beside her.

You must wake him. Her magic bellowed at her, carrying words of warning from the goddesses. *Find the kids. Something is horribly wrong.*

"Think, damn it!" she screamed at herself. "Don't crumple under your fear." She scrambled for her phone and called her sister.

"What's wrong?" Frankie's voice was laced with worry.

"Francesca!" Gia shouted. "I need you and Niko now, and Marie too. Whoever you can bring. Someone took the kids." She was certain of it. "And they...they did something to Hugh. He's here, but I can't wake him. Please, hurry."

She hung up, grabbed Hugh's phone, and dialed Drake, her fingers shaking as she fumbled with the numbers. "God damn it!"

"Drake, it's Gia. I need your help." She started crying then.

"What's happened? The kids?"

"Please come," she begged through her tears and her fear. "Can you get whoever you can and bring them? I can't wake Hugh. He's alive, but I can't wake him. It smells like terrible magic, like evil. Please. Whatever it is, took my kids."

It did smell like awful magic, a kind she'd smelled before. Only now was she able to recognize it for what it truly was. It was exactly how the room had smelled after Doug had been killed. An ancient desert, the ground cracked and dry and…screaming out the dust of broken bones. Evil incarnate. The scent stirred additional memories. They bubbled inside her, scrambling for attention.

Chapter Fifty-Eight

Francesca and Niko arrived first. Marie and Booth, Niko's groundskeeper and all-around amazing man, were a few seconds behind.

"I brought the hounds," Booth said. "Your kids love 'em and they may not be as powerful as vampires and werewolves at tracking, but every bit helps."

Gia had to choke back another round of tears. She threw her arms around Booth. "Thank you." Then she grabbed her sister's hand and ran up the stairs. The rest followed.

"Good God," Niko swore as he arrived behind them and saw Hugh on the bed, eyes closed, smile on his face, puffs of breath coming from his mouth as though he were somewhere extremely cold. It was all so strange and macabre and fucking frightening. Gia had to save him. She had to find her kids. And she didn't know how to do either.

"Hey." Francesca squeezed Gia's hand, sending strength into her body. "Look at me."

Gia turned, knowing her eyes were filled with fear. Her expression hid nothing from her sister.

"Take a deep breath. We're going to figure this out."

Marie moved to Hugh's body and felt for his pulse. "A powerful spell, indeed. Warped and awful. Something familiar, but I can't place it. Tell me exactly what you remember about the night," Marie demanded as she dug through her bag and began setting things around Hugh's body. "He's alive, but it's like something is freezing him to death from the inside out."

"I...I..." Gia could hardly speak.

"Close your eyes, honey," Francesca said. "Focus. Use your power. Lean into it, your connection with Hugh, to your kids, to Mother Earth and the moon and stars."

Gia did as her sister instructed. Then she stepped into her memories and spoke. "I came home from working with you. The kids were in bed. I checked on them. We went to bed and I..." The odd dream space she'd been in washed over her. She gripped her sister's hand harder and mentally threw her strength and focus toward remembering her dream. It hurt to be back there now, seeing it from outside. A slow freezing ache. It started on her skin, tightening in. Evil.

"I fell asleep and found myself in a weird dream. Something was pressing in on me. I can see it now, the extreme pressure, and the cold. It was difficult to come out of, but I dragged myself awake to find..." She opened her eyes then, the terror tightening around her heart. "Everything changed. I could tell something was wrong because everything smelled different. I called all of you."

Hugh's family arrived, yelling her name.

"Upstairs," Niko called. And a moment later, Drake was there with Grant, Ian, and Alexander.

"May and Addie are downstairs. Duncan and Harper are watching Connor. What's happened? Christ." Drake took Hugh's hand.

"A freezing spell," Marie answered and took Gia's hands while whispering words to herself. "Gia, you escaped. I believe you were meant to be in one too. Or maybe yours wasn't as strong. I can't tell. We need to get Hugh out quickly or he might not survive."

"What do we do?" Gia asked.

"We warm him from within. We need to find him, wherever he is, now."

"How?" Gia asked. Something niggled at her brain through the fear and worry.

"I got here as soon as I could." Augustus, Francesca's friend and co-worker slammed into the room. He'd helped them battle Francesca's demon. "What's happened?"

"Something put Hugh under a powerful spell of black magic, and took Gia's kids, something awful. We're not sure yet," Niko said.

Augustus stepped closer and leaned over Hugh. "Something full of hate. It's fierce. I've never encountered a force this strange before..."

"Can we talk about this later or is this going to help us?" Marie said.

"No, it can wait. By all means, what can I do?" Augustus asked.

"I need Gia and Francesca. Everyone else, please clear the room."

Reluctantly, they all walked out. Niko was the last, kissing Francesca. "Be careful, love. I'll take Booth and the dogs, see if we can scent anything outside."

"Gia, put your hand on his chest so he can feel you." Marie lit candles around the room and placed objects beside each candle, one for each element: fire, water, earth, and air. She took Francesca's hand. "Francesca, hold your sister's other hand. Gia, close your eyes and use your lunar connection to find him. I think only you can bring him back. It's your mated connection."

"I'm not strong enough yet," Gia said.

"You are," Marie and Francesca spoke at the same time.

"I can feel it in you," her sister urged.

"You've already been using it, I suspect," Marie said. "Like I explained, this part of your magic is not untrained."

Gia ignored the doubt in her mind because it didn't matter. Nothing mattered but getting her loves returned to her safe and sound. She closed her eyes and did as she was told while Marie chanted words around her and wove her spell. The magic, warm and earthy, spiraled around her. Her sister's powers soothed her heart with its blue healing salve, and Gia felt a pinprick of hope.

Carefully, she tiptoed backward into her dream. Out of nowhere, the same hollow, oppressive pain pushed in on her, but this time she wore a shield around herself, magic from Marie, from Francesca. Soon, her own powerful energy led her.

"Hugh, my love, where are you? Let me find you." She walked or floated. It was difficult to tell. Onward, forward as much as forward was a concept when everything around her was a bleak horizon of gray, circular and mind-numbing in its emptiness. Fear crept upon her and with it the cold. Her bones began to freeze.

"Focus. Claim your power." The words zapped through her hand, her connection to her witches, and struck right into her soul.

Gia stopped and called upon her magic from Mother Earth, from the goddesses, the sky, the air, the ground beneath her, water, and fire. The moon rose high in the barren landscape, her lunar connection to Hugh. Simmering sparks of energy loosened from her fingertips and her eyes. Soon pinks and reds and oranges ripped through the hollow world; pricks of heat zapped at her. Pinkish orange light led her out of the bleakness. Through the veil, she saw him. "Hugh!"

He slept, shivering in the woods, a gray, desolate woods. Using the moon to guide her, she shot arrows of warmth to him, calling on all her strengths, and her skill in knife-throwing. Then Gia flung a burst of wind to blow away the stagnant creeping onslaught of death, blasted lightning in brilliant streaks of red through the suffocating air to reach him and when she did, she focused on her heart, all the magic swirling there, covered his body with his, and kissed him.

CHAPTER FIFTY-NINE

"HELL!" HUGH SAT UP fast, grasping Gia to him as he took deep breaths, pulling air into his lungs. "Fuck! That hurts. Gia?" He smoothed his hand over her head, his heart racing a million beats a second. "Are you okay? What's going on?" Every muscle ached, and he didn't have the energy to stay sitting. Falling back to the mattress, he kept a hold on Gia. Sweat broke out on his skin as he went from freezing to overheated.

"Oh, Christ," Gia swore and wrapped her arms around him. Her tears wet his neck.

He cradled her head and kissed her, wiping away her tears, holding on, taking the power she shoved into him. Already his strength was returning.

"You were under a spell," Gia said, running her hands over every part of his body. "Are you hurt? We thought...you almost...what if I had lost you?" She scrambled into his arms and held on.

"Something evil put you under a spell and took the children. They have Danny and Ava," Francesca said. She and Marie stood in the bedroom.

Scents drifted around him of burning candles and powerful magic, and family and... "Someone took Danny and Ava?" he bellowed.

Gia shoved off his lap and raced to the closet. She had her knives strapped to her thighs and was pulling on her tight black pants.

He threw off the sheets, stood, and stalked toward her, naked as he was when he'd fallen asleep.

"Our cue to leave." Francesca covered her eyes and huffed out a laugh. "Hurry. We'll be downstairs."

"Who dared enter our home and take them?" His voice thundered.

"They put us both under the spell. I don't know why or how I woke, but I did and you were out," Gia said frantically. "I could smell...the house had changed. The kids were gone. I called everyone I could think of to come help me, help us, Hugh. What do we do? How do we find them?"

He gripped her and wrapped his body around hers. "Jesus, are you hurt?"

"No...just scared, Hugh. I was so afraid you were going to...that I..."

"I'm here and we are getting those kids back." He threw on his clothes and followed Gia downstairs.

"Son." Drake pulled him into a hug while his brothers slapped his shoulders. He gave May a kiss and wrapped Addie in a hug.

"I'm okay," he said.

"Bad news," Niko said, stepping back into the house without Booth. Hugh's friend Callum was behind him. "There's no trace of them outside anywhere. There's a wisp of evil, that's it. Whoever took them is gone. And the camera you had on the porch is smashed. I sent Booth home in case the children find their way to my house, by some chance."

"Niko called me. Said you could use all the help you can get," Callum said.

"Good to see you, Son," Drake said to Callum. "It's been too long."

"Not long enough." Hugh barely heard his sister Addy swear under her breath. Something was going on there, but he didn't have time for that now.

Hugh stalked outside to check for himself, whipping around the perimeter of the house and the yard before he raced back inside. *Fuck him.* It was the gross essence he'd noticed at her house before. And Niko was right. Only a thread remained, with no link to anywhere. Fuck, he hadn't been careful enough. He'd ignored his instincts the last few weeks when he knew, he *knew* he shouldn't have. "This is my fault," he said. He took Gia's hand.

"What do you mean?"

"I told you weeks ago about scenting something off here. I let the recent peace get in my head and ignore my instincts."

"How could this be your fault? I should have done something more, noticed more, protected my kids more."

"Augustus, you said earlier that you might have an idea?" Marie interrupted.

"I...yes. In Germany, in the 1500s when the witch trials were in full force, there was a man, a powerful demon, who could use witches and wizards for their power, leeching off of them basically. If they were close enough, he could steal their powers to use, but the powers never appeared in him. He was there, but he was like a ghost, or a disease. A mix of an erdhenne or doppelganger and a witch. For centuries, he went undetected by the witch hunters. He could be invisible, like the wind, or take the form of an older man. Short, gray hair, unless he dyes it, oddly pointed nose."

Gia gasped and covered her mouth.

"What is it?" Hugh said, reaching out to touch her, but she stepped back.

She looked at him with wide eyes, pale green and full of fear, and then he watched them change, grow darker in hue, and flicker with dark red sparks of rage. "It's Orin."

"Fuck."

"Who's Orin?" Marie asked.

"Gia's..." Hugh wasn't sure what to call him.

She swallowed and gripped her hands into fists. "My mentor, if you will." Each word sounded scraped through her rage to get out. "I've been working for him, secretly, for years. I thought...all this time that he was helping me find who killed my husband, but he...he's been using me," Gia seethed. "He trained me, he helped me. I thought..."

"Hush," Hugh said. "We're going to find him, and we're going to find those kids."

"How do you know?" she cried.

Hugh couldn't stand the agony spilling out of her. He wrapped his arms around her. "Because I feel it in my blood, just as I'm certain you are mine. So are they. And no one, human or creature, harms what's mine, what's ours," he vowed.

"Tell me everything you can about your work for him," Marie said. "Where, when, what you did. Leave nothing out."

Gia glanced at Hugh and nodded. And then his brave love spoke her truths. How Orin found her one month after her husband had died and said he had information about her husband's murder, how he lured her into working for him with the promise of finding the men who murdered Doug and more. How he trained her. When her missions were, what she did on those missions.

With every word she spoke, his heart broke a little more for her, for every wrong and trauma she'd endured.

"I was so desperate when he found me, so angry. I wanted to find Doug's killers more than anything. I thought my magic was my gifts with computers and numbers. I *killed* for him."

"You took out monsters," Hugh said, taking her hand. The open anguish in her expression was going to be his undoing. He was going to murder Orin Zeleb a million times over.

"I think you do have an affinity for numbers and code, dear," Marie said. "But I don't think there's magic involved with that. You're simply brilliant that way. However, these occurrences, or dates you've given me, align with full moons, each of them.

There was silence around the room while everyone waited.

"He's the one who's been using your lunar powers," Marie said. "I'd bet my life on it."

"Only those?" Francesca asked curiously.

"For some reason, yes." Marie nodded. "I think so. Perhaps because her storm powers were buried so deep, or because they sometimes align with lunar powers, camouflaging each other. Maybe he wasn't strong enough to sense them in her. I also suspect that he's the poison I saw in you, Gia. The one you thought was from the drugs you'd been given. The longer you've been away from him, the weaker that poison in you has become."

"You stopped working for him," Hugh said. "Effectively taking your source of power away."

"But I..." Gia rubbed her head. "I...*he's* the one who wrote me off after my last mission. He was so angry he wouldn't take my calls."

"What happened on your last mission?" Grant asked.

"I failed," Gia said simply. "I nearly got killed. Hugh saved me. But Orin had been acting weird before that." She paced.

He could see her mind racing to catch up with everything.

"He'd started to get furious, losing his temper when he never did before. Condescending comments slipped out of him. That I was distracted and couldn't handle my job. Everything pissed him off, even tiny things like me getting a manicure. He started calling me girl and commanding me to get my shit together. Making me feel guilty. It all started…" She stopped and gazed at Hugh. "When I met you."

"Because your lunar powers now had a true mate, a healthy connection, a connection bound by trust and love and life." Marie's voice sounded through the madness.

"Perhaps he wasn't able to access as much of your powers and started coming apart at the seams," Francesca said. "He sounds more dangerous than ever. So he…he took what matters most to you."

Gia nodded, her expression a mixture of agony and rage. "How do we find him?"

"We know where he lives." Niko pointed his gaze at Hugh. "But he could be anywhere and I'd bet he's effectively masked their scent with his?"

Hugh linked his hand with Gia's, let his warmth seep into her, calmed his mind, and let his instincts take control. The past few months raced through his mind, memory after memory until something caught on the edges. "We find them in their dreams."

"I don't understand," Augustus said.

"Gia and I are dream walkers," Francesca said. "She and I can enter each other's dreams. It's how I found her in Prague. Danny and Ava have the talent as well. They may even be more powerful."

"Some werewolves have the power too," May said, gazing at Hugh's father.

"Danny was in a nightmare when he found me as my wolf and invited me in. I wasn't sleeping or dreaming myself, but I was able to go into his dream. Ava showed up too like they'd both been doing it for years."

"But if we don't know where they are, how can you succeed?" Gia asked. "When it happened before, you were here with them."

"I think I can do it while sleeping too. Remember how I told you when I was a teenager and I got lost and my father found me?"

Gia nodded.

"Amazing that you can dream walk too, as a werewolf," Marie said. "I've never encountered such a thing."

"My great-grandmother was a witch," Drake said.

One more thing Hugh had been excited to share with Gia but hadn't had the chance yet.

"Impossible, isn't it?" Marie said. She reached for Hugh's wrist and closed her eyes. "My goodness. You have witch's blood in you as well. Astonishing."

"It doesn't have to be me, but it takes energy," Hugh said. "And I think Gia and Francesca should save their energy. I have a feeling when we find them, we are going to need lots of powerful magic. I think, if I can find them in their dreams, they might be able to tell me where they are, and if not I should be able to locate them anyway from there." Hugh took Gia's hand and brought it to his chest.

She reached her other hand to his cheek and said, "We need to hurry."

Chapter Sixty

They raced outside beyond Gia's backyard, toward the woods lining her property and the Webb's. All of them, werewolves, witches, demon, and vampire. All of them helping him and Gia. By God, he was grateful for family and friendship right now.

Francesca, Niko, Marie, May, and Augustus all waited by the woods while the werewolves and Gia stepped deeper through the thick trees and into a clearing. In an instant all the werewolves shed their clothes and shouted out their change, their bodies swirling through the air as they leapt and shifted, landing, each of them, safely back on the ground. In case Hugh needed help or got stuck in his dream, his family could bring him out of it.

Hugh shook out his fur and made his way to the center with Gia.

"Please be careful," she whispered into him.

Hugh lay down and talked himself to a slumber, surrounded by love. His heart told him this was the way. He suspected he would have to seek far and wide to locate them, but he was wrong.

In a matter of minutes through the clear, dark night, lit by the full moon, Hugh found them.

"Hugh," Danny whispered. He was lying on a cot in a basement with his sister next to him. They were huddled together, shivering under a thin blanket.

Hugh stood outside the large, ugly, black house where Orin lived. The monster hadn't taken them far at all. What in the hell was he playing at? Carefully Hugh entered the boy's dream, looking around for signs of danger.

"You found us," Danny whispered. "I don't know what to do. We're locked in. I fell asleep. I was so tired."

Hugh nuzzled into Danny's side. Danny found the note wrapped around Hugh's collar that Gia had tucked in.

It read: "We're coming to get you. Stay quiet. We'll find you, my loves. -Mama."

Danny hugged Hugh, the boy's tears wetting his fur. He gave one big lick along Danny's face, wishing he could speak, wishing he could take them with him now, but dream walking didn't work like that. Quickly, then, knowing time was of the essence, he turned and ran.

He woke, shifted, and explained what he'd found.

Chapter Sixty-One

"He has them at his home, here in Mercy? What the fuck?" Gia swore. "What is he playing at?" She hated every single second of this. Her kids being snatched from her, confusion, not knowing. She hated not knowing. Someone was messing with her, with her loves. She was furious.

"I wondered the same thing," Hugh said.

"Let's go, right now." She started toward the house at a run.

Hugh caught her and held her around the waist. "Wait," he whispered.

"He has my babies." She shook as she spoke, nearly doubling over with the pain.

"He wants you," Francesca said, her head tilted toward the sky. "It's a full moon. It's you at your most powerful. He's luring you."

Realization sank in like a twisted piece of barbed wire in her gut.

"I think Francesca's right," Marie said. "I think he didn't put you under the same strength of freezing spell initially. I think he intended you to wake and search for them without Hugh."

"But I wouldn't have known where they were." Gia threw out the words as if they were her knives.

"Who would you have gone to who has been instrumental in your life at finding bad people?" Francesca said, things clicking in her expression.

"Holy shit," Gia swore. "But why…why take them?" Her voice broke. Hugh set her down but stayed behind her, wrapping his arms around her, sending her his strength.

"They are witches too?" Hugh's friend Callum asked. He was taller than Hugh by an inch, with thick dark hair curling over his collar. Black tattoos laced around his arms; his eyes were as dark as the ink on his skin.

"Christ," Hugh's sister swore. Addy did look like a princess as Ava had said, but a dark, avenging one at the moment, fury pulsing off her. She stood, arms crossed at the other side of the clearing from Callum. "She doesn't need you to be scaring her, Callum." The way she spit his name, it was a wonder the earth didn't quake under their feet.

Callum turned his head slowly to face Addy, although Gia had a feeling he'd already been acutely aware of her. "Gia's already scared. What she needs is all the information, not any one of us holding back our theories."

"You think he took them to use their powers?" Gia asked. It was infinitely worse than she thought.

"I don't know," Callum said. "I'm gathering facts, keeping my emotions out of it. Something I'm told I'm exceptional at." He gave Addy one last glance and Gia caught the hint of staggering longing in his eyes before he turned and started pacing.

"It's a thought," Francesca said. "But he might not know they have any powers. Most witches don't develop theirs until they're older."

Gia nodded, hoping like hell her sister was right. But then everything coalesced in her mind. The weird instincts she'd had during the last few months, becoming in touch with her magic. Understanding was a white-hot light in her mind.

"He's going to kill me. He's done with me, and I must be eliminated. He's going to kill them too, I suspect. Or use them. It's always been about death for Orin. I...I've been so, so stupid. He *found* me, he used me, not to rid the world of evil, but simply to kill people."

The words shot around the clearing, shaking the trees like a flash of angry wind. Orin was luring her, and she would go. Walking right into a tragedy. She saw it now, the truth of it all, and she sank to her knees, hands on the ground, pebbles and pine needles under her hands. Her breath left her in a crying wind. Tightness banded around her lungs, for all that she'd done at his bidding. For trusting him and risking her children. Her children...she...she couldn't breathe.

Hugh covered her, murmuring to her. He wrapped his strong arms around her. "Breathe, love. Breathe. It's time to fight. The battle of our lives. You're not alone."

She closed her eyes and pictured Danny, the small grin at the corner of his mouth he wore more and more these days with Hugh around. The way she could practically see learning happening inside that brilliant mind of his. And Ava, how strong she was, her absolute curiosity about the world, her mind in such vivid color. Gia sucked in a breath. And another, each one steadying her heart. She let emotion twirl inside her with knowledge and felt the surge of her energy.

"Heart and mind, love," Hugh said. "That's how we beat him. Heart and mind."

The scent of trees, stalwart and humming with all the strength from underneath them, the entire world at their roots. The scent of wild and vibrant roses, her sister always beside her, now with Niko and his own aura full of power. There was energy and focus from all the werewolves, a brilliant bright candle-lit essence from Marie, her ancestor. A rock-solid aura that held many secrets, the deep abiding love of May and Drake, a broken heart or two. She couldn't tell who those belonged to. Vines and plants, growth and powerful magic twining together.

And Hugh. He surrounded her with his scent of overwhelming love and desire for her, for life, for what they were building together. He was the trees and the river and the glowing moon and the tides always returning to her. He was everything. Gia breathed them all in.

"And you, Gianna Reily," Mother Earth spoke to her. Gia felt it more than heard it in her soul. She nearly wept at the connection, the embrace. *"You are the scent of wonder and resilience, of motherhood and love, of desire and longing, of so much power, unlike any we've seen in centuries. Remember, Gia. Remember your wounds, your trials, and connections. Remember all your powers. Harness them, harness them now, and go."*

Gia linked her fingers with Hugh's and rose, her skin prickling with awareness, her magic simmering in anger, in anticipation. Pinkish-purple sparks zapped from her fingertips and up her arms. She turned and faced Hugh.

"Your eyes are on fire," Hugh said, his intense focus meeting her gaze.

"He doesn't know everything." She paused, filling her lungs with power, with intention. "My lunar powers, yes. He doesn't know about my other strengths."

"You're certain?"

She looked at Francesca and Marie, stepped toward them, and held out her hands, connecting herself with her blood, her ancestors, and all those who came before. "I am. And now I have the link to my magic and help from all of you."

"He's not going to give up easily," Augustus said.

"He's not going to give up at all." Gia knew it in her heart.

"Here," Francesca said. "It's quartz, for protection." Gia took the small piece of quartz and brought it to her nose. Roses and sisterhood. Her sparks wrapped around it, making it glow pink. Beautiful. Brilliant.

"When you bring a storm, this will help protect you from its effects."

"You'll need this too." Marie placed a necklace around Gia's neck. "Malachite also helps with protection. It's centuries old, handed down for generations. And take these." She folded a small vial into Gia's hands. "Gather some snow, some pine needles, and a few pebbles. These, along with your fire, and your lightning, can help cast extremely powerful spells. I suspect your knives will come in handy too. It's time now, time to fight for good. You'll know what to do."

"We're all with you," Hugh said. "Let's go get those kids back."

She nodded. "Let's go."

Chapter Sixty-Two

They surrounded Orin's house from the woods. Gia, Francesca, and Hugh fanned out in a semicircle in front. Drake, Ian, Grant, Alexander, Addy, and Callum, as their wolves, joined Marie and Augustus around the sides and the back. Niko was hidden, but Gia could sense him. The full moon guided them, illuminating the night.

"There's powerful magic here," Francesca whispered. "I can feel it."

"Mm," Gia acknowledged. She could feel it now too. Now that she'd broken any link Orin had on her and her powers, she could sense the weighted vacuum of emptiness around this place. It was wretched and frightening. Thank the goddesses it wasn't only *his* magic that was powerful.

She and all those who came to help her were magnificent. And they were prepared. The sky was clear, but not for long.

The front door opened, and Orin stepped out. Gia hadn't expected that, but he was clever. He had something up his sleeve. He walked toward her, glaring at Hugh and her sister, their linked hands. "I knew you'd come. Took you long enough. Your children have been waiting, Gia. What kind of mother are you?" He smiled. "Leaving them alone in their beds for me to take? And you too stupid to realize. I've been visiting your house at night, just in case I had to take from you."

She was long past the stage of intimidation. "Where are my kids? That's all I want," Gia said. "Give them back to me."

"You have to come inside and get them." He smirked.

Never. He was trying to antagonize her, but she could feel his powers were weak. And one scent was all it took to tell her her kids were okay. They were still in the basement. She gave Orin no hint of what she was feeling or thinking. He'd trained her well in that respect. *I'm coming, loves.*

Orin sniffed the air. "You think you can beat me, little girl," he said softly. Instantly, he lashed his hands toward her. But she was ready. They all were. They'd anticipated his obsession with powers and they knew he'd try to take theirs.

"Now!" Gia yelled.

They broke their link and moved. Hugh ran full-speed at Orin, shifting into his werewolf in midair. He tackled Orin, growling and snarling. Orin shoved with what strength he still possessed, but all it did was send them rolling and fighting together. Hugh clawed and bit at Orin, and slammed him into the ground, as if Orin were made of paper. Somehow Orin snaked his arm around Hugh's neck and started laughing.

"A wolf with witch's blood," he yelled. "I should have known. I should have taken you when I had the chance." He began chanting words. Black puffs of smoke circled his body, but Hugh was quick. In a flash, he sliced a cut across Orin's neck and shoulder with his sharp teeth, then leapt away into the forest, too far for Orin to use him anymore.

"Arggg!" Orin screamed in pain, in rage. "You were supposed to die, wolf. A long, slow painful death for Gia to watch. Vile creature. You seek to hurt me with his puny bite. I thought better of you, Gianna." Blood seeped from his wound as he took a step in her direction.

Her magic spun inside her with each inch he came closer.

"Hooking up with a werewolf," he spat. "I could smell him on you, making you distracted. Once you let him touch you, you were no good to me anymore. I thought Laszlov would be the end of you, but you survived somehow, you bitch!"

So, he'd sent her there to die. It made sense now. How Laszlov knew she was a spy, how he'd almost killed her. The knowledge did nothing but fuel her.

"He's completely unhinged, Gia. I can sense it," Francesca sent the words to her.

"I know."

"Time to hurry."

She didn't bother asking for her kids again. Their hearts beat in tune with hers. She had to get through Orin to get to them. Casting the contents of the small vial in a circle around her, Gia raised her hands and called on her connection to the air.

Wind kicked up from the ground, fierce and angry. She directed it carefully, at him.

Orin stumbled, looking around. There was nothing to see. Her connection to the wind was invisible. Bending forward into the wall of powerful air, he attempted to get closer.

"What did it do to you to realize I'd been using your powers all these years? Using you? All those men you killed, and your work to find them on my network allowed me right into their finances. So much money you'll never see! Because you tossed yourself and everything we worked hard for at a werewolf. How cliché." His laughter was like shattering glass, trying to slice its way into her heart.

"Focus, Daughter." Mother Earth's voice was calm but stalwart. *"Now is not the time for guilt. He seeks to weaken you with it. Cast it away. His ego speaks for him."*

Gia breathed through her sins and her guilt to the well of her magic. *Ego is powering him. This is how he will die.* "The ego always gets them in the end." Orin's own words.

"Now..." He shot out a hand and dragged Francesca to him in an instant, locking his hand around her neck.

God damn it, if he wasn't so predictable, he would have been frightening. But they weren't ignorant. She wasn't a little girl anymore. Neither was Francesca. Anticipation and preparation served them well.

"I'm okay," Francesca said through their silent way of communicating, then she grabbed the hand of Orin's that held her and dug her nails into his skin chanting out her spell, one they'd

worked out to send goodness into his soul. A healing spell. It would either work or enrage him.

"You think to use your magic on me?" Orin boomed. He flailed and tried to pull Francesca off of him, screaming out his pain. "You think because you're Bianca's daughter, you are stronger than I am?"

"Bianca's daughter? How does he know?" Gia asked her sister.

"You're weak, both of you," Orin yelled. "I'll kill you both as I killed your father and your mother."

"What?" Gia faltered.

Niko appeared in a flash, the avenging midnight devil, silver flames licking at his eyes and singeing the earth in his wake. He jumped through the air, kicked Orin, and swooped Francesca out of sight.

Orin crawled to his feet, that awful smug smile on his face. In all the years she'd never seen him smile and now it showed how evil he truly was, transforming his face from a stoic, cold businessman to something disgusting. His nose stretched out and parts of his cheeks turned ashen and paper thin, caving in on his bones. The blood from Hugh's wound bubbled and changed to a matching, sick gray. An imprint of Niko's boot was burned into his chest.

"Stupid, weak man, your father." With each word he spoke, blood oozed from his mouth. "Couldn't even protect his wife and kids. I had to go through him to get to your mother. She was mine!"

A sound like a banshee screeched across the landscape, nearly flattening Gia. She did a backflip and righted herself. Standing, she whipped her knives out. Chanting out her commands, using her love, her magic, her truth. "Air mine, heed my call. Wherever is a scourge, destroy it all."

The wind obeyed and pummeled the land, whooshing and twisting around them. Soon it formed a column and lowered to the ground, dragging leaves and branches, spinning debris into the sky. A deep moan tunneled across the land. A sleek tornado of purple air whipped its way toward Orin, forcing him back.

A memory rose inside her, from when she was a baby. Her father's death, the scent surrounding that space…was Orin, that barren, cracked earth, the lifeless gray dust made of witches' bones from long ago centuries. All these years she'd thought it was the scent of death.

And then it all coiled together, snaking up like vomit from deep within her gut. *All their deaths.* "You!"

"Stupid girl, you never put it together. You don't deserve your powers!" He screeched. "Those powers were mine. I made you powerful. I made you kill!"

Rage burned inside her. "You killed them all, our parents and…Doug. You monster." The wind spun sideways, increasing in speed, taking cues from her rage. Orin was barely upright. Hugh crouched low to the ground. The roar was deafening.

"Your mother was the most powerful witch in centuries. She and I could have ruled the world!" Orin raised his hands, gnarly bones protruding from the flesh dripping off his limbs.

A force pressed upon Gia. She knelt, trying to escape it. Hollow, emotionless, Orin. Powerful even as his body wasted away in front of her eyes.

"She should have come to me after your father died, but she ran. Tried to hide from me. I had to kill her. And then I waited for you, followed your stupid little life. Decided I would have you instead. You're not nearly as powerful as Bianca. My Bianca!" The crazed screeching nearly knocked her off her feet.

She looked up. Red flames licked at her vision. All this time, he'd seduced her into believing he would help her find who killed her husband, and it was him. All he'd ever done was steal love from her.

Fueled by a rage and anguish so fierce, Gia rose. The wind was a violent storm now, tossing rocks into the air, flattening trees, shoving Orin down to his knees as she gained strength and towered over him.

"I took everything from you," he hissed. "How are you doing this? You can move the wind?"

I can do a hell of a lot more than that. You killed my loved ones. You took my children!

"Love is the answer. Always remember." The Goddess' truth surrounded her heart, her mind, her body. *"It's in you now. Overflowing. Use it."* A steady warmth bloomed inside her.

Covering his dripping eyes with what was left of his hand, Orin tried to see through the air whipping around him. "Let me touch you one last time. Let me have your power." He was unraveling.

"Never!" she swore, moving with ease through the windstorm. It was her magic. She could bend it at will. It was time to end this. Her heart cried out for Danny and Ava. Clouds danced in a dark frenzy above them, feeding into her rage.

A movement caught her eye, Hugh nodding at her from the trees, the golden gleam around his eyes finding her, loving her, surrounding her with his strength.

Love is the answer.

Silently, stealthily, he made his way behind Orin toward the open front door of the house. The other werewolves, led by Augustus, crept behind Hugh, following. She had to pull it together. Their mission was to get her kids back safe and sound. Hugh was focused. It was her turn.

"Don't you want your kids?" Orin hissed. "I'll give them to you. Come, Daughter, come closer."

"I'm not your daughter." Each word she spoke echoed loudly through the wind tunnel.

He tried to rise, triumph blooming on his face. "No. If you were, you'd be smarter. Ahh, a wind witch is it? Did you know I can siphon your powers this way too? It's not..." He stood, growing in size. "It's not easy, but I can."

Never! Gia closed her eyes and yelled to the clouds. Rain fell in walls of water, tripping Orin and making him stumble again.

But there in the flood was his eerie cackle. "Not just wind. A weather witch! How extraordinary," he cried, getting to his knees. "Keep showing me your powers, dear."

"He's weakened, but he's using your powers as you throw them at him." Francesca's voice was clear and steady through the moaning wind and whipping rainfall.

"I know," Gia said. *"I've got this."* Clasping her hands together, the sound rang out along the ground and up, up, up into the air. The wind and rain stopped instantly. The ground flooded with water, and, with great strength, she drew it toward her, away from Orin, while he cried out for it.

His eerie laughter continued. "Oh, you shouldn't do that. You shouldn't take the water away from me. What if you need it? What if..."

"Kids are safe," Francesca said. *"Everyone's out. They left out the back and into the woods. Hugh and Niko have them."*

Orin sat back on his knees, cackling as he raised a small device. "What if I did this?" With one click, the house behind him exploded into a fiery whorl of flames. The thundering noise sliced through her and tossed Gia off her feet, spinning her into the trees. She caught herself mid-air, flipped, and sank to the ground. Pain ripped through her side where a flying rock sliced into her calf. But in her heart, she could feel the hearts of those she loved still beating.

In an instant she calmed her anxiety, re-channeled her magic, let it zap and simmer across her skin like flint and flame, like anger and love, like death and life, like truth, her truth twirling around her, swirling into a mass.

Gia breathed in slowly, all the scents surrounding her, the cold but steady dirt, the stalwart help of all her friends and family, the furious air, the long-lasting ache of her ancestors. And, burnishing along her body, her own unique essence emanated brilliantly, on fire as her magic filled her, pulsed in her. It leapt from her fingertips to her knives, knives that began to shimmer, hot as fire.

She extended the silver blades, felt the clamoring energy inside her body reaching for a way to get out. She aimed her arms to the sky and sought the lightning, calling on the ancient powers and ancestors, asking them for the light. A storm built heavier above them. Gia tossed her head back and screamed.

All around them, the air hung in silence for a second. With a deafening clap, the sky opened and rain fell in earnest. And Gia, witch of fire and water, witch of moon and stars, witch of love and heat, dragged the fire from the sky. Lightning struck Orin in the chest when she aimed her knives into the hollow void of his heart.

A million banshees' screams shook the night. And then he was gone, disintegrated into a billion pieces of ash.

Chapter Sixty-Three

A FEW HOURS LATER, they all, or most of them, hovered in the hospital waiting room together. They'd spilled out of cars and vans as the sky turned pink to await the birth of Duncan and Harper's twins.

Grant, Ian, and Ian's husband George, whom Gia had just met, sat at a small table playing cards with Connor and Danny. Alexander sat in one of the chairs, hands crossed over his chest, eyes closed. Gia couldn't tell if he was sleeping or not. Francesca and Niko sat together on one of the loveseats.

Francesca had her own sparkly glow about her that Gia could see now, teals and silvers woven together, her hand linked with Niko's, their noses practically touching as they whispered joyful words to each other. They had to be joyful words, Francesca's face was beaming.

Ava sat in Addy's lap, talking a mile a minute while Addy wove braids into Ava's hair. Drake and May had gone to get everyone coffee. Callum had disappeared before they'd arrived at the hospital. And Marie had left eventually, saying she'd love to meet the twins soon.

Gia rested her head on Hugh's shoulder. He had his arm snaked together with hers and their fingers linked. She was tired, but somehow also humming with energy. Marie said that was natural and that she might crash later and sleep for a while after using so much power. Gia anticipated that, but for now, she was simply happy. Both of her kids were smiling, both were comfortable. They hadn't even been scared when she'd finally gotten to them. All they could talk about was how a pack of pretty wolves had tiptoed into the basement and saved them.

"You saved my babies," Gia turned her head to Hugh.

"Marry me," Hugh whispered at the same time.

Gia's face warmed. "Honey."

"I mean it, love. You can bet I'll plan a special surprise to ask you, but I want you and I want Ava and Danny. More kids too, if that's what you want. And I didn't save them. *You* did with the most brilliant, powerful lightning I've ever seen in my life. My mate is stunning."

"I couldn't have done it without you, without all of you," she whispered, humbled at how much love surrounded her in this room, from Hugh, from her ancestors. She felt it all welling up inside her. This time, when her tears fell, they truly were tears of joy.

"Mama," Ava interrupted from across the room. "Connor says we're family, which means he's our cousin and the new babies can be our cousins too."

Gia looked at Hugh, squeezed his hand, and said to Ava, "That's right, sweetheart."

"This is the bestest family ever!" Ava cheered.

"Is that a yes?" Hugh asked her.

Gia leaned in and kissed him. "That's a yes, Hugh Webb. I would love with all my heart to be yours if you'll be mine."

"Gianna," he whispered and took the kiss deeper, cradling her head with his beautiful hands. Her magical werewolf had his own tears falling.

"Oh, my goodness." A musical voice lit up the waiting room.

Gia looked up. Willow stood there, her arms piled high with boxes of pastries and doughnuts. She practically floated on a puffy cloud of her unique pink magic.

Before Gia could say anything, Augustus stalked over to her and took the boxes from her arms.

"Hi," Willow whispered. Her eyes were wide and shimmering as she looked at Augustus.

For a moment Augustus stared. Then he quickly set the boxes on a table, turned toward the exit, and stormed out.

Just then, Duncan pushed through the swinging door, his hair askew and his shirt untucked, with a gigantic smile on his face. "One of each," he said, beaming at his family. "A girl and a boy. Both healthy. Adair Eileen Webb and James Ian Webb. Everyone's invited back for a peek, but...uh...maybe in groups?"

Everyone jumped up in cheers and congratulations. Hugh picked Gia up and swung her around, wrapping her up tightly in his arms. This truly was the bestest family ever.

***

After the early morning celebrations at the hospital, Hugh drove Gia and the kids to the farm. It was Gia's idea. She'd whispered it to him when they left Harper and Duncan beaming over their babies. They knew puppy adoption day was coming, but today felt like the perfect day. He agreed.

Danny and Ava raced up the steps of the farmhouse. Drake opened the door with a huge smile on his face. He'd just become a grandpa again with the twins and he already felt like Danny and Ava were his grandkids.

When they walked in, May was in the penned-off area with five of the puppies. A few had already been adopted, but not the runt, Bobo. Hugh reached over the gate and scooped up the chunky reddish brown Golden Retriever, Labrador mix. He may have been born the smallest, but he'd caught up quickly.

"Is he ours?" Danny asked, a wide grin on his face.

"Yep," Hugh said. He crouched down in front of Danny. "You and Ava named him. You helped bottle-feed him in the beginning when he wasn't getting enough food. Now he's ready to come home with us."

"He's so beautiful," Ava said, running her hand down Bobo's fur. The dog stretched out his head and licked Ava's face. "Do you think we're ready?"

Hugh handed the dog to Danny. "I know you are. The day started off scary, but you kept each other safe and led us right to you. I think we'll be a perfect little family for Bobo. What do you think?"

"I think it's only perfect," Ava gushed. "If you'll be part of our little family too."

Hugh glanced at a beaming Gia, gathered Ava and Danny and the dog in his arms, lifted them, and walked into Gia. She folded them all into a wonky, wonderful hug and said, "Ava, I think you have the bestest ideas ever."

Epilogue

It was Christmas Eve Eve, almost nine months since Gia had destroyed Orin, since she'd put down her assassin knives, along with her quest for vengeance. It was over now and she was...she was...

Gia smiled and turned around in Hugh's arms. "I don't feel it anymore."

"What, love?" Hugh tucked her in, just as he always did, their bodies creating that beautiful heat between each other.

"Afraid."

Ava, Danny, and Connor were tucked in their sleeping bags in the tent Hugh had set up in the middle of his loft. They were munching on popcorn and watching old Christmas movies on the projector screen. Ava had decided they needed a Christmas Eve, Eve tradition and so this was it. The first-ever, two nights before Christmas, cousins' movie night. Babies Adair and James were sound asleep in their car seats beside the tent, waiting for Duncan and Harper to pick them up any minute now. The new parents had had a date night mixed with last-minute shopping and were thrilled the twins had been invited to the tradition. Bobo was asleep in the tent, snoring soft and goofy puppy snores.

And Hugh was teaching her how to make his grandmother's cake. He was patient and funny and she was having a blast, even if it was more fun to watch him than pay attention to measuring.

"Mm." Hugh smiled, and she loved what that smile did to his eyes, warming them, sending sparks out toward her. "Therapy's helping. You're sleeping better too, no more nightmares."

"Therapy has been so helpful, especially to talk about everything I buried for so long. I'm glad I got the kids back in too for a bit," she whispered. "But I owe so much of my fear disappearing to you, Hugh. Even when…even when…that first night we met, you made me feel so, so alive, and safe. I'm never afraid with you."

"Darlin'." Hugh rested his forehead on hers.

"And I sleep better because you're fantastic at sex," she whispered softly in his ear.

Hugh busted out laughing.

"Pipe down!" A loud whisper came from the tent.

"You're the fantastic one. And you're all mine," he said. "Got a surprise for you."

"You always have surprises for me," Gia said, melting into his arms.

"House is finished."

"Oh! It is?"

For the last few months, Hugh, his sister, Addy, who was an amazing carpenter, Alexander, and a few friends had been working on Gia's house, updating the windows and the wiring, putting in new bathrooms, and sprucing up the kitchen a bit.

"So we get to spend Christmas there?"

"It's what you wanted," Hugh said. "Take the kids to cut down a tree in the morning?" They were going to keep the loft too, for now, maybe rent it out. They hadn't quite decided. They'd been having so much fun spending time together as a family, but they knew they wanted to live in the old farmhouse. Hugh had even put a gate in the back fence that connected to Hugh's parents' land. Connection, family, love. It was everything Gianna wanted and more.

***

Hugh

Hugh opened the back porch door and found Gia standing in the yard, surrounded by snow. She had her arms raised and was whispering the words to a spell he hadn't heard before. Connecting with the land, the earth, with her ancestors. She finished, sent kisses into the air, and stepped out of the circle she'd drawn around herself. When she turned and saw him, she smiled, then she ran and jumped into his arms. He caught her. He'd always catch her. She buried her face in his neck.

"All right, love?"

"Mm-hmm," she said. "Happy and sad."

December 26th. Today was her mother's birthday. She'd had brunch and mimosas with Francesca this morning at Adair's. May, Harper, Addy, Marie, and Willow had joined them, along with a friend of Francesca's from the hospital. Even Samantha had been invited but was out of town for Christmas. They were celebrating and honoring women and witches, those they'd lost, and those still living.

"I miss her. I think I miss her more now that I'm digging into my memories and letting them take up space in my heart. It's so good, you know, but it's also so, so hard."

"Yeah." He carried her inside. "Come inside so I can get you warm."

"Okay."

She snuggled into his arms and Hugh felt ten times taller being able to comfort her. And he loved knowing she now wore an engagement ring on her finger. Even more special to him were the additional bracelets circling her wrist. One with his name and one with Bobo's. Danny had made them the same day they brought Bobo home.

"I have one more gift for you."

"Hugh." She pulled her head out and kissed him. "What else could you possibly have to give me? You take care of me. You never give up on me. You brought me back to life."

"Here." He set her down on the newly renovated back porch. One side was screened in, perfect for Georgia summers.

The other end was closed in with windows on three sides and fully insulated so Gia could use it all year long. An office or studio or sorts for her to do what she wanted, learn about and practice her magic, nap, knit. He'd added something while she'd been outside.

"Alexander helped me make this for you. The kids helped a bit too."

"It's beautiful." Gia ran her hands along the top of the desk, made of pine. Simple with straight legs and two drawers. He'd set a vase of flowers on it, along with a bowl of her sour cherry candies, the crystals she loved and several small framed photos. "Oh, Hugh."

"It's those we've lost," he said. "Your mom and dad, my mom. I love this one of Doug holding Ava with Danny on his back. It's…I thought you might like an altar. You can decorate it, put what you want on it, or use it for something else or…" She was so quiet he didn't know what to do.

Gia fingered each photo carefully, then she faced him with shining eyes. "I love you so much, Hugh Webb. You keep giving and giving to me and I can't handle it."

He grinned and wrapped his arms around her. "Yes, you can, my stunning witch. You can handle anything."

***

Later, when they were in bed and the house was quiet aside from their lovemaking and Hugh was moving inside her, she whispered, "I hope you can handle anything too, my love."

He grinned. What was she talking about with that sexy voice of hers and that crooked grin he was addicted to? He lifted her leg to wrap it around him, free to caress her thigh and up her spine, free to watch her arch and smile and glow for him, while he swelled inside her. He tugged her head back and kissed that sweet, sweet mouth of hers. "Oh, yeah?"

"Mm." She writhed under his touch and he moved his mouth down her neck, felt her pulse hammering for him, moved back up, and locked their mouths together.

"You feel so good inside me, on me, moving over me," she hushed. "I love your skin. I love your muscles. I love everything about you, Hugh." She roamed her hands down his back to his butt and urged him to go faster.

He obeyed, picking up the pace. His own orgasm raced down his spine. He could feel it. He was so close. "Gotta give me one more, Gianna. Let me see you soar." One more thrust and he was done, spilling inside her. He reached down and caressed her clit, pushing on it, while she moaned out her orgasm around him, softer, quieter, her body languid and flushed.

"Beautiful."

"In the summer." She held his head to her neck.

He was coming down from the high, listening to their hearts galloping next to each other. She was sweaty and gorgeous and her scent... always the scent of her... Wait. Something was different. It wasn't just her familiar passion and love he smelled; it was... He popped his head up. Her eyes were shimmering pools of tears.

"No way?" he said, his grin growing wider.

She nodded. "We're going to have a baby."

"Christ." He kissed her. He had to. He peppered them along her face and her neck, down her chest. When he pulled out of her he placed his hands on her belly, the soft, precious skin there, marveling at her body. Then he lay by her side and took her face. "Gianna Violetta Reily, I am so in love with you."

"Webb," she whispered over her tears. "I want to be a Webb, Hugh before the baby is born."

"Ha." Hugh cheered. "A wedding and a baby. And a spectacular life together."

"Promise?" she asked.

"Promise," he answered.

ACKNOWLEDGEMENTS

I LOVED WRITING THIS book. The words came easy. I guess I have a thing for heroines especially who have survived trauma, including trauma passed down through generations. Gia carries trauma not only from things she's experienced but from all her witch ancestors. And how powerful is that?

But healing can be powerful too. Therapy is helpful for many. Positive supportive relationships can also be helpful. Although those two things are not always available to people. But one thing that has always struck me as profoundly helpful in my own life is art. Visual art, musical art, written art, all the art! So thank you to all the artists putting your creativity into the world. I am constantly inspired by you.

And to my own artists, Greg, Lily, and Jasper, I love you.

About Sara

Sara Ohlin lives on Whidbey Island with her husband and two kids. Her essays can be found at *Anderbo.com*, *Feminine Collective*, *The Manifest Station*, *Panorama: The Journal of Travel, Place, & Nature*, and in anthologies such as *Are We Feeling Better Yet? Women Speak about Healthcare in America*. She is the author of ten romance novels with Totally Bound Publishing. In the summer she ignores everyone to work in her garden and dream up new recipes. She once met a person who didn't read books and wasn't that into food and it nearly broke her heart.

Visit Sara Ohlin Online
www.saraohlin.com

ALSO BY SARA OHLIN

Enchanted Mates Series
Luscious Bite

The Graciella Series
Handling the Rancher
Seducing the Dragonfly
Flirting with Forever

Rescue Me Series
Salvaging Love
Igniting Love
Promising Love
Embracing Love

My Graciella Series
Hearts in Bloom
Harvest Moon Kisses
Winter Wonderland Love

Newsletter

Would you like advanced notification about upcoming releases and sales? Access to exclusive content and fun recipes? Sign up for my newsletter to keep up to date with the latest from Sara Ohlin.

www.saraohlin.com/newsletter/